Praise For
A Memorable Murder

"I wouldn't be too quick to open up *A Memorable Murder*, the newest book by John Schlarbaum because once you do, you won't be able to put it down. You will be catapulted into an adventure that will keep you from doing anything else you promised yourself. This isn't a book where you can pace yourself reading. Once you begin with that first page, you will be locked into a story that weaves together the twists and turns of political intrigue, murder and pay-back. Schlarbaum is a storyteller whose extraordinary grasp of plot and character and compellingly eerie and disquieting scenes will make you squirm. This is a murder mystery of immense talent. Once you finish with this book, you will want to read everything else by this writer."
~ Marty Gervais, Bestselling author of *The Rumrunners*

"A diabolical plot, well drawn characters and written in a quick and quick witted narrative. John Schlarbaum's *A Memorable Murder* is a pleasure to read". **~ Bob Steele - CBC Radio**

"With *A Memorable Murder* Schlarbaum has crafted a richly layered mystery with lots of unexpected twists and turns. I couldn't wait to get home to continue reading it. You never know what could happen on live television ..." **~ Annette Hamm, anchor and ex-crime reporter, CHCH TV**

"John Schlarbaum creates detailed characters we soon love to hate in his latest novel *A Memorable Murder*. He is able to delve into the psyches of his characters to show what motivates them and it isn't altruism. There is a little bit of each character we can all relate to and that's what makes *A Memorable Murder* so compelling. As we connect the dots on our way through the book, Schlarbaum continues to weave different relationships into the process and it is these relationships that twist the story into a sordid tale that jumps from the pages. Naivety, lust, greed and evil are all mixed in this mystery that will certainly have readers quickly turning the pages to discover the outcome." **~ Kathy Rumleski, London Free Press**

"*A Memorable Murder* is just that - memorable and compelling until the very last word. Readers can expect to be kept on the edge of their seats, guided by the clever and quick-witted detective Jennifer Malone. Nothing is what it seems in this page-turner where revenge, blackmail and murder drive the story to unexpected twists and turns."
~ Marie Jeannette, Mimetic Entertainment

"Schlarbaum has a unique gift of being able to deliver the kind of comfort that only a truly great mystery novel can give a reader, while also keeping us intrigued with all of the plot developments, and twists. The characters are a perfect marriage of dark humour, and likability making this a pleasure to read".
~ Alan Coombs, Astral Radio - CJBK London

"*A Memorable Murder,* is a fast-paced medical/political thriller. His new protagonist, Jennifer Malone, is a funny, quick-witted reporter who knows the ins and outs of the news business and how to get a story. The characters ring true. They are smart, witty, funny and sexy." **~ Stephen Gaspar, author of *To Know Evil***

"*A Memorable Murder* is an entertaining read with plenty of intrigue, deception, crime drama and a search for the truth. There is realism to the way main character Jennifer Malone is portrayed. *A Memorable Murder* allows readers to follow its' characters through the good, the bad and ugly of big business, political drama and media interaction."
~ Ron Giofu, Amherstburg Echo

"Schlarbaum has done it again, with the introduction of a new mystery series. Readers will be captivated with feisty reporter Jennifer Malone as she unravels a fascinating murder mystery while racing against the clock." **~ Lori Twining, Buzz 27 Blog**

"Breaking from his Steve Cassidy Series, Schlarbaum takes us into a deadly affair that keeps the pages turning while still amusing us with his jocular wit. Schlarbaum's resourceful ability to draw us into a mystery is addictive. His instinctive skill at allowing us to get to know and relate to each character makes for an enjoyable and yet, unsettling read; for in each character you may find a piece of yourself."
~ Tina Wells, TV Host - The Storyteller

A Memorable

Murder

A Jennifer Malone Mystery

Books by

John Schlarbaum

BARRY JONES' COLD DINNER
A Steve Cassidy Mystery #1

WHEN ANGELS FAIL TO FLY
A Steve Cassidy Mystery #2

* * *

THE DOCTOR'S BAG
A Sentimental Journey

AGING GRACEFULLY TOGETHER
A Story of Love & Marriage

A MEMORABLE

Murder

A JENNIFER MALONE MYSTERY

SCANNER PUBLISHING

WINDSOR, ONTARIO, CANADA

COPYRIGHT 2011 BY JOHN SCHLARBAUM

Library and Archives Canada Cataloguing in Publication

Schlarbaum, John, 1966-
A memorable murder : a Jennifer Malone mystery / John Schlarbaum.

ISBN 978-0-9738498-5-1

I. Title.
PS8637.C448M45 2011   C813'.6   C2011-906560-6

SCANNER PUBLISHING
5060 Tecumseh Road East, Suite #1106
Windsor, Ontario, Canada N8T 1C1

Cover design: Hawksworth Designs © 2011
www.hawksworthdesigns.com

Printed in Canada

Acknowledgements

I would like to thank all those who read preview copies and then gave me their unvarnished opinions. Your comments, ideas and enthusiasm for this novel helped shape this final version in ways I had never imagined.

As a former Private Investigator I obviously know a thing or two about the human brain and how it works ... oh wait ... nevermind. Fortunately for me, my dear friend Debra Kigar is a former McMaster University brain researcher who worked on Einstein's brain - yes, THAT Einstein. Thanks Deb for your technical medical input that makes me sound smarter than I really am.

As always I thank the readers who continue to encourage me to write. I trust you will take Jennifer Malone to heart as you have Steve Cassidy. She is easier on the eyes and doesn't carry as much emotional baggage - yet.

Finally, I'd like to thank those individuals who have stuck by me through the highs and lows of the past two years. You know who you are. I could not have accomplished everything I have without you.

John Schlarbaum
September, 2011

For Kevin Jarvis

*"It is by chance that we met, by choice
that we became and have stayed friends."*

A Memorable Murder

ONE

The voices were familiar yet distant, as if the speakers were communicating through bullhorns miles away. Their words drifted in and out of clarity, spoken in measured tones, although Lynn sensed an undercurrent of urgency in their manner. Rushing to tell their story; trying to convey a particular feeling - a scene - to those listening. As the stream of hopelessly unintelligible words droned on, Lynn thought she recognized a sound in the background. A police siren? Possibly an ambulance? Regardless of its origin, the disembodied noise did not reassure her in the least.

Her head began to pound as she opened her eyes. It took a moment for them to adjust to the semi-darkened room. Although her vision was blurred she saw the walls were bathed in a faint blue light that flickered sporadically, creating a strobe effect. She found it near impossible to lift her upper arms or body, which felt like they were filled with concrete.

Where am I? she thought.

Lynn turned her neck toward the source of the mysterious light. The twenty-inch television on the bureau answered many of her initial questions. On the TV was a split-screen showing a well-dressed man and woman at an anchor desk and a female reporter outside a large building. At the top of the screen "NCN Special Report" appeared.

Lynn strained to hear their conversation. Their mouths moved, words came out, yet she was unable to decipher what they were saying.

A Memorable Murder

Was it in code? Frustrated, she studied the images, trying to piece together what was important enough to have interrupted the afternoon soaps.

Was it afternoon?

Lynn's eyes moved from the screen to the tiny window where curtains hung haphazardly. Through the numerous rips in the material and at the centre where the curtains didn't quite come together, she could see the blue light strobing off the glass. Beyond it, however, it was completely black.

No streetlights.

No headlights.

No moon.

No sun.

Nothing.

Panic set in as an increasing sense of doom engulfed Lynn's mind. While certain she wasn't restrained in any way, she still couldn't move.

She quickly resolved she was in a rundown motel room, one that she couldn't remember checking into, or ever wanting to check into. Not knowing the time of day, Lynn willed her left arm across her chest and stared at her watch which read 8:15.

Her body went limp, the exertion leaving her both mentally and physically drained.

Was it morning or night?

What day of the week was it?

Why am I here?

The answers were not forthcoming.

Again, Lynn turned her attention to the news report. The words were slowly getting clearer. She was determined to learn all she could before the station cut back to its regular programming. As her vision also focused, Lynn realized the people at the news desk were Jason

Morris and Susan Donallee, the co-anchors of the National Cable Network's evening newscast.

"When was the last time this type of incident occurred, Tanya?" Jason asked the reporter.

The screen went full-frame showing Tanya Grahame, an extremely photogenic young woman, in front of what Lynn recognized as the network's flagship station, WCNY. The building's huge two-storey windows, which served as a backdrop, were part of the morning show's much-publicized new set, allowing the public to view the show as it aired live across the country.

It was at this moment Lynn noticed the sun was shining brightly.

It must be 8:15 a.m., she thought.

She glanced again at the darkened window.

Was this place located where the sun hadn't come up yet? It would mean a difference of time zones if that were true, her mind screamed.

She tried unsuccessfully to put the thought aside, as she concentrated on Tanya's answer.

"Televised incidents like this have occurred before, but this type of gangland-style shooting is thought to be the first of its kind for a nationally broadcast program. Other shootings have taken place during local news reports, where a distraught family member or friend has shot an alleged killer being transferred through an airport or courthouse. And although those killings may have subsequently received national exposure, today's shooting was seen live by millions of people, many tuned in to see Presidential candidate Douglas Adams."

Was Douglas dead? He couldn't be, Lynn thought frantically. *I was just with him last . . .*

The thought drifted away as she wasn't sure if last night was now this morning, or if it was, in fact, a couple of days ago, or even last week. Almost immediately she felt a sudden tightness in her chest as she experienced a shortness of breath. Desperately she gulped for air in

an effort to fill her lungs. With one final intake of precious oxygen, the seizure passed and she began to feel tingling in her arms and legs.

She lay on the bed stiff as a board, not daring to move a muscle until her breathing returned to normal and the prickly sensation subsided.

"Thank you for that report, Tanya," Susan Donallee said as the screen cut back to the studio. "We will hear from Tanya again as new developments arise in this tragic story." Susan turned to her co-anchor. "Jason."

Jason Morris had been a fixture on the national news scene for over thirty years. In his mid-60's and with dignified grey hair appearing at his temples, he was the epitome of a ladies' man: handsome, intelligent, muscular, warm and caring. Almost secondary to his looks was his talent to sniff out a news story. As a reporter he'd covered every worthwhile war, election, assassination attempt and breaking story with the same intensity of a cub reporter looking for his first big break. Even though he'd made enemies over the years, his reputation was unassailable.

So today, as whenever a major story broke, households across the country turned their news channels off and switched to their one and only source of the facts: Jason Morris.

"For those of you joining us, *The Nation Today* has suspended its operations. This after an unidentified man was shot in the head as he was preparing to ask Presidential candidate Douglas Adams a question. The man, described as in his mid-40's, had stepped up to the show's street microphone when an unidentified woman came up from behind and shot him in the right temple. An explosion then detonated from within a gym bag placed amongst the crowd gathered to view the show through its new bulletproof windows.

"In the ensuing confusion, the woman escaped from the scene in a grey 4-door vehicle, possibly a Volvo. The woman is described by witnesses as being in her 40's, approximately 5'7" tall, with a slim figure. At the time of the killing she was wearing a blue and white dress, dark glasses and a blonde wig. The victim was pronounced dead at the scene and his identity is being withheld until his family is notified.

"Our reporter Tanya Grahame was told by officers at the scene that a clue to the shooter's identity was recovered. However, police are withholding that information from the public at this time.

"What we don't know yet is if there's a connection between the victim and Presidential candidate Douglas Adams, who is also the head of the powerful Health and Welfare Committee. Upon observing the shooting, Mr. Adams was rushed out of the studio by armed bodyguards and his whereabouts are not known."

Lynn felt sick to her stomach.

Douglas was safe but where was he now? Was there a connection with the dead man? More troubling she thought, *was there any connection to why she was in this room?*

The answers her brain feverishly provided didn't make sense. Neither did her current situation. With her tired mind now fairly clear, Lynn clutched the bedspread with both hands and pulled herself upwards. The room, its walls, the TV, the bureau, the menacing blue strobe flicker, all began to spin out of control.

You have to hold on, Lynn kept reassuring herself. *It'll pass.*

A moment later, Lynn stood tentatively. She took small steps toward the bathroom, putting her outstretched hand against the wall for support. Behind her, Susan Donallee was telling viewers that the scene they were about to replay was of the actual killing and small children should leave the room. The co-anchors then talked for a short time, allowing those conscientious parents throughout the nation to shepherd their children away from the TV set.

Lynn made it to the bathroom door and stood against its frame. She turned to witness the murderous footage, as the anchors described what was taking place. As she swung her head around, something caught her eye above the bathtub. There on the shower rod, was a . . .

"The woman was wearing a blue and white dress."

neatly hung blue and white dress.

Lynn gasped at the sight.

She next looked on the vanity and saw . . .

"She also wore a blonde wig and dark sunglasses."

a blonde wig and dark sunglasses.

The room began to revolve slowly around her. Steadying herself, trying to rationalize a logical explanation, she turned her full attention back to the TV.

The screen cut from a two-shot of the smiling morning show host and candidate to a close-up of a man on the street at a microphone. His head was tilted slightly downward and the fedora he was wearing obscured much of his face.

"I have two questions for Mr. Adams," the man said.

Before he could utter another word, the woman in the blue and white dress was upon him, placing a gun to his head and pulling the trigger. As he felt the barrel make contact with his skin, he looked up in startled surprise. An instant later, he became a nationally televised murder statistic. This was immediately followed by an explosion heard off-camera which engulfed the area in smoke around the dead man.

Lynn collapsed to her knees. She again began gasping for air, eerily emulating the crowd's coughing and feeling their confusion at what they'd observed. Yet it wasn't the bystanders she was concerned about; it was him. The split-second full-face image of the murdered man became etched in her mind.

With a sickening thud Lynn fell onto her side and fainted dead away.

The last thoughts that flashed through her mind frightened her beyond belief.

Where am I?

JOHN SCHLARBAUM

How did I get here?
Why am I here?
And finally, *why would I kill my husband?*

7

TWO

There was turmoil inside and outside the television studio. For the people who hadn't witnessed the shooting, the immediate interest was that of a motorist passing an accident. Their dismay at narrowly missing out on the year's biggest story wouldn't hit them until they heard the news at their office or were asked by a security guard if they had seen *The Nation Today*.

For those who'd stood next to the mysterious orator (who now lay face down on the sidewalk at the base of the microphone), only one question ran through their collective minds: *What if I had asked the first question?*

The smiles they'd been wearing when the outdoor camera's red light flashed on had been replaced by lost expressions and tear-stained faces. Their once-waving and animated arms now hung silently at their sides. Those not openly showing their emotions stood uneasily, shifting from foot to foot, unsure of what to do next.

What if I had asked the first question?

He was dead. Everyone knew this. There was no need for a good Samaritan to step forward to comfort the man. He ceased to exist the moment the shot rang out. He wouldn't have to worry about money problems, finding a job, finding romance or simply trying to keep going until the sun rose again.

He also wouldn't have to carry the horrific memory of seeing a man shot in the head as he was about to ask a question on a network morning show.

What if I had asked the first question?

Stanley Unger stood so close to the window that the fog his breath produced on the glass obscured his view. He didn't seem to care as he absently watched the scene before him. As the newly appointed producer of *The Nation Today*, he knew he was to blame, or that he would be blamed for this. It had been his suggestion to go back to the winning formula that had suited the show in the mid-60's. It was his idea that the public should see what goes on behind the scenes and allow them to be part of the show, instead of merely as observers. He'd pitched these radical ideas to the network bigwigs who decided they had nothing to lose. That was why they had hired the 32-year-old hotshot from the competition in the first place. Although $15 million to renovate the main studio seemed a bit excessive, it was a better idea than replacing one of their hosts. In the past that tactic had temporarily boosted ratings until the public caught on the show remained virtually the same. Interchangeable talking heads couldn't hide that detail.

"Have the police been notified?" Stanley asked no one in particular.

"They probably saw it on TV like the rest of the country," a voice in the background mumbled.

Stanley slowly turned and surveyed the group who made up the crew. No one moved. Stanley fixed his unflinching gaze on a television assistant who stood near the set. The TVA wore a smirk on his face which he unsuccessfully tried to hide. Stanley saw through the charade and was not amused.

"What was that, cue-card boy?" Stanley asked. "You have something to say?"

"Not really," Carl Taylor replied. "It was—"

"What—a joke? Is that what you were going to say, Carl?" Before getting a reply, Stanley was running full-out toward the man. Members of the crew grabbed Stanley as he reached his target. "You won't be laughing when you're looking for another job after the network shuts us down!" He twisted his way out of the burly arms that held him back and returned to the window.

"Calm down, Stan. This wasn't your fault," a production assistant said.

Stanley wanted to throttle her.

You don't have all the facts yet, he thought.

He had to keep his attention focused. Blowing off steam at a bunch of unionized technicians wasn't going to help in any way, so he began to do what he'd been hired to do: take control.

Seeing that both police and ambulance had arrived, his first directive was to pull the curtains across the wall of windows. Onlookers had begun to press against the glass hoping to catch a glimpse of anyone they recognized from the show. This type of voyeuristic atmosphere was not what Stanley needed. He next ordered the entire crew back to their positions.

"If we go live again, I don't feel like hunting down a cameraman or a tape guy who thinks he can slack off because the rest of today's show is cancelled." Stanley looked at the crew before him. "And under no circumstances is anyone, regardless of how low on the food chain you are," he said glaring at Carl, "to talk about what has happened to anyone. That means no calls out of this studio or the control room for personal reasons. Is that clear?"

A muttering of agreement came as the reply.

"One more thing."

The sternness drained from Stanley's face as he watched the

curtains close off the outside world.

"I know some of you are really shook up and that's understandable. However—and don't think I'm a cold, unfeeling prick for what I'm about to say—we are in the news business. There is a time to reflect on this horrible incident, unfortunately, now is not that time." He pointed to the curtains. "If you thought we were in a fishbowl when the show began, you had better believe that bowl has now been transformed into a giant microscope."

With the crew looking nervously at each other, Stanley left the studio and briskly walked up the hall toward the newsroom. His head felt like it was about to detonate.

What happened wasn't your fault, he repeated to himself, although not totally convinced. *A random act. It had to be, because nothing like this ever happens in real life.*

He pushed his back against the wall and took a deep breath. His entire body began to shake. He lifted a hand and watched, mesmerized, as it quivered uncontrollably. Painfully aware that if his connection to the dead man became known his days in the industry would be over, he summoned his remaining strength and walked into the newsroom to face his peers head on.

* * *

Through a stroke of luck Jason Morris and Susan Donallee were at the anchor desk. The two anchors, whose Q-rating for recognition amongst the viewing public rivaled Brian Williams and Katie Couric, had been scheduled to do an early morning promotional shoot for the new fall campaign. On any other news day, these two network powerhouses wouldn't have been anywhere near the studio until early afternoon.

This small gift from the heavens only momentarily soothed Stanley's nerves as he began to contemplate the significance of what they were

telling the viewers at home.

"Not since Lee Harvey Oswald was killed in the basement of a Dallas Police Station has a televised murder been seen by so many people," Jason said with a grim expression on his face.

"That's right, Jason," Susan cut in. "Back in 1963, however, there were only a small percentage of TV sets in use and the signals were broadcast mainly for the North American viewing public. Today with satellites and cable, a network's signal is truly global. Although millions will have seen this tragedy unfold throughout the country, there is no way of determining how many untold more witnessed it around the world."

Where the hell did she pull that out of? Jason thought. *What a load of crap. I'll show her. Take this, honey.*

"For those of you *old enough* to remember, at the time, Jack Ruby claimed he shot Oswald in a fit of passion out of concern for Jacqueline Kennedy, as he didn't want her to have to return to Dallas to suffer the further ordeal of a trial. Was today's shooting also an act of passion? As a reporter covering the crime beat for many years, I can tell you that for a woman—such as today's shooter—to gather the internal strength to carry out such an act of violence, it is highly probable there was a relationship between her and the victim. Was this an act of jealousy? Of love? Revenge? Or simply an act of passion?" Jason paused dramatically before adding, "We may never know."

The camera had slowly zoomed into a single shot of Jason, thus not recording for posterity Susan rolling her eyes in disbelief at what she was hearing.

Great, she thought. *The crusty old crime reporter turns pop psychologist. What's next, Jason—a psychic reading?*

The director (who playfully thought of airing Susan's theatrics before being outvoted by the other control room technicians) cut back to a two-shot when Susan had sufficiently regained her composure.

With live reports such as these, there were no scripts to follow. There was only one rule that had to be followed at all times: Don't blink.

As the shooting had taken place during one of the network's shows, it was quickly decided that, as a duty to the audience, there would be no commercial breaks. With the two nightly news anchors already in the building, the decision not to use the morning show's newscaster was pretty simple. During a major crisis the public didn't want to see a former football jock giving them updates and analysis. They wanted the best money could buy and that happened to be Jason and Susan.

A news anchor is like a computer: information in equals information out. Along with having the director and production team giving them updates and subject ideas in their earpieces, the anchors have to contend with their surroundings. Only a few feet away from the set there was a small army of people running from desk to desk, furiously typing copy or on the telephone. Each person had a job to do, which today entailed only one thing: to make the anchors appear knowledgeable. Promotions and raises hinged on one's performance during a crisis situation.

Using all available land lines, cell phones and smart phone devices, reporters and junior news directors tried desperately to schedule guests who could give their "expert" opinions on why the morning's events had occurred. On the line at various times were police sergeants, psychologists, criminal behaviourists, car experts, gun dealers and so forth. Susan would have smiled to hear the psychic who was claiming she knew the identity of the killer and that it was not a woman! The reporter who had the misfortune of taking her call insisted he didn't think they could afford her services.

"Not at $4.99 a minute in any case!" he'd laughed, before putting her on hold indefinitely.

Stanley watched the media circus unfold in front of him. Listening to the anchors relate the recent events over and over made him nauseous. It was the phrase, "Not since Lee Harvey Oswald," that stuck like an ice

pick in his mind.

This thing is bigger than the Kennedy or Reagan or Lennon shootings, he thought.

There were millions of witnesses who had seen it happen—live—and he now believed he'd been party to the whole thing.

Feeling physically sick for the first time, Stanley rushed to the nearby men's room where he vomited violently. As he lay partially on the floor at the base of the toilet, he gave thanks the room was empty.

A short time later, he pulled himself off the tiled floor and walked to the vanity, where he splashed water on his face. He looked at himself in the mirror, noticing his paleness and realizing that being sick was only part of the reason.

As he stared at his mirrored twin, he saw raw unbridled terror looking back at him. He tried to banish the image from his head as he exited into the hallway. Yet, he could only think that if he couldn't look at himself now, how would others view him if the truth ever came out?

He shuddered at the thought and decided that now was an excellent time for a smoke.

THREE

Forgotten by all except the television crew was the morning's distinguished guest: presidential candidate Douglas Adams. Almost as the gunshot outside had rung out, Adams was forcibly removed from his chair. To the dismay of the audio techs, Adams ripped off his lapel microphone and threw it to the floor, where one of his entourage immediately stepped on it, rendering it useless for all time.

The Nation Today's co-host, Evan MacLean, sat in his chair across from Adams in stunned silence. He watched Adams' handlers whisk him into the hall. As the studio door closed behind them, MacLean saw one of the men yelling into a walkie-talkie, "This is a code white situation! THIS IS NOT A DRILL!"

As the sidewalk explosives went off, MacLean's attention was directed toward the huge wall of windows, which shook from the blast.

We're under attack! he thought as he dove to the floor. *They're going to kill us all!*

He risked a look at the street scene and wished he hadn't. He saw mass confusion as people ran for their lives, many running up to the windows and pounding on them violently. Their faces etched in fear as they realized they were stuck outside.

MacLean wondered what they must have thought seeing a roomful of people secure from the mayhem, staring blankly back at them.

"Heaven help us all," he said aloud, before closing his eyes to await the next bomb blast that never came.

As the limousine pulled out of the station's parking lot, candidate Adams' head was pushed between his legs by one of his guards.

"Is this necessary?" he demanded.

"It's what you pay us for," came the reply.

"Don't take Huntington," head of security Terry Jameson said to the driver. "They may have anticipated that."

"Anticipated what?" Adams cried, shoving the huge forearm off his neck and sitting upright. "They weren't after me, you idiots! They were after the guy asking the question!"

Jameson turned and faced Adams.

"Did you know that man?"

"He was a stranger off the street—how would I know him?"

"We can't take any chances, sir," Jameson said. "When we turn this corner there'll be a blue car waiting for us. I want you to get into that car as quickly as possible. The driver will take you to a safe place."

Adams looked bewildered.

This is from a bad spy movie, he thought.

"Is that advisable?"

Jameson turned back to the front and said, "This limo is a bit conspicuous, don't you think?"

Adams failed to reply.

I pay these guys to think at times like these. Trust them. They know what they're doing.

The limo turned onto Addingham Lane and sure enough, the blue nondescript car was idling by the curb.

"The driver is one of us, so do what he says. I'm staying with this car as a decoy and will meet up with you in a few minutes," Jameson advised.

The limo door was pulled open by a man dressed in street clothes, who watched over Adams as he ducked into the backseat of the car. As it fled the area, he slumped down in the seat in an effort to make himself invisible.

His thoughts were a mixture of panic and sheer excitement. The Reagan assassination attempt replayed in his mind; how the Secret Service had shoved the President into the back of his motorcade car while others joined the melee to restrain John Hinckley.

A split-second later however, this terrifying thought was overtaken by a more agreeable one.

If the voting public hadn't known me before, they surely would now. This will be the biggest story of the campaign, overshadowing policies and both parties.

The possibilities were endless. He was now a direct link to a national tragedy. He could take a stronger stand on gun control and not have to worry about backlash from the NRA. He could make it a personal crusade to see that the shooter was brought to swift justice, although he knew he had no real clout over police matters. Regardless, he understood people loved politicians who talked tough.

In light of what happened, he could position himself with the "little guy" who can't even ask a question of a presidential candidate without having to fear for his life.

This is potent stuff, all right.

With thoughts of sugar plum voters still dancing in his head, the car came to a sudden stop in front of a dilapidated house.

"What are you doing? Why are we stopped here?"

The driver exited the car and opened the back door.

"We're going inside, sir."

A black station wagon drove into the driveway and Jameson got out. Seeing Adams still in the car, he instructed, "Out—come on!"

From outside the house looked like a real fixer-upper, but inside resembled something torn out of *Architecture Achievements Magazine*. Adams was stunned. After downing a shot of scotch in the living room, Adams was relieved to see his campaign manager, Harold Green, enter the large living room.

"Is all this spy stuff really necessary?"

"As there has been no apparent attempt on your life thus far, probably not," came Green's reply, stepping to the window overlooking the street. "Pretty efficient though, don't you think?"

"I haven't had time to think," Adams said irritably. His features loosened slightly and he added, "That's not true. I have been—"

Green cut him off.

"Been thinking about the polls, right? Voter recognition. Name recognition." He turned on his heel and faced his boss with a mile-wide smile plastered across his face. "You can't buy publicity like this!" he claimed as he took a seat beside Adams. "Don't get me wrong—I feel genuinely sorry for that schmuck who got offed. He was probably a drug dealer or something."

"Is that true?"

"Who knows? Who cares? Who would shoot a guy on national television who didn't deserve it? And the bomb—don't forget about the bomb."

"What bomb?"

"The one that detonated right after the broad blew the guy away." Green saw Adams' confusion. "You were probably being led out when it went off. No matter. The fact is this thing was an organized hit. It was meant to send a very—how would you say—*persuasive* message to an individual out there in TV land."

"You think it was a mob hit?"

"I don't care if the guy was killed for stealing candy from a baby.

He's dead, you're alive and this campaign is about to go through the roof." With a salute, Green added, "Mr. President."

Adams was startled by Green's certainty. The more he pondered the situation, however, the bigger the smile on his face also grew.

"This thing is huge. With only three weeks left, the President is now a lame duck candidate. How is he going to explain to John and Jane Public that after four years people still feel the need to—and have the means to—kill a fellow countryman? He can't." Green stood and began to pace the room, his arms flailing in front of him. "Our whole strategy has been to show the administration's shortfalls and what better way to do that than a guy getting blown away during *The Nation Today*?"

"That's all well and fine, but what about right now? How long are we going to stay in hiding?" Adams was becoming edgy about the house, not having a clue where he was.

"Only until the press release is ready," Green replied. "We should be out of here within the half-hour."

The thought appalled Adams.

"You're issuing a statement while that dead man is still warm?"

"We really have no choice. If we don't get our message of condolence to the family and our commitment to make sure this never happens again out there, the other camp will. And personally, I'd rather have Jason Morris read our statement with the whole nation riveted to the coverage than have him read Travers' spin on things first. This is politics and I play to win."

Adams knew his top man was right although the feeling didn't sit well in his stomach.

"Whatever you have to do, do it. I'll play along," he conceded.

Green turned on the giant plasma television set in the corner of the room and switched to NCN.

"There is still no word from the police on the identity of the slain man," Susan Donallee was saying.

The screen cut to a two-shot.

"This just in," Jason Morris stated authoritatively. "We have been handed a press statement issued by presidential candidate Douglas Adams."

Sitting on the overstuffed couch, Adams marveled at how quickly events were unfolding. The statement was relatively short in its length yet long on emotion and commitments. The last line slid out of Morris' lips as though it were a personal pledge from God himself.

"In the days ahead, I will do everything to ensure that this kind of tragic incident never befalls another citizen of this great country."

"Ha!" Green said triumphantly. "Try and top that!"

His self-congratulatory mood faded slightly when his cell phone went off.

"Hello. No, candidate Adams cannot speak at this moment. Who is this?"

The female voice on the other end was almost a whisper.

"Tell him Robert Barker's killer wants to talk to him—privately."

"Robert Barker?" Green turned to Adams and mouthed, *Crank call.* "Robert Barker isn't dead. Now I don't know how you got this—"

"Don't you watch *The Nation Today*?" the throaty voice countered.

"Of course . . ."

Green's face went blank as the pieces at last fell into place. His worst fears were confirmed as he glanced over at the TV and saw a frozen close-up of the man at the microphone.

It couldn't be, he thought.

Even though the face was partially covered by his hat, there was something about the man's sly smile that almost floored Green.

"What do you want?" he demanded.

"To talk to the candidate, of course." There was a pause before the caller added, "I know he's with you, so don't give me the runaround."

"I wouldn't do that," Green stammered. "Give me a moment."

"Take your time. I'm not going anywhere."

Seeing Green's ghostly white face, Adams became very concerned. "What is it?"

"The dead man is Robert Barker."

This news caused Adams to momentarily stop breathing.

Before the shock really set in, Green continued.

"Remember how I said the shooting was a message for someone out in the TV audience? It would appear I was right. Unfortunately, that someone is you." He held the phone out in front of him. "There's a woman who wants to speak with you. As your campaign manager, I strongly suggest you take the call."

With hands trembling, Adams took the phone and placed it to his ear.

"This is Douglas Adams."

"Dougie, how are you holding up? I guess you'll think twice about appearing on another morning show any time soon, huh? Well, let's talk the talk for a few minutes. What happened to our mutual acquaintance Mr. Barker is a tragedy beyond compare but also a necessary evil."

The woman spoke with a quiet intensity. Her manner was almost nonchalant, one moment speaking as if threatening and then switching to a gentler, yet deeply sarcastic tone.

"You see, Mr. President—I hope you don't mind me being too presumptuous—we have a case of *you scratch mine and I'll scratch yours.* Funny thing is I've already scratched your back, as you're now well aware. Okay, enough of you—let's talk about me and my needs. What I'm looking for in a man, Dougie, is someone who can use all his power to shut down Mantis Pharmaceuticals."

"That's Barker's company," Adams said, fear falling off each syllable. "How am I going to shut down a dead man's company?" he asked swiping his brow.

"I'm sure an influential man like yourself can do anything you set your little mind to. Otherwise, the press will be very interested in certain campaign donations—or should I call them by their real name: kickbacks—from the Litchfield Corporation. You know—the guys in direct competition with Mantis for those big government grants you and your cronies are always giving out."

Green snapped into action, seizing the phone before it hit the floor as Adams sat on the couch, shaking uncontrollably.

"This is Harold Green again. I don't know what you've told Douglas but I assure you whatever it was, we can work this out. We all know what Douglas is after and as his right-hand man, I know whatever you're after is attainable."

Green listened intently as the caller reiterated her business proposal.

At its conclusion, he said, "I'm not sure how we're going to manage that. You have our word though, that as soon as Barker is identified, we will begin to resolve your situation to your satisfaction."

"Stop with the lawyer jibber-jabber. I know you'll come through, otherwise Adams will have a lot of explaining to do, won't he? Kissing the presidency goodbye will only be the beginning of his troubles. Now put the old guy back on."

"Yes?" Adams said wearily.

"Your yes-man said we're in business, even though I don't trust him wholeheartedly, if you know what I mean. So, as a final inducement to get the deed done before Election Day, I want you to remember one thing." An extended pause almost caused Adams to have a seizure as the anticipation built. "Just so you know, the press kits I've made up not only document your questionable dealings with Litchfield, they also contain some lovely photos of you and your wife—oops, a little Freudian slip there. I meant to say you and Robert Barker's wife, Lynn."

Douglas Adams' heart rate skyrocketed. What remaining blood

was in his cheeks drained away, leaving him with the facial mask a refrigerated corpse would be proud to call its own.

"Why are you doing this to me?" he wept into the phone.

"Because the bigger they are, the harder they fall."

"Please leave Lynn out of this. I'll do anything you want," Douglas pleaded. "By killing her husband you've caused her enough pain."

The voice laughed.

"Did I say I killed Mr. Barker? Well that is simply not true."

In a voice now weathered by life, Douglas asked the fateful question, knowing the answer would surely kill him.

"Then who did?"

"I can see the giant headline dancing in front of me as we speak: 'Wife Kills Hubby on National TV. Senator's Mistress Hoping to Become First Lady.'" Hearing only Douglas' laboured breathing, the woman's tone turned serious once more. "If you play straight with us, you won't have a care in the world."

Douglas' wheezing intensified.

"Think about it, okay? You kill Mantis and we won't kill your career, your reputation or your mistress."

The wheezing stopped.

"What do you mean *kill my mistress*?"

The connection was abruptly terminated.

Seconds later, Harold Green was frantically dialing 911.

"Presidential candidate Senator Douglas Adams is in the midst of a medical attack of some kind and emergency attention is needed immediately!"

* * *

She placed the phone in her pocket and walked to the car.

"How'd it go?" the male driver inquired.

23

"Let's just say the campaign manager is currently asking one of the security guards to loan Adams his underwear for the day."

"That well, huh?"

"Couldn't have gone better." She searched through her purse and asked, "Got a smoke?"

"These things'll kill you," the driver said, handing her a pack from his shirt pocket.

She lit a cigarette and inhaled deeply.

"What do I care? I'm about to become a multi-millionaire."

"No, *I'm* about to become a multi-millionaire," the driver corrected her. "*You're* about to become my wife."

"Keep talking like that and I may soon afterwards become a widow." She laughed and smiled broadly. "If you know what I mean."

The drive would take less than half an hour, during which would be a chance to reflect—individually. Talking would come later. Basking in personal satisfaction for a job well done came first.

Their thoughts, however, were nearly identical.

* * *

After the initial adrenaline rush of the shooting and the subsequent getaway, they had to act fast—dumping the Volvo off and then racing back to the motel.

For Melanie Fields, it had been the longest day of her life. Aside from not being able to sleep the previous night, the most frustrating part was the waiting. Once *The Nation Today* began, the news report, the weather report, centenarian birthday greetings and the always asinine host chit-chat seemed to go on endlessly. It was only after the first commercial break that Melanie made her move.

With the gym bag strapped over her shoulder and the gun in the pocket of her sundress, she made her way to the front of the crowd outside the studio. From the huge monitors above them, the curiosity seekers could see the events unfold through the glass and then how they appeared on TV. When Douglas Adams appeared on screen the onlookers became excited and talked animatedly amongst themselves. For many, this would be the closest they'd ever get to a man who one day soon might become their president.

After Adams restated his various platform positions, Evan MacLean announced that after the commercial break they'd be going outside to get reactions and questions from the voters.

In two minutes it will all be over, Melanie thought, as she placed the bag on the sidewalk.

It was then she saw Robert Barker being positioned in front of the outdoor microphone, that Melanie decided to move a little closer. As she ducked under a wooden barrier, a security guard appeared and told her to stand back.

Without thinking, she said, "I'm with him," pointing to Barker.

She was terrified that Barker might turn and see her.

Then what?

Luckily his attention was glued to a small television monitor on a table in front of him.

"Okay then," the guard said as he turned back to the crowd, watching for more gate crashers.

Melanie adjusted her blonde wig and calmly flicked the safety off the gun. Waiting for that idiot MacLean to throw the broadcast to the street became excruciating.

"And now let's go outside to see what the voters think of your views, Senator Adams."

The words were music to her ears.

Barker stared at the microphone in front of him, making sure the fedora he was wearing covered much of his face. The idea to wear a hat was brilliant.

A Memorable Murder

I'll have to thank Jerry when I get to the office, he thought.

The plan was to keep his features obscured as much as possible until he actually asked the first question. He would then discard the hat and look straight into the camera, ensuring Adams knew who he was.

After clearing his throat, he began, "I have two questions for Mr. Adams."

Melanie quickly took the three steps that separated them and pulled the gun from her dress. She heard a gasp from behind her as she squeezed the trigger, sending the bullet into Barker's right temple. Before his body hit the ground, she turned and ran toward the street, leaving those behind screaming and ducking for safety.

In a surreal state of mind, Melanie ran as fast as her legs could carry her. The world around her was in chaos, yet she still felt in total control. She had one goal and one goal only: get to the car. Running with the gun tucked against her side, she thought she knew what football players must experience sprinting toward the end zone to win the big game.

She jumped into the backseat of the Volvo, which was driven speedily out of the area. As her accomplice Jerry Steele navigated through the congested morning traffic, Melanie tore off the blue and white sundress, as well as the wig and glasses. After placing them in a bag she changed into a track suit.

"Any problems?"

"Not that I can see," Jerry said, checking his mirrors.

By the time they neared the airport, the shooting was all over the airwaves.

Jerry pulled into an alley behind a burnt-out bar. After changing the vehicle's plates, they continued to the airport where Melanie—using her middle name, Alison—returned the car to the rental office. The car was virtually untraceable and if everything else fell into place, the police would soon be looking for Lynn Barker and her car with a vengeance.

Back at the motel office, Jerry intently watched the colour monitor.

"Is she still there?" Melanie asked.

"Yep and sleeping like a kitten," he said with a smile. "Do you have time to put that stuff in the room?"

"Yeah, no problem. The gas will keep her under for another half-hour at least."

Melanie grabbed the bag and walked to unit #2. She unlocked and eased the door open, terrified Lynn might be waiting to ambush her.

Lynn, for all intents and purposes, however, was lost to the world.

Using the sunlight coming in from the doorway, Melanie watched Lynn's chest rise and fall before entering the bathroom to hang the dress and place the wig and glasses on the vanity. As she was preparing to leave, an idea hit her and she walked to the bureau. She switched on the TV, turned it to WCNY, the local NCN affiliate, and set the volume low.

"You've been a very bad girl, Lynn. What will the old gang say now, Prom Queen?"

Melanie closed the door behind her, locking it from the outside.

"Sweet dreams, sucker."

FOUR

Television viewers from sea to shining sea watched in reverent silence as Jason Morris brought the country up to date on the morning's tragedy. The network's coverage was into its second hour, although for everyone present in the conference room, it already felt like the second day. With no quick resolution in sight, the identity of the victim still unknown and no rational explanation for the shooting, the news executives were frantic to keep the story going without looking as though they were enjoying all the attention. As today's incident had occurred during one of their shows, the news status code was immediately elevated to that of a Presidential assassination: Code Blue.

"We've got to make a statement, Colin," the head of marketing said.

At 65, Colin Doherty was no stranger to pressure situations. As the President and CEO of the network for 15 years, he'd taken a hands-on approach to every major crisis. Using a remote, he turned down the television volume and joined the seven other men and women at the conference table. This team represented the brightest and best and it would be their job to help him decide how to proceed for the remainder of the day.

"I'm going to go around the table," Doherty finally said. "Let's start with public relations. Beverly?"

"A statement has been written," Beverley said as she handed out photocopies. "Simply put, we state that we are very concerned *The Nation Today* was used as a deliberate backdrop for this killing and that we are co-operating fully with the authorities. It's short and sweet, plus we don't assume any liability."

"Joel?" Doherty inquired in the direction of the network's chief attorney.

Joel re-read the statement.

"My only concern is the *deliberate* part. It sounds as though we know for a fact this thing was staged. I recommend we drop that one word and keep the rest."

"Done," Doherty stated putting the paper aside. "What kind of manpower do we have on this story, Kenny?"

WCNY's news director looked up from the statement.

"Well," he stammered, "Mary and I have assigned eight reporters to get information from the police, witnesses and passersby."

"Tanya is our main network correspondent and has already given several live updates," Mary, the assignment desk director, added. "We've also called in three camera crews that were scheduled off today."

"Okay, keep on top of this, because I don't want to be scooped on any information. This is our story and cost is not a factor." Doherty turned to Ryan and smiled. "Ryan, if we stay live for the rest of the morning, what type of money are we talking about?"

Roberts pulled out his calculator and started inputting figures.

"As a network roughly $2 million," the accountant said, "and as a station roughly a hundred thousand."

"We're losing most of that money for commercials that would have run during *The Nation Today*," Kim, the head of marketing, added. "If this had happened at the tail end of the show, our losses would have been a lot smaller."

"So, Stanley, as the show's producer and segment scheduler, I guess this is your fault, isn't it?"

Stanley didn't know how to respond. He wasn't sure if Doherty was trying to lighten the mood or if he was simply stating what everyone else was thinking. The notion of rushing to the washroom to vomit again washed over him.

Hoping the comment was meant as a joke, he said, "I'll bring it up at our next production meeting."

He was too nervous to look around the table to see anyone's reaction.

"Very well," Doherty said with a sly smile before proceeding. "So, Charlie, that only leaves you. As president of the station, what do you think of this mess?"

"I hope the police locate this psychopath soon and that she gives us an exclusive interview before the trial. Other than that, it looks like everything's under control at this point."

"All right then, here's my view," Doherty said, leaning forward in his chair. "First, let's get that statement on the air. Next, get those extra crews out on the street, instead of reading papers in the newsroom. Send a couple of them down to police headquarters with whatever other anchors or reporters we've got covering this thing. Make sure any information reported is first confirmed by one other source. I don't want any wild theories masquerading as fact. Leave that to the tabloid shows. As far as our continuing coverage, we stay with the story until the victim's identified and his family is notified. After that, we'll air special reports throughout the day whenever any new information comes to light. Also, let's get a reporter covering our co-operation with the police—show the cops screening tapes etc. etc."

"What about our on-air personalities?" Kenny asked.

"Jason and Susan until the end. They're both professionals, they know what they're doing." Doherty looked at Mary. "Keep those experts coming. There's nothing duller than two anchors babbling to each other—although that 'not since Oswald' stuff played pretty well. Let's do some research on how often this type of thing actually happens. Remember, you've got the network's archives right downstairs with 40 years of murder and mayhem at your fingertips." Doherty looked at the faces before him. "Any questions?"

"What about tomorrow's show?" Stanley asked tentatively. "Do you want two hours rehashing this thing or say, the first hour—depending on what happens today, of course."

"The studio windows will be covered and the street microphone is gone," Doherty said without hesitation. "Those are certainties. The rest we'll play by ear as the day's events unfold. The killer may be in jail by noon and then we'll have to decide how much coverage the killing warrants. Regardless, the first guest will be some eminent psychologist who can help counsel those viewers affected by having witnessed a live execution." Standing, he added, "And don't think people aren't calling their employers right now saying there's no way they can come in today. Whether we like it or not, this thing's going down in television history." He let that sink in before adjourning the meeting.

As everyone rushed back to their posts, Doherty asked Stanley to stay behind.

"Stanley, I know you're living through your own personal hell. I want you to know I'm not holding you or anyone else responsible for this incident."

"I appreciate that, although I'm not so sure everyone shares that view."

Doherty walked toward the door.

"You're probably right," he said before disappearing down the hall.

Stanley slid back into his chair and stared at the ceiling tiles.

A Memorable Murder

In a near whisper he said, "If anyone finds out how Barker came to stand before that microphone this morning, Colin, your opinion of me is going to change drastically."

* * *

"Come on, let 'em through," the officer said as he watched the ambulance attendants make their way toward the body.

The onlookers were now over two thousand strong with more joining the group with every bus that stopped near the studio. The four corner subway walk-ups were also jammed with the arrival of each new train.

Then there were the small independent groups of people actually making the news. Crews from every television and radio station were on the scene, all clamouring to get the best shot or a great sound bite for their bosses.

In no time, agents from all the major crime squads were flashing their credentials to the cops securing the immediate area. FBI, DEA, the terrorist unit, the bomb squad. Their bickering about jurisdiction came to an immediate stop with the arrival of Detective Michael Speers.

"This is an everyday occurrence in my neighbourhood, gentlemen. That it was televised doesn't change that. Now, everybody out of my way!"

Speers was a very imposing individual, standing 6'4" and weighing a muscular 270 pounds. His chestnut brown eyes, crooked nose, scarred right cheek, pursed thin lips and cropped black hair relayed to everyone within striking distance he meant business.

Speers walked to the body, bent down and lifted the blanket. He saw the man's right temple had been blown away and congealed blood was everywhere.

"Where's forensics?" he barked at the officer in front of him.

"On their way, sir."

"ETA?"

"10 seconds?"

Speers glared up at the officer and was ready to question him when the forensic team descended upon him.

"Very well, officer."

While forensics took pictures, measurements and samples, Speers listened to the station's security guard giving his statement to an officer.

"Yeah, I saw her," he insisted. "Came right under the barrier. I asked her to move back but she said she was with the dead guy."

"So you believed she was his wife or girlfriend?" the officer asked, jotting the information into his notebook.

"Wouldn't you? This microphone thing's been going on for a month and every day I see this happen. Not the killing part, mind you but some relative is always trying to get behind their husband or wife or friend so they can be on TV too."

"What did this woman do next?"

"She kinda stood there a few seconds. Nothing unusual like. Then the man he startin' to talk and she comes toward him. It was then I seen the gun in her hand. Without even hesitatin' she brought it up to his head and blew him away. They've got to have that on tape," he said shaking his head. "You know, this ain't the first person I've seen killed. Growing up I seen lots of people die but this was different."

"How?"

"I don't know . . . maybe it was her expression when she did the deed. It was cold, hard-like." The guard looked at the officer and then at Speers. "You knows — like she *enjoyed* it."

"After she shot him, what did she do?"

"Starts runnin' away. Wouldn't you? I gave chase but stopped when the bomb, or whatever it was, went off. The last I seen her was when she got into a grey Volvo."

"Get the plate number?"

"I only gots a 5 and a 3. I couldn't tell ya what order though. Someone else musta seen the car leave. She wasn't being very careful."

After a few more questions, Speers stepped forward.

"You found something, didn't you?"

"How'd you know?" the guard replied.

"The look in your eyes. You shouldn't be this excited unless you've got a bombshell to drop. So what is it?"

"You's good," the guard smiled. He quickly surveyed the area. "If you all don't mind, I think I should show you what's I got inside." He looked at Speers' perplexed expression. "Away from the TV cameras."

Speers and the uniformed officer turned and saw the sea of media behind them.

"Fine, but let's make this quick," Speers agreed reluctantly.

Once inside the building, the guard led the men to the empty security office.

"I think this'll help you out." The guard pulled a gold bracelet from his pocket. "I saw it drop off her wrist when she was running away."

"You've got to be kidding," Speers said as he was handed the bracelet. He let out a long whistle when he turned it over. "To L.B Love R.B. - Aug. 9th."

"Pretty nice clue, huh?" the guard said triumphantly.

"Not bad at all," Speers concurred.

Speers left the uniformed officer to complete the statement and went outside. Seeing forensics were gone he went over to the body.

"We confirm his I.D. yet?"

The officer guarding the dead man took out his notebook and began to read.

"Robert Barker of 378 Whitecastle Boulevard, New Liston. They found a couple of business cards in his wallet indicating he was the president of Mantis Pharmaceuticals."

"The drug company?" Speers asked, more to himself than to the officer. "That place is worth millions."

"If you say so, sir."

"Was he carrying much cash on him?"

"A couple hundred and change."

"Anything else of note?"

"Guy's dead—officially, that is."

For the second time, Speers was about to take the officer to task until he saw the big stupid grin. "Very well, officer . . . ?"

"Kendall. Barry Kendall, 56th Precinct."

"Make sure he gets to the morgue safely," Speers said walking away. He strolled over to another plain clothes detective. "Mario, what have you got?"

"Hey, Mike," Mario replied with a smile. "You tell me yours and I'll tell you mine, all right?"

"Deal," Speers laughed.

"From the witnesses we've talked to, the shooter was either a Caucasian or Hispanic or Asian female in her 20's, 30's or 40's, between 5'3" and 5'11" in height, with a petite to muscular build. The only thing everyone agrees on is she was blonde. The problem is some think she's a strawberry blonde, some think she's definitely had a dye job, and quite a few think she was wearing a wig."

"What about the gun?"

"Anything from a .22 to a .38 to a .45. One guy said he thought he heard her pump it once before she did the guy."

"A shotgun?"

"What do you expect this early in the morning?"

"What about the explosion? Got any ideas?"

"The bomb guys said it was a harmless pipe thing. Homemade. Strictly by the book using household cleaners and stuff you can buy at any electronics store."

"Was it hooked up to a timer?"

"A low frequency detonation. Our girl turned the bomb on, dropped it on the sidewalk, killed our boy, then sent some kind of shortwave back to the bag and ka-boom. Timed it perfectly, too."

"I haven't had the pleasure of watching the replay yet," Speers said. "I think I'll meander up to the control room. I might as well view what everyone else in the civilized world has already seen a hundred times by now."

Speers began to walk away and felt the bracelet in his pocket.

"One more thing, Mario. No one talks to the media until I say so. 'No comment' will have to hold them over."

"Sure thing, Mike."

After watching the replay of the killing, Speers gave a short statement saying only that the victim had been identified and next of kin still needed to be notified.

Speers proceeded to Whitecastle Boulevard where he discovered that 378 was a mansion on a large estate. Accompanied by a uniformed officer, Speers pressed the front doorbell several times. A few moments later, a small woman with long dark hair opened the door.

"Can I help you?"

The woman, who was wearing an apron, looked nervously at the officer.

"Is this the residence of Mr. Robert Barker?" Speers said in a soothing voice.

"Yes. Is there something wrong?"

"Is Mrs. Barker home?"

"No, she isn't. Has something happened to them?" she asked alarmed.

"Is something wrong?" Speers asked back.

"I don't know." Her voice cracked with emotion. "I've worked for the Barkers many years and they always tell me if they're going away but not today. When I got here this morning, no one was home and there were no notes for me. I get very worried and then you showed up."

"What is Mrs. Barker's first name?"

"Lynn."

"Can we come in, Miss . . .?"

"I am Francelina Lopez. Yes, please come in."

The foyer was the size of Speers' backyard and decorated with Italian marble and sculpted statues in each of the four corners. In the room to his right, he saw a large fireplace and a baby grand piano. On top of the piano were several portraits that caught his eye.

"Could I look at those pictures?"

"Yes, yes."

After confirming the two pictured people were the Barkers, Speers began to study them as he continued to ask Francelina questions.

"What does Mr. Barker do for a living?"

"He owns a big drug company. Mantis Pharmaceuticals."

"And his wife?"

"She doesn't have a job but is on many boards and, how you say, committees? She especially likes the arts."

"Is that so?"

Speers came across the one thing he'd been hoping to find. Turning to face Francelina, he held up the security guard's find: a gold bracelet. When she saw it glittering in his hand, she gasped aloud.

"Is this Mrs. Barker's? The same one she is wearing in this photo?"

"Yes, yes," Francelina said, her eyes beginning to water.

"When was the last time you saw Mrs. Barker?"

"Yesterday."

"You haven't seen or heard from her this morning?"

"No. Please tell me what's going on, I beg you."

"I'm sorry to have to break this news to you. Mr. Barker was shot and killed this morning by a woman who was wearing this bracelet."

"No—it can't be. You are mistaken! Mrs. Barker could never do such a thing. Never!"

"Excuse me, I have to make a call," Speers said stepping away, taking out his cell phone, all the while ignoring the maid's theatrics.

Speers was quickly connected to the crime scene.

"Mario, this is Mike. If you're done there, get your butt to 378 Whitecastle Boulevard—the dead guy's place."

"You find something out there?"

"Only the killer, Mario."

"Get outta town!"

"She isn't here at the moment, although that doesn't surprise me. After dropping your bracelet at a crime scene, it kind of puts a crimp on any airtight alibi plans you may have made."

Within the hour the Barker mansion was tied off with yellow police tape and Speers and his men were awaiting a judge to issue them a search warrant.

FIVE

Mitch Carson stood in his office doorway and scanned the assembled faces before finding the one he was seeking.

"Malone, get in here!"

The early morning chaos in *The Telegraph* newsroom momentarily broke as Mitch's voice bellowed across the large room.

"Some gals have all the luck," the paper's Lifestyle editor said as Jennifer Malone walked past her desk.

"I'll keep that in mind next time I'm home alone on a Friday night," she shot back.

Jennifer Malone was a tall, slender woman in her mid-30's with shoulder length brown hair. She had made her mark the day she stepped into the city's second largest daily.

After having won an investigative reporting award at a small weekly tabloid, she arrived at her junior reporter job interview with the silver-plated statuette in her oversized purse. When the editor asked for her current resume, she first pulled the award out and placed it firmly on his desk, making sure the gold plate stating her name and the category faced him. Without missing a beat, she produced her resume and put the award away, never mentioning it for the remainder of the interview.

"You've got bigger balls than most of my guys out there, Ms. Malone," Mitch had said, pointing to a gathering of male reporters.

"My mother always told me that it's not the size that matters, it's how you use them."

"Well I think we can use them around here—if you think your mother would approve."

"I can't see a problem," Jennifer said with a smile. "I'll tell her the news at her next parole hearing."

That successful interview was ten years ago.

"Did you see that?" Mitch said excitedly as he continued to watch the TV coverage on his small set on the counter.

"I'm usually a *Good Morning America* kind of person," Jennifer smiled. "After this morning though, I'm a total *Nation Today* convert. Of course I'm shocked they would book such an elaborate publicity stunt this close to sweeps."

Mitch looked up from the screen, still not knowing how to take her sense of humour.

"I want you to get down there and find out everything you can about the shooting. I've got Levison working the Senator Adams angle, if there is one. I'm also going to assemble a team of eight to help co-ordinate all the information you both send back, as well as anything we get off the air."

"I've already asked Manny the copy boy to have the Batmobile ready for me in 30 seconds."

"Would you get out of here already!" Mitch ordered. "It's not every day a major news story breaks before eight in the morning."

"And a darn good thing too," Jennifer said as she walked out of the office. "Can you imagine what that kind of stress could do to the editor-in-chief's blood pressure? It'd kill him."

Unwilling to confirm the obvious, Mitch nevertheless knew she was right.

"Very funny, Malone."

He glanced at his secretary who was watching him with a smirk.

"Problem, Amy?"

"No, Mitch. It's just I love a man in charge who faces danger head on. A man who knows his life is screwed for the next couple of days and thinks nothing of it."

"The only person that'll be screwed is you, if you don't get me Girard, Millar, Mascoll, Daly, Papp, Israelson, Crane and Harding in my office in two minutes."

"Did you really mean that part about being screwed?" she asked with a sly grin.

"Could you please get them in here?"

"Yes, sir," she replied efficiently, as Mitch went to his desk and began making phone calls.

"One other thing," he said over Amy's intercom. "Are we still on for Monday evening?"

"If that's what your daily planner says, it must be true."

"Okay, good. Now can you get me some coffee?" he asked, returning to his old gruff self. "This is going to be a long day."

The Daily Telegraph's office was located a few short blocks from the National Cable Network's headquarters, where *The Nation Today* was shot. As Jennifer came into view of the rival *Star* newspaper's front doors, she recognized three reporters exiting the building, all of whom began jogging through the maze of stopped traffic.

"You better run," she called out to Mark Orr, *The Star's* crime reporter, as he crossed to her side of the street.

He glanced over his shoulder and gave her a quick wave.

"And why's that?"

"Because as soon as I arrive on the scene, the only leads you'll be chasing are ones that I feel you guys can handle."

41

"We at *The Star* will keep that in mind, Madam Malone."

She watched him continue up the street. Noticing she was about to pass The Brewing Cup, she thought, *What the heck,* and entered the nearly empty café.

"The usual," she said to the young bleached blonde waitress behind the counter.

A look of surprise came over the girl's face as she turned her head away from the radio on the shelf behind her.

"Shouldn't you be covering the shooting?" she asked.

"You're not my editor's illegitimate daughter, are you?" Jennifer said with a smile. "You know, checking up on me?"

"If she was Carson's daughter, do you think she'd be working as a waitress in a place like this?" a male voice said.

Jennifer turned and saw Andrés Gonzmart, the always impeccably dressed Columbian owner, coming out of the back room.

"Yeah, I guess you're right. Even Carson's kid would have some level of standards."

"What makes you so mean?" Gonzmart asked as he handed her a cup of coffee. "Man problems?"

"I wish."

"Maybe someday you'll find the man of your dreams—you know, right under your nose."

"Working in a quaint coffee shop perhaps?"

"If you're lucky."

"Are you coming on to me, Gonz?"

"Heaven forbid," he said with a laugh. "Even I have—what did you say again?"

"Level of standards?"

"That's it—a level of standards."

"Touché."

"Now, getting back to my niece's question—"

Jennifer looked at the blonde.

"You're his niece?"

"That's what I've been led to believe," she said with a soft voice and wide grin.

"My condolences."

"Thanks."

"Can we cut the girl chit-chat and get back to business?" Gonzmart asked. "Why aren't you down at the shooting?"

Before answering, Jennifer took a sip of her coffee.

"I'm on my way. I mean, that guy has only been dead for what—15 minutes?"

"He's dead?" Gonzmart asked. "I hadn't heard that."

"Well if he took a bullet to his temple and survived, the surgeon who put a metal plate in his head should come forward. He'd make a mint from referrals alone."

"So why aren't you rushing to the scene?" the blonde asked, genuinely interested in the conversation.

"I am. Really. I like to take my time sometimes. My deadline is approximately 17 hours from now. I'm sure two minutes isn't going to kill me." Jennifer paused before adding, "Maybe *kill* isn't the right word under the circumstances, huh?"

She finished the last of her beverage and put a bill on the counter.

"With a fire in my stomach and the desire to properly inform the people of this great city what happened on their TV sets, I bid you both adieu."

"Good luck, Malone," Gonzmart called to her as she exited.

"Thanks, Gonz. I think I'm going to need it today."

SIX

Arriving at a crime scene was one of Jennifer's favourite things in the world. There was a charge in the air that could only be matched by the exhilaration of a seventh game of the World Series tied in the bottom of the ninth with the bases loaded, two out, and a full count at the plate. Other than that, murder, mayhem and chaos were in a league all of their own.

She estimated the crowd had swelled from the usual hundred spectators to a couple of thousand.

Don't these people have jobs? she mused to herself.

She knew the show's sidewalk layout, where the outdoor microphone was situated and how the crowd control barriers were set up. In this kind of mob though, there was no way she could get near the action for an initial look.

She surveyed the immediate area and decided to enter the nearest skyscraper to her south, taking the elevator to the fifth floor. As expected, several office doors were open, all without receptionists sitting behind their desks. She walked into a realty office and proceeded to make her way unnoticed to the windows overlooking the chaos below. For several seconds she stood silently alongside three women dressed in business attire before one of them noticed her.

"Can I help you?"

"That depends," Jennifer said as she pulled out her media identification card. "I'm a reporter from *The Telegraph*. Did you see what happened?"

The other women now turned their full attention to Jennifer.

"Ah . . . no. We got into the office a few minutes ago."

"What about the bomb? Do you know if anyone was injured when it went off?"

"I'm not sure." The woman pointed to an area in the middle of the crowd that was cordoned off with yellow police tape. "I think that's where it exploded. There have been a couple of CSI people using tweezers to pick fragments off the sidewalk."

"And what is your name?"

"Anita Byers."

Jennifer scribbled her name in the notebook she'd taken out of her coat pocket.

"Am I going to be in the newspaper?" Ms. Byers asked, full of life.

"Not unless you shot that guy down there," Jennifer replied nonchalantly. She took another quick look at the scene below and planned her next move. "Thank you, ladies. You've been more help to me than you could know."

Jennifer exited the building and backtracked down the street away from the crowd. She proceeded to a side entrance of an old art deco structure - The Kingdom Entertainment Building - adjacent to the NCN complex, and took the stairs to the third floor. The building, a city landmark, was built in the 1950's and still had outdoor fire escapes running down the sides.

She entered the third floor lobby and made her way through a small throng of people huddled near the windows.

"Is this fire exit alarmed?" she asked no one in particular, pointing to a door at the end of the hall.

A handsome male in his mid-20's turned toward her.

"No. That's where we have our smoke breaks," he said, eyeing her from head to toe.

"Thanks," she said, hoping to bump into him at a more opportune time.

Without another word she walked down the hall and pushed the door open. She scanned the windows of the building across the street and noticed Anita Byers and her friends watching her. She gave them a quick wave and flashed a smile in their direction, which they returned.

"See, I told you you've been helpful," Jennifer said as she began to descend the stairs of the metal fire escape.

Stepping off, she quickly checked her reflection in the windows of the NCN building.

Harried looking, yet still intact, she thought.

As she was technically behind the police-sanctioned perimeter, she had an unobstructed view of the scene of the crime. Sure enough, there was a deceased male bleeding from the side of his head, only a few inches from the stand-up microphone. And as her new office girlfriends had pointed out, several forensic techs were scouring the area where a ratty gym bag lay on the sidewalk, a faint line of smoke emanating from it.

She scanned the crowd and also noted the officers present. She knew two of them well: Barry Kendall and Detective Mario Stancu, both of whom were standing near the body.

A promising sign, Jennifer reasoned.

She turned her back on the crowd, pulled a small micro-recorder out of her pocket and pressed the record button. She then placed it into a specially-made pocket sewn inside her jacket close to the collar. After stating the date and time, she walked toward the crime scene, hoping no one in authority would stop her before she reached her destination.

"And what do you think you're doing?" a male voice asked.

Jennifer turned and came face to face with Michael Speers, who had exited the building behind her.

"Detective Speers, I thought this looked like your handiwork."

"You know the rules, Malone," he said, unsuccessfully trying to convey his disapproval.

Jennifer looked around and pleaded innocence, which both of them knew had been lost many stories ago.

"Do you mean . . . that I'm on the wrong side of the police tape? I don't know how this could have happened, Detective Speers. As you know, I'm a simple farm girl from a small town where these big-city crimes don't happen."

"You're telling me you're lost?" Speers asked as a smirk crossed his lips.

"No. I'm telling you that if I don't find out what happened here today, my big mean boss is going to send me back to Kansas on the first available bus."

"Carson is right. You do have bigger stones than most men."

"Well, I don't like to brag . . ."

"You know, Jennifer, I could stand here and talk all day—"

"Really? I thought you had a murder investigation to run."

"As I was about to say . . . but I have a murder investigation to run."

"You know I'd never think of getting in your way while you're doing your job, right?"

"Enough already, Malone. I'm going to escort you right to the front of the line, where you can have the best view in the house. And do you know why I'm not sending you all the way back to 103rd?"

"Because you respect me as a woman?"

"Hardly," he laughed. "Because I respect you as a reporter—unlike some of your colleagues."

Walking beside the swelling masses, both saw Mark Orr pushing his way to the front of the tape, still a hundred feet away from the action.

"Speak of the devil," Speers said with a smile.

Orr stood in disbelief as he watched Jennifer and Speers pass him.

"I hate to say I told you so . . ." Jennifer said to Orr, letting the sentence trail off, satisfied with the dumb look on his face.

During the next 15 minutes, Jennifer interviewed five shocked eyewitnesses to the shooting. By day's end, their faces would be familiar to everyone who owned a television set.

None had spoken to the man before he'd stepped up to the microphone, although one elderly woman recalled watching him briefly, as he kept fiddling with the brim of his hat.

"What do you mean *fiddling*?" Jennifer asked.

"Tugging it a little at the front, as if he were trying to cover his eyes. You know—so no one would recognize him."

"You think he was hiding from someone?"

"I don't know. It happened so fast. Maybe he was getting the brim the way he liked it."

Jennifer wrote down the woman's account and drew a star beside it. Although it could be nothing, something about the hat had piqued her interest. She turned and scanned the multitude of people behind her. Not a man with a hat in sight.

Was the man trying to hide something? And if so, why do it in front of millions of viewers?

Jennifer also circled the statement to remind her to keep its contents front and centre in her mind. She saw Barry Kendall looking in her direction and flashed him a smile.

"Officer Kendall—any word on the getaway vehicle?"

"I've been instructed only to say, 'No comment,' Ms. Malone."

"What fun is that?" she replied.

"It was a grey Volvo," she heard a man say to her left.

She pivoted in his direction and immediately spotted him. His eyes were wide with electricity and his face was that of a schoolboy who knew the answer to the teacher's question.

Pick me! Pick me! it conveyed.

"And you are?"

"J.J. Monteleone."

"And you saw this vehicle?"

"Yeah, it was parked on Elm Avenue."

Now this was something interesting, Jennifer thought.

"Was there anyone in it at the time you saw it parked?"

"A man. I saw a white man sitting behind the wheel."

"What about the woman? Was she in the car?"

"No, only the man."

"Can you give me a description?"

"Not really. He had the visor down and was wearing sunglasses. I really only glimpsed him as I crossed the street," the man said, almost apologetically.

"And what time was this?" Jennifer asked as she wrote down the information.

"I guess around 6:45 or so."

"Was there anything about this Volvo you can recall—some distinguishing marks, scrapes, cracked windshield—that kind of thing?"

"There was one thing. I think it was a rental or used to be a rental."

"Why do you say that?" Jennifer asked, about to jump out of her skin with delirium.

Eat your heart out, Orr.

"Well . . . I worked at a rental place for a while and all the companies put their logos on the front bumper. Extra advertising, you know. Then the vehicles were targeted by carjackers who saw the rental sticker and assumed the occupants were tourists."

"I remember that," someone beside him said.

"Anyway, when the Governor changed the law last year, we had to scrape all the stickers off."

"Are you saying this car still had a sticker on the bumper?"

"A partial one really—you know, a corner piece."

Please have the answer to this next question. Pretty please with a cherry on top.

"And do you remember what colour?" Jennifer asked calmly.

"A reddish-orange."

Reddish-orange. Which company had those colours?

Jennifer's mind began to mentally picture the logos of the well known rental companies, only to draw a blank.

"You wouldn't possibly know which company used a reddish-orange logo, would you?" Jennifer held her breath as she watched Monteleone begin to roll his eyes, obviously a side-effect brought on by deep thinking.

"Queen City's logo has a reddish-orange tinge to it."

Jennifer was staring so intently at Monteleone that when the answer to her question came, she was briefly mystified how he'd said the words without moving his lips.

"Miss, I said that Queen City has a reddish-orange logo."

Jennifer snapped back to attention and realized the speaker was an old Italian gentleman standing six feet away from her.

This is like playing Jeopardy *with a thousand people—not all of whom have a buzzer,* Jennifer thought.

"Are you sure?" she asked as she faced the gentleman.

"They might have changed it."

Jennifer heard a woman gasp to her right. She turned to see the coroner load the dead man into a body bag.

"Did he die instantly?" Jennifer asked the men zipping the bag closed.

"Quicker," the older of the two said.

"No comment," bellowed Detective Speers, who had come up behind them.

Barry Kendall was standing alone watching the body placed into the coroner's vehicle.

It's now or never, Jennifer thought, noting Speers had re-entered the NCN building.

With the dexterity of a prize fighter climbing through the ropes into the ring, Jennifer ducked under the two rows of police tape and was quickly at Kendall's side.

"Don't hate me because I'm beautiful," she said, as a startled Kendall became aware of her presence.

"No comment."

"To my statement or to any questions I'm planning to pose to you?"

"Both."

"I need a name."

"I need the shooter."

"The car is or was a rental."

"What?" Kendall asked, a shocked look on his face.

"The getaway car is a rental or was at one time."

"And how did—"

"A guy in the crowd said it was parked on Elm Avenue at 6:45 with a white man behind the wheel, trying to remain inconspicuous."

"You're bluffing."

"His name is J.J. Monteleone."

"The driver?"

"No—the witness, you idiot." She pointed Monteleone out to him. "The guy with the blue blazer."

"You're not kidding, are you?"

"What's the dead guy's name? I know you have it."

Kendall looked around to see if he was being watched.

"Not a word of this to anyone, not even your editor, until Speers confirms it. Are we understood?"

"Understood. Now what's his name?"

"Robert Barker."

"Why does that sound so familiar?"

"Think pharmaceuticals."

"Kendall!"

Speers' voice sliced through the air as he came upon them with a look of fire in his eyes.

"What did you tell her?" he demanded.

"No comment, sir."

"Malone?"

"That's it, Mike. Tough as an acorn this one. And you know how talented I am at cracking nuts."

"Well as far as you're concerned, the show is over."

"I was leaving anyhow. With all these people, a dead body and a bomb, I was thinking of getting away from it all for a while. You know—to clear my head."

"Just stay out of my way. Deal?"

"Your wish is my command, Detective."

As they watched Jennifer make her way through the crowd, Speers turned to Kendall.

"Nothing but trouble, that one," he said.

"I couldn't agree with you more," Kendall concurred.

Speers shook his head and began to walk away.

"One more thing, sir," Kendall said tentatively. "Ms. Malone said a man in the crowd saw a grey Volvo parked on Elm Avenue at 6:45. He said a white male was behind the wheel."

"Have Mario take a statement and follow it up. I'm going to talk to the press and then head to Barker's house to see if we can figure out why he was here in the first place."

Jennifer half-jogged back to *The Telegraph* and made a beeline to Mitch Carson's office.

"I'm onto something really big. The only thing is I can't tell you what," she said, out of breath.

"What do you mean you can't tell me? I'm the editor-in-chief!"

"Time's a-wastin', Mitch. Trust me on this. It'll only be for a few hours."

"Fine. Now if time really is a-wastin', what are you doing here?"

"I have to take a little trip and won't be back until noon at the earliest."

"Are you kidding?" Mitch protested. "You're my best reporter. That's why I didn't hesitate to give you this thing. Now you want to bail?"

"All I need is someone to cover the crime scene—you know, take notes of times, talk to witnesses. One of the interns could do that."

"You really can't tell me where you're going or why?"

"Right."

"All of a sudden, I'm thinking I'm the crazy one."

"It's 8:00 now. I'll call you later this morning, say 10:30, with an update."

"You'd better. 'Cause if I don't hear from you I'm going to give the byline to Girard."

"That hack?"

"I heard that, Malone," Arnold Girard said with a smirk as he passed the doorway.

"I meant 'hack' in a positive way," Jennifer called after him.

"Now that's settled, do you need anything for this secret journey?"

Jennifer thought for a few seconds.

"Got a hundred bucks for expenses?"

SEVEN

As she drove one of the paper's cars to Mantis Pharmaceuticals, a number of issues continued to entertain Jennifer's thoughts:

Why was multi-millionaire Robert Barker standing outside The Nation Today's *studio and from whom was he hiding?*

Who was the man in the grey Volvo parked on Elm Avenue? The getaway driver?

And where was the female shooter during this time?

These questions especially gnawed at her because if she'd kept working the crowd, she was certain she'd have learned more about the shooter's actions—before and after the killing. As it was, she was simply assuming things from the few seconds of the show she'd watched in the company of her newspaper brethren. She was amazed she had witnessed it at all, as *Good Morning America* had a Brad Pitt/ Angelina Jolie interview scheduled for the same time. Unfortunately for Brangelina, she'd been outvoted by Levison and his political pals.

Pulling into a visitor parking spot, she took a deep breath and kept telling herself that this trip was more important than any old crime scene.

She walked through the giant glass doors of the main building and was greeted by a woman behind the reception desk.

"Good morning," the woman said cheerfully. Her name tag read *Kimberly*.

"It is, isn't it. How are you today?" Jennifer replied in an equally chipper tone.

"Very well, thank you. Do you have an appointment this morning?"

"Actually, I'm doing some research for a college course I'm taking at Shelton Academy. I'm looking into the manufacturing and testing of new medicines, drugs—that kind of thing."

"And how can we help you?"

"Would there be anyone who could answer a few questions, so I can better understand how your industry works?"

"Well, I'm not sure," Kimberly said hesitantly. "We usually don't give out such sensitive information."

"I think you're getting me all wrong. I'm not doing an article on the industry—or even your company. I'm simply looking for someone to give me a very general overview how things are done. At no time would I ask specific questions about Mantis Pharmaceuticals. Because you see, between us, I think I'm way over my head in this course. I thought it would be easy to write, not realizing how technical everything is."

Jennifer saw a look of sympathy come over Kimberly's features.

"Just an overview, right?"

"Exactly."

"Please have a seat."

Soon a balding gentleman in his early 50's stepped off the elevator and strode confidently toward Jennifer.

"Jennifer? I'm Kenneth McIntyre from the public relations office."

Jennifer stood and shook McIntyre's hand, who continued to hold hers for a couple of beats longer than was necessary.

"Very nice to meet you," she said, flashing him a winning smile.

"I'm sorry I didn't call ahead."

"No need to apologize. All that matters is you're here now. Why don't we go up to my office and I'll try to answer any questions you have."

If that's the way you want to handle this, you dirty old man, then that's the way it'll be, Jennifer thought as she got in the elevator with Mr. PR.

For the following 45 minute period, Jennifer asked all the general pharmaceutical questions she could possibly think of. Unfortunately, her eager host filled in the other 40 minutes with what passed as extremely boring small talk about the industry. Knowing she had less than a half-hour before having to call Carson at the paper, she decided to turn on the charm and get down to business.

"What about new drugs? Does Mantis have any new and exciting drugs ready to hit the market?"

"Oh, we have a few on the back burner," McIntyre said with pride, as he sat back in his chair.

"What's the process for getting a new medication to the public?"

"It's very complex."

"Could you give me the basic steps involved?"

"Certainly," he said smoothly. "The first step is to develop the drug. We have our own research and development program that is continuously testing new formulas."

"Is it at this stage you test the drugs on mice or other animals?"

"After a time, yes."

"When do you begin tests on humans?"

"This is where it gets complicated. You see, after initial testing proves successful, the next stage is often testing it on humans. To do so however, the company must first get approval from the federally run ethics committee."

"The FDA?"

"No, the ethics committee is actually an offshoot of the Health and

Welfare Committee."

Federally run? The Health and Welfare Committee? What did these two things have in common? Jennifer asked herself.

Before this thought was fully formed, the answer came to her like a bolt of lightning.

Douglas Adams.

"Are you saying that before one of your new drugs gets approval, Mantis has to go before a committee headed by Senator Douglas Adams to get permission?"

McIntyre was taken aback by Jennifer's sudden intensity and apparent knowledge of the Washington power structure.

Jennifer cursed herself for letting her reporter side become so aggressive.

"That's correct," McIntyre said reluctantly. "You're from what university again?" he asked cautiously.

"It's actually an academy—Shelton Academy, upstate."

"I've never heard of it."

"It's pretty small."

She could tell this meeting, regardless of how interested McIntyre had appeared to be in her earlier, was rapidly deteriorating and drawing to a close.

"Do you have any more *general* questions about our industry?"

She smiled and tried to avoid eye contact as she looked for some way to continue the conversation, even though a connection between Barker and Adams had been made.

Throughout their conversation, she had been discreetly studying McIntyre's affects. There was a large wall calendar to his right, and more interestingly, a date planner that lay open on his desk. After years of covering the police beat, and in some instances political affairs, she had become quite adept at reading documents upside down.

As a last-ditch effort, she focused on a strange word written in red ink. Figuring she had nothing left to lose, she attempted to turn on the girlish charm for one final kick at the can.

"What about Memoradium?" she asked casually, making direct eye contact with McIntyre.

"What was that?" McIntyre replied dumbfounded.

Jennifer knew she'd hit a raw nerve.

"Isn't Memoradium scheduled for review in the near future?"

A combination of terror mixed with anger registered on McIntyre's suddenly tired face.

He glanced at the planner in front of him and slammed it closed.

"Who are you?" he demanded. "And what do you know about Memoradium?"

"Only that it's being hailed as the new wonder drug," she bluffed, hoping she was on the right track.

"This is preposterous!" McIntyre exclaimed as he bolted from his chair.

He walked swiftly around the desk, in the process scaring the living daylights out of Jennifer. She jumped to her feet, not wanting to be seated submissively in the chair.

"Is it, Mr. McIntyre? It seems to me a lot of people are willing to go to great extremes to get this thing to the market as soon as possible."

She continued to pray her instincts about this were not wrong.

Seeing McIntyre's face redden, Jennifer produced her media identification card and stepped away from him.

"All I'm looking for is confirmation Memoradium exists and that it's being prepped to go before Senator Adams' committee."

"Where did you get this information? This is top secret!"

"Either you tell me what I want to know or tomorrow's *Telegraph* will be filled with innuendo about a secret drug, which may be connected to the threat against Senator Adams' life on *The Nation Today*."

"There was no attempt—" McIntyre began to argue, clearly appalled this reporter had information on the Memoradium project.

"That's not the way my article will read, Mr. McIntyre." Jennifer glanced at her watch: 10:20. "You've got 10 minutes before this thing goes into the stratosphere. I promise any information you tell me will remain between the two of us. I will not use the information unless there is a clear connection between what happened this morning and Senator Adams."

"This is blackmail!" McIntyre cried out. "If I say nothing, you'll write all about it. Yet if I do tell you about this project, you'll have information that could severely harm this company if it becomes public."

"Nine minutes, Mr. McIntyre."

McIntyre paced the room trying to figure out his next move. Finally, he slumped into his chair, resigned to defeat, although nevertheless defiant.

"I will give you the bare essentials. Only a *general* overview."

It's a swing and it's going, going, going. It's out of here! Jennifer thought, a satisfied smile escaping her lips.

"Very well," she said noncommittally. "I'm all ears."

He finished with 30 seconds to spare.

"And no one else is currently testing this type of drug?"

McIntyre let out a sigh.

"There have been rumours—unsubstantiated thus far—that another company is developing a similar drug."

"And that company would be?"

McIntyre hesitated and then looked at the steel determination in Jennifer's eyes.

"Litchfield Industries," he said with a sigh.

"Is it standard practice to develop the same drugs as a competitor? Isn't it easier to make a knock-off after the original hits the market?"

"Not since the government imposed what is referred to as the Cloning Act. It states the company that develops any new drug has an

automatic 10 year patent on it."

"Meaning . . . if Mantis gets approval first, Litchfield would be left out in the cold."

"That's not the main reason in this case, however."

"Then what—money?"

"I don't think you realize the overall potential of Memoradium, Miss Malone. It is not another form of aspirin. This is a revolutionary drug that, from all indications, may reverse the effects of memory loss brought on by old age, Alzheimer's, strokes, as well as certain brain damage caused in auto accidents or falls."

The impact of the multiple uses of Memoradium began to flood Jennifer's mind.

"This thing is going to be bigger than a cure for cancer, isn't it?" she asked.

"When it comes to the brain and its capacity for memory, there are what is known as the three R's: Registration, Retention and Recall," McIntyre said. "With the advent of Memoradium, we are confident a fourth 'R' will be added—Reconfiguration.

"As I understand it, reasoning and intellectual ability depend upon pathways or routes among the cells of the brain. When a pathway becomes blocked, information from that cell cannot connect with other cells. So, for instance, you may be able to identify an object and explain its use, but aren't able to come up with the object's name," McIntyre paused, then added, "This is because the name is contained in a cell assembly which for whatever reason, is functionally disconnected from other assemblies. In animal lab tests with Memoradium, we've been able to unblock those pathways that no longer send information to other cells."

It took Jennifer several seconds for the drug's ramifications to register.

"And if Memoradium works on humans, Mantis would presumably

have a monopoly on the memory drug market forever."

"And make billions of dollars of profit along the way."

They sat and passively watched each other, no longer the adversaries they had been a short time ago.

"What are the odds of getting approval from Senator Adams' ethics committee?" Jennifer inquired, breaking the silence.

"We assume our application will be rubber-stamped."

"Don't be too sure about that, Mr. McIntyre. The politics of pharmaceuticals became much more volatile this morning."

"How so?" McIntyre asked intently.

After what he'd given up, Jennifer was tempted to tell McIntyre the boss was dead and his public relations job was about to become a lot more interesting. There would be no time to lounge around talking to pretty female students about the drug industry.

"I have a reporter's instincts for these things, nothing more." She could tell he wasn't buying it for a second, yet gave him credit for not pursuing her statement further. "One final thing, Mr. McIntyre. Who owns this company?"

"Robert Barker. President and C.E.O. He's the son of the founder and owns 90% of the stock."

"And if he were to leave the company for some reason, who would take over control?"

"If you mean if he were to die today, I'm really not sure. I presume his wife might—Lynn Barker."

"Does she own any stock?"

"I'm not sure. I'm guessing Robert would will his stocks to her. Again, I don't know any specifics."

A frown came over Jennifer's face.

"Is there something wrong?" McIntyre asked nervously.

Jennifer ignored his question and glanced at her watch: 10:45.

"One last thing. Do you have a year-end company report I can take with me? You know—one the company hands out to the public."

McIntyre hesitated.

"Why do you need one of those?"

"Reporter's instincts. I just want to have a current copy that has factual figures in it. Nothing more, honest," she lied again.

McIntyre reluctantly took a glossy report from the top drawer of a filing cabinet and handed it to her.

"Thank you," she said, giving him a brief smile.

Jennifer grabbed her coat off her chair, hoping against hope her recorder didn't drop to the floor.

"I really do have to leave now, Mr. McIntyre."

The look of foreboding manifested itself afresh on McIntyre's face, as he grabbed Jennifer's arm and turned her toward him. She could see perspiration beginning to form at his temples.

"You promise that the Memoradium project will not appear in any of your articles?" he implored.

"You have my word, Mr. McIntyre. I will hold this conversation in the strictest confidence," Jennifer replied, gently pulling her arm out of his grip. "The only time you'll see any mention of Memoradium is when it becomes public knowledge. However," she added, "if I hear about it on the street and believe another news organization is going to print or televise some aspect of the project, I will go public with what I know. Does that sound fair?"

McIntyre still had a look of a man buying a used car from a shady salesman.

"I guess it will have to do, won't it?"

Jennifer left McIntyre alone and made her way to the lobby where Kimberly met her warmly.

"Was Mr. McIntyre able to answer your questions?"

"All of them and then some," Jennifer replied. "Thanks for your help, I really appreciate it."

She exited the building and used her cell phone to call the paper.

"You're late, Malone!" Mitch advised her.

"Have they ID'd the dead guy yet?"

"Not yet. Girard is running down a lead we picked off a police scanner. It seems there's a lot of police activity on Whitecastle Boulevard in New Liston."

"Get hold of him and say I'll meet him there, okay?"

Jennifer terminated the connection as Carson excitedly asked, "What about your big lead?"

Driving to New Liston, Jennifer had a gut feeling that when the police arrived at Robert Barker's house, Mrs. Barker wouldn't be home. It was only a feeling but some days, especially days like this, instincts were all a reporter had to go on.

Then thinking of the implications of the wonder drug she'd just been told about, she mused to herself, "No matter what, this is going to be a memorable murder investigation," and pressed the gas pedal down a bit further.

EIGHT

With her head still groggy, Lynn began to stir. She managed to get to her feet and stumble toward the bed, listening to the news anchors blathering on about the shooting.

"We have just received new information," Susan Donallee said seriously. "Jason?"

"Police have identified the man shot during *The Nation Today* broadcast," Jason Morris began. "He is Robert Barker, president of Mantis Pharmaceuticals, the country's largest pharmaceutical company. Police have also issued a warrant for Lynn Barker, the deceased's wife. She has not been seen since yesterday and is considered armed and dangerous.

"Police are also looking for a male accomplice who drove a grey Volvo from the scene of the crime. The car's license plate, 503 TJE, is registered to Mrs. Barker. The vehicle has also not been seen since yesterday.

"In other developments, NCN has learned Mantis Pharmaceuticals has applied for a hearing before the very committee of which Senator Douglas Adams is the chairman. As you know, it was Senator Adams whom Mr. Barker was addressing when he was shot in the head. Police are trying to contact the Senator at this time to see if there is any further connection between the two men.

"Authorities state a clear motive for the killing has not yet been established. However, a search warrant has been issued for police to search the Barker residence at 378 Whitecastle Boulevard in New Liston. To repeat this late breaking news, police have identified . . ."

Jason's voice drifted off as Lynn stared at the set. She was a wanted fugitive, although she had no memory of committing any crime.

Robert and Douglas—what if the police find the connection?

Lynn began to shake uncontrollably. She was stricken with dread at the idea of police ransacking her drawers and closets.

They will only see the bad side, she thought. *They are going to put me away for life!*

As Jason continued his narrative, Lynn saw a photo of her and Robert. It had been taken the previous Christmas after Robert had given her the gold bracelet seen in the portrait.

Lynn looked at her wrist. It wasn't there. It was *always* there.

Where the hell is it?

Jason's voice filtered back into her consciousness.

"Police say a piece of jewellery left at the crime scene helped to determine the woman's identity."

"No! No! No!"

Lynn grabbed the lamp above the headboard, ripped it out of the wall and threw it at the TV. The screen shattered, as smoke and flames began to rise from within the broken unit.

They'll find my charred remains in this room and think I committed suicide, she thought. *This can't be happening!*

She got off the bed and unplugged the TV, which didn't seem to have any effect. Confused and frightened, she ran into the bathroom and closed the door behind her. There were no towels. She grabbed the sundress off its hanger and doused it in water from the sink. After putting the dress at the bottom of the door, Lynn climbed into the bathtub waiting for the flames to enter the room. She stared at the sides of the door looking for signs of smoke and fire, but saw none.

Looking up, she noticed smoke coming from the ventilation fan in the ceiling. This smoke wasn't the right colour though. It was pinkish, not grey. And the smell—it didn't smell like burning wood or carpet.

"Why are you doing this to me?" she asked. "Why?"

As the fumes began to overtake her, thoughts about the news report swam in her mind.

Robert was dead.

Douglas is missing.

There's a warrant for my arrest.

I'm being held prisoner in this room.

This doesn't make sense!

Before passing out, her final thought was a silent cry for assistance.

I really wish Melanie was here to help me.

NINE

SIX WEEKS EARLIER

It would only be the second time they'd seen each other in public—the first since beginning their affair—and Lynn was as excited as a schoolgirl. Having discovered her darling husband had been fooling around with a beautiful young lab researcher, Lynn had methodically set out to have a dalliance of her own.

Lynn Barker was an extremely attractive 40-year-old. Her slim build, collar-length light brown hair, aqua-coloured eyes and dazzling smile had been causing men to crane their necks at parties for years. The fact that she was happily married only made these men more envious of Robert. After dating in high school, they'd married while in college, much to Robert's parents' dismay who had hoped he'd marry within his own class. The Barker family fortune was piled high from the sale and development of drugs which relieved everything from the common cold to treating HIV/AIDS. The business was a century old, started by Robert's great-grandfather who'd sold medicines, potions and miracle creams from the back of a horse-drawn wagon. Today, Mantis Pharmaceuticals

was worth over a billion dollars and growing each year.

The idea that Lynn was merely a gold digger was never far from anyone's mind, yet it never stopped her from being the perfect daughter-in-law and consummate wife. After the death of his parents, as their only child, Robert was willed the company, having been its acting Vice President at the time.

With business doing well and no apparent problems on the home front, Lynn was devastated to learn of Robert's affair. Not devastated enough to ask for a divorce, mind you—as such things became much too publicized—yet hurt enough to give him back some of his own medicine.

The first opportunity presented itself at a campaign fundraiser staged by the pharmaceutical industry to show its support for Senator Douglas Adams.

Lynn arrived in the most revealing red dress she could find.

Elegant, yet slutty, she thought as she'd looked at herself in the mirror.

When introduced to Adams, as they shook hands she could feel the heat pass through their bodies.

He was a distinguished-looking man whose mannerisms conveyed to everyone that he was a powerful person. Recently widowed, in speeches he'd often speak of his wife, saying how she'd always dreamed of living in the White House. She'd supported him tirelessly although cancer was slowly killing her. Her passing was front-page news and Adams' tears at the funeral, followed by his determination to win the election for her, had boosted his campaign to a higher level.

That they truly hated each other was widely known to political reporters, although never divulged to the public.

By the gala's conclusion, Lynn and Douglas had made it discreetly known that a private get-together would be mutually enjoyable.

On the ride home, Robert shocked Lynn by saying, "I see you and the candidate hit it off pretty well."

"What do you mean by that?" she said defensively.

"Take it easy. I didn't mean anything by it. It's just that at this stage any advantage we have over Litchfield is key."

"You think I was talking to Adams in an effort to influence your grant application?"

"Weren't you?"

The irony was too much for Lynn. Here she was setting up a sexual liaison with Adams and Robert thought she was being the faithful dutiful wife.

Let him think what he wants.

"You know me too well, Robert." She paused before adding, "I was going to sleep with him to *guarantee* his approval. What do you think of that?"

Robert laughed.

"You'd do that for me?" he said sweetly.

"Twice, if necessary."

There was another couple who had taken great interest in Senator Adams and Mrs. Barker. Standing off in a corner, not mingling amongst the drug industry's movers and shakers, were Jerry Steele and Melanie Fields.

As Robert Barker's administrative assistant, Jerry had been bored to tears at numerous flashy parties. However, when he started to bring Melanie along each event became at least bearable. They were an odd pair. He was tall and gangly with a thin moustache. She was of medium height and weight with an attractive face that caught men's attention. It was this last physical quality she used to her advantage. The fact she had no scruples about sleeping her way to the top also proved helpful on occasion.

Jerry had met Melanie at a pharmaceutical convention the previous summer. At the time, she was working for a small mail order company,

hustling generic drugs to shut-ins. Her goal was to make a few bucks and then get a marketing position at one of the big drug companies. When she met Jerry and slept with him every day of the three-day convention, she felt sure her career was about to go somewhere. Unfortunately, Jerry wasn't able to find her work at Mantis and suggested she try rival Litchfield Industries.

Although he didn't like sending her to the competition, Jerry couldn't bear not having her near him.

After a few "interviews" with the personnel manager, Melanie announced she had joined the Litchfield marketing team. Her emphasis would be on lobbying the government for regulation changes and to ensure Litchfield would continue to receive grants for research and development projects.

Jerry and Melanie decided that unless asked point blank, for obvious reasons they would keep their relationship private.

"Who's that talking with the Senator?" Melanie asked Jerry as she sipped from a flute of champagne.

"Lynn Barker, Robert's wife."

"Really?" Melanie had never met the woman. Seeing her now made the hair on the back of her neck bristle. "Does she attend all of these things with him?" Melanie asked, trying to sound merely interested.

"Most times." Jerry looked at Melanie, who appeared to be sizing Lynn up. "I think this is the first time the two of you have been in the same room together. Are you impressed?"

Melanie's dislike for the woman in the red dress was absolute but she couldn't tell Jerry that without having to explain why. Then something extraordinary happened: Lynn looked in their direction and her eyes met Melanie's glare, if only for a split second.

It couldn't be, Melanie thought.

"Hello—Earth to Melanie."

"Something familiar about her," Melanie said absentmindedly.

"The way she's flirting with Adams? Maybe she reminds you of yourself."

"What did you say?"

"Nothing, dear."

Melanie continued to stare at Lynn's profile.

"It's not the flirting—although I do like that quality—it's a physical thing. She looks familiar."

"Maybe you've seen her in Mantis literature or on television."

The final tumbler finally fell into place.

"Or at the prom."

"Whose prom? Your prom?"

"Do you know her maiden name?"

"I've heard it before . . . something like Foster or Fester or—"

"Fletcher. Lynn Fletcher."

"That's it," Jerry said astounded. "You two know each other?"

"It's been a long time. Over 20 years, I guess."

Melanie stood silent for a moment, shaking slightly as a rush of adrenalin burned through her veins.

Would this nightmare ever end? she asked herself.

Looking into Jerry's probing eyes did nothing to calm the rage which was welling up within her.

"Were you two classmates?" Jerry asked eagerly.

Knowing there was no way of getting around this situation, Melanie figured she'd have to go with the flow of conversation.

"A few classes. Although I was never in her class, if you know what I mean."

"Small world, huh?"

Claustrophobic, Melanie almost blurted out. She lit a cigarette and inhaled deeply. *Calm down, girl*, she thought, *keep your cool.*

Melanie ignored the question and instead asked, "When did Robert start banging that lab technician?"

Jerry was startled by the sudden change of topic.

"I don't know—January, early February," he stammered.

That bastard! Melanie silently fumed. *His wife wasn't going to divorce him. He had only found another playmate to screw around with!*

As if by magic, Robert appeared at Lynn's side and escorted her away from the Senator. Jerry noticed Melanie's eyes narrow.

"You don't like Lynn, do you?" he asked.

"I don't like either of them much right now." Melanie threw her half-smoked cigarette onto the carpet and stamped it out with her high-heeled pump. "She was a real bitch, who as Miss Popularity regularly looked down on the little people who didn't belong to her court."

Jerry began to laugh.

"I'd have never guessed you'd let anyone treat you like that, Melanie. It's very big of you to divulge this information to me."

"Big, my ass! If I could have killed her back then, I would have. Unfortunately, fate made me a nobody. Unlike Lynn, I didn't need a bunch of fake friends to make me feel worthwhile."

"Sure, sure."

"Stop that!"

"Look, why don't you introduce yourself? Your issues with her were a very long time ago, Melanie."

"The scars remain."

For the rest of the evening Melanie drank heavily, while trying to figure out when she had gotten so stupid. During her affair with Robert she intentionally avoided knowing anything about his wife. She didn't search for images of her on the internet or in trade publications. Her belief was if he was with her, it didn't matter what wifey looked like or which committees she ran. Robert didn't care for her, so why should she?

Ignorance is bliss, she rationalized.

Until now.

Near the gala's close, Melanie saw something which piqued her interest: After writing on the back of his business card, Senator Adams had very carefully handed it to Lynn. As they parted company, Melanie saw Lynn shove the card under the edge of her bra.

"Jerry, does Lynn know about Robert's bimbo?"

"Not that he's aware of. Robert's very careful. Why?"

Melanie related the card exchange.

"There's something going on with her and the Senator," she said.

"She was flirting a bit, I concede. Anything more and Robert would know about it."

"Just like she would know if he was having an affair."

"Okay, so she may or may not be having an affair with Adams. So what?"

"So what?" Melanie tossed her hair back in disbelief. Her words became slurred with excitement. "Our futures are riding on this, Jerry. Don't you get it? She sleeps with him and he gives Mantis the next big grant, instead of to Litchfield."

"Boy, that would teach Robert a lesson not to fool around anymore," Jerry deadpanned.

"So I haven't thought this through yet. Give me time." Melanie took a final swallow of champagne and got up unsteadily from the table. "If my dear old friend is having an affair, I am going to use that information to my advantage."

"To what end?" Jerry asked as he helped Melanie on with her coat.

"Whichever end justifies the means."

"You're drunk," Jerry laughed.

"Yeah, I guess I am." Melanie looked up into Jerry's face. "Even you're starting to look pretty handsome."

TEN

Two weeks after the gala, Melanie entered her house, slamming the door behind her and flinging her briefcase to the floor. Aside from the theatrics, Jerry knew solely by the strained expression on her face that all was not well.

"Slow down," he said tentatively.

"Screw you! I'm not in the mood to listen to your passive nonsense right now, Jerry."

"Fine," he replied and exited the room.

"Get back in here!"

"Look, Melanie," Jerry said re-entering the room, "I'm not in the greatest of moods either, so stop pulling my chain like I'm your lap dog." Jerry fell into one of the chairs across from the couch where Melanie sat. "What's the problem?"

"Your boss and his sleazy prom queen wife, that's what's the problem. Give them any more rope and we're going to be out on the street or in jail."

"Mind elaborating on that?"

"During lunch, I mentioned Mrs. Barker's behaviour to Gloria.

Told her about the card exchange, blah, blah, blah, and my theory about sleeping with Adams to get grants for Mantis. So it's all kind of funny you know and we go back to work. Next thing I know, I'm called into Manard's office."

"Howard Manard? As in CEO Manard?"

"Bingo. I had no idea why he wanted to see me. I've only passed him in the hall a handful of times. I was certain he didn't know who I was or what department I worked in." Melanie let out a long breath and tried to calm down, with questionable results. "Anyway, the first thing he says is, 'I heard about Robert Barker's wife and the Senator. I need to know everything you saw. Don't leave *anything* out.' I was flabbergasted. I couldn't see Gloria phoning him, so I figure someone in the lunch room overheard our conversation and went right to Manard."

Curious, Jerry asked, "So did you give him the lowdown?"

"Of course. You should have seen his face, Jerry. It got whiter and whiter as I went on. The man looked terrified."

"Maybe he's already sleeping with Lynn and is worried about communicable diseases."

"After what he told me, I bet he wishes he were. It certainly would simplify things."

"So you tell your little conspiracy story and what happens?"

"Manard asks his secretary to hold all calls and not to disturb him unless war is declared."

"Does he have a hide-a-bed in the office?" Jerry smirked.

"Would you please shut up."

"Fine."

"What's that memory drug Mantis is working on?" Melanie asked, leaning forward on the couch.

"Memoradium, why?"

Jerry abruptly had a bad feeling about this conversation and sensed his joking mood was about to be replaced by a much darker one.

"Guess who's also developing a memory retrieval drug?" Jerry stared blankly at her. "You got it—Litchfield Industries."

"No," was all Jerry managed to say.

The Memoradium project was classified Top Secret and had been in development for eight years. It was only recently that the results required to get approval for human testing had been achieved. In fact, the public announcement date was only weeks away, at which time Mantis would reveal its research to the scientific community. The statement, as well as a grant application, would be simultaneously made to the Health and Welfare Committee outlining Mantis' long-term goals. The latest lab results would not only revolutionize the drug industry, they'd turn the medical community on its ear. There was hope that approval of the experimental drug by the Committee's ethics panel would be automatic. However, Melanie's statement had put that in jeopardy.

Jerry got up and began to pace.

"You're kidding me, right?"

"I haven't even got to the best part."

"There's more?" Jerry asked.

"It seems Litchfield has staked more than its reputation on this drug. From what Manard told me, trying to catch up with Mantis has almost drained the company. All other R & D projects have been shelved and their budgets reallocated to this memory drug."

"That's fiscal suicide," Jerry said.

"Manard claims it's a gamble he had to take. He believes the implications of this wonder drug are so far-reaching, that the first company to the market will shut out every other Johnny-come-lately. He muttered, 'Look at Microsoft—how there's dozens of other operating systems out there but Joe Blow hears the name Microsoft and that's the end of the story.' He stopped and said, 'When the dust clears, Litchfield is going to be the Microsoft of the medical world.'"

"Where is he getting his information? Memoradium has higher security clearance than anything yet devised by the Pentagon. This research has been going on for years—how could Litchfield close the gap so quickly?"

There was a tinge of terror in Jerry's voice. He felt betrayed and violated. It was obvious something his company had worked so hard on had become the victim of industrial espionage.

For the first time since returning home, Melanie's face relaxed and she wore a wry smile.

"Remember those reallocated research funds? Not all of it went to more technicians and test tubes. Some went directly into a slush fund of sorts. Instead of cash for coffee or postage stamps, it apparently went toward bribes and blackmail." She paused for effect, as she saw surprise on Jerry's face. "Your people are pretty easy to buy, honey."

"What people?" Jerry demanded.

"Low-level techs."

"They don't have all of the data in front of them. Only a handful of people are privy to everything."

"Manard knew the top dogs couldn't be bought. However, by obtaining small bits of information from a few mutts, Litchfield was able to piece the puzzle together—or at least get a reasonable idea in what direction they should be concentrating their efforts."

They sat in silence for a moment. It was like a plot from a James Bond movie.

"Why did Manard tell you all of this?" Jerry asked, puzzled why a CEO would tell a new employee information so sensitive that if it became public knowledge, it would undoubtedly ruin his company. "It doesn't make sense, Melanie. Maybe he was trying to—"

"He knows about us. That's the hard truth," Melanie said somberly, "and he's threatened to expose us to Robert."

"That's blackmail."

"Haven't you been listening to anything I've said? This man is desperate and he's got something on us."

Jerry's mind clouded.

"So we live together, big deal."

"He showed me photocopies of documents outlining the drug research Mantis is doing."

"And?"

"They've got your signature on them. They're setting you up as the fall guy. You're the informant, Jerry."

Jerry was visibly shaken by this revelation. The colour drained from his face and his body, once tensed, became limp.

"So . . . what does he want from us?" he finally said softly, his voice cracking with emotion.

"He wants us to shut Mantis down."

"Is he insane? Why not ask us to stop the world from spinning? That's at least doable with the right nuclear weapon."

"There is something else to consider," Melanie said. "If we pull this off, Manard will pay us both a million dollars from the slush fund."

Not entirely surprised by this promise, Jerry asked the inevitable follow-up question.

"And if we don't?"

"He'll have us killed."

"He actually said those words?"

"Not exactly. The threat was implied though, believe me."

"And how does he think we can accomplish this feat, barring some natural disaster?"

"With another million dollars and by any and all means possible."

"I wonder how big this slush fund is."

"When billions are at stake, a few million is small change."

The afternoon sun slowly sank into the horizon as Jerry and Melanie tossed around various scenarios, although Melanie's heart really wasn't in it. She knew what they would have to do and relished the thought, yet there was no way she could come right out and tell Jerry her idea. She'd have to coax him a bit, which would begin later in the evening.

Until then she would play along as his co-conspirator.

Their ideas were ingenious but not entirely workable. The lab had so many safeguards that unless they could get their hands on a scud missile, trying to destroy it was not feasible. Various Mantis labs across the country were working on the same project, so taking out the main lab would have little overall effect.

They next considered a computer virus to disable the company's mainframe. However they decided this would take too long to implement, as they'd first have to develop a virus the Mantis computer couldn't detect. As hard copies of the research would still be available, it would only slow Mantis' progress as they re-entered the information.

By the time they went to bed, Jerry was emotionally and physically exhausted. He was well aware that shutting down Mantis was virtually impossible, yet to fail might mean certain death.

Laying in the dark, Jerry soon became aware of something else: Melanie's silky smooth hand slowly moving from his chest into the waistband of his boxer shorts.

"What are you doing?" he asked as she began to kiss him.

"All this espionage talk got me thinking of doing some undercover work of my own," she whispered softly. "Any objections?"

If this could happen to James Bond, why not to me? he thought.

Jerry closed his eyes and said, "Not that I can think of."

* * *

Even after a very pleasurable evening together, by morning the full implication of what they were up against started to take a toll on Jerry. His hands shook slightly as he lifted the coffee cup to his lips.

A Memorable Murder

This is ridiculous, he was thinking. *There's no way we can shut Mantis down, regardless of the consequences.*

Not knowing Manard, Jerry couldn't decide if his death threat should be taken at face value. The threat itself was disturbing though. He knew people were killed every day for a couple of bucks but never by a millionaire executive. Of course, if Manard had gambled his whole empire, he was probably now thinking like a street thug.

What would possess a man to do such a thing?

The more Jerry thought of how desperate Manard was, the sicker he felt.

On the other hand, Melanie awoke refreshed.

During the night a plan that would solve all their problems had begun to come together in her mind. The only obstacle was its complexity and that it depended on people behaving in certain ways at specific times. What especially fascinated her was that every detail would have to be thought through. Everyone involved would have to be manipulated in such a way that their actions seemed logical to the outside world. In addition, she needed to make sure there'd be no trail back to her and Jerry.

"Do you think Manard was serious about killing us?" Jerry asked before leaving for work. "Doesn't that seem a bit extreme under the circumstances? Even if he exposed us and revealed that I was the mystery source of information, we'd be thrown in jail for insider trading or corporate espionage by the feds. So why kill us?"

"He isn't thinking rationally, I grant you," Melanie said. "Let's take it to the next logical step: we're small fry and Manard is the big catch. The feds would love to take down a guy with his stature. Besides the espionage charges, there's bribing an elected official, threatening us with bodily harm and who knows how many other charges they'd manufacture against him."

"Did I hear you right? Did you say bribing an elected official?

When did Manard do that?"

"He hasn't—yet."

At her office desk, Melanie began to write out her idea. By the time she was finished it read like a murder mystery, which, in fact, it was. She was certain Jerry wasn't going to like it.

Under the circumstances, he really had no choice.

The threat of being exposed as an informant had already shaken him. That Manard had no such documents in his possession was not the issue. However, his unequivocal participation in her plot to exact revenge upon the Barkers was paramount. For her, lying to Jerry was akin to telling a kid Santa Claus existed. Melanie's strategy had always been tell everyone what they wanted to hear, especially if the truth would never come to light. In the case of the forged documents, there was no way Jerry would ever need to see them. When this unseemly business was over, she would tell him she'd personally shredded them. End of discussion.

Melanie reread her notes. Bribery, kidnapping, murder.

This will be fun, she thought.

Upon reading the same notes that evening, Jerry went ballistic.

"There is no way I am going to kill anyone, Melanie!"

"You're not going to, Jerry. I am," Melanie replied in a calm cold voice. "You see, I value my life more highly than anyone else's, including yours. Therefore, when my life is threatened, I'm going to do everything in my power to stay alive."

Melanie walked across the room with her right hand behind her back. Sitting on Jerry's lap, she said, "Right now we're in this together. That doesn't necessarily mean things between us won't change."

Melanie brought her hand around and showed him the small gun she'd picked up that afternoon.

"What are you doing, Melanie?" Jerry asked, beginning to panic as she drew the barrel of the gun across his chest. "I've got as much at stake as you." Melanie lifted the gun to Jerry's temple. "I don't care how we accomplish this thing, let's just get it over with."

Melanie threw the gun onto the nearby couch and began to laugh. As Jerry looked as though he was about to cry, she planted a wet kiss on his trembling lips.

"You didn't think I'd shoot you, honey, did you?"

Flustered, Jerry pushed Melanie off his lap.

"I don't know what you were trying to prove, Melanie, but I am against this idea. One—I don't think it'll work, which means Manard will track us down and kill us. And two—even if it does, the police will be searching for us until the end of time. This is too damn complicated!"

"Leave the complications to me," Melanie said as she poured herself a double bourbon.

They stared at each other across the room.

"I need some air," Jerry said, breaking the silence. "I'll be back later."

He grabbed his coat and left, presumably heading to the condo he still kept. From the start, he'd told Melanie that keeping two separate residences would ensure neither of them felt trapped. Although they spent most of their time at her more spacious house, days like these made paying two mortgages worth the money.

Melanie watched from the front window as Jerry drove out of sight.

That wasn't so hard after all, she decided.

In a way, she felt sorry for him. She would love to tell him why the notion of putting a bullet into Robert Barker's head was so enticing. Or why framing Lynn for the murder was so tantalizing. She knew she couldn't, at least for the time being. Someday, she would probably tell him all the sordid details.

Then again, she mused as she emptied her drink, *Jerry may not be around to relay those details to in the near future.*

With details, sordid and otherwise, racing through her mind, Melanie grabbed a pad of paper and started to refine her plan. She soon realized Jerry was right about it being too damn complicated.

That's what they said about the Wright Brothers' airplane though, right?

When Jerry returned in the early morning hours, he found a note taped to the fridge.

Dear Jerry,

I know you're not in favour of my plan, however, I believe it's the only hope of shutting down Mantis, if only for a short time. Remember, that is our goal. If we fail, I'm convinced Manard will kill us. The thought frightens me and in drastic situations like this, I believe drastic measures have to be taken.

I love you and would never do anything to hurt you. We are a team through and through.

Love, Melanie

While drinking at various local bars, Jerry had come to the conclusion that no matter what they did, they were in a no-win situation. So if Melanie wanted to give her idea a shot, fine.

After reading the note, he hid it in one of his favourite books for safe keeping. He figured for her plan to get to the point of killing anyone, several things had to happen. He was betting most it wouldn't come to fruition and the plan would soon be scrapped for a more sensible one.

Jerry was wrong.

ELEVEN

Jerry arrived at the office and began to organize Robert's appointments for the day. Next, he stepped into Robert's spacious oak-walled office and placed several documents requiring a signature on the desk. This was Jerry's routine each and every business day, except during his four weeks of vacation, which were often interrupted by Robert, who couldn't find vital information at his fingertips. Their working relationship was entering its seventh year, which made Melanie's radical ideas hard to justify.

As was his morning ritual, Robert strode briskly through the lobby's glass doors at 9:15, a coffee in one hand and his briefcase in the other hand. Although some executives were in their offices before many of the staff, Robert always felt that caused problems in the long run. His strategy was to act like a man in charge with complete faith in those who worked around him. He had already achieved wealth, respect and, in a small way, fame—so there was really no reason to come to work early. His father had worked himself ragged to get the company to where it was today.

Robert had no intention of doing the same.

"Morning, Jerry," Robert said, as he took off his coat. "Anything of major importance today?"

Jerry grabbed his scheduler and stood at the head of Robert's desk.

"You have a 10:00 with Barry Miller to discuss financing the Serkel research. At noon there's a conference call with our Houston, Seattle and Florida heads of engineering to discuss expansion plans in their regions. Then at 2:30, Melvin Black has requested your presence in the lab regarding some facet of the Memoradium Project."

"He gave no details of what he wanted to discuss?" Robert asked, looking up from the documents set out before him.

"He said it was imperative, whatever that means."

"Is that all for the day?"

"For now."

Jerry began toward the door when he was stopped by Robert.

"Would I have time to sneak away for some personal business?" Robert's eyes never left the papers he was reading, knowing Jerry knew exactly what was being asked.

Jerry turned and only then did Robert look up.

"Morning or afternoon business?" Jerry asked, trying to suppress a smile.

"Well. . ." Robert began as he leaned back in his chair. "I think this afternoon would be better for Alysha," he finally said. "Hold on a sec."

Robert pressed one of the many memory buttons on his desk phone.

"Alysha Foster."

"Alysha, my love, how are you this fine morning?"

The woman's voice went from a friendly business tone to an almost giddy teenage girl's in a split second.

"I'm fine," she said demurely. "Is this call business or personal?"

"As personal as two people can get," Robert replied with a wide smile, "without having to pay by the minute." Alysha began to laugh on the other end. "Actually, I'm calling to see if you were free this afternoon. I'd like to go over a couple of briefs with you," Robert added, winking mischievously at Jerry who finally smiled.

"When you put it that way," Alysha purred in agreement, "I guess I won't be missed for an hour . . . or two."

"How about 1:30 then?"

"The Highland?"

"No problem."

"It's a date then. I'll see you later, Robert."

"I can't wait," Robert said softly, as he ended the call. "This won't cause any problems, scheduling-wise, will it?" he asked Jerry.

"Not really. I'll bump the conference call up an hour and Melvin Black back an hour."

"You're the man, Jerry."

"Thank you, Robert."

"I'm not kidding," Robert said as he came out from behind his desk and walked to Jerry's side. "Do you know why I wanted a male assistant?" He didn't wait for an answer. "Because I've found they're more trustworthy than females. Gossip less. The way you've handled my relationship with Alysha has been extraordinary and I want to thank you." Robert patted Jerry on the back. "Come Christmas, I think you'll like the bonus I have in mind for you."

"I look forward to it," Jerry responded with a smile.

Jerry felt the time was ripe to implement one of Melanie's ideas.

"Are you certain Lynn knows nothing about Alysha?"

Robert was startled by the question.

"Not that I'm aware of. Has she acted suspicious when you've dealt with her?"

"Not at all," Jerry answered with a shrug, as he sat behind his desk. He saw relief on Robert's face. "It's only that—and I've never told anyone this before—late last year I thought my girlfriend was fooling around on me. I could never prove it, which drove me nuts."

Robert tried to camouflage his panic, which he knew must be

turning his face red. Luckily, Jerry seemed more interested in searching for the hotel's phone number. Robert took several steps away from Jerry's desk, grabbing a magazine off a nearby table as he did so.

"Really?" Robert managed to say. "I had no idea. You said late last year, right?"

"Yeah, I'm guessing between September and December. After the first of January I got the feeling everything was back to normal."

"How could you tell—about the affair, I mean?" Robert asked anxiously, trying to act nonchalant about the whole subject.

"I don't know, little things. Her cell bill skyrocketed. She seemed to be working late more often. Then there were receipts for jewellery I never saw her wear."

The chain that hung around Robert's neck began to feel like a white hot branding iron. His mind now dizzy with fear.

Had Melanie told Jerry of their affair? It wasn't possible, was it? Why would Jerry keep working for me if she had?

"You said you couldn't prove an affair. Did you suspect anyone in particular?" Robert stammered.

"No. Maybe one of those faceless men Melanie works with at the agency and talks about on occasion. Guys I've never met."

Jerry looked up at Robert who seemed out of sorts.

"Are you all right?" Jerry asked uneasily.

"Me? Oh, I'm fine," Robert said, running his hand through his hair. "You got me thinking, that's all—about Lynn." Robert paced for a moment, clearly agitated at the thought. "Are you sure she hasn't acted suspiciously?"

"Of course not," Jerry replied enthusiastically. "I'm sorry I brought it up. It was—"

"What?" Robert interrupted.

"Well, I was thinking about that gala a couple of weeks ago."

"I remember. The one for Adams, right?"

"Right. I know you're going to think this is stupid and it was probably my imagination but I saw her talking quite a bit with the Senator."

"Adams? Yes, yes, I remember," Robert declared with a laugh. "They were talking business—about our grant application for Memoradium—although I'm sure she never mentioned it by name." Robert felt relief sweep over him. Lynn's efforts to boost Mantis' chances had not gone unnoticed. "Lynn told me all about it on the way home and we had a laugh over it."

Jerry sat silent, unsure how to proceed. Part of Melanie's plan hinged on the fact Robert was unaware of Lynn's flirting with Adams. He was supposed to become suspicious, which would in turn cause friction at home. Melanie had been wrong though. Robert obviously knew about Lynn's actions and had even discussed it later that night.

So much for Melanie's grand plan, Jerry thought.

"I guess the business card the Senator gave Lynn was part of the act then, huh?"

Robert's calm composure appeared to crack with this revelation.

What business card? Lynn had never mentioned that.

Not wanting to appear out of the loop, Robert quickly said, "Actually, she gave me the card. You know, in case I wanted to speak to him personally when we file the application."

Robert's nervous smile and awkward laugh hadn't fooled Jerry. Something was amiss.

He hadn't known about the card.

Jerry's spirits immediately rose. It was as if on the last play of the game he'd managed to snatch a victory from the jaws of defeat.

"That should come in handy when the time comes," Jerry said with a grin.

Although staggered, Robert willed himself to laugh at Jerry's statement. As Jerry reached for the phone, Robert said, "Could you make sure there's a bottle of wine waiting for us?"

"The usual then," Jerry stated as he began to dial the hotel.

Robert returned to his office where he folded into his chair. In reality, over the past two weeks, Robert had begun to suspect something strange about Lynn's demeanour. She was too *up* lately, with no apparent reason for the sudden change in attitude. After hearing what Jerry had said, Robert's inclination to dismiss Lynn having an affair as inconceivable slowly became believable. It was then he remembered a snippet of their conversation after the gala.

I was thinking of sleeping with him to guarantee his approval.

As he stared blankly out the large window behind his desk, Robert wished he was with Alysha that very moment, so she could ease the tension in his neck which he found almost paralyzing.

Shifting in his chair, he felt the gold chain Melanie had given him the previous Thanksgiving slide across his chest. She had been the first woman, aside from Lynn, he had made love to in over 15 years. Their affair was a real eye-opener. The possibilities seemed endless. Lynn had become cold over time (or so he thought) and had stopped satisfying his sexual needs. Melanie, on the other hand, was the complete opposite. Nothing was taboo with her. When it came to her body and having sex, she was the freest person Robert had ever encountered. After their first tryst, Robert knew why Jerry often came to work looking totally exhausted.

As the new year dawned, however, Robert became attracted to one of his lab technicians, who was as full of vitality in bed as Melanie but whose body was 10 years younger. He'd tried to let Melanie down easily, claiming Lynn had found out about them and had threatened divorce. If she succeeded, so the story went, she would take control of the company and oust him as President and CEO.

It was a threat he couldn't take lightly and therefore they would have to stop seeing each other.

A Memorable Murder

At the start of their fling, Melanie insisted there would be no talk about their work. Aside from their connection with Jerry, neither discussed any other personal or family matters. So even when they went their separate ways, Robert still had no idea where Melanie was employed (aside from the vague marketing aspect of her job).

In many ways, they were strangers who decided to get together for a roll in bed every once in awhile.

Friends with benefits.

With Alysha, Robert was trying to keep the same "no strings, no commitment" rules in effect and so far things had worked out quite nicely. However, as he watched the sun disappear behind a band of storm clouds, his cheerful mood courtesy of Alysha, slowly darkened as well. He wondered if Lynn had really started her own private dating service.

Robert stood and grabbed some papers he would need for his 10:00 meeting. He closed his eyes and rubbed his temples the way he'd ask Alysha to do later in the day; still his head continued to throb.

Walking out of his office, Robert felt an involuntary shiver run through him as he unexpectedly heard Lynn's annoying grandmother's advice ringing in his head.

What's good for the goose is good for the gander.

TWELVE

Melanie's first encounter with Lynn was during a Grade 11 gym class. Melanie had transferred to Glenridge High School and knew no one. At the time, she was what her mother referred to as an ugly duckling, who was only now blossoming into a beautiful swan. She was a bit pudgy, wore glasses and her breasts still resembled her stepfather's: all fat, with no symmetry. Although not unattractive, Melanie knew the quarterback of the football team wasn't going to be asking her to the Christmas dance.

"Everyone line up," Mrs. Brothers said after blowing her whistle. "Lynn and Debbie, you'll be the team captains."

With an air of condescension surrounding them, Lynn Fletcher and Debbie Sutherland walked to Mrs. Brother's side. They were the two girls to whom every boy wanted to lose their virginity. They were tall, slim, athletic, with full-formed bodies that made college girls envious. Looking at the other students, it was apparent they already knew which team they'd be on. The only difference today was that there was a new girl in line.

The predictable choosing order came to an abrupt halt when

destiny stepped in and Sherri Webster was called to the guidance office.

Disappointment registered on Lynn's face as she stared at the last girl on the green line.

With a twinge of resentment Lynn said, "I guess I'll take *her*."

Due to her looks and/or general lack of co-ordination, Melanie had taken a fair share of ridicule over the years. To have Miss Pom Pom directing slights her way on the very first day of school, however, made Melanie livid. It would be a feeling that only grew in intensity over the next two years.

Now two decades later, Melanie was about to do the unthinkable and call the old hag up. Hearing of Robert's reaction to Adams' business card hand-off was like a sign from above. It was looking like her plan was not as foolhardy as even she'd first thought.

"Hello, Barker residence," a woman with a slight accent said.

A maid, how domestic, Melanie thought.

"Hello, I'm calling for Mrs. Lynn Barker. Would she be home?"

The sound of her own sugar-coated voice made Melanie sick to her stomach.

"Mrs. Barker is out. I expect her back soon. Can I take a message?"

I don't know, can you? Melanie said to herself.

"No, that's okay. I'll try back later this afternoon."

"Would you like to leave your name?" Francelina inquired.

Melanie almost declined the offer, then decided to say, "Please tell Mrs. Barker a friend from Glenridge High called."

"Glenridge High? Is that a company, ma'am?" Francelina asked, sounding confused.

Melanie suppressed a laugh.

No, it's a state of mind, you idiot.

"Mrs. Barker will know what it means," Melanie said sweetly as she hung up the phone.

The morning dragged as Melanie's head was filled with possibilities for the weeks ahead. Although her desire to make contact with Lynn now verged on the fanatical, she was uncertain of Lynn's reaction to her call.

Would she be happy to hear from an old high school classmate? Would she politely say it was great to hear from her but had no intention of getting together? Would she even remember Melanie Strauss?

Of course she will, Melanie thought.

A smile formed on her lips as she silently thanked her mother for letting her stepfather adopt her, even if no one outside of the family knew. From Grade 12 onward all legal documents pertaining to Melanie were directed to Melanie Fields, instead of Melanie Strauss (although she continued to use that name until she left for college). Now as long as Robert never saw Lynn with Melanie—which would put an end to everything rather quickly—there would be no reason for her plan not to go forward. Unless, of course, Lynn didn't want to see her.

Any fears quickly disappeared after only a few seconds speaking with Lynn.

"Melanie Strauss? From Glenridge High School? I don't believe this!" Lynn said excitedly over the phone. "How in the world did you find me?"

Gotcha, Melanie mused.

"I saw you at a gala for Senator Adams," Melanie said, trying to sound equally thrilled. "I asked around and they said you were married to Robert Barker. A few calls later and I got your number. I hope you don't mind me calling you at home."

"No, this is fine." Lynn took a deep breath and sighed. "How has it been two decades? It's gone by so fast."

"Time waits for no one, not even for the Prom Queen." Melanie hoped Lynn hadn't picked up the sarcasm in her voice. "And if you don't mind me saying, you still look like you could run for the title."

Melanie tried not to gag.

"I don't know about that," Lynn said modestly. There was a short awkward silence before Lynn continued. "We should get together to talk about old times."

Hook, line and sinker, Melanie thought gleefully.

"That would be great. When are you available?"

Lynn checked her calendar, telling Melanie of all the committees she sat on and how it seemed she was always preparing for the next meeting.

They finally agreed they'd meet for lunch in three days.

"It certainly is nice to hear from you, Melanie. You know I never really kept in touch with anyone from back home."

"Me neither," Melanie replied.

"So I'll meet you at Spinoly's at 12:30."

"I can't wait," Melanie said.

As Lynn put down the phone, Francelina entered the hallway and asked, "Is everything all right, Mrs. Barker?"

"It couldn't be better. The woman who called is a friend of mine from high school. We haven't seen each other since graduation."

"Were you close?"

"Now that I think of it . . ."

A puzzled look came over Lynn's face as she began to recall in more vivid detail memories from the past.

"Are you okay, Mrs. Barker?" Francelina asked, concerned by her employer's change of expression.

"Yes, I'm fine." Lynn entered the luncheon information into her cell phone's scheduler. "I'll be having lunch with Melanie on Thursday, so you needn't fix me anything that day."

Lynn left Francelina and went to her bedroom to change into more comfortable clothes. She was both excited and apprehensive about

Melanie's call. They had been more *acquaintances* than friends. Lynn remembered that when Melanie transferred to Glenridge she was a tad overweight and was instantly deemed unfit to join her clique, made up of fellow cheerleaders and jocks. As one of the most popular girls in school, Lynn knew that being voted Prom Queen wasn't about getting respectable grades. It was about hanging out with the right people. This was the reason Melanie never got to compete for the brilliant-looking tiara in her final year.

* * *

Melanie had been a loner during her first year at Glenridge. Then in her senior year, a fantastic metamorphosis took place and she was unexpectedly the centre of attention. During the summer break, she had exercised daily until she had the body of a dancer. She'd also worked at the beach Burger Hut and made new friends who partied with her every night after closing time.

When school reconvened, Lynn was feeling a bit threatened. Although never revealing her dislike for Melanie, her friends knew and remained loyal to her. After she'd made a play for Lynn's boyfriend, it was this same staunch loyalty that doomed Melanie.

Before there was Robert Barker, there was Peter Elliot.

If Lynn was every guy's fantasy, Peter was her equal with the entire female population, except maybe Melanie who thought he was kind of simple. His choice in girlfriends only confirmed this notion.

For her final year, Melanie had higher sights already set, none of which involved Peter and Lynn. Yet, as had happened so many other times in her life, fate stepped in.

At the first dance of the year, Melanie's attention was squarely focused on the new shop teacher, Mr. Francis, whose pro football career was cut short by a blown kneecap during a bowl game. Although she'd flirted with him all night, he kept rebuffing her advances, saying any relationship between teacher and student would not be condoned.

"Only if we're caught," Melanie said with a smile, to no avail. "Well then, you just made one guy here tonight very happy."

She could feel Francis' eyes watching her as she walked away.

You had your chance, stud, she thought, now surveying the gym.

Horny and annoyed, she decided on the only male present rumoured to know his way around the female anatomy.

"Hi, Peter, how are you tonight?" Melanie asked. "Where's our future Prom Queen tonight?"

"Sick," he said making sure Lynn's friends weren't monitoring him. "The flu or something."

"So you're all alone? Poor baby." Melanie could see Peter's uneasiness. "Don't be afraid, I won't bite."

"That's not what I heard," Peter chuckled, his nervousness subsiding.

He and Lynn had actually fought that afternoon and she'd decided to visit a cousin. When Peter said, "You'll miss tonight's dance," Lynn replied, "Oh, I'll still be dancing tonight, just not with you."

If she wants to screw around, let her, he thought.

"You wouldn't know where to get a real drink, do you?"

Her purring voice sent waves of pleasure through Peter's body. The idea of getting back at Lynn through Melanie's thighs had an unmistakable appeal to it.

"Maybe."

Melanie noticed several pairs of eyes looking in their direction.

"Meet me at the Burger Hut."

"It's closed for the season," Peter stated, thinking this scene was some kind of set up.

"Not if you have a key," Melanie replied pulling out her key ring. "I'll be there in a half hour."

Passing Mr. Francis near the stage, Melanie said, "I'm about to find out if one of your shop students knows how to use his tool properly. I would have much preferred his teacher but c'est la vie."

By Monday, rumours were rampant about Melanie and Peter. Lynn, tormented by suspicion, decided to believe in Peter's fidelity, even though her friends kept telling her otherwise. Peter wisely kept his mouth shut about the whole affair which continued twice a week for the remainder of the school year.

Unfortunately, all good things must come to an end and so it was one warm April evening Peter told Melanie he had to end it because he wanted to marry Lynn.

He's dumping me for her? Melanie thought, astounded. *I should be dumping him for Mr. Francis!*

In her worst nightmares, Melanie was never the one being given the old heave-ho, as that would mean she was no longer in control.

"You can't do this to me, you ungrateful bastard!"

"If I don't, Debbie will tell Lynn everything," Peter cried.

"Debbie Sutherland? What does she have to do with anything?"

As if confessing murder to a priest, the true story about his engagement plans streamed out of Peter's mouth.

"Debbie followed me to the Burger Hut on several occasions and is going to expose us to Lynn."

"You said it would teach her right if she ever found out!" Melanie reminded him, venom dripping off each word.

"I love her, Melanie," Peter sobbed. "I can't hurt her like that."

"And it's okay to hurt me? You are a pathetic worm, Peter Elliot. I've seen bed sheets with more backbone than you."

The following day Melanie pulled Debbie Sutherland aside.

"What gives you the right to stick your nose into other people's business?" Melanie demanded.

"Lynn's my friend," Debbie replied, pushing Melanie away, "and

I'm not going to let her get hurt."

"Maybe I'll go tell Lynn myself. What do you think about that, darling?"

Debbie's face went hard.

"You wouldn't dare."

"And why not? I don't have anything to lose."

"But Mr. Francis does."

The words came out of Debbie's mouth icy cold and their effect was immediate.

"Peter wasn't the only one I was following around." She let the implication seep in. "I'm sure the school board would be very interested in some photos I have." With a huge smile she added Melanie's favourite catchphrase, "If you know what I mean."

"Give me the pictures," Melanie said in a controlled, yet strained voice, "and I'll leave precious Lynn and Peter alone.

Graduation could not come quickly enough for everyone involved. Peter and Lynn were crowned Prom King and Queen and Debbie spent the final month of school in traction, after the front wheel of her bike mysteriously came off, sending her beneath the wheels of a bus.

Melanie Strauss, upon writing her final exam, had enough of small-town life and disappeared. She later surfaced as a college student majoring in marketing.

To complete her transformation, she also decided to start going by her adopted surname.

Thus, Melanie Fields was born.

THIRTEEN

"I had quite a surprising phone call this afternoon," Lynn said at the dinner table.

"Really," Robert replied absentmindedly, as he placed a piece of T-bone steak into his mouth. "Anyone I know?"

"Her name is Melanie."

Robert began to cough violently, as the steak momentarily lodged in his windpipe.

"Are you all right?" Lynn asked.

Robert quickly downed his glass of water and stood up from the table to catch his breath.

First Jerry had brought up an affair he'd suspected Melanie of having and now over dinner her name had popped up again.

What in the world does this woman want from me?

"And what did she want?" Robert asked, not hiding the contempt in his voice. "Money?"

Lynn was taken aback by Robert's reaction.

"Why would she want money?"

Robert put both hands on the table and leaned forward, staring

directly at Lynn.

"Why don't you tell me?" he said in an almost sinister manner.

"What has gotten into you?" Lynn asked as she threw her napkin onto her plate. "One, you don't know Melanie Strauss, so I'm not quite sure why you're acting this way. And second, I don't care for your tone. It's as if you're accusing me of something. Obviously you've got something on your mind, so come right out and say it, Robert."

Robert stood dumbfounded.

Who in the world is Melanie Strauss?

His eyes remained locked in a stare with Lynn's. Everything he had worked so hard to keep under wraps had inexplicably begun to unravel. He knew Lynn was not about to be placated by some weak excuse. Unfortunately, he had nothing else to give her.

"I thought you said Bellamy, dear. Which in no way justifies my actions."

"Who is this Bellamy woman?" Lynn shot back. "And why would she be calling me for money?"

"She wouldn't—I mean I got confused," Robert stuttered.

"Who is she, Robert?" Lynn demanded.

She knew all about Alysha Foster and the Highland Hotel, yet her spies at the office had never mentioned anyone named Bellamy.

Robert's mind started to shut down. All he wanted was to leave the house and drive far away. Not only had he almost spilled the beans about his affair with Melanie, he'd made his wife suspicious about a possible affair with a woman who didn't exist.

"Bellamy is a name she gave me over the phone," he finally said. "She says she has high-level information about the Memoradium Project and wants me to buy it from her. Otherwise she'd sell it to the highest bidder."

Robert paused and tried to read Lynn's expression.

"Go on."

"So . . . when you mentioned a woman named Bellamy had contacted you, I thought it was the one I was dealing with and that she was going to blackmail you." Robert could feel his face getting redder. "See, it was a big misunderstanding, as you apparently said Melanie, not Bellamy — which is certainly better than if it had been Bell . . ." Robert's voice trailed off as he realized he was starting to sound like a bizarre Monty Python or Benny Hill sketch.

"Are you through?"

"I think so," Robert said resigned.

"I hope so," Lynn said shaking her head in disgust. "I've never seen a man pitch so much manure in my direction since I visited my uncle's cattle farm. At least he warned me that I should stand clear. Not you, though. That would be too easy. You really are a tiny man, Robert — at least in my eyes." Lynn got up from the table and walked toward the door. "I'm going for lunch with Melanie Strauss on Thursday. Who knows, maybe she really is the mysterious Bellamy. What do you think?" Getting no response as she exited the room, Lynn added, "Of course, I'm not sure you can think anymore, at least not with the head on your shoulders."

After Lynn left for parts unknown, Robert sat by himself in the silence of the dining room for over an hour. Lynn's final words indicated she knew he was fooling around, although he couldn't bring himself to believe it.

Maybe she was only testing me, he thought.

Either way he was screwed. If she wasn't suspicious before, he'd given her every reason to be now.

After calming his nerves with a substantial amount of scotch, Robert recalled what Jerry had said earlier in the day.

I guess the business card the Senator gave to Lynn was all part of the act then, huh?

The operative word was 'act.'

A MEMORABLE MURDER

As the alcohol took effect, Robert became more convinced the Senator and Lynn were having an affair. Unlike his babbling this evening, however, he had no proof of such a relationship. Unless . . .

With Lynn gone, Robert did something he'd never felt obliged to do during their marriage. His search of Lynn's bureaus, dressers, vanities, closets and purses was thorough. Finding nothing, he felt ashamed of himself. Here he was trying to justify his extramarital affairs by rifling through Lynn's personal belongings—in the hope of finding a simple business card.

During those galas, he routinely gave out his Mantis business card. That was how business was done. It didn't mean he wanted to sleep with every woman he gave his card to.

Robert quickly replaced Lynn's things back to where they belonged, trying to keep everything as orderly as possible.

This was a very stupid idea, he scolded himself.

He made his way to the kitchen and started up the coffee machine. Walking into the den to catch a football game on the tube, something at the back door caught his eye: a white purse.

Don't do it, a little voice in his head implored. *You've already done enough damage this evening. If the card isn't hidden in her underwear drawer, why would it be in this purse, out in the open? It doesn't make sense, Robby boy.*

As most people who've been drinking too much can attest, logic has no meaning at certain times.

This was one of those times.

Robert grabbed the purse and opened the top flap. Inside was the main compartment and two smaller zippered compartments. Learning his lesson from his bedroom actions, Robert slowly took each item out of the purse and laid it on the floor. A wave of relief passed through his body as he found no card in any of the three compartments.

Having replaced its contents, he picked the purse off the floor and again set it on the table near the back door. As he did so, his hand lightly brushed against the back side of the purse. The material was not smooth. Turning the purse over he discovered a fourth compartment. There was no zipper and the opening was camouflaged, as there was no lining on the top of it. A quick glance and you'd have thought it was all one piece of leather.

With his heart racing, Robert slipped his fingers into the compartment. When they touched a business card, his pulse quickened even more.

The first words he read were written by hand.

The Palace. 2:00 p.m. Room 1845. The Presidential Suite.

Robert turned the card over and read the bold type engraving: **Senator Douglas F. Adams**.

FOURTEEN

The only bright spot in Lynn's life was her scheduled lunch with Melanie. Robert had been unbearable to be around and made excuses for working late—none of which Lynn believed.

I hope Miss Bellamy is servicing all your needs, she thought.

Lynn arrived early at Spinoly's - the city's trendiest restaurant on the strip - hoping to catch a glimpse of Melanie as she walked in. Of course, Melanie had the advantage of knowing what she looked like from the party. Lynn had been too preoccupied with Douglas' advances to concentrate on anyone or anything else that evening.

Melanie beat Lynn at her own game, arriving a half-hour early and taking a stool at the bar. She wanted to make sure the soon-to-be widow actually showed. When Lynn appeared in the lobby, Melanie quickly downed her drink and exited to the street via a side door. A few minutes later, she casually re-entered the restaurant.

As the hostess checked the reservation book, Melanie and Lynn's eyes met and 20 years instantly vanished.

"I can't believe this is really happening," Lynn said as Melanie made her way to the table.

You can say that again, Melanie thought.

"It has been awhile, hasn't it?" she said with a smile.

They stood in the aisle looking at each other, feeling an awkward moment pass between them, unsure if a "welcome hug" was required.

"Oh please, Lynn, sit down," Melanie finally said. "I'm not used to people getting up when I enter a room. I think you're only supposed to do that when a lady approaches—and I'm sure you don't remember me as a lady."

"Times change," Lynn laughed. "I'll give you the benefit of the doubt."

Oh thank you, your highness.

"You always were the diplomatic type."

Whatever hard feelings Lynn may have harboured in high school, Melanie didn't detect any during their lunch. In fact, much to her dismay, she was actually having fun reliving the good old days—even if it was with her arch-rival. What truly surprised Melanie was how Lynn had softened over the years. Gone was the superiority complex. Her husband may have millions in the bank but Lynn's days of being better than everyone were now over.

Even a prom queen's reign only lasts one year, Melanie reflected with a smirk.

"So, you mentioned you don't keep in touch with anyone back home?"

"Not really. I don't get back much. We still get the Examiner every week, although I don't know why. After five years, all the names were of people I don't know. Every so often a picture of the town council pops up or an award is given out and I'll recognize someone from school."

"Like who?"

"Well, let's see. Do you remember Teresa Findlay?"

"Thick glasses, curly hair? Kinda mousy?"

"That's the one. There was a write-up in the Police Journal about how one night she shot her husband after he came home late."

"Did they say why?" Melanie asked.

"Does the name Sharon Hardy ring any bells?"

Melanie laughed aloud.

"Are we talking about the same Sharon Hardy whose jeans were so tight we swore she coated her legs with lubricant to get them on?"

"That's the one," Lynn laughed. "It seems that for years she's been having affairs with several men in town. Teresa finally had enough and decided to show Louie who wears the pants in the family. Unfortunately, Louie—remember Louie Dobson?—well, he won't be wearing pants for a while until his groin heals sufficiently."

To the other restaurant patrons, they were the perfect picture of two old friends reminiscing about the past. Once Lynn and Melanie had caught up on former classmates and neighbours and dessert had been served, the conversation finally came around to their personal lives.

"I haven't had much luck in the marriage department," Melanie stated, "although after three divorces, I certainly do know my way through the court system."

"Maybe you can give me the number of your lawyer," Lynn said in a low tone. "I guess you never know when you'll need one."

"Problems at home?" Melanie asked.

As she waited for Lynn to finish her coffee, Melanie felt a twinge of trepidation regarding her affair with Robert. It wasn't often that the other woman gets to hear the wife's side of the story. Most women take the cheating husband's word at face value, with no way of substantiating his claims about why their affair has to stop. Today, however, Melanie was going to revel in the truth, straight from the horse's mouth.

"I don't want to burden you, Melanie," Lynn said resigned. "After three divorces I'm sure the last thing you want to hear about is another woman's marital problems—especially from someone you haven't seen since you were 18."

"Don't be silly, Lynn," Melanie replied.

She reached across the table and placed her hand on top of Lynn's.

"I might have had better luck in love if I'd had someone to talk to when things were troubling me."

She took her hand back, seeing Lynn had been genuinely moved by the gesture.

"The fact is," Melanie continued, "I didn't have any girlfriends who wouldn't blab my problems in a heartbeat. I'm certain the women at those fundraisers of yours are all social snobs. The type who, at the first whiff of scandal, transform themselves into wolverines, ready to eat one of their own, if you know what I mean."

There it was—The Phrase, Lynn thought. In school she'd overheard Melanie say it a thousand times and always thought it was just a way for her to act tough. A catch phrase that implied knowledge Melanie may or may not have possessed. Today, it sounded authentic and surprisingly sincere.

"Wolverines at least have the courage to bare their teeth when they decide to attack," Lynn said with a nervous laugh. "Most of the high class socialites I meet don't give any warning when they decide to turn on someone. One day they're all chummy with you and the next you're a pariah. Of course, if you grovel long enough, they'll accept you back into the fold—lucky you."

"That's what I figured," Melanie agreed quickly, still anxious to get Lynn talking. "I, on the other hand, have no vested interest in your personal or public life."

"Then in theory I can trust you with my deepest darkest secrets?"

"Who would I tell?" Melanie quipped. "Sharon Hardy?"

Lynn only smiled back.

Melanie could sense she was still weighing her options. After

savouring the last forkful of her cherry cheesecake, any apprehension vanished from her face.

"At first I ignored the tell-tale signs," Lynn confided, unloading a burden she'd been carrying alone for much of the past year. "Working late, alcohol on his breath when he came home, being unable to reach him at the office in the afternoon. It wasn't until last Thanksgiving when I noticed he was wearing a gold chain, all the pieces fell together."

At the mention of the gift she'd given Robert, Melanie almost choked on her coffee.

"Are you okay?" Lynn asked, worried by the sudden fit of coughing.

"Fine—really. It's only that what you described happened to me several years ago—Husband #2. One day, out of the blue, he starts strutting around with a chain around his neck. When I asked him where he got it, he said he'd bought it for himself. He claimed he'd seen it in a store window on his way home from work."

Melanie saw Lynn's face go white.

"That's exactly what Robert told me," Lynn said in an uncertain voice. "When I confronted him about the price and the store he began to stammer. It was all the proof I needed."

"Did he ever tell you where he bought it?" Melanie asked, knowing full well Robert had told Lynn he'd purchased it at the upscale King & Co. store.

"Only after he became very defensive toward me."

"Fits the pattern. My husband claimed he bought it at King & Co. on 57th Street and then he—"

"Did you say King & Co.?" Lynn asked incredulously.

"Yes, why?" Melanie replied, trying to remain calm. "Robert didn't say the same place, did he?"

A blank look momentarily came over Lynn's face.

"I can't believe after all this time apart, we're here today relating an identical experience we've both had to endure. It's uncanny."

Like flippin' incredible, Melanie mused to herself.

"Spooky is more like it," she said aloud. "What happened next?"

"Well, knowing he'd been caught, things settled down for a month or so. Maybe he broke up with the little tramp, I don't know. What I do know is that he became eerily sombre, walking around the house as if on egg shells. Then out of nowhere he became talkative again, more outgoing—happier, you know."

After hearing herself described as a little tramp, Melanie almost lost it.

That wouldn't help things along, now would it? she thought. *Remain calm. Act civil. Act interested.*

"So the two of you patched things up?" Melanie asked, knowing full well Alysha Foster was now on the scene.

"Hardly," Lynn said with a wave of her hand. "He started to screw around again."

"No."

"Oh, yes. This time with a lab technician from the office."

"How did you find out?" Melanie inquired, almost giddy that Robert's second fling had been discovered almost immediately.

Lynn began to laugh.

"When a man has sex on his mind, the rest of his brain becomes oatmeal. For instance, take those memory buttons on your telephone. Common sense would dictate you don't put your home number next to your bimbo's number."

"You mean he—"

"Uh-huh. Pressed my button when he really wanted to press hers." Lynn paused for a second. "There's something Freudian about that last sentence, isn't there? Anyway, I picked up the phone and lo and behold, I hear Mr. Faithful saying, 'It's me, honey. Can't wait to see you at the Highland.'"

"What did you say?"

"I was too shocked, so I hung up."

"Did you ever confront him?"

"I couldn't be bothered," Lynn stated matter-of-factly. "Why fight for a lost cause? I decided the best defense was a better offense."

"I don't get it. Obviously you haven't filed for divorce, so how are you making him pay?"

Come on down, Senator Adams, Melanie hoped.

"Let me put it this way," Lynn said in a low whisper. "What's good for the goose is good for the gander, as my grandmother always said."

"You mean you're having an affair?"

"Men have affairs. I like to think what I am doing is an extra-curricular romance with no strings attached, which is fine with—" She stopped herself as the word *Douglas* was forming on her lips. "Well, let's say it's also a suitable arrangement for the man I'm seeing."

But the damage was done. Melanie could read Lynn's lips saying Douglas, even if the actual word never materialized.

Bingo, Melanie thought. It was all she needed for her plan to proceed.

The rest of the luncheon was now inconsequential, although not unimportant. She would still have to remain on friendly terms with Lynn for everything to come together.

As their waitress left the bill, Melanie checked her watch and was surprised two hours had passed by so effortlessly.

"I wish I'd had the nerve to do that when I was married. Does Robert suspect anything?"

"Not as far as I know. I think he's too busy with his young plaything to suspect." Lynn also checked the time and realized she had a board meeting to attend in an hour. "I really hate to leave, Melanie, since we are having such a pleasant time. I've got to get uptown for a meeting though."

Against Melanie's objections, Lynn paid for lunch and they quickly planned to get together the following Monday.

"When do you see *your friend* again?" Melanie asked as they waited for their cars to be brought by the valet.

"Saturday night with any luck. He's pretty busy at the moment."

"A business tycoon?"

"Actually, he's trying to keep his present job." Lynn laughed; the thought that being a Senator was a real job amused her.

The cars arrived and the women faced each other. Knowing this moment would be a defining one in Lynn's ability to put her utmost trust in her, Melanie stepped forward and embraced her prey.

Lynn was overwhelmed by the simple gesture.

"You don't know how much this lunch has meant to me, Melanie," she said with a smile. "You're like a breath of fresh air compared to the other women I know."

"I'm glad I called," Melanie replied. "They say you can never go home, yet today was just like that, only with better food, if you know what I mean."

"I know exactly what you mean, Melanie, and I can't wait for Monday."

Both women drove off the lot feeling better than when they'd entered Spinoly's. Lynn was ecstatic she was able to talk to someone about her problems without being judged or condemned. The fact Melanie had turned out to be such an attentive listener, especially considering their past, had also been a pleasant surprise.

Getting on the freeway, Melanie was extremely pleased with herself. Over one lunch, she'd not only wiped clean years of possible animosity, she had gained Lynn's implicit trust. Which in the dark days ahead would be her biggest ally and Lynn's worst nightmare.

FIFTEEN

"We'll have him right where we want him," Melanie said as she poured a drink for herself and Jerry.

"Manard went for it?"

Melanie handed him a glass and went to the sofa.

"What choice did he have? He wants this Mantis locomotive slowed down and I told him what was needed to start applying the brakes."

Jerry took a swig of his drink and thought of the ramifications.

Wasn't bribing an elected official a felony?

"Do you really think Adams is dumb enough to go through with this?"

"Adams is definitely not dumb. What he is, though, is running for office and that means money. Lots of money."

"It also means audits and full disclosure of assets, doesn't it?" Jerry asked.

"That's not our problem, is it? How he wants to handle the disbursement of the bribe is his business. He's a career politician so I'm sure he knows how to hide illegal donations." Melanie said with a wide smile.

"Maybe," Jerry said unenthusiastically. "It's still a big if, as far as I'm concerned. He may look at you and laugh. Like you said, he's a career politician, who can probably see a con man a mile away."

Melanie stood and let her terry bathrobe fall to the floor, revealing her naked body.

"Not one like this."

She walked to Jerry's chair and straddled him.

"Are you saying if I came into your office and offered you two hundred thousand dollars *and* the use of my body, you'd turn me down?"

"You're kidding about the use of your body, right?" Jerry asked half-excited, half-fearful of Melanie's answer.

Melanie's response was to press her body against Jerry's chest as she exchanged a deep lustful kiss with him. In an hour, exhausted by Melanie's unquenchable thirst for sex, Jerry fell asleep with a million-dollar smile on his face and his question still unanswered.

As she had planned all along.

* * *

"I have a problem, Senator," Melanie said as she sat in a plush leather chair in front of Douglas Adams' desk.

They were sitting in a spacious office set up within Adams' otherwise drab campaign headquarters. The large mahogany desk was uncluttered; the only items on it were a stylish halogen lamp, a pen set and a portfolio binder which was opened to a blank piece of paper—as if ready for the Senator to write down suggestions brought to him by one of his many supporters.

Adams walked to the rear of the desk and took a seat behind it. His large frame in its blue pinstripe power suit immediately drew attention away from the size of the desk and its sparse contents. Once comfortable, Adams leaned forward and flashed his award-winning smile. Melanie quickly felt she was in the presence of a snake that had somehow manifested itself in human form.

"Well now, I hope I can be of some assistance to you."

Without consciously meaning to, Adams' eyes lowered and stared momentarily at Melanie's ample bosom, which was practically spilling out of her tiny dress with its plunging v-neck.

"As we are both busy people, Mr. Adams, I'll make this short and sweet." Melanie paused and crossed her legs, giving Adams a brief glimpse of thigh. "You have something I want and I have something you want. Actually," she added, noticing the location of his stare, "I have a couple of things you want, if you know what I mean."

Adams looked up to Melanie's face and smiled a knowing smile.

"So, what's the deal, Ms. Fields, if that is your real name? Are you recording this conversation to sell to Travers' campaign manager? Or how about the tabloids—did they put you up to this?" Adams leaned back into his chair and stretched his arms out in front of him. "I can hear it now: Candidate pays for sex with hooker! Exclusive audiotape on the next *Gotcha!* show."

Melanie simply smiled back at him.

"I've got two hundred thousand reasons for being here today, Mr. Adams," Melanie said.

"That's how much they're paying these days? That's incredible," Adams said with a look of genuine astonishment. "Of course, for you to collect I would have to unwittingly play along with your little charade, something I think both of us know is not going to happen. So if that's everything, I'll show you out."

Adams stood and began toward the office door. Noticing that Melanie had not moved, he added, "I really am a very busy man."

"Who said I was the one going to be richer at the end of this meeting?" Melanie asked coolly.

"As we are the only two in the room, I assumed you would be the beneficiary of the money, as I'm quite sure no one wants to pay me that kind of cash." A look of enlightenment crossed Adams face. "Oh, I get it now. You're not here to tempt me with sex, you're here to bribe me. Am I right?" Melanie didn't reply. "Still, I think paying you a couple of hundred grand is rather steep for a cheap bribery story."

"You talk too much, Mr. Adams."

Adams leaned over Melanie's shoulder and whispered in her ear, "I don't want you to go away empty-handed, audiotape-wise."

He straightened himself up and gave her a wink.

"We're obviously not going to continue this meeting until you're certain I'm not here to set you up," Melanie sighed. "Therefore, as a sign of goodwill I'll prove it to you."

Melanie picked her small purse off the floor and emptied its contents onto the desk: a set of keys, a lipstick and a ten-dollar bill. She then threw the purse to Adams who crushed the tiny piece of leather in his hand.

"This proves nothing," he said.

"Maybe this will convince you."

Melanie grabbed the bottom of her dress and lifted it over her head. Adams appeared dumbfounded as she stood before him stark naked.

"What are you doing?" he said as he ran to the door and activated its lock. "Put that back on!"

Melanie stood like a statue.

"Do you believe me now when I say I'm not here to record this conversation?"

"Yes, yes—please put your clothes on."

Melanie quickly threw the dress over her head and sat down again.

"Give me one reason why I shouldn't call the police?" Adams asked, his face flushed and his air of confidence gone.

"Because you want to know what I have to offer—other than my body, which you've already seen. As I said when I arrived, I want to keep this short and sweet. So here it is: The company I represent is Litchfield

Industries. We manufacture a number of pharmaceutical products, as you're well aware, being the Chairman of the Health and Welfare Committee and all." Adams nodded in agreement. "Well we have a problem and think you can help us out. Of course you'll be compensated for your trouble."

Adams laughed.

"Let me guess. Is it in the ballpark of say, two hundred thousand?"

"You're not as dumb as Senator Travers makes you out to be, you know that?"

"And what exactly would my role be, if I were as dumb as Mr. Travers claims?"

"It's simple actually. We'd like you to approve a new drug proposal which we are developing."

"You've got to be kidding," Adams said, astounded by the mere suggestion. "This wouldn't happen to be a new memory-enhancing drug, would it?"

It was now Adams' turn to enjoy his guest's shocked look.

Hit them when they least expect it, his father always told him. *You may not knock them out, but you'll be in a better position when they're dazed and confused than when they're clear and sober.*

Melanie, who thought she'd had the upper hand, realized what an amateur she was. For once it appeared Jerry was right. Adams could smell a fraud a mile away.

After a few moments of stunned silence, Adams smiled and again slid easily back into his chair.

"Never try to con a con, young lady. It's like trying to catch a greased pig. Sure, once in awhile you'll get lucky. For the most part though, the pig usually wins. And do you know why? I'll tell you. It's because the pig is used to running around in muck. You, on the other hand, are used to walking the streets in high heels." He paused and added, "High heels aren't very practical in mud though, are they?"

"I get your point," Melanie said dryly, trying to compose herself while formulating a new sales pitch.

"I can tell that you're worried I haven't heard a word you've said. Let me put that notion to rest right now. I've heard everything and I understand where you are coming from—"

"How did you know about the memory drug?" Melanie interrupted him.

"The same way Litchfield found out one of its competitors may be developing it: sources. Unlike them, I didn't have to pay for my information."

Melanie felt panic surge through her veins.

How many people outside of Litchfield knew the whole operation had been mortgaged to the hilt in the name of competition? If Adams knew, it meant his cronies did. Which meant they would all have to be bribed too.

"My informants are very discreet," Adams said, as if reading Melanie's thoughts. "You needn't worry that there will be a huge story in *The Times* any day soon. However, if Mantis self-destructs in the near future, I guarantee you that it'll be the biggest story of the year hands down."

"This conversation hasn't turned out to be short or sweet, has it?"

"And it's not over yet."

Melanie shifted in her chair and took a deep calming breath.

"Although you know far more than I ever expected, our offer remains unchanged. Over the next few weeks at regular intervals, we'll put money into your general campaign collection fund. Each donation will be completely legitimate and untraceable back to Litchfield." Melanie paused. "Or we can set up a numbered Swiss account and pay one lump sum. After the election, win or lose, you can withdraw what you want, when you want it."

Adams contemplated the offer. It was a pitch he'd heard a thousand times before with only the names, conditions and amounts being different.

A Memorable Murder

In political circles he was known as the Deal Maker - a man who could broker any agreement with another party and always come out ahead. In other, more sensible circles, he was known as the Teflon Man, as no matter what mud was flung his way, somehow—sometimes against all known forces of rational and better judgment—Senator Adams would emerge unscathed, with not so much as a speck of dirt on him.

"When would I be paid?"

"Tomorrow by noon."

Adams tried to restrain his surprise. He was used to being paid half up front and the other half upon completing his end of the bargain. With this amount of money involved, a payment in full was highly suspect.

"You're willing to gamble all that money on my ability to convince fellow committee members to approve your drug proposal?"

"That appears to be the case," Melanie said calmly, knowing the deal was done. "That we're still talking indicates you already know how such a plan could be implemented. Of course the only stipulation is that this favour be completed before you resign your seat as Chairman."

"This is truly extraordinary," Adams said, walking to a window overlooking a park. He knew with the right paperwork and by calling in a few favours, he could have any Litchfield proposal approved.

A quarter of this bribe could have had the same outcome, so why such a steep offer? he wondered.

"What are your company's real motives, Ms. Fields?"

"We want to win."

Adams nodded approvingly.

"And what if another drug company beats you to the punch?" he asked, still staring out at an empty playground.

"That's not going to happen, I can assure you."

The confidence in her voice was absolute, which was something he greatly admired in a woman.

Adams was about to say something when he turned and watched as Melanie bent forward to retrieve the items on the desk. As she placed each object into her purse, he was certain one of her breasts would pop out of her dress. At that moment he was equally certain if that were to happen, he would most likely be the one to put it back in its place . . . eventually.

Any misgivings about the deal vaporized when Melanie walked toward him and leaned against the corner of his desk. She was so close he could inhale her breath.

"For a recently widowed man you certainly give off an aura of availability."

"If that's what's going to win me the election then that's what I'm going to project," Adams replied in a laboured voice as Melanie placed her long fingernails on his crotch.

Melanie put her lips against his before pulling away slightly.

"I'm not much into politics," she purred into Adams' ear, beginning to nibble on his earlobe. "Are you a talker or a hands-on politician?"

Over the next 10 minutes, Adams showed her he was very much an action-oriented candidate and that he cared deeply about the electorate.

When it was over, Melanie gave him a smile and walked to the door. Unlocking it she heard him gasp, "When can we see each other again?"

"Who knows, maybe never."

"What if I call you in three weeks when I'll be back to appear on *The Nation Today*?" Adams asked in an almost desperate tone. "I'll even mention Litchfield's name on the air," he added, trying to sweeten the deal.

He hadn't experienced such a sex-charged adrenalin rush since his youth. The woman was absolutely incredible.

Before opening the door, Melanie adjusted her dress and blew Adams a kiss across the room.

"Your money will be in the Swiss account tomorrow. I'll courier the account number this afternoon." She turned and walked out into a room full of volunteers who stopped what they were doing to catch a glimpse of her.

As she strode to her car she allowed herself to crack a smile. It had been perfect. Her plan, once thought to be preposterous, was slowly becoming a reality. Even Adams wasn't half bad for a geezer.

Heading home, a thought came to her that she knew must have been lying in wait all day. The irony was sweet. After what happened this afternoon, she was certain every time Adams and Lynn jumped into bed, Douglas would be thinking only of her.

Melanie laughed out loud.

Twenty years later and prissy Lynn Fletcher was still playing catch-up to that little bitch once known as Melanie Strauss.

Turning into the underground garage of Jerry's condo, Melanie knew Jerry would enjoy this evening's bedroom escapades immensely. He would be happy she hadn't spent the night with Adams, while she would be reliving the glorious days of her adolescence.

Memories of the Burger Hut and Peter Elliot would be sweeter tonight than ever before.

SIXTEEN

Jerry awoke exhausted. Where Melanie got her sexual prowess was beyond him.

She'd returned from the Senator's office ready to devour him on the couch. Not until morning did he realize Melanie's plans were slowly coming together, meaning he needed to start convincing her killing Robert was not a viable option to shutting down Mantis.

When he oh–so-delicately broached the subject, Melanie knew she'd have to play her trump card and hope for the best.

Jerry was in the living room droning on about a new virus to install on the Mantis computer mainframe.

"We use our remaining money to buy the services of some computer geek to put it in for us. Okay, not all of it. We might as well keep most of it as profit. Still, there's got to be—"

Jerry's voice dropped as Melanie entered the room, a Scotch in one hand and a cigarette in the other. Her face was drained of colour, making her look more like an apparition than a flesh-and-blood woman.

She slumped onto the couch.

"Melanie, what's wrong?" Jerry asked, walking to her.

A Memorable Murder

"Stay away," she ordered, shooing the hand holding her drink out toward him. "We have to talk and I don't want you near me."

Jerry was at a loss for words. What could they possibly have to talk about? Last night was fantastic and everything seemed fine since. Jerry sat down in his favourite chair and looked at Melanie.

"What's the matter? What do we have to talk about?"

Melanie observed the concern for her in Jerry's eyes.

Like a lamb to the slaughter, she thought.

"I got my period," Melanie finally stated, finishing her Scotch.

Jerry watched as tears began to roll down her ashen cheeks.

"And that's a problem how exactly?" he inquired.

A look of disgust registered on Melanie's face.

"All men are pigs!" she shouted, practically spitting out each word. "All you care about is yourselves!"

"What are you talking about?" He'd heard the *men are pigs* ideas on numerous occasions, only not this early in the day. "We don't want kids, so your period showing up is a good thing, right?"

Melanie glared at him.

"That's typical. What is it with you? Your girlfriend gets her period and it's a cause for celebration. What happens when that same blessed event doesn't show up? Are there celebrations then, huh?" Melanie stopped for a moment, as if not sure how to continue. "Maybe that happens in other women's lives. Not mine."

Melanie completely broke down and began to cry as she'd never cried in front of Jerry before. It was of award-winning calibre, leaving Jerry dumbfounded. After a few awkward moments, he ventured cautiously out of his chair to sit beside her. Putting his arm around her shoulder he pulled her gently to his chest, where she continued to bawl.

"I never meant to hurt you, Jerry," she said between sobs. "It just happened and we got swept up in the whole thing. Honest."

"We? Who is we?"

Jerry could feel a deep pain-like sensation course through his chest, where his heart now pounded like a jackhammer.

An affair?

At first he didn't know how to react, as Melanie told him of her infidelity. As she spoke haltingly, gulping for breath between sobs, everything crystallized.

He remembered what Melanie had said when he confronted her with his suspicions. The way she had laughed about it and made him feel guilty for entertaining such thoughts.

Realizing she'd played him for months, his anger exploded in a stream of obscenities, as he pushed her away and paced the room.

"I have to be the biggest sucker in the world and you—you think it's all some big joke, don't you? All this time believing it was only you and me."

"I wanted to tell you, Jerry."

"Why should I trust anything you say? What do you care how I feel, as long as you're getting screwed?" Jerry's face was crimson and the veins in his neck were as taut as tightrope wire. "It's the best of both worlds. Having me at home to take care of your mundane needs, all the while having some guy doing you over his desk at work. Is that about right?"

Melanie did recall that once Robert had done her over a desk but it wasn't his—it was Jerry's. She concluded that raw honesty might send poor Jerry over the edge.

"He said he'd ruin your career."

Jerry stared at Melanie, who sat wide-eyed on the couch.

"Does this stud have a name?"

"Don't make me tell you," Melanie cried. "It's not important."

"Well I'd really like to know who my enemies are—especially ones you like to sleep with."

"It's over. That's all that matters."

Jerry's rage was boiling.

"You're the one who started this," he countered. "Coming in crying about your period! Every month it shows up should be a cause for celebration. Not this month though, when we have death threats hanging over our heads from Manard."

Jerry felt his self-control slipping away. Weeks of suspicion and inner turmoil were rushing to the surface. For a brief moment, the fury he'd wanted to restrain exploded and he turned away to punch a hole in the wall.

As drywall crashed to the floor, Melanie looked up in horror to see Jerry coming toward her. This was more than she'd bargained for. She never believed Jerry would ever become physically violent.

"I'm going to ask you one more time," Jerry said, pulling Melanie to her feet. Their eyes met and Jerry knew for once in their relationship she was actually taking him seriously. "What does your period and cheating on me have in common?"

Jerry squeezed Melanie's arms, causing tears to form in her eyes.

"You're hurting me, Jerry!"

"I'm hurting you? Isn't that interesting. How does it feel to be hurt by someone you supposedly love? Well?"

"Jerry, stop!"

"Tell me who he is—now!"

"Please, let me go."

"Tell me!"

"It was Robert Barker! I was screwing your boss and he made me have an abortion!" She watched Jerry's face go blank as he loosened his grip. "Are you happy now?"

Free, she pushed him away.

The words hit Jerry as hard as a sledgehammer would smash a thumbtack. He fell into a chair, the room slowly spinning out of focus.

The frenzied wrath that had overtaken him moments before dissipated. Next, he began to hyperventilate as the full weight of what Melanie had said sank in.

They sat for several minutes, in the bewildered silence that sucks the life out of a room in which unspeakable things have been spoken of, or unmentionable deeds have been admitted to.

Melanie's mind was as distracted as Jerry's. She had figured he'd get mad yet never to the point of nearly killing her. The hate in Jerry's eyes was truly frightening. Thankfully his rage was now gone, replaced by confusion.

If it wasn't for the bruises that now painfully appeared on her upper arms, she might have felt sorry for the poor bastard.

Pity is such a waste of time, she thought. *Time that is slowly getting away from both of us.*

It was Melanie who broke the silence.

"Now you know why I hate him so much," she began cautiously, noting that Jerry still appeared to be a bit dazed. "I don't know why I did it—the affair I mean. We were—"

"I don't want to hear the sordid details," Jerry snapped. "Don't you think you've made enough of a fool of me for one day?"

Melanie remained silent, wanting Jerry to come to some conclusion as soon as possible. In the past, she'd been able to sugarcoat any bad news with an energetic romp in the sack. Jerry, male homosapien that he was, always seemed to come around after that. She was hoping he would somehow forgive her now and turn his anger toward their mutual nemesis: Robert Barker.

That no abortion ever took place and Manard possessed no documents proving Jerry was an industrial spy was of little significance to Melanie. Her sole goal was to convince Jerry that her plan was now the only way for them to go.

Three days passed before Jerry returned to Melanie's house. Where he'd been and what he'd been doing, Melanie was not sure. He hadn't gone to work, of that she was certain, having called in the hope of straightening things out. A temp informed her Jerry was home sick with the flu.

I don't think so, honey.

Late in the evening on day four, Melanie could tell things had changed when he walked through the bedroom door. He was no longer the pushover. He stood in front of her with an air of confidence she'd never seen him display. For once he was more man than child.

Melanie sighed as she thought back to when he was squeezing her arms. She realized it was the terror in *her* eyes which had changed his outlook forever.

Great, she thought. *I've created a monster.*

Jerry didn't say a word as he approached the bed and took off his clothes. When he removed his briefs, Melanie could feel the heat rise in her body.

For the next hour not a word was exchanged as they engaged in the best lovemaking session they'd ever had.

Maybe a monster isn't so bad after all, Melanie thought when it was all over.

As he turned out the table lamp, Jerry said, "If we're going to kill Robert Barker, we're going to do it right and we're going to do it my way."

In the darkness a small satisfied smile crept over Melanie's lips as she blissfully drifted off to sleep.

SEVENTEEN

"Everything hinges on Adams' appearance on *The Nation Today*," Jerry said as he pulled his tie over his head. "We have to find a way to get Robert and the Senator together."

"Without them suspecting anything, right?" Melanie asked, still fuzzy on Jerry's updating of her plan.

"Not exactly. Robert will definitely have an agenda. The Senator, however, has to think Robert is simply there as a concerned businessman. He's already well known across the country so no alarm bells should start ringing in Adams' camp."

"Won't Adams be suspicious?"

"Sure he will," Jerry laughed. "Wouldn't you be if you came face-to-face with your lover's spouse?"

Silence enveloped them. Although the night before had been great, it hadn't changed anything.

Forgiven, not forgotten, Melanie thought.

"Anyway . . ." Jerry said, picking his briefcase off the kitchen counter, "we have to find out how the show runs. In the meantime, why don't you call Lynn and see how she's doing."

Melanie frowned at the thought.

"Do I have to?" she whined.

"Only if you want this to work." Jerry pocketed his car keys. "Because the way things are progressing, Lynn is going to be more crucial to us than Robert."

* * *

With Robert at a conference, Jerry was able to make several phone calls to the network, trying to piece together how *The Nation Today* selected its guests.

"As you know, Miss Dow, Mantis Pharmaceuticals is the largest company of its kind in the country. What I'm proposing is to have Robert Barker appear on your program to show how the election will affect the medical industry. As I'm sure you know, health care is one of the major issues this year."

"As it should be, Mr. Steele," Miss Dow, the Talent Co-ordinator responded in an overly-friendly manner. "However, during the past few weeks we've already focused on your industry quite a bit. I'm not sure how Mr. Barker's appearance would benefit our audience." Miss Dow paused before continuing in a hushed tone, "Off the record, we're going to start focusing on the candidate's tax reform proposals, as a run-up to election day."

"I see," Jerry said, trying to connect the two issues in his head. "When Senator Adams appears on October 15th, will tax reform be the only issue you'll be dealing with?"

There was silence on the other end of the line.

"Who did you say you were working for again?" Miss Dow said uneasily.

Something is wrong, Jerry thought.

He was sure Adams had told Melanie he'd be on the show in three weeks. Had that changed?

"My name is Jerry Steele and I am Robert Barker's Administrative Assistant at Mantis Pharmaceuticals."

Another long pause, as Jerry heard Miss Dow furiously writing down this information.

"Is there a problem?"

Sounding a tad flustered, Miss Dow assured him nothing was wrong and she only needed the information to give to the show's producer.

"He makes the final call on any guests."

Jerry didn't believe her. Something was up. Before Miss Dow hung up, he was able to glean one more piece of information from her.

"And who is the producer of your program?"

"Well, it's . . . I mean, his name is Stanley Unger."

* * *

That afternoon two men in dark suits and mirrored sunglasses entered Jerry's office.

Secret Service? FBI? CIA?

"Mr. Steele?" asked the one who looked like a redwood with excellent taste in tailors.

"Yes," Jerry said as he stood behind his desk, "I'm Jerry Steele. Is there something I can help you gentlemen with?"

The other redwood took off his glasses and pulled a notebook from an inside jacket pocket. He flashed Jerry a smile.

"Mr. Steele, my name is Rollins and this is my partner, Hastings," he said. Hastings remained silent and didn't try faking a smile.

"Am I in some kind of trouble?"

"Did you place a call to *The Nation Today* television program earlier today, speaking with a Miss Dow?"

"Are you government agents?" Jerry said with a sinking feeling.

Did they know about Melanie? Or Manard's bribery to the Senator?

Rollins ignored Jerry's question.

"During your conversation did you state you knew Senator Adams was to appear on the program October 15th?"

"I may have," Jerry replied coolly.

"Let's say you did, Mr. Steele—hypothetically, of course."

"Okay."

"How is it that a personal secretary—"

"Administrative Assistant," Jerry clarified.

"Okay, how is it an *administrative assistant* working for a drug company obtains such information? Information usually known to a select few? Can you tell us that?"

"You're Adams' thugs?" Jerry said trying to suppress a smile.

"Security Operatives," the tree stump known as Hastings said.

"Yeah, whatever," Jerry replied dismissively.

While trying to put on a brave face, Jerry's mind was swimming.

Had the information Adams given Melanie been top secret? Had Adams' appearance actually been finalized at all?

Knowing these guys had no real pull—it wasn't as though he'd threatened the President's life—was of only minimal comfort to Jerry. Regardless of what he said, if Robert were killed near Adams' presence, a direct link between the two would lead straight back to him.

"I overheard it at an Adams' fundraiser—you know, the one held at the convention centre." Jerry looked for any adverse reaction. Both stumps remained stoic.

A good sign, Jerry thought.

"I don't remember seeing you there, although as *security operatives*, I wasn't supposed to, right? Probably hanging out in the shadows."

Jerry's attempt at humour fell on deaf ears.

"Who'd you hear this information from, Mr. Steele?" Rollins asked.

"I didn't say I heard it, I said I *overheard* it. There's a difference."

"Which is?" Rollins stated, visibly agitated that their intimidation routine was not working.

"Look, I could talk to you guys all day but the short and skinny of it is while walking to the bar, I passed a group of suits talking campaign strategy. As I came into earshot, I heard one of them say the Senator would be appearing on *The Nation Today* in three weeks. That's it. That's all I *overheard*. I didn't know for certain it was the 15th—I guessed really."

Rollins scribbled notes into his pad before placing it back into his pocket.

"I'm sorry if we've inconvenienced you in any way, Mr. Steele. It's just that this appearance is somewhat delicate. I can only ask you to keep this information to yourself—for a week or two at the most."

"Yeah, sure," Jerry said with a shrug and a smile. "Anything for national security."

It appeared Rollins was going to add something, then a look from Hastings stopped him.

"It was nice meeting you, Mr. Steele."

"I'm sure it was," Jerry replied as the men exited the room.

He waited an hour before calling *The Nation Today* back, not wanting the redwoods to return to ambush him again. This time he tried the general public hotline, a number given out at the end of each program. Jerry was certain Miss Dow wouldn't be answering this line.

Mindy was with the network's public relations department and was more than willing to give out information. Her friendly voice and easy answers often distracted Jerry from his real mission, which was to find loopholes in their operation. After 10 minutes of breezy conversation, only one question remained.

"You know those people who ask questions of the program's guests—the ones outside on the sidewalk?"

"Yes."

"Who picks them? Is it the security guards or that rotund weatherman who is always out there?"

Mindy had heard all of these questions before.

"Actually, it's one of the show's floor managers. They're constantly talking to the crowd during segments and commercial breaks to find engaging people with interesting questions. Then they escort them to the microphone to interact with the hosts and the guests."

Jerry got the feeling Mindy was reading that last one straight off a response card.

"Are there any times when the producer, what's his name again — Mr. Unger — gets involved with the crowd?"

Mindy thought the question was out of the ordinary as most callers could barely remember the regular hosts' names, let alone the producer's.

"Yes, Mr. Unger is the producer. However, I believe his duties keep him in the studio throughout the show."

With no further inquiries, Mindy informed Jerry of the network's new website and pleasantly bid him goodbye.

Jerry had been tempted to confirm which day Senator Adams would appear but decided not to press his luck. He'd find other ways to get that information. His next call was to Steve Faylen of Scanner Enterprises, a television and video production outfit Mantis used to shoot promotional videos.

"Steve, this is Jerry Steele at Mantis Pharmaceuticals. How's business these days?"

Steve's face broke into a smile. With business relatively slow, a call from Mantis was what he needed to get through winter. Not only did they pay on time, the money was fantastic. Their videos were shot on film and consisted of a week's worth of shooting, not including the consultation and prep time, plus editing fees.

January's starting to look a whole lot warmer.

"What can I do for you, Jerry? I hope you're gearing up for a new product launch. Last year's Adalin kick-off was a real success, if I say so myself."

Always the suck-up, Jerry thought.

"Actually, we are getting ready for a big announcement and there's no one I'd rather have shoot the presentation than you. I'm finalizing the budget right now. Funny you mentioned the Adalin video. As I was comparing the two budgets, I discovered this new campaign is about triple the expenditure, which I'm sure will be music to your ears." Jerry could almost hear the drool exiting Steve's mouth and falling onto his shoes. "However, the real reason I called is about someone in the industry—the television industry that is—I thought you might know."

"Shoot. I still have some TV friends in low places. Who are you thinking about?"

"Stanley Unger, the producer of *The Nation Today*. Know him?"

"Linus?" Steve began to laugh.

"I thought his name was Stanley."

"It is—his nickname at college was Linus."

College?

"And why was that?" Jerry asked trying to contain his exhilaration.

"The most self-conscious guy you'll ever find. Like Linus in the Charlie Brown cartoons, he always had a security blanket with him. Instead of a blankie though, he carried around his datebook—you know, an organizer. He could tell you where he was going to be the following Easter at 9:23 p.m. if you asked him."

"A control freak?"

"Not exactly. More like an insecure guy who found some inner peace by mapping out his life down to the second."

"When did you last talk to him?"

"A few months ago? I remember—it was right after he took over *The Nation Today* job. I called to congratulate him. Why are you so interested

133

in him anyway?"

"I've got a niece who's thinking about a broadcasting career and she knows of Unger's reputation," Jerry lied. "She joked she might proposition him over a candlelight dinner to get a job."

Steve laughed over the line.

"It would have to be a very dark room."

"And why's that?"

"Because he's gay."

"I'll have to tell her the bad news," Jerry said nervously. He paused a second as another thought came to mind. "If she's such a big fan of his, why wouldn't she know that? Hasn't he come out of the closet?"

Steve laughed again.

"You know in your closet, behind the hanging clothes, behind the piles of shoes, behind the boxes, behind that hideous outfit your mother-in-law gave you for Christmas a decade ago—the one your wife won't let you throw out—there is a small hole in the back wall, about the same size as a lab mouse?" Steve stopped for a beat to make sure he hadn't lost Jerry. "There, inside that small hole in the wall is where Stanley Unger keeps his deepest darkest secret. Understand? Now does that answer your question?"

"Perfectly," Jerry said with a satisfied smile. "And if this information ever became public?" he asked tentatively.

"Professional outcast," Steve replied.

"C'mon. There's got to be scores of openly gay and lesbian people working at the network."

"You're right, there are. The problem for Stanley Boy is that much of his career has been advanced because of his background. I would think your niece knows he is married with two young children. It's that classic family unit, coupled with his unquestionable abilities as a producer, that has got him so far so fast."

"And it would all crash down if he was outed?"

"Like a flame thrower to a house of cards. Now, if there aren't any more questions about my college classmate, when can I expect a package from Mantis?"

Jerry was confused by Steve's request.

"Package?"

"The film shoot? Remember, the one you called about?"

"Oh, that," Jerry said, startled by his own absentmindedness. "Give us to the end of the month, all right?"

"Sure thing," Steve responded, thoughts of Bermuda dancing in his head. "Are you okay, Jerry? I wouldn't have believed revelations about Stanley Unger's sex life could have thrown you for a loop."

"I was thinking what a terrible strain that must be on a man—or a woman for that matter. Knowing one slip-up, one bad encounter, could ruin your life."

"No one forced him to stay locked up in the closet."

"True."

For the second time that day, Jerry's mind was swimming.

"One last request. Just curious, you know, as to where a recognizable individual like Stanley Unger would go to seek out partners?"

"I've heard of a place called Buttons on the east side—some other TV types talk about it. It's an upscale gay social club where no one knows your real name. The exact opposite of Cheers then, huh?"

"Yeah, I guess so. Anyway, thanks for your help. If my package doesn't arrive, call me and I'll see what the delay is."

"I'll be looking forward to it."

Jerry put the phone in its cradle, walked to the window and took in an amazing panoramic view of the city.

"Somewhere out there is a man who desperately wants to get rich, and I'm the man to make all his dreams come true."

EIGHTEEN

The previous evening's televised debate had not gone well although expectations were low in both camps. President Travers stood on his four-year record in office, while Senator Adams continued to push his reforms, many of which had the support of the electorate. Adams' problem was one of incumbency. The people were not worse off than four years ago and the economy was growing. Interest rates and unemployment were both at their lowest levels since the 1970's. With numbers like that, many in the public credited the President's "stay the course" rhetoric.

What Adams had successfully injected into the campaign was the issue of character. Unfortunately, an all-out personal attack on the President was inconceivable, as the public had demanded an issue-oriented election that didn't resort to dirty tricks or false allegations against the other candidate. Although a double-edged sword, Adams had instilled enough doubt about Travers' personal and legal follies to keep within 10 points of the President in every poll.

With election day nearing, however, Adams had taken on a problem that, if exposed, would derail his campaign train to the White House.

Her name: Lynn Barker.

"I'm telling you, Douglas, you are playing with fire," Harold Green stated, visibly irritated Adams was going to meet *that woman* again.

Adams checked his bow tie in the mirror.

"Give me a break, Harold. You're my campaign manager, not my mother." He turned and looked at Green. "In fact, you're starting to sound like my dead wife, God rest her soul—and you know how much she got on my nerves."

Theirs had been a stormy partnership. Adams would often joke that at their shotgun wedding he'd made the tactical error of shooting himself in the foot, instead of the head.

"We both knew it was over," he'd say, "when she asked me if we'd fallen out of love and I replied, 'Fallen? Hell, I jumped!'"

Since meeting Lynn, public references to Judith Adams had been cut back noticeably. The official explanation was simple: continued references to his dearly departed wife were taking their toll on the candidate's psyche.

The unofficial reason: Adams, who had despised his wife in life, had gotten sick of talking about her in such glowing terms in death.

What couldn't be ignored was that, by invoking her name throughout the campaign, his poll numbers had risen 15 points. It was decided to place his reforms before the public while his support was at its peak. The result was his numbers stabilized within striking distance of the President's.

With the race now too close to call, Green predicted Adams' resistance to dredge up the spirit of Judith Adams in the final days. The trade-off would be, if elected, Green promised her name would be banished forever.

"Do the words 'Gary Hart' mean anything to you, Douglas?"

"He was a fool, as I remember. Telling the press to try and catch him—and surprise, surprise, they did. And you know why?"

"He was a fool," Green responded blandly. "What about Clinton then?"

Adams scoffed. "Elected twice to the Presidency. You have a problem with that?" He didn't wait for a response. "If you haven't noticed, I'm not that stupid. In fact, it appears the media is still focusing on Travers' behaviour. They're leaving us alone because in the Year of the Issue, no one dares to start poking into the sex life of a recently widowed man." Adams looked up at Green. "It would be sacrilegious to do such a thing—even to a politician. Downright un-American," he said with a smile. "If they want to believe I'm still in mourning, I'll let them."

Green knew Adams was right. The legitimate press was printing only articles about the Senator's ideas for the future. On the other hand, tabloids were digging into Adams' past to show how concerned he'd been as his wife fought a losing battle with cancer.

It truly was a win-win situation.

"You can't understand how Lynn makes me feel, Harold."

"Actually I do, Douglas," Green said sarcastically. "Fortunately, I was a 16-year-old with no responsibilities, aside from passing my algebra tests." He pointed a finger at Adams. "You, though, are running on a platform of family values as a candidate for the leadership of the free world." Green's voice began to rise. "And if you don't keep your hands out from under the skirt of a married woman whose husband happens to come to your committee for grant money, the only election you'll ever win is leader of the Idiots Are Us club—formerly chaired by Gary Hart!"

Adams stood and came face-to-face with Green who was certain they were about to come to blows.

"Weren't you listening? I hired you to be my campaign manager, not my priest. Got that?" Adams words were short, clipped and to the point. "Your job is to get me elected. So you do what you need to do and I'll do the same."

They stared at each other for several moments before Adams turned and walked toward the door.

"After my *meeting*, I'll be back here at 10:30 to go over tomorrow's speech to the League of Women Voters." He shot Green a look that would have shaken lesser men to their core. "And one other thing: if I see my wife's name anywhere in that speech, you're fired."

Adams slammed the door behind him.

A veteran of many campaigns, Green had never come this close to the Holy Grail of politics. Nor was he about to throw in the towel to satisfy his own, sometimes questionable, ethical views.

Green smiled at his own musings.

Ethical politics. Now there was an oxymoron if there ever was one.

* * *

Having given a very appreciative Francelina the night off and Robert presumably working late (on Alysha Foster, no doubt), Lynn had the house to herself.

By 9:00 Lynn was ready to go. Her spirits were soaring on two levels. First, she had received a call from Melanie to set up a lunch get-together the following day. Second, came a call from Douglas, who also wanted to see her.

Meeting Douglas on the sly at the last minute had become somewhat of a routine. Never knowing when he'd have free time, Adams would often call only an hour ahead, telling her how badly he needed to be with her.

She looked at her full-length bedroom mirror and almost didn't recognize herself. Her brown shoulder-length hair was now pushed up under a bob-style wig she'd had in college. Even her trademark haunting aqua-coloured eyes were now a chestnut brown, thanks to designer contacts which were currently all the rage. Only her slim figure remained the same, although the little blue number she was wearing didn't hug her hips as much as she'd liked.

Staring at her slightly altered twin, she couldn't help wondering why she went to such lengths for a man. If Robert had asked her to change her appearance, she would have snapped, "If you don't like what you see, maybe you should be looking elsewhere."

Of course, if truth be known, that was exactly what he'd done.

Maybe it was the thrill of the chase. Being the mystery woman no one knew existed. Keeping one step ahead of the press.

For a millisecond, the notion that maybe it was love flashed across her mind.

If not love, she mused, *then lust on a scale of unbelievable proportions.*

She stopped and laughed. Even Douglas' catch phrases had rubbed off on her.

She concluded the real reason was that the danger level was as high as the satisfaction level she felt when they were together. Knowing Robert and his little lab partner were enjoying each other's company at her expense, she almost wished Robert would become aware of her extramarital activities.

Sweet revenge would then be hers.

Nineteen

Lynn gathered her purse and walked out the side door, commonly known in the area as the servant's entrance. Anyone passing would figure the maid was done for the evening, never believing the well-to-do Mrs. Barker was incognito, en route to a hotel to meet her lover.

"There she is!" Robert said excitedly, pointing to the figure walking down the driveway. "Can you believe it? She's dressed like a schoolgirl!"

"The servant's door was a nice touch, you've got to admit."

"Whose side are you on, anyway?" Robert said to the man sitting with him in the back of the van.

"Yours of course, Mr. Barker. You're paying me, which means I work for you."

"And don't you forget it," Robert said as he watched Lynn leave the area.

As had become her custom, Lynn walked several blocks until she was outside her neighbourhood. She would then enter the Black Russian diner and call for a cab. She always made sure to call a different company so as not to attract attention to herself or become known

to a particular driver. It usually took only a few minutes for a cab to arrive. The last precaution was to be dropped at an address near the designated hotel and walk the remaining distance. Tonight would be no different.

"Why aren't you going in after her?" Robert asked excitedly when Lynn entered the Black Russian. "We're going to lose her."

This was a bad idea, the P.I. thought to himself.

Jeffrey Hamill was in his mid-50's and had been a private investigator for over 25 years. During this period, he'd watched his weight balloon from 150 to over 250 pounds and seen his hairline retreat faster than an overmatched army. He blamed both situations on the lack of exercise one could do confined in a vehicle all day. Also the advent of drive-thru fast food joints hadn't helped either.

Tonight was the first—and presumably last—time he'd let a client come along on surveillance. That this was a marital case was also an excellent reason for not bringing the injured spouse along. Hamill knew the possibility Barker would jump out to confront Mrs. Barker was high.

That couldn't be allowed for a number of reasons: first and foremost, their discreet surveillance would no longer be discreet. Second, Hamill wasn't sure that his licence couldn't be yanked for allowing a non-licensed individual to work on an investigation. The third was the reason that worried him most: what would happen if Barker went completely bonkers and in a jealous rage confronted his cheating wife? Or killed or injured her? Or killed and injured Mrs. Barker's lover (if one existed)?

These doubts were less significant earlier in the week, when Barker threw $5,000 on his desk; a retainer five times the going rate. Barker's only stipulation was that he be allowed to tag along.

Hamill reluctantly accepted the money and terms.

"Let's get one thing straight, Mr. Barker. I've been in the P.I. biz for a long time. I know what I'm doing and also know *why* I am doing it in such a manner." Hamill turned his large frame around in the driver's seat. "Tonight's surveillance could last one hour or one week. Either way, I'm prepared to stick it out. As that television show used to say, the truth is out there. You're paying me a lot of dough to keep tabs on your wife. All I'm asking is you stop yelling and relax already."

Robert knew Hamill was right. He felt far too hyperactive to keep his head clear, which would be required to make rational decisions.

"I'm sorry," he said. "It's not like this happens every day."

"Oh, trust me, it does, Mr. Barker. Every single day I get a husband or wife darkening my doorway—"

"To me! This kind of thing doesn't happen every day *to me*."

"I'd hope not," Hamill said off-handedly as he continued to watch the diner's front door.

Robert peered through the van's tinted windows.

What is she doing in there?

"What if she's meeting someone at the bar or for dinner?" he asked, unable to remain silent any longer. "We're never going to see them in the act from out here."

Hamill shot Robert an amused look.

"As I don't think you're going to keep quiet the whole evening, I'll tell you what—if you stop barking suggestions, I will more than gladly let you in on some basic investigation techniques. So how about it, Mr. Barker? Deal?"

Robert had hired Hamill to do a job and he was now hindering him from doing it.

"I'm sorry."

"You said that a few minutes ago," Hamill countered.

"This time I mean it."

Their eyes met for an instant and both men smiled.

"Okay, so, the whole idea of surveillance is to remain discreet. If I

walk in there and the Missus sees me, there would be no problem. I'm a stranger to her. Now let's say she leaves the bar and we follow her downtown. Then, due to traffic or whatever, she looks in my direction and sees me stopped at a light. Again, this is no problem, as more likely than not she'll assume it's a weird coincidence the guy she saw earlier is heading in the same direction as she is. Following me so far?"

Robert nodded.

"Because here comes the tricky part. Like baseball, you only get three chances before you're burned—meaning your subject has clued into your presence. When that happens, you better hope they don't have access to a tire iron, because most people get real riled up 'bout someone following them.

"Your wife's next move is likely to go to some hotel and what we really want to know is what room she enters, right? Unfortunately, if she's already seen me a couple of times, it'd be foolhardy of me to get on the elevator with her. Does that sound reasonable? The investigators who push their luck usually end up talking with the cops."

A look of disbelief crossed Robert's face.

"Trust me, it happens."

"What if she stays in there for a long time?" Robert asked picking up a pair of binoculars and training them on the Black Russian's windows.

"Nothing is cast in stone. If she hasn't come out in, say, 15-20 minutes, I stick my head in and take a look around. If she's having a drink or meeting someone for dinner, she won't notice a big galoot like me at the front door."

A City Taxi pulled up to the diner.

"Get ready," Hamill said to Robert.

"For what?"

The words were barely out of his mouth when Lynn stepped into view. As she entered the cab, Hamill couldn't resist saying, "Aren't you

JOHN SCHLARBAUM

glad we didn't go barging in?"

Pulling away from the curb, Hamill grabbed his cell phone and pushed one of the stored numbers.

"Who are you calling?" Robert asked.

"A friend. Don't get your panties in a knot."

After several rings, the line was answered and Hamill put the phone on speaker.

"Is Salvador working tonight?" Hamill asked. A few seconds passed before his friend came on. "Sal, how's it hanging tonight?"

"Not too bad, Mr. Hamill. What can I do for you? The usual?"

"If you would be so kind."

"What number?"

"1579."

Robert looked up the street and saw the identification plate of Lynn's taxi was 1579.

"15534 Ellis Blvd."

"Got it."

"Anytime, Mr. Hamill. Take care."

"You too, Sal. And remember, there'll be a little something extra in your pay envelope this week."

Hamill disconnected.

"How much did that cost me?" Robert inquired.

"Fifty bucks, which is a bargain, if you ask me."

"What's at 15534 Ellis Blvd?"

"If memory serves, a sleazy strip club called The Beaver Box, or something equally ridiculous."

Robert was beside himself.

What in the world is Lynn doing? She leaves the house dressed as a teenager and is now taking a taxi to a strip club? This doesn't make sense.

"If it means anything, if duty calls I'll only look at your wife's face while she's doing table dances."

145

A look of terror, coupled with rage, passed over Robert's face.

"I was joking, for Pete's sake," Hamill quickly added. "She probably won't even go in. From what you've told me, I don't think a mid-life crisis would include becoming a peeler. I'm guessing she'll get dropped off there and then walk to their rendezvous location."

At a stoplight, Robert looked into the back seat of the taxi and saw Lynn applying lipstick.

Has our marriage deteriorated to this? he thought, equally disgusted with himself and Lynn.

Another quarter-hour passed before they turned onto Ellis Boulevard.

"There it is," Hamill said, pointing to a flashing neon sign. "The Eager Beaver. So close."

"How cute," Robert said as he watched the taxi pull in front of the club and Lynn get out. "What now?" he asked anxiously.

"As it's highly unlikely she'll take another cab, my guess is she'll be walking—which means I'll be walking."

Hamill parked and began to get out of the van. Lynn was now a block and a half down the street.

"You can't just leave me!" Robert shouted.

"Sure I can."

Hamill pulled a second cell phone out of his pocket.

"When we get to where we're going, I'll call." Hamill saw Lynn crossing the street and scribbled his number on a card, which he handed to Robert. "Stay here," he ordered. "This shouldn't take too long."

Robert locked the door as Hamill waddled quickly down the sidewalk.

Since finding Adams' card in Lynn's purse, Robert had agonized about what to do. He didn't want to confront her on the off-chance she would return the accusation. After his stupidity at dinner regarding the name Melanie, that was one area he'd rather leave alone.

It was only after Lynn had "disappeared" on two occasions that he'd known something was happening. On both occasions, she said she'd been shopping and had new purchases each time. Still his mistrust persisted. It got to the point where he felt there was no choice other than to hire an investigator to settle the matter.

As the minutes ticked by and dance music blared from the strip club's outdoor speaker, he wasn't sure if he had temporarily lost his mind.

The cell phone rang.

"She's at The Omni Spirit."

"Which room?" Robert demanded.

"Let me worry about that. The last thing I need is you running in and screwing the whole thing up." Hamill let the words sink in. "By the sounds of it she's alone. I doubt that'll be the case for long."

"What do we do now?"

"You stay in the van while I hang in this stairwell."

The line was disconnected by Hamill, leaving Robert alone with his thoughts.

Hamill soon heard the elevator door open and saw three gentlemen emerge. The oldest man, who looked vaguely familiar, walked to Lynn's room and knocked softly. A moment later, he gave his associates the thumbs-up and entered the room, locking it behind him. The other two men re-entered the elevator.

Hamill quietly closed the stairwell door and called the van.

"I need you to park the van at the rear of the hotel. Make sure you then have an unobstructed view of the back doors."

"What's this about?" Robert asked, his heart beating uncontrollably.

"Just do what I say! When you're in position, take note of anyone exiting the hotel and any cars that pull up or have been left running."

"Is that everything?"

"No," Hamill said, remembering the size of the two men entering the elevator. "Take special note of any football linebacker types who have impeccable taste in expensive suits. Got that?"

The line went dead as Hamill began running (to the best of his ability) down to the main foyer. Before opening the lobby door, he tried to compose himself, which was easier said than done; his forehead was dripping sweat and his shirt was hanging over his pants.

Once presentable, he quickly walked to the front of the hotel and checked the sidewalks. No sign of the football players.

Maybe I beat them down after all, he thought.

Next, he walked to the rear of the hotel and saw his van parked on the lot. He immediately knew something was wrong. It took only a moment for it to hit him and he quickly pulled out the cell phone.

"Cut the engine and turn off the lights, you moron!" he screamed under his breath into the mouthpiece.

Swearing profusely, Robert turned off the engine and pushed the light switch so hard he thought it might go through the dash.

"Any signs of the fancy dressed goons?" Hamill asked exasperated.

"Not yet."

"Keep your eyes open. Can you do that?"

The line went dead in Robert's hand.

As he re-entered the lobby, Hamill saw them step out of the elevator. They briefly looked around as if casing the joint. Hamill picked up a nearby pay phone and put it to his ear waiting for them to pass.

His cell phone rang.

"They came out and got into a black Lincoln."

"Can you see the licence plate?"

"Yes."

"Write it down and drive to the front of the hotel."

Robert was confused.

"What if they go back inside?"

"The next time that car moves, the guy who entered your wife's room will be in it. Now get the lead out and pick me up!"

Starting the van, Robert realized Lynn was in a hotel room with another man and he was more confused than ever.

Hamill was soon on the phone calling a friend at the 12th Precinct.

"You have a good night too, Sergeant. And if you have any more problems with the wife straying, you know who to call." Hamill closed his cell phone and said, "If I were his wife, I'd fool around too."

"What about the car? Did you find out who it's registered to?"

"Strangest thing," Hamill said as he stared at his notebook. "It seems our black Lincoln is registered to a Judith Marie Kelly."

There was a blank look on Robert's face.

"Why is that strange?"

"Well, if memory serves me, once a person has died the heirs must transfer all title of ownership to the new owner within a month."

"How do you know this woman is dead?"

Hamill turned and looked Robert in the eye.

"Do you only read the business section?" He was greeted by a bewildered stare. "If I'm not mistaken," he continued, "Judith Marie Kelly is the recently deceased wife of Douglas Adams."

A look of astonishment crossed Robert's face.

"Yeah—now you got it. Douglas Adams—as in Senator Adams—as in soon-to-be President Adams." Seeing Robert's expression go from puzzlement to clarity, Hamill added, "But you knew that, didn't you?"

After several more seconds of silence, Hamill tossed his notebook on the dash and began to laugh.

"Well, ain't this a kick in the head!"

TWENTY

The soft knock on the door startled Lynn.

"Who is it?" she asked innocently, not bothering to look through the peephole.

"Douglas."

She opened the door and Douglas entered.

"I was worried the notice was too short," Douglas said as he kissed Lynn lightly on the lips. "I hate having you sneak around like this."

Lynn led him to the bed where she fell onto her back, pulling Douglas on top of her.

"Did I say I minded?" she said, returning his kiss a little more aggressively. "This is like a magical mystery adventure for me. Not wanting to get caught by Robert, and all the while not wanting the press to find out about us."

"If either ever did," Douglas chuckled, "I don't think this adventure would continue to be very magical or mysterious for much longer."

"Are you saying you'd deny everything?" Lynn asked playfully.

"Well, not everything. I would make sure the electorate knows their next President still enjoys the company of women—especially hot-looking ones."

"Won't that turn off some voters who think you're still in mourning?"

"I'd make certain the spin Harold put out was something like 'Senator Adams is now ready to look to the future and to the enormous challenges that face this God-fearing and proud country.'"

After pulling her blue dress over her head, Lynn watched as Douglas stepped out of his suit pants.

"If I didn't know better, Senator, I'd say all this talk about politics is getting you rather worked up."

Douglas smiled as he climbed under the sheets.

"You know what Kennedy always said before bedding Marilyn Monroe, don't you?" Douglas asked as he began to caress her neck. "He'd say, 'Don't ask what your President can do to you, but ask what you can do to your President.'"

As they both began to trace each other's bodies with their fingertips, Lynn sighed loudly.

"He certainly knew how to sweet talk a lady, didn't he?"

* * *

With droplets of perspiration trickling down her back, Douglas watched Lynn walk to a table where a bottle of wine rested in an ice bucket. It was only as he followed her naked body that another female encounter came to mind.

Melanie Fields, he thought. *What a piece of work she'd been.*

Not only had she been a perfect afternoon lay, she'd actually paid him $200,000 for the pleasure! The irony that he was now sleeping with two women who were loosely working for two competing companies hadn't escaped him.

Gone were the days when he was juggling the passions of two

farmers regarding which side of the road a new municipal ditch would be built.

No doubt about it, he'd come a long way.

His thoughts returned to his earlier conversation with Harold.

You're right, as usual, he mused.

Lynn (and for that matter, Melanie) was exactly like playing with fire: a heat you'd feel well after the sex was over and a heat that would burn you to a crisp if the press ever found out.

He remembered a line from a Pete Townshend song: *No one respects the flame more than the fool that's badly burned.*

Was he a fool or only human? He didn't know and at this point in time, lying naked in front of a gorgeous woman, he didn't much care.

Lynn handed him a flute of wine.

"To us," she toasted.

"Who knows," he said lifting his glass, "come January, maybe we'll be doing this in the living quarters of the White House."

"Don't you have an election to win first?"

"A mere formality."

They sipped in silence, each enjoying a soothing state of being.

Finishing his wine, Douglas kissed Lynn before heading to the shower. They were now back to the *business before pleasure* mode, having reversed their sequence for about an hour.

He soon reappeared, a towel around his waist. He carried the bottle of wine over to Lynn and refilled her glass.

"Before I came over, Harold suggested I quit seeing you."

Lynn's eyebrows went up.

"Is that right?"

"Doesn't want you to become the next Donna Rice or Monica Lewinsky."

"How considerate. Did you tell him where to go?"

Douglas laughed.

"Even gave him directions!" Douglas looked at his watch. "Speaking of Harold, I've got a meeting with him in 15 minutes. I have to speak to those militant housewives tomorrow afternoon."

"Are you referring to the League of Women Voters?" Lynn asked. "A group of which I am a card-carrying member?"

The remark made Douglas stop looking for his underwear.

"You're going to be there tomorrow?"

"That depends," Lynn smirked.

"On what?"

"If my cake turns out or not. You never want to go to a militant housewives' meeting with a burnt Bundt cake, now do you?"

Douglas ignored Lynn's laughter and located his underwear, which he quickly put on.

"If you were on my staff, I'd have you fired for such a remark."

Lynn bent forward and stroked the front of Douglas' underwear.

"If I were on your staff, you'd be too exhausted to campaign."

A smile broke across Douglas' lips as Lynn gently pulled him back onto the bed for a few more minutes of campaign strategy.

TWENTY ONE

"I thought you'd forgotten about me," Lynn said as she met Melanie at the front door.

I wish I could, Melanie said to herself, returning Lynn's hug.

When Lynn had suggested coming to her house for lunch, Melanie jumped at the idea. Robert hadn't been man enough to bring his mistress home for a quickie, even when his suffering wife was out of town.

Looking at the antique figurines and statuettes, as well as the expensive paintings, Robert probably thought bringing her here would only cause trouble between them; the mystique of the house would be lost, the happy pictures on the piano would have to be explained. As she looked around the modest opulence, another thought came to mind: he was probably afraid she'd break something and he'd have to explain it to the Prom Queen.

A coward through and through.

"I dug out our old yearbooks. I thought after we've eaten we could go down memory lane."

Great, Melanie thought. *This was your miserable life. Brought to you by Glenridge High School and hosted by Miss Teen Dream 1975, as elected by her equally hairspray-challenged classmates.*

"Sounds like fun," Melanie said, keeping the sarcasm to a low roar.

* * *

"How is life on the marriage front these days?" Melanie asked as Francelina took her salad bowl away.

"What day is it again—Wednesday?"

"That bad, huh?" Melanie replied, giddy inside. "Let me ask you this then - how's your love life?"

Lynn put her fork down and allowed herself to smile at the question. The thought of last night's romp at the Omni Spirit was still fresh.

"No complaints."

As Lynn began to blush, Melanie's temperature rose ever so slowly. *You think you have the whole world by the tail, don't you little Miss Popularity? Well, we'll see about that.*

"Does Robert know?"

"About me and Douglas—" Lynn stopped, knowing she'd never mentioned Douglas' name before. Fear set in.

"He does have a name then. Douglas, huh? It could be worse," Melanie laughed. "His name could be Adam."

She enjoyed watching the blood drain from Lynn's face.

"How did you—just by his first name, I mean," Lynn stammered across the table.

Francelina entered with their entrées and was shocked by her employer's appearance.

"Are you all right, Mrs. Barker?" Francelina looked at Melanie, who sat looking as cool as the cucumber she'd bitten into.

"We were talking politics," Melanie said with a devilish grin. "And I mentioned that one of the candidates running on a family values campaign was cheating on his wife."

155

A look of astonishment registered on Francelina's face.

"Is this true, Mrs. Barker?"

Lynn unsteadily brought her water glass to her lips.

"I'm afraid so," she answered uneasily. The worried look on her maid's face remained. "It is nothing to concern yourself with, Francelina."

"If this man says one thing while doing the exact opposite during the campaign, why should we trust that he'd do the right thing once in office?" Francelina looked at both women briefly and threw her arms up in disgust. "This man—and the woman he's fooling around with—will both pay later on." She pointed to the ceiling. "When they meet their maker they'll discover He doesn't believe in stuffing election boxes."

"I couldn't have said it better myself, Francelina," Melanie said as she raised her glass in a mock toast. "All men are pigs!"

"You know, I like your friend very much, Mrs. Barker," Francelina said. "She knows what she's talking about."

Francelina left the room muttering that men were pigs and she was glad she wasn't eligible to vote.

The room was deathly still as the two old friends mentally continued to size each other up.

For Melanie, it was the moment she'd been denied years earlier by Debbie Sutherland. From Lynn's expression, Melanie knew she'd achieved her objective of cutting the Queen off at the knees.

Never to jump so high again.

To have one's hired help unknowingly chastise you to your face, well that was priceless. Lynn now knew what it was like to be called "the other woman." She'd casually referred to Robert's extracurricular partners as tramps. Now to be told she too was going to Hell in a handbasket hurt.

Lynn also flashed back to her adolescence. There was a reason she and her friends had never associated with Melanie: she couldn't be trusted. Not with secrets, friendships or boyfriends.

A sickening thought burst into her mind: *What is she going to do with this information? Blackmail me? Tell Robert? Tell the press?*

"I don't know what to say. I'm not very experienced at this kind of thing," Lynn said slowly.

She was humbled by this? You've got to be kidding!

"There's nothing to feel sorry about," Melanie countered, sounding as concerned for Lynn's well-being as her voice would allow. "I'm not here to judge."

Tears began to well up in Lynn's eyes.

L.o.s.e.r.! Melanie's heart sang out, as she watched the fruits of her labour begin to cascade down Lynn's face.

"His campaign manager thinks we should break it off."

"You can't do that!" Melanie said with such force Lynn looked up startled. "I mean," Melanie began more gently, "listen to your heart, not some dweeb worried about his job."

Lynn's features softened.

"You aren't going to tell anyone about this, are you?"

The vulnerability in Lynn's voice almost had Melanie feeling sympathetic.

Almost.

"Why would I do that?" she answered in her most reassuring tone yet. "We're friends and friends don't do things like that to each other."

"You really are my friend, aren't you?"

Someone save me before we have a group hug, Melanie pleaded to any poltergeists in the room also enduring this pathetic display.

"Only if you want me to be." Melanie saw Lynn begin to smile. Melanie smiled back. "Of course, if you'd rather, I could be that bitch you hated in high school. It's your choice. I do both really well."

"No thank you. I'll take a friend over an enemy any day."

A Memorable Murder

After lunch they looked through the yearbooks and talked about old classmates. Melanie made sure to give her most unflattering critiques for those part of Lynn's inner royal circle.

"My friends weren't that bad," Lynn said, closing the final book. "We were running in a different direction than you and your friends."

More like running over my friends, Melanie thought silently.

All in all, as with their last meeting, Melanie had to admit that memory lane wasn't all that bad to travel down. However, somewhere between looking at Grade 11 and Grade 12 pictures, a thought began to creep in and out of her mind.

It was only when Lynn started talking about the old neighbourhood that the thought crystallized; a perfect solution to the one gaping hole in her plan: how to kidnap Lynn before the shooting.

"Why don't we go back?"

"What are you talking about?"

"Let's take a road trip to Glenridge and East Haven."

"You're kidding?"

"Come on, Lynn, it'll be fun. You and me retracing our steps. We'll see if our hometowns have changed any." Melanie could see Lynn was quickly warming to the plan. "Back to when cheerleading and being crowned Prom Queen meant something."

"You're serious, aren't you?"

"You don't like the idea? Afraid of who you'll see?"

"No, I love the idea," Lynn said enthusiastically. "I think it would be wonderful to see some old friends. You know—the ones we said we'd always keep in contact with, only never did?"

"Then it's settled. A Back-To-Glenridge-High road tour it is."

Melanie saw the absolute joy in Lynn's eyes. For the first time she actually wanted to embrace the woman for her complete and unequivocal stupidity but knew such an embrace would have to wait.

When it did finally happen though, it would be one to die for.

JOHN SCHLARBAUM

TWENTY TWO

Robert arrived at work in a rage. Jerry sat at his desk, perplexed, after his boss insisted he not be disturbed for any reason—great or small.

At 1:00, Jerry was summoned into the office.

Upon entering, he saw Robert behind his desk looking dazed and dishevelled.

"How could she do this to me?" Robert demanded.

"I'm not sure I follow," Jerry said, worried about Robert's mental state. He glanced at the bar cart and noticed a half-empty bottle of whiskey. "Would you like another drink?" Jerry asked, seeing the empty tumbler on the desk.

Robert flung the glass across the room where it exploded against the wall.

"I don't want another drink!" he bellowed. "I want answers!"

"If I can help, I will," Jerry said, taking a step back toward the door. "First, you have to tell me what the problem is."

"Women—that's my problem!"

The odour of alcohol drifted across the desk to his nostrils and almost made Jerry throw up.

"Why not sit back down and tell me what's wrong, okay?" Jerry suggested soothingly.

Robert's face went blank as he slumped into his chair.

Jerry took a seat in a corner leather chair, wanting distance between them in case Robert started throwing things again.

"I can't believe she's fooling around on me."

Not sure which female he was referring to, Jerry guessed.

"Alysha is fooling around on you?"

"Is that a statement or a question?" Robert demanded. "What do you know?"

Seeing Robert reaching for a paperweight, Jerry quickly stammered, "It was a question—relax. I have no clue what you're talking about."

"Lynn is cheating on me, you idiot!" Robert paused, contemplating what he'd said. "And you'll never guess who with," he challenged.

How about that nice Senator Douglas Adams, Jerry thought.

"I have no idea."

"Adams, that bastard!"

Jerry tried to look baffled.

"Douglas Adams?"

Robert jumped from his chair.

"I never saw it coming," Robert said walking to Jerry. "You did, though. You saw it from the start, didn't you?"

"I really don't know what—"

"The card! You saw Adams slip Lynn a business card at the fundraiser. And do you know what?" Jerry shook his head. "I found that very card in her purse. Do you know what it said?" Robert didn't wait for Jerry's reply. "It said 'The Palace. 2:00 p.m. Room 1845. The Presidential Suite.' Can you believe it?"

Robert's words were beginning to slur. He patted Jerry on the chest and headed to the bar cart.

Melanie had been right all along, Jerry thought.

With Robert's confirmation of Lynn's affair came the realization that their plan to eliminate the Barkers—and take control of Mantis Pharmaceuticals—was at the point of no return.

Watching Robert drown his sorrows, a deep sense of satisfaction swept over Jerry.

The man had no shame, he thought. *No sense of honour.*

It was impossible to dismiss the irony of the situation. Robert unburdening himself about his wife's infidelity to the man he'd deceived for months while bedding Melanie on a regular basis.

Robert took a long swig from his glass and Jerry hoped he'd choke and die on it.

Where was the adventure in that? he decided.

Robert next told Jerry of the previous night's surveillance with Jeffrey Hamill. How Lynn left the Omni Spirit with a huge smile on her face after Adams had been driven off by his security goons.

Rollins and Hastings, no doubt, Jerry thought.

"After she got home, I waited in my car up the street for an hour to *allow* her time to transform back into a 40-year-old woman—after getting laid while dressed as a 16-year-old!"

Robert shook his head in disbelief.

"Did you confront her when you went inside?" Jerry asked, wanting to hear about all the fireworks.

"You know what she did? She completely ignored me!"

"You didn't exchange any words at all?"

Robert took another gulp of whiskey.

"The only thing she said was, 'I hope your meeting was a bang-up success.'"

"That's it?"

"Then she locked me out of our bedroom! Do you believe it? The nerve! Treating me like I was the one getting banged last night!" A look of comprehension came over Robert's face. "A *bang-up* success—that's what she said. She was implying I was out with someone, wasn't she?"

"Well . . . I guess that's—"

"I'm going to kill her!" Robert slammed his fist on the desk.

Not according to our plans, Jerry wanted to say.

"Robert, that's dangerous talk. You have to keep those sentiments to yourself," Jerry said in an authoritative tone, checking the lobby to make sure no one had overheard the outburst.

"She's going to pay, Jerry," Robert replied in a low mumbled attempt at a whisper.

Jerry sensed Robert was teetering on an emotional ledge and there would be no better time than to give him a little push.

"I know exactly what you're going through, Robert. Do you remember me telling you of my suspicions that Melanie had an affair last year?"

An expression of terror appeared in Robert's eyes. Suddenly, he was as sober as a judge. He could only shake his head affirmatively.

"On the weekend she confessed to it."

"Confessed?" The word sputtered out of Robert's mouth. "She confessed—to you?"

"Let's say I have an idea who the sleazeball is she was with."

Jerry let the sentence sink into Robert's alcohol-impaired brain. He could actually see Robert bracing himself against the desk, readying himself for a fight if one were to begin between the two of them.

You're such a spineless, hopeless, human being, Jerry thought.

Before he could stop himself, Jerry let out a tiny laugh.

"What's so funny?" Robert demanded.

"You are," Jerry said grinning ear to ear. "Both of us actually."

"I don't understand."

And he didn't.

Why would Jerry stop before confronting me about my affair with Melanie? The man should be beating me to a pulp.

"I don't see the humour in this, Jerry."

"It's that we both find ourselves in the same predicament."

"How's that?" Robert snapped.

"We've both been cheated on. Now in my case, I was able to walk out and leave the little whore behind."

"You and Melanie aren't together?"

"For the time being."

Robert was confused.

"How is that the same as my situation? I can't move out. My reputation would be ruined and Lynn would get half of the company. Half of the Memoradium profits! It would cost me billions!"

Ah, Memoradium. The reason for all this insanity, Jerry thought.

"What I meant was while our relationships are most likely beyond repair, we could still focus on the root of our problems."

"Which is?"

"The men who felt obliged to take our women to bed. They didn't care that Melanie and Lynn were in relationships!"

Jerry stood and slowly leaned across the desk, giving the impression he might haul off and hit Robert with a left hook. Robert braced for the contact which didn't come.

"They didn't think we'd fight back."

"You want to physically beat up these men?"

"I want the guy who slept with Melanie to die a slow, painful death—that's what I mean." Jerry didn't attempt to get out of Robert's face. "I'm sure you can understand that. Can't you, Robert?"

Robert swallowed hard as his mind raced for an answer. To his inebriated brain, Jerry might as well have asked a variation on the trick question *When did you stop beating your wife?*

When did you stop screwing around with Melanie?

No response would satisfy the seeker of truth. Damned if you do and damned if you don't.

"What do you mean?" Robert asked weakly.

One more gust of hot wind and Jerry knew Robert would fall off that fragile ledge inside his head.

"I mean the only outlet left to vent our anger is *through* these parasites. Think about it, Robert—wouldn't you love to bring Adams to his knees? Embarrass him to the point of begging for mercy. Sounds fun, right?"

He doesn't know it was me, Robert thought.

Jerry poured himself a drink, in the process glancing over at Robert who was looking mighty relaxed. Emotionally drained, yet relaxed.

He thinks he's off the hook, Jerry mused. *Big mistake, Robert.*

"We can get Adams," Jerry said coldly.

"He's running for President, if you haven't noticed," Robert countered, feeling like his old self again.

"No one has more skeletons in their closets than politicians. It's just that no one is looking this time around, as the poor Senator was recently widowed."

"If I could be so lucky," Robert snarled, remembering Lynn's glowing face as she left the hotel.

"We're going to have to find something in his business dealings. I'm sure he's made plenty of shady drug deals in the past."

"What about the fact he's sleeping with my wife? Doesn't that carry any weight?"

"Sure, we could alert the media about that, and no doubt the wheels on Adams' family values campaign would come off quicker than a kid's toy car on Christmas morning . . ."

"Then let's—"

"Problem is," Jerry interrupted, "it's your name everyone will remember—and this company's name. You'd be the laughing stock at every pharmaceutical meeting in the country."

"Yes, of course, of course." Robert pushed his tumbler of whiskey away. "I'm not thinking straight. You're right, we have to look at his business dealings."

"We still have one major problem looming."

"Which is what?"

"Memoradium. We are scheduled to appear before Adams' ethics committee before they recess for the election."

"Why is that a problem? If I was in Adams' position I'd make certain that grant was approved. Because if he doesn't and it's later revealed he was with my wife, the conflict of interest allegations would drive him out of any office—including the White House."

The logic was fuzzy yet still true, Jerry thought.

"Conversely, what happens if we're approved and the affair with Lynn is exposed by some third party? Conflict of interest allegations would still hound Adams out of office, however, it would also mean the project's approval might be revoked."

"An end to the Memoradium project—at least momentarily. Maybe only long enough for another company to get their memory drug on the market first," Jerry added.

Robert pounded his hand on the desk and Jerry was certain he'd heard a bone snap, although his boss gave no indication of being injured.

"I'll kill both of them!" Robert declared. "Mark my words, Jerry, they're going to wish they'd never set foot in the same room together."

Robert picked up the tumbler, emptied its contents and threw it against the same wall as the one he'd smashed earlier. Shards of glass again exploded onto the carpet.

"Get the cleaning staff in here to pick that mess up," Robert ordered. "And find a way to get some dirt on Adams that doesn't include my wife. Money is no object."

Robert grabbed his suit jacket and headed into the lobby.

"I'm going to see if Jeffrey Hamill knows where to start. Last night he said the truth was out there. Well, I want it found and exposed because there's no way Adams is going to be President!"

Robert stormed down the hall, out of sight.

Jerry poured himself a drink and sat in Robert's leather chair.

It's a nice fit, Jerry thought. *I could get used to this.*

Now that Robert was running around like a madman poised for revenge, his next step was to shore up plans for Adams' television appearance.

After finishing his drink, Jerry returned to his desk and began to study *The Post's* classified section. Finding an ad that looked promising, he dialed the number listed.

"Hello, you have reached the Man-To-Man Escort Service and Talk Line. What is your credit card number?"

Minutes later, Jerry hung up the phone and checked his watch. He hoped Raoul, his date for the evening, wouldn't mind his girlfriend coming along for the ride.

"It's me. Meet me at a bar called Buttons on Willis Street at 7:30."

"Isn't that a gay club?" Melanie asked mystified by Jerry's request.

"It had better be or we're going to look pretty stupid standing at the bar talking to each other."

"What is going on?"

"Meet me and Raoul at 7:30. I'll answer your questions then."

"Who's Raoul?"

The line went dead.

Frustrated, Melanie slammed the receiver into its cradle.

She began to check her closet for clothes suitable for Jerry's little surprise party.

What had he been up to during those three days? she continued to ask herself. *And what did he have in store for them tonight?*

TWENTY THREE

A full week after their meeting at Buttons, Melanie was still thrilled by Jerry's self-initiated plan.

"This thing with Raoul is perfect."

"Only if it works," Jerry corrected Melanie as she turned the car onto a dirt road. "He hasn't made contact yet."

"He will," Melanie stated.

Two hours out of the city and they found themselves on an abandoned roadway.

"I'm not sure this is such a good idea," Jerry complained. "We'll be so far away from Lynn anything could happen. Then where will we be?"

"Stop worrying," Melanie scoffed. "During the times Miss Teen Dream is alone, she won't know if she's coming or going anyway."

"Time is running out and there's a ton of stuff we still have to organize."

"Over there," Melanie said, ignoring Jerry's whining.

"You've got to be kidding. It's the Bates Motel."

The Chandler Motor Lodge was once a popular, well-run ten-unit motel located on a busy highway. However on May 16, 1963, the day the new freeway opened, it ceased to exist for all intents and purposes. By all appearances, the owners locked the front door, got into their Chevy and drove away—presumably heading toward the freeway, never to return.

"It's like a time capsule," Melanie laughed as she peered into the former office's dirty window. "Where's your sense of adventure?"

Jerry cautiously wiped the grime from one of the guest room windows and held his breath, certain he'd see Norman's mother rocking in her chair, still stuffed to her gills with sawdust.

"Tell me again how you know about this place," Jerry said, straining to see the room's contents which included a bed, a desk, a chest of drawers and a bureau.

"My uncle ran the place for a summer in its heyday."

"But he never owned the place, right?" Jerry worried there might be a way to trace the place back to Melanie.

"No, he was the handyman. Probably paid cash under the table"

Jerry looked around. Desolate only began to describe the empty highway stretching endlessly to the north and the south.

It's like a one-building ghost town, Jerry thought.

"Let's get started," Melanie said. "As you so eloquently reminded me, we've got a lot to do and time is a-wastin'."

After deeming the former office as their command centre, Jerry set up the surveillance equipment as Melanie nailed wooden boards over the windows of Unit #2.

Who knows dear Lynn, this might very well turn out to be your final resting place, Melanie thought, hammering the last nail into place.

By late afternoon, Jerry had the portable generator working and was running the final gas lines into the bathroom's heat duct and ventilation fan. The idea was to give Lynn a needle or use an inhaler to knock her out for the initial ride out to the motel. Once there, they'd control her consciousness by filling the room with a sleeping agent called Diltroicide, which Litchfield had been developing before funding was diverted to the Memory One project.

"Did you plug in the TV?" Melanie asked.

"It's ready to go. If you're worried about her trying to toss it out the window, don't bother—I secured it to the bureau. Anyway, she's going to be so weak a stiff wind could push her over."

As they headed out of the area, Jerry asked, "Are you sure no one ever comes out here?"

"Did you see tire tracks anywhere around there? The answer is no. That's because no one remembers the Chandler Motor Lodge existed. Look around," Melanie said sweeping her hand toward the countryside in front of them. "We're in the *middle* of the middle of nowhere. No one cares anymore and that's exactly why it'll work to our advantage."

As they approached the city lights, Melanie allowed herself to drift off. She began to dream about the look on Lynn's face when it was broadcast she had killed her husband.

It would be awful, Melanie dreamt with a smile subconsciously pulling at the corners of her mouth. *From Prom Queen to Prime Suspect in one short lifetime. Oh how the mighty will fall.*

TWENTY FOUR

"Have you got anything yet?" Robert asked over the phone.

"It's only been a couple of days since your visit, Mr. Barker. These things take time to find."

"I don't have much time left, Hamill."

Hamill didn't immediately reply, knowing Robert was in the mood for a fight and nothing else.

"I've got a friend at *The Telegraph* checkin' some campaign donations. She's supposed to get back to me today. Other than that, aside from a few unsubstantiated rumours, it looks like Douglas runs a tight ship."

"Any skeletons in his personal life?"

"Well . . . it was no secret his marriage to Judith was no picnic. She kept him on a very short leash. If she got a whiff of any type of flirtation with another woman, she was all over Adams like a pit bull on a mailman."

"So those stories she was tough as nails were true?"

"Tougher. It seems the White House was more her idea than her husband's—like she badgered him until he finally caved."

"Where's that bitch with her leash now when I need her?"

Robert stopped himself instantly. Even he was appalled by this callous remark. Being in the pharmaceutical industry most of his life, he knew Judith's last days were filled with great pain and misery. While testing new drugs, he'd visited enough cancer wards to know no one deserved to die that way.

"Are you all right?" Hamill asked as the silence continued.

"I'm tired of playing this game, that's all."

"I'll keep digging and —" Hamill began.

"Just keep me informed," Robert said as he hung up.

Jerry knocked on the open door of Robert's office before entering.

"Did I hear your investigator hasn't been able to find anything?"

"Essentially," Robert said dejected. "What we need is hard proof, something tangible."

This was what Jerry had been waiting to hear. It was Jerry and Melanie's hope Hamill would uncover something. If not, they were prepared to step in at a moment's notice.

"I'm sure he'll turn something up."

* * *

Sitting in his office, Hamill took a bite of his ham sandwich. All his political contacts had dutifully returned his calls, although most of their information wasn't of much use. Now he was waiting for his newspaper friend to call back.

On the phone's third ring he picked up and bellowed, "Malone, what took you so long?"

"Is this Jeffrey Hamill, the private investigator?"

The female voice was smooth and sultry. It definitely didn't belong to his friend Jennifer Malone.

"Yes it is," Hamill stammered. "I'm sorry, I thought you were someone else. Please forgive my rudeness."

A Memorable Murder

"Is it that you so rarely receive calls to your office you were surprised when it rang, or is this Malone person a drinking buddy?"

A feisty one, Hamill thought.

"Neither, but I'm sure that's not the reason you called, is it?"

"Does the name Douglas Adams ring a bell?" the voice asked, getting straight to the point.

Startled, Hamill threw his sandwich aside and grabbed a pen.

"Is this Senator Douglas Adams we're talkin' about?"

"I've heard you've been looking for some dirt," the voice replied, ignoring his question, "and thought we could make a trade."

"I'd have to see the dirt first."

"In about five minutes, a courier will drop off a photocopy of a deposit receipt made out in a roundabout way to the Senator. The exceptional private dick you are will immediately notice some of the information has been blacked out."

"How much will it—"

The line went dead.

Hamill went to the hallway, his head dizzy with anticipation.

Sure enough, a few minutes later a flamboyant black male courier arrived at his door carrying a manila envelope.

"Who sent this?"

"I can't give you that information," the courier replied as Hamill signed the delivery sheet. "I deliver the stuff. I don't do dispatch."

Hamill locked the office door behind the departing courier and ripped open the envelope. It took him a few moments to decipher what the single sheet meant. When he did, he shook his head in disbelief.

The phone rang only once before he picked it up.

"I got the package," he said excitedly.

"Don't you ever say hello? For all you know I could be Malone, who'd probably want to know what you were talking about. Not the brightest move at this stage."

"Let's quit the chit-chat. How much for the blacked-out info?"

"Fifty thousand to start."

"What do you mean *to start*?"

"Every additional piece of paper will cost you five grand."

"I'll only pay on delivery."

"Half up front, half on delivery."

"How many pieces are we talking?"

"So far, ten."

"How do you want the payoff?"

"Small bills. I'll even be generous and give you three hours to get it. I'll call back to arrange the drop-off."

Once again the line went dead.

Hamill made several hasty phone calls to banking friends before calling Robert.

"From what I can tell it shows some kind of large donation."

"From whom?" Robert demanded.

"That's the part blacked out. Everything looks authentic. It's a receipt for funds wired into an account held, I assume, by Adams."

"For how much?"

"Two hundred thousand dollars."

"Why is this so earth-shattering? Is it illegal?"

"Here's my theory, based on what I've got right now. This is only a theory, remember," Hamill said, trying to make Robert aware that without the blacked-out information everything was speculation. "It has to do with the account number of the sender. The only information I could get on such short notice is that it's a Hong Kong company. The bank the money was transferred from has a different set of numbers for personal accounts and business accounts. My thinking is this is some sort of campaign donation, which is illegal regardless of the amount, since donations from foreign citizens or companies are prohibited."

"I'll be damned," Robert said, completely floored by Hamill's revelation. "Pay whatever it takes. Adams is going down and it's going to be on my dime."

At 1:00, Jerry entered Hamill's office carrying a briefcase filled with cash, knowing full well he and Melanie would be home counting it together that evening.

At 1:15, Hamill's phone rang.

"Hello, Jeffrey Hamill Investigations."

"I'm impressed. You learn quickly," the voice said.

"Everything is ready for delivery."

"In that case, the courier you met earlier will return with an envelope. It will contain the blacked-out information. You'll then give the briefcase to the courier. Are these instructions clear?"

"Crystal."

The line went dead.

Two minutes later, there was a knock on the door. When Hamill opened it, he discovered the sour-looking face of the courier.

"Someone is trying to punish me down at the depot," the courier said without a smile. "Sign here."

Hamill signed and took the envelope, which he immediately opened. The once blacked-out name read: Nagitoki Pharma.

This meant nothing to him.

"I'm supposed to pick up a briefcase," the courier said curtly.

Hamill looked at the document and then handed over the briefcase.

"Thanks," the courier said walking out of the office.

"Don't I get a receipt or something?" Hamill asked, playing the game, knowing full well the man was no delivery person.

"Not today," was the smug reply.

Hamill shut the door and looked at Jerry hovering nearby.

"Do you know anything about Nagitoki Pharma?"

Jerry grabbed the sheet and looked intently at it for a moment. "Get

Robert back on the phone now!" he ordered Hamill.

When Robert came on speaker phone, Jerry tried to sound as surprised and as outraged as he possibly could.

"This is no campaign donation. It's an out-and-out bribe, Robert."

"I don't believe Manard would stoop to such a level."

"Who's Manard?" Hamill interjected.

"The President of Litchfield Industries," Jerry replied.

"The competition? So who is this Nagitoki Pharma then?"

"It's an Asian subsidiary of Litchfield," Robert said. "What does Manard have to gain? The only application we'll have before Adams is for Memoradium. There's no way Litchfield has any knowledge of it, nor could they have a similar drug ready. So what's the point?"

"What's Memoradium?" Hamill asked.

The phone line was silent and Jerry gave Hamill a blank stare.

"It's a new drug," Robert finally said. "I can't say more than that."

"Fine with me. I was just askin'," Hamill said with a shrug. "Now what do you want to do with this stuff? I can leak it to the press, no problem."

"When is the other documentation being delivered?" Jerry inquired, knowing no further documentation would ever be produced.

"She didn't say."

"Then we'll have to go with what we've got. Bring it to the office, Jerry. We don't have much time," Robert directed before hanging up.

"Send us a bill for your services and we'll pay it by the end of the day," Jerry said as he left Hamill's office.

"No problem," Hamill said with a smile, accustomed to having to wait a month or more for most invoices to be paid.

Jerry arrived at the office a short time later and was met by Robert at the door.

"If we expose this thing, not only can Adams kiss the White House goodbye, it will also mean a new chair for the committee."

175

A Memorable Murder

"I never thought of that," Jerry said uncertainly.

He was unexpectedly doubting their plan, although he knew what the next move would be. Robert, however, was still a wild card. With this information before him, it would take all of Jerry's powers of persuasion to convince Robert to sit on it until *The Nation Today* program aired in less than two weeks.

"I'm going to crucify him!" Robert declared with delight. "First we'll expose him as a dirty politician and then as an adulterer. It'll be the best 1-2 punch since Ali-Frazier." Robert turned and saw Jerry lost in his thoughts. "Didn't you hear me? This is going to destroy Adams."

"Sorry, Robert . . . I was thinking of something I learned a few days ago which might help our cause."

"What is it?"

"Adams is scheduled to appear on *The Nation Today*, probably to announce some new reform."

"That's all well and fine but what do you propose I do—break into the studio and confront him on live TV?"

"As a matter of fact, yes."

"Are you crazy?"

"Hear me out, Robert," Jerry said smoothly. "I think you're going to like this."

Robert sat behind his desk as Jerry outlined his idea.

"Adams knows me. He wouldn't participate in such an ambush."

"Think of it this way, Robert - if Adams recognizes you, so will the director. You are well-known to the news media."

"I don't know, it seems too risky. First off, how am I going to get into the position to ask a question? And second, even if I did, who's to say they wouldn't cut away from me? Hell, Adams could simply walk off the set."

"I know people, Robert. I can set this up. As for someone recognizing you, disguise yourself a bit."

"Don't be ridiculous! What—am I supposed to rip off a fake moustache at the last second? Everyone would think I was mentally unbalanced and forgive Lynn for going outside our marriage for some comfort."

This from a man who carried on with Melanie for months under my nose, Jerry thought bitterly.

"What about a hat then? Tilt your fedora forward to cover your eyes. That's the kind of disguise I was talking about. Chances are Adams won't even be watching the outside monitor until the last second. By then it'll be too late to cut away."

Robert thought about this scenario for a moment.

"The element of surprise might work for me."

"Exactly."

Robert still looked undecided, although Jerry thought he saw a glimmer of light begin to appear at the end of the tunnel.

"I'm telling you, Robert, even if you're recognized from the very start, no director worth his weight would cut away. It would be great television. Live, unrehearsed and spontaneous. Even if Adams ignores you, there'll be tons of reporters getting off his bus to talk to you."

"And then it wouldn't matter what Adams' reaction was," Robert said slowly. "I'll expose him either way, won't I?"

They shared a smile.

"This is brilliant, Jerry. Is there really a way you can guarantee I'll be allowed to ask the first question?"

"I have a friend at the show who owes me a favour."

"And who's that?"

"The producer—Stanley Unger."

Jerry was about to leave when Robert said, "I like the hat thing. I think this could work out beautifully. Adams and Lynn will never forget this day for the rest of their lives."

Nor will you, Jerry thought, exiting the room.

TWENTY FIVE

Although they now occupied the same room, Robert and Lynn only grudgingly acknowledged one another, each suspicious of the other's motives.

Robert was livid. Lynn was supposedly going back to Glenridge for a few days. Her and an old friend from school.

Friend, my ass, Robert thought. *Don't you mean dearest Douglas, sweetheart?*

Lynn, on the other hand, was looking forward to her trip with the anticipation of a child going to the zoo for the first time. Not only would it get her out of the house, it would allow her time to resolve her feelings for both of the men in her life.

Robert had walked into their bedroom and saw Lynn packing a sweater into a suitcase on the bed.

"I don't remember Glenridge being all that cold this time of the year," he said sarcastically. "Are you sure you're only going home?"

"It cools down at night, you know that," Lynn stated in a clipped tone. "You should go back home more often. Maybe you could find the man I married."

Robert ignored the comment.

"And who is this Melanie person you are going away with again?"

"What's it to you? As long as I'm away from you I think we'll both be happier—at least for a few days."

"Ha! A moment ago I was thinking how empty the house will be without you."

"Probably not for long," Lynn said under her breath, envisioning little Alysha sprawled on the bed as open to Robert as her suitcase was now.

"What was that?" Robert asked as he stood from the corner chair he'd been sitting in.

Lynn remained silent as she continued to fold slacks and tops.

"I asked what you said." Robert's voice took on a more menacing tone.

Lynn turned and stared at him.

"I said," she began in a calm measured manner, "I wouldn't be gone long."

"Do you think I'm that stupid?"

"I'd rather not get into such debates right now, Robert."

Robert started toward Lynn, who immediately felt afraid. Although he had never hit her during their marriage, she knew there was a first time for everything.

Robert grabbed the blouse Lynn was holding and threw it on the floor.

"Look at you, always portraying yourself as Little Miss Innocent."

Lynn began to back away from Robert, who tried unsuccessfully to grab her arms.

"Robert, you're scaring me. Please get away from me," Lynn began to plead, not wanting a full-blown confrontation. "I'll be out of your life in two hours, okay. Let me finish packing and I'll stay out of your way."

Robert had backed her up against a night table in the far corner of the room. He continued to glare at her, enjoying the sight of her squirming. It was then he saw her right hand reaching for something behind her back. By the time he realized what she was grabbing, it was too late.

The heavy vase came out of nowhere and smashed against the side of his head, shattering into tiny fragments.

"I warned you," Lynn said as she watched Robert fall to his knees.

Stunned bewilderment briefly crossed his face before one of rage replaced it. Lynn held the broken vase base in both hands and brandished it at Robert.

"I'm serious, if you don't walk out of this house right now, I'll—"

"You'll what—call the police?" Robert asked mockingly.

"I'll slit your throat," Lynn replied coldly, never letting her eyes stray from his.

They were both very still for a few moments as the weight of Lynn's words sank in.

"Okay, we'll play it your way tonight," Robert said as he pulled a handkerchief from his pocket and wiped the blood trailing down the left side of his face. "You go and *play around* in Glenridge. You and *Melanie*, if such a person exists. Say hello to your old piano teacher, if you see her—wink, wink, nudge, nudge. And to Pastor Clark at the church. You remember him, don't you?"

"Leave, Robert," Lynn began. "I'll call Melanie and meet her right now. I'm not in the mood for a knockdown fight with you tonight."

"No, he wouldn't like that, would he?"

"If you have something to say, say it."

It was Robert's turn to surprise Lynn.

"When I have something to say, you can bet everyone in the country will hear about it—and I mean everyone," he emphasized.

"Whatever, Robert. Keep talking gibberish."

Lynn quickly walked over to the bed and closed the suitcase, unaware Robert had stepped into her walk-in closet.

"Robert!" she called out, fearing he'd gone to get a butcher's knife.

"I'm right here, dear," Robert said, unusually soft-spoken as he stepped out of the closet.

Lynn noticed Robert had something hidden behind his back.

What in the closet could be used as a weapon? she wondered.

At the moment Robert brought his hand into view, the wishful idea he might kill her with shoes or scarves vanished.

"Don't forget this," Robert said, throwing the bob-style wig at Lynn's chest. "We both know how cranky politicians can be when they don't get their way."

The wig bounced harmlessly off Lynn's body and fell silently to the floor, although from the stunned look on her face, Robert knew a bullet through her heart would have produced the same effect.

As Lynn continued to stare hopelessly at the wig at her feet, Robert began to leave the room.

"I have a feeling the White House won't have a new tenant after all. A shame, don't you think?"

It was all over, she thought. *Her marriage. Her affair. Her life.*

She sat in a trance until she heard the front door slam, which brought her back to reality.

She picked up the telephone and dialed Douglas' number.

"Hello."

"Douglas, I have to see you right now."

"Who is this?"

Lynn recognized Harold Green's voice.

"Harold, I need to speak with Douglas."

"Lynn?" Green said, finally figuring out who was babbling over the line. "I can't get hold of him right now."

"Don't lie to me, Harold! This is an emergency that could cost Douglas everything," Lynn pleaded.

During his years in politics, Harold Green had seen many politicians go down in flames over an affair or in some instances, alleged affairs. He'd overseen these liaisons from their genesis but there always came a time when something went wrong. When the woman wanted more attention, more money, more cars or a bigger apartment—that was trouble. It was at this stage he would take complete charge of the situation regardless of his candidate's feelings.

Listening to Lynn blather on, Harold assumed she was drunk or high on some drug her hubby may have brought home from the lab. Either way, on the eve of a major campaign announcement, there was no way he was going to allow Adams' mind to wander to things domestic.

"I'm not lying, Lynn," he lied. "Douglas is flying over the Rockies at this moment and communication to the plane is impossible."

"The airports then. Contact him through regional control towers. I have to speak to him. This is urgent."

Did you break a nail while making a pitcher of martinis? Green thought.

"Look, Lynn, as soon as communication is restored, I'll forward your message."

"It's about tomorrow," Lynn implored. "I think something is going to happen during *The Nation Today* appearance."

"The only thing that's going to happen is our poll numbers are going to go up several points," Green said thinking ahead. "I've got to go. I'll tell Douglas you called."

"Don't—"

Green hung up.

"No!" Lynn pleaded. "Don't do this to me!"

She slammed the phone down and crumpled onto the bed.

Everything's ruined and there's nothing I can do.

She glimpsed the wig on the floor and was overcome with rage.

Just get a grip, she told herself. *Going crazy isn't helping. Calm down and think things through.*

She jammed the wig in her suitcase and then picked up the broken pieces of glass. Next, in a moment of clarity, she picked up the phone and began to dial.

"Could we get together earlier—like right away? Things have got a bit out of control and I don't want to be around when Robert returns."

"No problem," Melanie said as she threw a pillow at Jerry, who was asleep on the couch. She mouthed the words *Lynn wants to leave now*. "I need to pack a few things, so come over now. You've still got my address?"

"Yes, it's right here."

"One other thing," Melanie began. "Will you still be driving the grey Volvo?"

Lynn thought it was a strange question.

"Yes, the grey Volvo. Is that a problem?"

"No," Melanie said with a smile. "Now get your stuff over here. Glenridge here we come!"

The enthusiasm in Melanie's voice brought a smile to Lynn's tear stained face. The thought of Robert's ominous threat briefly re-entered her mind, although it now seemed childish.

All sound and no fury, she concluded.

This trip was going to be very therapeutic for her. Getting away from Douglas and Robert would not be as hard as she thought it might.

What better place to do some deep thinking than in the small town where I grew up?

Yes, this was going to be a trip she would never forget.

TWENTY SIX

"You can pull into the garage, Lynn," Melanie instructed as she walked to the driver's side window. "It'll be safe in there."

As promised, Melanie was ready to depart, having already put her things in the Jeep.

"I can't believe the things he said to me," Lynn said. "I honestly thought he was going to hit me."

How horrifying, Melanie thought, trying to suppress a smile.

An hour later, although she'd been planning this moment for weeks, the roadside Rest Area sign made Melanie's heart rate quicken.

"I really have to go," Melanie said, pulling off the interstate. "Do you?"

"No, I'm fine," Lynn said.

"Why don't you stretch your legs while I'm in the bathroom?"

"Yeah, maybe I'll get us some sodas from a vending machine," Lynn said cheerfully. "We can make a toast to the great trip ahead."

You won't be in the mood for drinking, much less celebrating, in a few minutes, Melanie thought. *Me, on the other hand . . .*

The parking lot was empty. No vehicles. No bikers. No hitchhikers.

"I'll only be a second," Melanie said as she walked to the far side of the main building, out of Lynn's sight.

Lynn turned on the overhead light and began searching for change in her purse. Stuffing a handful of quarters into her windbreaker pocket, she flipped off the light and pushed her door open.

Before her foot touched the ground, Jerry was on her.

The specially-designed plastic nose cup he was holding went over her nose and mouth. Next, he pressed the top button of the Diltrocide-filled aerosol-type canister, and held onto Lynn from behind as she frantically inhaled the gas.

Moments later, he pushed her sideways across the seat, where she lost consciousness.

Painless and precise, as they had planned.

Melanie saw two cars arriving and cursed their timing.

"Leave her there," she said in a low voice as she saw Jerry beginning to lift Lynn out of the Jeep. "There's no time."

Melanie got behind the steering wheel and slammed her door shut.

"Take that stupid thing off," she said, seeing Jerry was still wearing the cheap mask he'd bought as a disguise. "Meet me at Tucker's Corner. There's a roadway no one uses off the east side road. We'll do the switch there."

"This is nuts," he said to himself as he entered the Volvo parked in the picnic area.

Tucker's Corner was a few miles off the interstate, the name for six houses, a rundown variety store and a gas station that had gone out of business years earlier.

Jerry killed the lights as he rolled toward Melanie's parked Jeep.

"How long before she comes to?" he asked as he lifted Lynn's limp body into the Volvo's trunk.

"Did you give her a full shot of that stuff?" Melanie replied, nervously watching the area for vehicles or movement.

"I did like you showed me. She gulped it down like it was liquid chocolate."

"Then about two hours. Plenty of time to get to the motel, where we'll give her another shot of it. Let's get out of here, and remember do the speed limit. The last thing we need is a cop pulling you over and deciding to check the trunk." She stopped and glared at Jerry. "Do you understand?"

"I'm in this as deep as you. I'm not going to botch it now, so let's go."

With the abduction of Lynn Barker, they had added kidnapping to their growing list of crimes that included bribery, industrial espionage and conspiracy to commit murder.

And all for what? Fortune? Fame? Their lives?

Jerry was too pumped to think about such things as he drove up the laneway of their imitation Bates Motel, where guests checked in but rarely checked out.

Carrying Lynn into her room, the idea he might still be a dead man walking crossed his mind. Howard Manard, a man he'd never met, continued to hold his and Melanie's lives in his hands. Then again, if they completed their task satisfactorily, he'd make them very rich.

Fortune? Undoubtedly.

Fame? No question.

Their lives?

Jerry inspected the room, making sure nothing had been tampered with since their last visit. With everything still in place, he exited the room alone, leaving Lynn on the bed.

"How is her breathing?" Melanie asked as they watched the monitor in the former office.

"Like a baby," Jerry said with a smile. "Our billion-dollar baby."

"It ain't over yet, lover boy. We still have a busy day ahead of us tomorrow." She turned and held out her hand. "Did you get it?"

"Right here."

Jerry reached into his pocket and retrieved Lynn's bracelet.

"Do you want it as a souvenir or something?"

Melanie looked at the bracelet and smiled.

"No, Jerry, this is our insurance policy."

Jerry shrugged his shoulders and dropped the topic.

By midnight they were heading back to Melanie's house.

As she lay in her bed staring up at the ceiling, Melanie felt a rush of cool relief come over her.

It's almost over. My involvement with Robert. With Lynn. With Jerry.

The girl who'd been ridiculed in school would show the world that brains beat beauty every time.

"If only they'd listened then," Melanie said to the empty room.

She began to laugh at the precarious situation she'd placed herself. It was insane to think her plan was about to come true.

You never know 'til you try, right? she mused.

As she drifted to sleep, her only hope was that when this was all over, Jerry would see the humour in the fact she'd been Howard Manard's mistress for the past six months. Regardless, the poor fool would have lots of time to think about such ironies while awaiting his death sentence to be carried out.

First things first.

She still had to take Robert and Douglas down before putting Jerry's head on a stick. Who knew—maybe Jerry would have a fatal accident, which would save the taxpayers a great deal of money on appeals.

Dilemmas for another time, she thought.

With sunrise only a few hours away, her mind embraced the idea of getting rest, knowing that in the days ahead, there would be no rest for the wicked.

No matter how smart they were.

TWENTY SEVEN

PRESENT DAY

As night descended on the Chandler Motor Lodge, both Jerry and Melanie were feeling pretty cocky.

They'd actually pulled it off.

Not only had they got away clean, there was no indication that anyone except Lynn Barker and her mysterious accomplice were responsible for Robert Barker's terrible murder.

They'd committed the perfect crime.

Once police gained access to the Barker residence, new clues supporting Lynn's guilt began to pile up.

It started with a match of the dropped bracelet to one shown in a picture found on the Barker's piano. Then came a development both Jerry and Melanie could have only hoped for: a bedroom floor covered in glass fragments from a vase which had been thrown at a wall. Police deduction: domestic fight causing injury. Robert's blood was found on the carpet and an examination of the shoes he was wearing at the time of his death revealed the same glass caught in the tongue and laces.

Next was the matter of the missing grey Volvo.

After dropping their rental off at the airport, Melanie took Jerry to work, where he assumed the role of shocked co-worker. Once home, Melanie temporarily put the Jeep's plates on Lynn's Volvo, which she drove to a secluded industrial area. After replacing Lynn's plates, she walked several blocks before taking a taxi back to her house. Secure in her mind that everything was fine, she placed an anonymous call to the police, telling them where Lynn's car could be found.

Within minutes, video of the abandoned car was being broadcast live on every TV channel.

Since the shooting, Jason Morris and Susan Donallee had been on the air longer than any other network news team. They finally signed off to allow NCN to run their nightly primetime programming, however, were still required to do updates.

"Now I know how Cronkite felt covering Kennedy's assassination," Jason said to Susan as the tally lights on the studio cameras were finally extinguished.

"At least he had something knowledgeable to say during his broadcast," she scoffed as she removed her microphone and began to walk off the set.

Furious, Jason snapped back, "Oh yeah, I forgot—you watched the whole thing from your crib. Probably right after your mother spoon-fed you some strained carrots!"

The studio went silent as Susan stopped in her tracks, turned and glared at Jason, who sat at the anchor desk with a victor's grin on his face.

"That's pretty tough talk from a man whose last erection only measured four inches and was brought on by a picture of your sister's head superimposed over a Playboy bunny's body."

The smile drained from Jason's face. Then, like a cartoon character, a wave of redness moved up his neck, across his cheeks, over his ears and

finally onto his forehead.

"You ungrateful little bitch!" he responded. "After all I've done for you!"

"Unfortunately four inches doesn't go as far as it did in olden times, Jason," Susan replied.

She didn't wait for his response and walked out of the studio, leaving Jason to face the crew on his own.

Fifteen minutes later, the colour in Jason's face still hadn't returned to normal. The director had contemplated having Susan do the first update alone but decided to go with Jason, crimson face and all.

"Good evening. Our top story remains the gangland-style killing of millionaire Robert Barker, owner of Mantis Pharmaceuticals, outside the studios of *The Nation Today*. The police have confirmed that a grey Volvo found in an industrial park is registered to Lynn Barker, whose whereabouts are still unknown. A warrant has been issued for Mrs. Barker's arrest on a count of first-degree murder, after police determined the couple had a violent domestic argument last evening in their New Liston home. Police are not giving out details regarding this apparent dispute, however, reporter Tanya Grahame has learned more. Tanya. "

The screen cut to a shot of Tanya Grahame standing outside Robert and Lynn's house.

"Jason, after speaking with several sources here, I've learned that pieces of a glass vase were found in a wastebasket in the bathroom off the Barker's master bedroom. Shards of this vase were also found on the bedroom carpet and it's reported a piece was embedded in the room's south wall."

"Was there any evidence of personal physical violence, Tanya?"

"There's an unsubstantiated report that blood believed to be that of Mr. Barker was found on the bedroom carpet as well."

"Is it possible the blood is Lynn Barker's and not her husband's?"

"Again, Jason, there is speculation the coroner typed the blood at the scene, comparing blood from Mr. Barker's body and there was a match."

"Thank you for that report, Tanya. In other developments, Presidential candidate Douglas Adams is reported to be doing well, after what his campaign manager, Harold Green, said was a mild case of food poisoning. Senator Adams was on *The Nation Today* when Mr. Barker was shot in the temple while preparing to ask the Senator a question. Why Mr. Barker was outside the studio has yet to be determined."

"Turn that off!" Adams barked to one of his security guards. "Food poisoning? That's the best you could do, Harold?"

"Well, let me see, Douglas. I guess I could have told them you had a minor heart attack upon learning your mistress killed her husband on national TV—but somehow I don't think the electorate would take too kindly to that, do you?"

"What about the paramedics who treated me? What if they say something?"

"With their kids' education now paid for? I don't think so."

"We're buying off kids to get votes? Have we stooped that low?"

"Apparently," Green said casually.

Adams remained silent, staring at the blank screen as Green continued to speak.

"From the brief polling we've been able to do, all indications point to a very positive reaction to your quick response to the shooting. As more people learn about your professional connection with Barker, I believe it can only enhance your ratings."

Adams got out of his chair and walked to the corner bar. The Regent Hotel was much better than Harold's safe house. Although it had been useful at the time, Adams hadn't felt comfortable there. A spacious hotel suite though was like a second home. After years on the road campaigning for one office or another, he figured a full third of his political life had been spent in rented rooms.

A MEMORABLE MURDER

He poured himself a two-finger shot of whiskey, emptied the contents and thought, *Where the hell is Lynn?*

* * *

Not knowing if it was day or night, Lynn slowly began to regain consciousness. The first thing she noticed scanning her eerily silent surroundings was that the television set she'd blown apart was gone. Obviously someone had entered the room to remove it, although she had no recollection of it. She did recall collapsing in the bathroom after seeing pink smoke—was it really pink?—start to billow into the room from the ceiling fan.

For now, she remained on the bed, slowly remembering how much damage she'd done to herself and the room the last time she'd stood upright.

What is going on? her mind continued to ask. Regrettably, her brain could not summon any rational answer. *How could it,* she thought, *nothing so far has been rational.*

The last sane memory she had was calling Melanie to say she'd be coming by earlier than arranged for their trip to . . .

Panic began to overtake her.

Where is Melanie? Is she in another room? Is she alive?

The pieces began to reassemble in her head. The fight with Robert. Trying to contact Douglas. Going to Melanie's house. Packing the Jeep. Leaving the city behind. Stopping at the rest area. Melanie getting out of the Jeep. Looking for change for the pop machine.

Then nothing.

A total blank.

She didn't recall getting the sodas or anything else for that matter. As for Melanie, Lynn was sure she hadn't come back to the Jeep.

She lay perfectly still, staring at the crumbling ceiling above her bed and attempted to hold back the tears she felt coming on. She tried to calm herself, to little avail. As a full-blown anxiety attack overtook her, she gripped the sheets with both hands, her back arched off the bed and she began to gulp air into her lungs.

There must have been two or more of them waiting at the rest area. Hoping for an easy target. Looking for quick cash.

WHERE IS MELANIE?

Thankfully, Lynn's attack soon subsided, leaving her completely drained. She turned onto her stomach and buried her face in the pillow, squeezing it with her hands.

Why is this happening to me?

Without wanting to, Lynn slipped back into a deep sleep, as the relevance of this seemingly illogical situation continued to elude her.

* * *

"What do you think about putting another TV in her room?" Jerry mused as he watched the monitor of Lynn's room. "You know—to keep her abreast of the police investigation."

The idea of continuing to mentally torture Lynn appealed to Melanie immensely.

"Not yet. Let's give her a day or two to think things over," Melanie said. "I've heard solitary confinement can do wonders for one's psyche," she laughed.

Jerry turned away from the monitor and switched on the portable television sitting on the counter.

"Too bad they don't have cable out here in the sticks," he said as he pulled the set's rabbit ears back and forth.

"Stop complaining. You can get the networks, screw CNN. WCNY had more coverage yesterday than the others stations combined."

"It's not the same," Jerry said dejectedly, as one of the four stations they could pull in came into focus. "What's that you're reading — *The Telegraph*? What do they have to say?"

Melanie had begun to read Jennifer Malone's front page story.

"Same as all the rest, pretty much." She continued to scan the story when something caught her attention. "This is interesting," she said as she flipped to the centre fold of the first section, where the shooting took up the entire two pages.

"What's that?" Jerry asked.

"It may be nothing. Listen to this: 'Mantis Pharmaceuticals is one of many pharmaceutical companies which maintain an in-house research and development operation. They manufacture new drugs, as well as so-called knock-off drugs of other established products. However, it does not appear that Mantis is developing any generic drugs at this time.'"

Even Jerry didn't like the sound of the last sentence.

"She's implying Mantis is only working on developing new drugs."

"Which in itself is primarily true, right?" Melanie asked.

"Then why did she go out of her way to bring up knock-offs?"

"Maybe there were space constraints and she had to kill a line or two."

"Or maybe she knows more than she's writing about and is leaving herself an opening to do a follow-up story. So why did you find that particular section interesting?"

"Because of all the stories that mention Mantis and its connection to our friend Senator Adams and his Health and Welfare Committee, no one else cites anything about what Mantis is currently developing — let alone not developing. It's all a rehash of the company's past."

"Which means that moron McIntyre in PR is actually doing his job," Jerry said.

"Speaking of doing his job, don't you have to reprise your role as the grieving secretary this morning?" Melanie inquired.

"Administrative Assistant, thank you very much."

"Yeah, whatever. Try and stay out of the firing line of reporters and television cameras."

"What—you don't want to see me on TV?"

"Not until everything is in place."

Jerry put on his coat and checked outside for nonexistent traffic.

"I hope the police are done with me. That Detective Speers is one intense cop."

"He bought your story, right?"

"Hook, line and sinker. Anyway, what would a CEO's assistant know about a gangland-style killing? It's not like I'm going to inherit the company," he said with a laugh.

"Exactly. How many CEO's leave their companies to their secretaries? Especially ones they haven't been boinking. And I'm almost certain you and Robert weren't doing the horizontal bop, now were you, Jerry?" she asked, almost accusingly.

Ignoring her annoying tone, he was about to correct her on the secretary thing, before deciding on a parting shot of his own.

"Only those nights he wasn't pretending to enjoy screwing you, dear," Jerry said as he turned and walked out the door.

Melanie was momentarily stunned by Jerry's comment.

He's getting too big for his britches, her grandfather would have said.

"Don't worry, Gramps," she said aloud. "He'll get his comeuppance soon enough, if you know what I mean."

TWENTY EIGHT

Jennifer walked into the newsroom and was immediately overwhelmed by loud applause and cheering. She acknowledged her fellow reporters and co-workers with a low and gracious bow.

"My loyal subjects, your Queen thanks you!" she said, sweeping her right hand into the air as she straightened up.

Laughter briefly broke out throughout the room and soon everyone was back working on the next edition's copy.

Jennifer made her way into Carson's office and found him eased back in his chair.

"Tough life, Mitch," Jennifer said taking a seat on the battered leather couch across from his cluttered desk.

"Just savouring our exclusive," he replied.

"Don't you mean *my* exclusive?"

"Sure, if you want to get technical."

"I wasn't aware you'd been adopted by the owners. Does Old Man Hollingsworth personally take you to the park and to ball games or does his chauffeur?"

"Not even you can spoil my upbeat mood this morning, Malone.

The fact that we were the only media outlet—electronic or print—with information about the parked Volvo will go down as one of the biggest scoops in news journalism."

"At least until someone else's scoop comes out tomorrow, right?"

"Again, if you want to get technical about these things . . ." Mitch replied slowly. "So what's on your agenda today?"

"I'm thinking of scoping out *The Nation Today*. I watched most of this morning's show—essentially a rehash of the endless hours of drivel that Morris and Donallee spewed yesterday."

"You know one of them, right?" Mitch asked, sensing a new story angle.

"Yeah—I once slept with Morris' wife to pay off a poker debt," Jennifer deadpanned. "I could have sworn that last card was going to be a King of Hearts. Regardless, Morris is a strange fellow. Does a helluva job reading news though, don't you think?"

"So I take it you know Donallee then?" Mitch asked, deciding not to encourage any more tall tales, no matter how amusing they might be.

"You're no fun when you're in a happy mood. Has anyone ever told you that?"

"Only once," Carson said seriously. "It was during a conjugal visit with your mother, which I'd rather not get into right now."

They stared at each other for a second and then broke into laughter.

"I always wondered why writing news stories was in my blood. Do you mind if I call you Pop?"

"I'd rather you not call me at all," he said with an easy smile. "Susan Donallee on the other hand . . ."

"I'll see what I can do." Jennifer got off the couch. "I'm hoping she doesn't remember that I stole her boyfriend during our first year at college."

"Students are notorious for fooling around on each other."

"Who said anything about a student? This guy was the Ethics prof."

"Oh."

Jennifer left Mitch with a puzzled look on his face and went to her desk to find Susan's number. Once in hand, she decided a personal visit would be better than a telephone call.

After all the previous day's commotion, she was pleasantly surprised how easy it was to gain entry into the NCN building. The powers-that-be must have concluded Barker's killing was an act of revenge against him, and not aimed at the network.

She walked through the rear receiving door and was confronted by a handsome guard in his early 20's sitting behind a desk watching several security camera monitors, as well as the station's feed.

Looking at him, she was reminded of the good-looking male she'd encountered in the Kingdom Entertainment building.

I've really got to get out in the neighbourhood more, she thought.

"Hello, I'd like to see Susan Donallee."

"Your name?"

"Candice Mathews."

Knowing NCN's parent company also owned the *Star*, Jennifer was pretty certain a copy of today's *Telegraph*, the one with her picture above the by-line, would not be found at the guard station.

"Your company's name?"

"*Architecture Monthly*. We want to do a cover story on Ms. Donallee's house."

"Is that right?" The guard picked up the phone and paused. "With all the excitement yesterday, Ms. Donallee wasn't taking any calls, being on the air and all."

"Yes, the shooting was awful," Jennifer said, trying to act both sweet and concerned, always a daunting task for her. "You weren't working when it happened, were you?" she asked, figuring any information he might provide was better than none at all.

"No, Eugene was on duty."

"Eugene? I used to know a security guard named Eugene," Jennifer said playfully. "What's his last name?"

"Murphy. Is that your friend?"

"No."

"Too bad," the guard said as he punched in Susan's extension, which Jennifer memorized.

"Hello, Susan, this is Michael at the security desk. I have Jennifer Malone from *The Telegraph* here to see you." He flashed a smile at Jennifer, who sheepishly smiled back with a shrug of her shoulders. "Says she's an old friend of yours. Can I send her up or would you like to come down to greet her yourself?" He waited for an answer and then hung up the phone. "She'll be right down."

"You saw right through my whole 'Candice Mathews' thing. You're the whole package, aren't you?" Jennifer said with a slight laugh. "Brains and looks."

"I could say the same thing about you."

"Then why don't you?"

"It's not in my job description."

"And a sense of humour." Jennifer pulled out a business card and scribbled her personal number on the back. Handing it over she said, "Whenever you're not in uniform and would like to discuss our common attributes, call me."

As Michael put Jennifer's card in his jacket pocket both became aware of Susan Donallee's presence.

"Jennifer, I didn't see what I think I just saw, did I?"

"It's called networking," Jennifer said calmly.

"It's called desperate," Susan replied with a smile.

"You TV people have a different word for everything, don't you?"

They turned their attention to Michael, whose face was beginning to turn red.

Jennifer looked back at Susan and smiled.

"For once I think we're both right. What just took place here could definitely be classified as desperate networking."

Both women laughed as they saw Michael's expression change.

"Thanks for calling me, Mike," Susan said as she led Jennifer down the hall.

As they rounded the corner, Jennifer turned her head back to the guard desk, gave Michael a wink and mouthed, *Call me.*

"Why do you torture the boy so?" Susan asked in the elevator.

"Who said anything about torturing him? Although the image of him buck naked, handcuffed to my bed and a riding crop on the nightstand does have some appeal, you have to admit."

"Only in your dreams," Susan laughed. "Speaking of handcuffs and riding crops—how is Professor Walmesley doing these days?"

They spent the following half-hour talking in Susan's office about old times and fellow reporters, even though both knew the true purpose of Jennifer's visit.

"I'm not sure how I can help you, Jennifer. Hell, I'm not even sure you being in this building, let alone my office, is allowed these days. You being the enemy and all—especially after your scoop this morning."

"I got lucky with that one. I even told the police about it as soon as I heard it."

"Out of the kindness of your heart, I suppose?" Susan asked, casting a suspicious stare in Jennifer's direction. "You didn't get Barker's name several hours before the rest of us by any chance, did you?"

"Officer Kendall's got a big mouth," Jennifer replied.

"That's not the only big thing he's got," Susan said with a smirk.

"Okay . . . " Jennifer said, blushing slightly. "So, what I really need is an interview with Unger, the show's producer."

"Best of luck with that. The guy's a basket case. The brass sent him home for a week."

"Why?"

"Once we—meaning that dickhead Morris and I—were on the air, I guess he totally lost it. The top guys decided to get him away from the whole situation and put an associate producer in charge."

"Nice break for the associate, after all the hype of bagging Unger."

"From what I understand he's taking the shooting personally, because it was his great idea for the outside microphone, yadda, yadda, yadda. As far as I'm concerned, he's simply another pretender going down in flames when the fire gets too hot."

"I can't believe that's the only reason."

"Find another one and you'll have yourself another scoop."

Susan's desk phone rang and she picked it up, speaking briefly.

"They want me to do a quickie voice-over. It shouldn't take long."

"Take your time," Jennifer said cheerfully.

As soon as she heard Susan's footsteps trailing down the hall, Jennifer was out of her chair and looking at the papers on the desk.

"They've got to have one," she muttered as she gently looked under several stacks of papers. Then she saw it.

"Right under the phone, how clever."

She picked the network's internal personnel directory up and scanned for the names Stanley Unger and Eugene Murphy. Quickly memorizing both numbers and listed addresses, she replaced the directory and scooted back to her chair. Not hearing any footsteps, she quickly called *The Telegraph*.

"Mitch," she said in a whispered tone, "it's Jennifer. Don't ask why, just text me something in a few minutes."

Sitting back, she began to laugh at the thought of Mitch slamming down his office phone and calling her every name in the book.

"Where were we?" Susan asked, closing the door behind her.

"Well . . . as this Unger guy has apparently flown over the cuckoo's nest, is there anyone who could give me the lowdown on how *The Nation Today* works—security, booking arrangements, that kind of thing?"

Susan began to scroll through her cell phone's contact list.

"No one on the current staff will talk to you. I think Rosanna Rhames might if you're nice."

Susan rattled off her phone number.

"Who is she?"

"You mean who *was* she."

"Is she dead or something?"

"She is as far as the network is concerned. You see Miss Rhames—a nice enough woman by all accounts—was the associate producer of *The Nation Today* before the shakeup. When they fired then-producer Harvey Stoltz, Rosanna felt she should have been named his replacement."

"Then the big boys passed her over for Stanley the wunderkind and she quit."

"Almost. She threatened to sue for sexual discrimination."

"Talk about a career suicide mission."

"Not exactly. The last thing NCN needed was a high profile discrimination suit, so they paid her off."

"Do you really think she'll talk on the record?"

"She'll give you the kind of dirt usually found at the bottom of a sewer."

Susan's phone rang again and by her expression Jennifer knew their visit was over.

"I have to take this call, Jennifer," Susan said, knowing a fellow reporter would decipher the code and leave graciously.

As if on cue, Jennifer's phone beeped, indicating an incoming text.

"Duty calls," she said looking at the readout: 911-911-911. "Once this Barker thing is over, let's get together away from the office, okay?"

"Sounds good to me."

Jennifer exited the building using a side entrance, not wanting to talk to Michael the security guard (at least not yet). Then it was back to the paper where she filled in a very high-strung Mitch about her new leads.

"Do you think it's wise to go to Unger's front door and start hurling questions at him?"

"I'm not sure he's still in the country, Mitch. If I call I'm only going to get a machine. There may be a small army of reporters camped out at his house already."

"Check it out anyway. Maybe he's too scared to leave the state."

"That's my guess. From what Susan told me, he had a nervous breakdown or something frightfully similar. Add the fact that an associate is now running *his* show, I'll bet he's still in contact with the network on an hourly basis. I'll go so far as to say he'll be back on the job tomorrow or the day after. He doesn't want to appear to have abandoned ship."

"What about the security guard, this Murphy fellow?"

"Probably minor league stuff. If Unger doesn't work out I'll track poor Eugene down. Same with Rosanna Rhames."

Jennifer took an unmarked company car and drove an hour out of the city, using the GPS to locate Lincoln Park, an affluent planned community with a population of a thousand people.

Not your normal rural types out here, Jennifer assumed driving through the town's wide streets, fascinated by the mansions to her left and right. She noticed the vehicles parked in the driveways—a Lexus here, a couple of BMWs there. She was almost hit by a Porsche driven by a boy who Jennifer swore didn't look a day over 16. The houses, the lush manicured lawns, the tennis courts and the swimming pools all declared *Rich People Live Here!*

TWENTY NINE

Stanley Unger's mini-palace was no different from the others in the vicinity. The street was empty and thankfully there were no reporters or satellite trucks milling about. She was about to turn into the driveway when one of the three garage doors opened. She could see an attractive woman in her early 30's hurrying a boy and a girl into a new black Cadillac.

"Where's Poppa Bear?" Jennifer inquired to herself.

She watched in her rear view mirror as the Caddy was driven quickly out of view. Jennifer made a U-turn and headed to the Unger residence.

In the driveway, Jennifer switched on her mini-recorder and walked to the front doors. Would there be a housekeeper to greet her? She pressed the bell several times with no response. Detecting no movement from within, she decided to check out the back yard, where she heard music playing.

This looks promising, she thought.

There, stretched out on a poolside lounger, was the man whose picture Jennifer had seen in an NCN hallway.

I think that's him, she pondered.

The physical features were the same—high cheekbones, prominent nose and shaggy shoulder-length hair—yet the look of loneliness which clouded his face and creased his brow made a positive identification impossible.

"Mr. Unger?" Jennifer said in a soft, engaging voice, stopping several feet away from him.

The man was startled at the mention of his own name. Clearly still lost in whatever tortured thoughts he'd been thinking, he turned his head in Jennifer's direction and stared at her as if she were the Grim Reaper.

"I'm sorry to bother you like this," Jennifer said apologetically. "I rang the front bell several times."

His eyes were bloodshot and for a fleeting second Jennifer wondered if Unger's wife and kids had left forever, simply packing a few items and driving away.

Does he even know they're gone?

"Are you the caretaker my wife arranged?" Unger asked in a low, strained tone.

Jennifer's first instinct was to say 'yes,' however, she knew professional ethics wouldn't allow her to lie about her identity, at least not in this case.

"Actually, Mr. Unger—can I call you Stanley?—my name is Jennifer Malone. We met briefly at the NCN media banquet last December."

One little white lie never killed anyone's career, Jennifer thought, although she *had* been at the banquet, albeit only for the cocktail hour.

A passing look of recognition swept over Unger's face and his eyes lit up as if remembering actually meeting her.

"Do you work for the network?" he asked.

"Actually I work for a newspaper."

"Oh."

From his continued vacant stare, Jennifer knew this information wasn't completely registering with him. The way he looked, however, would not come across on the micro-cassette turning in her jacket pocket.

I've identified myself and that I work for a newspaper.

"I'm a reporter," Jennifer added, trying to cover all of her bases.

"Then I guess you heard about the shooting yesterday."

"Yes—yes I did. A real tragedy."

"A Shakespearean tragedy, if you ask me." Unger tossed his head back and began to laugh, an almost insane cackling.

Jennifer took a tentative step closer.

"Do you mind if I sit down?"

"No, go ahead. I could use the company," he replied, gesturing to a lounger on his left. Without coaxing, he continued their conversation. "I always liked Shakespeare, you know. He'd always show you both sides of any story, allowing the audience to decide which one they wanted to cheer for and which one they wanted to revile. The trick was to never allow the characters to see what was really going on—the big picture. Because if they could glimpse even a few seconds into the future, they'd probably make different plans. That way they'd always be on the *right side* of the play and feel morally justified in their actions."

Unger stopped rambling to absently watch a small bird land on a nearby birdbath.

"Maybe I can help," Jennifer offered innocently.

"How?" Unger asked, turning his full attention back to the beautiful stranger who had walked into his life.

"We can rewrite yesterday's tragedy."

"That's not possible!" Unger protested, now wide awake. "A man is dead and I helped kill him!"

The statement left Jennifer temporarily speechless.

Was it really this simple? Had Unger set up Barker to be killed and was now overwhelmed with guilt?

Over the years, Jennifer had witnessed hundreds of ordinary people blame themselves for not being able to stop unforeseen tragedies. She knew the only way to handle such fragile individuals was with kid gloves and a lot of understanding.

With her reporter's instincts primed to the max, Jennifer made a split-second judgment: there was no way Unger had set Barker up and he didn't have knowledge of the plot beforehand.

It just wasn't possible.

"You didn't kill Mr. Barker, Stanley," Jennifer said, trying to console Unger. "It was a freak occurrence."

"Do you call me planning to have Barker step up to the microphone at a specific time, on a specific date, a freak occurrence? I don't!" Unger straightened up in the lounger, turned his body toward Jennifer and placed his bare feet on the patio tiles. "If it wasn't for my selfishness, Robert Barker wouldn't have been there yesterday. He wouldn't have been shot. He'd still be alive today if it wasn't for me! Don't you understand that?"

Jennifer braced herself believing Unger might leap to his feet and begin to shake her to make her understand. Instead, he buried his face in his hands and began to sob.

So much for my fabulous reporter instincts, Jennifer reflected.

There was still a nagging feeling about this scene that didn't gel. If Unger had been involved with Barker, what was their connection? Jennifer checked her watch and wondered how much longer wifey and the kids would be away.

"Why would you kill Robert Barker?" Jennifer asked bluntly, hoping reality might filter back into Unger's mush of a brain. "Why did he have to die?"

The sobbing stopped and Unger lifted his head out of his hands. Nothing happened for several seconds and Jennifer worried that she'd

once again been too aggressive.

Then Unger began to laugh. It was the same odd cackling that only someone at the end of their rope could produce. He clapped his hands a couple of times, somehow thoroughly enjoying a joke to which only he knew the punch line.

"That's what's so tragic," Unger bellowed to the sky. "I never even met the man! I didn't know Robert Barker from Adam, yet because of me he's dead! Isn't that hilarious?"

Not the word I would have used but sure, why not, Jennifer thought.

"If that's the case, why arrange his appearance with Senator Adams?"

"They said they'd send the pictures to my wife and email copies to every television station and newspaper in the country."

"This is about blackmail?" Jennifer asked, completely astounded. "Someone has pictures of you and another woman, is that it? I don't see the big deal."

Unger's expression went blank for a moment. Although drained of emotion, he slowly became serious and frightened.

"Another woman my wife could handle," he said slowly.

"They're gone, aren't they? Your wife and kids."

"I told her everything," Unger said as he tried holding back an avalanche of tears.

Jennifer didn't know what to say. Here was a man leading some sort of double life, seemingly at the top of his game career-wise, respected by his peers, with a wife and kids, yet now left entirely alone to fight his innermost demons.

"Are you going to write all of this down, Miss Malone? It's the scoop any reporter would give their right arm for."

For the second time in as many days, Jennifer was faced with holding the key to many people's futures. It was a feeling she wasn't at all comfortable with.

"Did you get the pictures?"

"And the negatives," Unger said hesitantly. "I did what they said—you have to believe me. I had no idea they were going to kill him. Please believe me," he pleaded.

"I do, Stanley. For some reason, I do."

Jennifer looked at the broken man before her and contemplated her next move. In her heart she knew if she'd postponed this trip until the afternoon, Stanley Unger would no longer be available to answer any of her questions, or anyone else's.

She concluded she could not play God in this situation and whatever decision Stanley Unger made would be his alone.

"I can't imagine what you are going through. Let me assure you I won't publish any of this information unless it is completely relevant to the Barker story. You have my word on that. I really do want to help clear your name. I have a few more questions and then I'll leave, if that's all right?"

"I won't be talking to anyone about this again, so you had better ask your questions now."

"Thank you. First, do you know who was blackmailing you?"

"I haven't a clue."

"What about the man—I'm assuming—in the pictures?"

"His name is Raoul and I met him at a gay bar called Buttons. I'm not sure if he was party to this or not." Unger sighed. "Although I guess he'd have to be in some manner."

"And the only demand was that you arrange for Robert Barker to ask the first question of Senator Adams, is that right?"

"Which at the time was kind of strange, as no one from the show or Adams' campaign had publicly announced the appearance."

"Meaning what?"

"Meaning very few people knew Adams would be there—especially a few weeks beforehand. Whoever needed Barker dead wanted him to die in front of Senator Adams."

"You think this shooting was politically motivated?"

"I don't think so, but the shooting has meant an immediate rise in Adams' numbers—enough to get him into the White House."

Jennifer wanted to discuss the role Memoradium and the Health and Welfare Committee might have played in the killing, then thought better of it. No matter how unlikely, she didn't need Unger to somehow make a full recovery and get word back to the network newsroom.

They sat in silence, both surveying the large yard, with its expensive landscaping and huge kidney-shaped pool.

"You have a wonderful place here, Stanley," Jennifer said sincerely.

"It is, isn't it?" he replied as if in a dream.

"I really should be heading back. I appreciate your time and hope you and your wife can patch things up." It was an old ploy she'd heard a cop use while talking to a would-be bridge jumper. 'Personalize their situation,' he'd told her later. "Your children are about school age, aren't they?"

Unger gradually looked up and Jennifer saw a genuine smile cross his face.

"Owen is five and Kara will be four in November."

"They're cute at that age, aren't they?" Jennifer saw tears begin to form in Unger's eyes again. "Cute, innocent and best of all, forgiving. Their whole world is their mother and father. And somehow, even at that stage in their lives, they inherently know neither parent would ever do anything to hurt them."

Unger stood and wiped away some of the tears that had fallen down his cheeks.

"I'm really glad we met, Miss Malone," he said, extending his hand.

As she shook it she said, "It's Jennifer." Letting go, she added, "I hope everything works out. Maybe we can get together after all this chaos is relegated to the trash."

Unger laughed.

"You may have to travel a fair distance. I doubt if I'll be working in the city much longer."

"My schedule's flexible. Take care."

As she departed Lincoln Park, she realized the smugness she'd felt toward the *mansion people* as she'd driven in, was surprisingly muted as she drove out.

With the city skyline in view Jennifer was still plagued by one nagging thought: *Had that jumper she'd watched so long ago jumped to his death or had he been talked down to safety?*

Back at *The Telegraph*, Jennifer's reporter's juices were at a boiling point. She walked into the newsroom, went straight to her desk and climbed atop it, bringing the activity around her to an unexpected standstill.

Seeing she now had everyone's attention, including Mitch's, in her loudest voice she demanded, "My loyal subjects. I don't care how you know but your Queen needs the address and everything you've got on a gay bar called Buttons and she needs to know it right freakin' now!"

THIRTY

By week's end, the story of Robert Barker's murder had only slightly subsided. The police were still following every lead that jammed their hotline, although ultimately each turned into a dead end. Lynn's mysterious disappearance and speculation about her male accomplice, remained a fixture of television and radio talk shows. It was obvious Lynn had taken up with another man and decided the only way out of her marriage was to kill her husband.

Case closed.

Why she'd do such a thing in front of millions of TV viewers was unclear.

More troubling was why Robert Barker was at *The Nation Today* microphone in the first place. To the media there was only one explanation: he wanted to confront Adams for some reason. Regardless of how hard they looked and how much they paid their anonymous sources though, no concrete motive emerged. Mantis employees, as well as the remaining Board of Governors, were cautioned by the police to reveal nothing about the company, its current production load or any feelings about Robert.

Jerry had to admit Kenneth McIntyre was a better PR man than he'd given him credit for. Not only had he kept a lid on the Memoradium project, he'd also held an employees-only memorial service. During this hastily organized service, Jerry had stressed Robert had worked hard to make Mantis a world leader in pharmaceuticals. Struck down on the eve of realizing his dream, it was everyone's duty to remain united behind the company—if only until the police found Robert's killer.

At the conclusion of the speech, there was not a dry eye in the auditorium and Lynn Barker was never mentioned.

With the police and investigative reporters evidently stymied, Jerry and Melanie decided it was time to act.

Back at the motel, they initiated the next step of their master plan.

"So help me, Jerry, if you screw this up, Manard won't be the only one ready to put a bullet in your head."

"Shut up and stop moving."

Melanie gave Jerry one last glare as he placed duct tape over her mouth. He stepped back and smiled.

"This is the first time since I met you that you're speechless. I kind of like it."

Melanie didn't try to respond, concentrating instead on remaining calm and breathing through her nose. She'd let him have his little fun, knowing there was a day in the near future when he'd understand how painful payback could be.

I'm gonna kind of like that, she thought.

Back in the motel's office, Jerry watched Lynn's room monitor.

"Wake up already," he said. He rechecked the items on the counter waiting to be utilized. Picking up the black ski mask briefly, a sensation of electricity coursed through his blood.

We're almost there, he thought.

Loading the .22, Jerry realized he'd helped kill Robert not for money and power but for honour.

With this pleasant idea dancing in his head, Jerry noticed movement on the screen.

"It's show time," he said as he put on the rubber gloves and ski mask.

As her mind-fog began to clear, Lynn intuitively knew something was different. Still groggy, she turned onto her side and in the semi-darkness saw what she'd only sensed.

"Melanie!"

Melanie, pretending to be asleep in the chair Jerry had tied her to, snapped her head upright. Her eyes were wide with a combination of fear and excitement. When she tried to speak Lynn's name, only a terrifying muffled sound escaped into the room.

Overwhelmed that Melanie was alive, Lynn jumped off her bed and ran to her friend. She hadn't got three steps before the door flew open and a man in a black ski mask burst onto the scene.

Lynn screamed in horror, falling backward. Along with her captor, the daylight blazed into the room, instantly blinding her. She instinctively covered her eyes, as she lay crumpled at Melanie's bound feet.

The man walked across the room and picked her off the carpet, throwing her back onto the bed.

"Please don't hurt us!" Lynn pleaded. She saw Melanie rocking back and forth in her chair. "We'll do anything you want!"

Lynn couldn't bring herself to watch the man as he walked back to close the door. A low buzzing sound began to fill the room. It was only then she ventured a look.

The sound came from a small hand-held object.

What is that—a stun gun, or something worse?

Her eyes readjusted to the now-darkened room and she realized it wasn't a taser.

There are no poles for the electric current to pass between.

She watched carefully as the man placed the vibrating device against his throat.

Lynn realized it was an electronic voice box, used by people who had lost the ability to project their own voice. She shuddered at the grotesque sound it made as the man spoke.

"I know you'll do anything I ask, Mrs. Barker," the menacing machine-like voice said. "Otherwise your friend Melanie here is going to become part of history."

Jerry pulled the gun from his waistband and set the barrel against Melanie's right temple.

"Does this look familiar?" the man asked. "It should. It's the gun you killed your husband with."

"I didn't kill my husband!"

The impact of knowing Robert was murdered and the police believed she'd done it was still too incredible for Lynn to accept. Now, however, with the gun being waved in Melanie's face, a part of her knew the man wasn't lying. That was the weapon used to kill Robert and if she didn't do as she was told, it would also be used to kill her and Melanie.

Lynn had no idea how many days she'd been in captivity but understood her captor(s) had treated her well under the circumstances. It was clear she was the reason for the kidnapping. As she tried to concentrate on what the man was saying, Lynn caught sight of Melanie's eyes and locked onto them.

What had they done to her? Lynn thought. *Had she been bound and gagged all this time?*

We're going to get out of this together, Lynn tried to convey. *Together and alive.*

Melanie's eyes softened a bit, as if she'd received the message.

"Why don't you let her go?" Lynn asked. "It's me you want, anyway. Melanie can't help you."

"Oh, but she can. She's helping right now in fact by being here."

"What do you want? Money? If not, what?" she asked tersely.

She noticed Melanie's eyes widen in surprise.

I know what I'm doing, she tried to relay.

"It's very simple. I want your signature on a piece of paper."

What was this all about? Lynn thought, failing to see how her signature would bring this ordeal to a close.

"I'll sign whatever you want."

"I wasn't too worried about that," the man replied, "although Melanie here was a little bit concerned, weren't you, sweetie?"

Melanie looked up into the mask's eyeholes and conveyed a message of her own: *You will die for this.*

Not intimidated by Melanie's gaze, Jerry withdrew a single piece of paper from his pocket and carefully unfolded it.

"One false move and I'll blow your friend's head clear off. Am I understood?"

The tension that had filled the small unit earlier returned with a vengeance. All three of the room's occupants felt threatened by the others' presence.

Jerry walked over to the desk and set the sheet and a pen on top of it. Never losing eye contact with Lynn, he reached into the top drawer of the desk and took out a dust-covered Gideon Bible, placing it over the top half of the paper. Waving the gun in Lynn's direction, he instructed her what to do next.

"Slowly—and I mean slowly—walk to the desk and sit in the chair. Then pick up the pen with your left hand—I know you're left-handed, so no funny business—and sign your name at the X. Next, put your initials beside the date which is typed there." Jerry returned to Melanie's side, again placing the gun against her temple. "And remember, Mrs. Barker, I know every nuance of your signature, so don't try to disguise it."

He pushed the butt of the gun hard into Melanie's head, her eyes and face flinched in pain.

Lynn got off the bed and sat at the desk. Looking at the paper, she tried to figure out how her signature would be advantageous to anyone. However, as with most questions she'd asked herself since arriving here, no logical answer was forthcoming.

Taking the pen, she calmly wrote her name and initialled the typed date. As she put the pen down, she looked more closely at the date.

This couldn't be right, she thought. This date was two weeks *before* her fight with Robert, which meant *before* he was killed.

Her mind raced for an explanation only to come up blank again.

"Slowly get away from the desk."

Lynn did as she was told, taking a seat on the bed. Jerry cautiously went to the desk and examined the signature. It was perfect. He slid the paper out from under the Bible, folded it and placed it in his pocket.

"You have done yourself a great service, Mrs. Barker."

"Now will you please let Melanie go?" Lynn asked.

"I'm not done with her yet."

Lynn could see the terror in Melanie's eyes.

"I did what you wanted, now leave her alone. She can't help you in any way."

"You know what—you're right."

Finally the man had seen the light, Lynn sensed.

Before she knew what was happening, the man opened the door and violently dragged Melanie and the chair out into the brilliant sunlight. Melanie's eyes widened and looked in desperation toward Lynn. Only muffled screams came from her mouth as her whole body began to buck wildly against the ropes that held her arms and legs in place.

"What are you doing?" Lynn asked finding herself on her feet. "She can't help you!"

"Exactly." Jerry slammed the door shut and locked it.

"Don't do this! Please don't do this!" Lynn cried as she began to pound her fists furiously on the inside of the door.

"Maybe your friend has a few final words to say," the man called out.

Lynn inhaled deeply.

Final words?

Her ears were filled with the sound of the duct tape being ripped off Melanie's mouth. Then in a voice charged with hysteria, Lynn heard Melanie begin to yell.

"Lynn, don't let him—"

The blast from the gun silenced Melanie in mid-sentence.

"No!" Lynn wailed. "Melanie—talk to me!"

Lynn took several deep breaths in an effort to hear what was going on outside. Greeted with silence, she began to lose her mind.

"You bastard—you killed her! I did everything you wanted. Why did you have to kill her?" Lynn fell to the floor. "Why? Why?" she continued to cry out, as if the mantra would bring Melanie back.

Still on the floor and sobbing uncontrollably, Lynn didn't notice the pink smoke which had begun to filter into the room.

This was fine with Jerry and Melanie, as Lynn's wailing was starting to get on their nerves.

THIRTY ONE

They waited until Lynn slumped over before speaking.

It was Melanie who started the conversation.

"You son of a bitch," she said under her breath.

Taking Jerry by surprise, she put her full force behind her right fist which she embedded in his stomach, doubling him over. But it was Jerry who really surprised her, forcing himself upright to unleash a vicious slap across Melanie's face, sending her falling into the nearby couch.

"You said make it look real and that's what I did. So back off!"

Melanie brought a hand to her face, stupefied by Jerry's response. He'd never come close to hitting her in the past and to show this side when they needed each other the most was unthinkable.

Then again, she thought, amused, *I did give him a pretty good shot of my own.*

Jerry staggered to a chair as Melanie slowly repositioned herself on the couch.

"I've never been hit by a man in my life," she said finally.

"That surprises me," Jerry replied slowly, catching his breath.

They remained silent, each assessing their current situation, before

A MEMORABLE MURDER

Jerry pulled the signed paper out of his pocket and tossed it on the table. Their eyes met and all was forgiven.

"There it is. Everything we've worked for is right there on that contract," Jerry said with a smile.

"Not quite," Melanie said. "Give me the pen."

Jerry threw it to her and she signed her name on the line underneath Lynn's signature. She also initialled the date.

"With a credible witness of Lynn's signature on this Power Of Attorney, *now* everything is in place."

"What about Lynn? How long are we going to wait to fry her brain?"

"Tomorrow night," Melanie replied with a note of perverse delight in her voice. "From Prom Queen to Vegetable Queen in a few easy steps."

Having given Lynn an extra dose of gas to keep her quiet overnight, Jerry and Melanie left for the city to finalize the business plans they'd been working on.

It was these plans that would bring Mantis Pharmaceuticals to its knees, as well as untold millions into their bank accounts.

* * *

"Are you sure this is the right way?" Anthony said as he tried to catch up to his friends.

"I'm telling you," John called over his shoulder, "it's up past the bend."

"It'd better be," Donnie said, "I'm getting tired of peddling."

With no school and no other pressing issues in their young lives, the Grade 6 students had left their homes in hopes of finding adventure at a fabled abandoned motel off the main road.

They had packed a lunch and happily sucked water out of their sport bottles. It wasn't their first time out this way, although they'd never ventured quite this far before.

"There it is!" John exclaimed. "Do you believe me now?"

Anthony exchanged a glance with Donnie and shook his head.

"Yeah John, we believe you. Let's just get there."

It looked exactly the way John remembered it, even though it had been two years since he'd seen it from the back seat of his father's car.

"The Chandler Motor Lodge," Donnie said, reading the dilapidated roadside sign. "I wonder who the Chandlers were?"

"Who cares?" John said, throwing his bike on the ground. "Let's see if any of the rooms are unlocked."

Anthony and Donnie also dropped their bikes and ran to where John was standing.

"It looks like someone is trying to fix the place up," he said, noticing splotches of black paint on the walkway outside Unit #2. Footprints in the dirt also indicated the building might not be abandoned.

"Let's get out of here," Anthony said anxiously.

"What's the point of riding all the way out here if you're not going to look around?"

"What if someone lives here, John?" Donnie asked. "They could charge us with trespassing or something."

"Yeah—and maybe you two are 'fraidy cats," John shot back, seeing the apprehension on his friends' faces. "Okay fine, but let's at least take a quick look around before heading to the railroad station, all right?"

"Fine with me," Anthony answered quickly.

"Me, too," Donnie chimed in.

"Let's go around the back," John instructed, as all three began to walk to the north side of the building.

It must be a dream, Lynn thought. *There's no one here—at least no one who would want to help me. Still . . .*

Feeling unsteady and not yet fully functioning physically or

221

mentally, Lynn pushed herself off the floor and fell back against the wall.

There are three of them, her mind was trying to tell her. *Three distinct voices coming from outside the door.*

Had they come to dispose of Melanie's body?

The thought sent a shiver down Lynn's back.

She scanned the room from her new vantage point and didn't notice anything different. There was no one bound and gagged in a chair to greet her this time. The time of day was, as always, a mystery.

Had the masked man been in the room yesterday or last year?

It didn't seem to matter anymore. She closed her eyes to clear her head, thankful she was alive.

It looks like someone is trying to fix the place up.

She was positive that was what one of the voices had said.

What's the point of riding all the way out here if you're not going to look around?

Look around for what? Lynn's mind asked, still lost in a daze.

What if someone lives here, John?

One of them mentioned a name, Lynn thought, beginning to see that something *was* different about her surroundings. It wasn't inside her room, it was outside of it.

Yeah — and maybe you two are 'fraidy cats.

'Fraidy cats? Who says 'fraidy cats anymore?

As if hit in the forehead with a Louisville slugger, Lynn fully awoke from her dream-like state and stood up.

There are kids outside!

"Help! Someone please help me!" she demanded, pounding on the door. "I'm in here! Please get me out!"

"Did you hear that?" Donnie asked, cocking his head in the direction of the road.

"Hear what?" John asked, continuing to look at a new generator at the back of the lot.

Anthony spoke up.

"I heard it too. Let's get outta here!"

John watched as his two friends made a beeline for their bikes. Jogging after them he heard the voice for the first time and stopped.

"There's someone in that room," he said. "Maybe she's trapped or something."

Donnie and Anthony remained poised on their bikes, as they watched John walk to Unit #2.

"Hello?" John asked tentatively.

The room went silent.

"It's a trap, John. Get outta there!" Donnie shouted.

"Shut up!" John pressed his ear to the door and heard someone sobbing. "Lady, are you okay?"

Lynn took several deep breaths before replying. Her prayers had been answered.

"Please help me get out of here. The door is locked and the windows are covered."

"There are boards nailed across the windows."

"Can you take them off?"

"We can try."

"What's your name?"

"John Hawksworth."

"Thank you, John. Thank you."

"I think I saw a crowbar on the ground near the generator," John said. "Between the three of us, I think we can loosen up the boards."

"Please hurry—I don't know how much longer I can take this."

The boys ran to the back lot where they found a crowbar and rusted axe.

"Let me try first," John said, motioning his friends out of the way. "We found an axe. Stay away from the windows."

Lynn dashed across the room and into the bathroom.

"Okay, go ahead!"

John's first swing had the axe bounce harmlessly off the sturdy wood boards, sending him to the ground.

"This isn't going to work," he said, dusting himself off. "Gimme the crowbar."

After wedging it under one of the boards, John pushed on the bar but couldn't manage any movement.

"If we all push, I think it'll come."

The boys stood side by side, each setting their legs in a fighting stance and pressing their palms against the bar.

"On three," John instructed. "One . . . two . . . three."

With their combined strength, the board loosened and popped outward.

"We did it!" Anthony declared triumphantly.

They grabbed the end of the board and pulled. When it splintered, all three found themselves on the ground in a pile of dust.

"What's happening?" Lynn inquired after hearing the board snap. For a split second, she'd thought it was another gunshot.

"The board broke in two," John called back. He stuck his head in the opening they'd made, expecting to see inside the room. Instead he was met with total darkness. Reaching into the space, he cautiously touched the window. "Someone painted over the window."

"Break the glass. Please, just break the glass!" Lynn shouted.

"If you say so."

John picked up the discarded axe and with a forceful jab penetrated the window, which shattered onto the room's carpet. Sunlight streamed into the unit like a spotlight piercing the night sky.

It was the most beautiful thing Lynn had ever seen.

A jab at a second window had the same effect. Finally, John smashed a third window and after checking that no glass could fall down and decapitate him, he stuck his head into the room.

"Are you okay?" he asked.

Lynn stepped forward and squinted her eyes.

Is this really happening? Am I really getting out of here alive?

"I am now," she said softly, as tears began to cascade down her cheeks. "Can you take off another board or two so I can climb out?"

John had no real idea what to expect when he peered into the room. The sight of a dishevelled woman his mom's age wasn't one of them though. The fact she wasn't mad at them was all the incentive he needed to tear off two more boards.

Still overwhelmed by this turn of events, Lynn took John's hand and carefully stepped out into the sweet sunlit air. Satisfied she was steady enough to stand on her own, John, Anthony and Donnie backed away from her, not completely sure they'd done the right thing.

Lynn took stock of her young saviours. From the way they stood beside each other, she knew which were 'fraidy cats and which one was the leader.

"I can't thank you boys enough. You saved my life. I'm sure of it."

"Do you own this place?" Anthony asked timidly.

Lynn laughed.

"I don't even know where this place is. Are we far from the city?"

"It's a couple of hours on the interstate," John replied.

As the words left his mouth, Lynn gasped at the sight of the wooden chair Melanie had been strapped to. Overturned and discarded, a fresh wave a dread invaded her thoughts.

"When you were out back, did you find—I mean, see—anybody else? A woman perhaps?"

"There's no one else here," Donnie chimed in.

Knowing she didn't have time to search the property, nor the stomach for such an abhorrent undertaking, Lynn looked around the lot. Noticing their bikes, she asked if they'd observed any vehicles.

All agreed they had seen no cars or trucks.

"Obviously, if you're riding bikes, you can't live far from here."

"It took us an hour from Delta but we were kinda taking our time," John said, looking down the deserted road. "It would probably take a couple of hours to walk. Do you want to stay here while we—"

"No!" Lynn cried, scaring the boys. "I'm sorry. I didn't mean to frighten you. It's that I can't stay here."

"If you want," John said, looking at his wristwatch, "we can ride double—each of us taking turns giving you a lift back home."

Tears began to form in Lynn's eyes again.

"You would do that?"

John and the other two boys nodded in agreement.

"If we pick up the pace, we should be able to get there in 45 minutes," John added.

As they walked toward the road, Lynn glanced back at the Chandler Motor Lodge.

When this is all over, she thought, *I'm going to personally bulldoze this place to the ground.*

"Why don't you start riding with me?" John offered. "When I get tired, Anthony will take you and then Donnie."

Lynn paused to examine the three of them again, knowing they'd got more adventure than they'd bargained for today. As she climbed aboard the seat of John's bike, a feeling of safety filled her.

The road was surprisingly smooth for one not travelled for quite some time. The boys all began to open up to Lynn the further they ventured from the motor lodge. It was during their conversations Lynn was told how the interstate had taken all the traffic away—at least, according to their parents.

What a perfect place to hide a kidnap victim, Lynn thought. *They are obviously professionals of the highest order.*

Shortly into their ride, John saw something encouraging in the distance: a large vehicle coming toward them.

"Maybe we won't have to take turns after all," he said to Lynn.

The sight of the car was like a second answer to her prayers—not that she minded riding on the back of John's bike. However, the thought there was an adult driving a vehicle capable of doing 100 m.p.h., instead of the current 10, filled her with elation.

"Let me off," Lynn said to John, who stopped the bike.

She dismounted and continued to look up the road. The car was picking up speed as it closed in on them. It was only when the vehicle was close enough to identify the make that panic gripped Lynn.

"It's them!" she told the boys. "The ones who held me in the room. They're coming back!"

The boys looked wildly at Lynn, then at the black Jeep roaring down on them and finally at each other. They didn't need Lynn's prompting to begin peddling in three different directions.

"Get out of here!" Lynn cried. "They're only after me. Go!"

While the other two were still within earshot, John told Anthony and Donnie to meet up at the railroad station as soon as possible. With that, each boy took a different path and disappeared into a small forest which bordered the road.

Lynn began to search for her own escape route. With the Jeep's engine roaring in her ears, she also headed for the forest.

"You're going to hit her!" she heard a woman yell.

Lynn dared to take one last look at the fast advancing Jeep and couldn't believe her eyes.

"Melanie?" she asked, as she lost her footing on an uneven piece of pavement, falling helplessly into the ditch. The impact of hitting her head on a rock jutting from a small pool of water only momentarily dazed her.

Was that really Melanie in the passenger seat? her mind wondered. *That's not possible—she's dead.*

In her confusion, she thought the driver also looked familiar.

As she slipped into unconsciousness, Lynn heard the Jeep's occupants beating back the brush around her.

"Please help me," Lynn said slowly. "Don't leave me here to die."

Her final disjointed thought was to wonder how her captors had poisoned the outdoor atmosphere with their mysterious sleeping gas.

These people were really, really scary.

"What if she sees us?" Jerry questioned frantically as he made his way into the ditch.

"Who cares about that?" Melanie cried. "What if she's dead?"

The blood on the rock near Lynn's head was not a good sign. Melanie made it to her first and felt for a pulse.

"She's still alive. Help me carry her to the Jeep."

Jerry lifted Lynn's limp body by the shoulders while Melanie grabbed her feet. Nearing the road, Jerry checked the surroundings. No cars and no kids on bikes. They hoisted Lynn's body into the back seat and before leaving Jerry jumped on the roof and looked around. He thought he saw movement by a tree not far from them. As time was now of the essence, he decided the quickest course of action was a verbal warning.

"I know you're out there and I know what you look like. It wouldn't be hard to track you down. Do yourselves a favour and keep your mouths shut—because if you don't, I will personally hunt you down and kill you with my own two hands."

The movement stopped in the area he'd focused his comments.

"Damn kids," Melanie said seeing the broken windows and boards on the ground. "Okay, let's set this place ablaze and get out of here."

Torching the motel would not only eradicate their fingerprints and any other traces, it would also indicate to the meddling Boy Wonders that the crazy woman's captors meant business.

Watching the motel in their side mirrors, Jerry and Melanie

contemplated how close their house of cards had come to being leveled. That there were witnesses who could identify Lynn was also not comforting.

Jerry pulled to the side of the road several miles away from the blaze to allow Melanie to hop into the back seat.

"Are you sure this stuff is going to work?" Jerry said, as he watched Melanie tie a rubber tube around Lynn's left arm.

"The Diltroicide will wear off in two hours, at which time Lynn will wake up and start to stumble aimlessly through the streets."

"With no memory at all, right?" Jerry asked nervously, always aware that this final step could put them most at risk.

"How many times do I have to tell you? This dose of Tramendoite acts as a permanent memory masking agent in the brain. I've seen the lab tests at Litchfield. They'd give this stuff to mice who had mastered one of the toughest labyrinths ever constructed. They could fly through this maze like they were doing the hundred-yard dash." Melanie stopped to take a full syringe out of her bag, which she inserted into Lynn's freshly raised vein. "Anyway, one shot of this and they might as well have been blind. No memory at all. Complete zombies."

"If you haven't noticed, Lynn isn't a lab rat."

Melanie took the needle out of Lynn's arm and unstrapped the tubing.

"You're completely right, she isn't a lab rat. However, after this stuff begins to swell and impair her brain cells from communicating with each other, she's going to wish she were. Why don't we stop the chit-chat and drop little Miss Prom Queen off at the ball, okay?"

Jerry took a final look at Lynn and put the Jeep into gear. They had places to go, people to see and money to be picked up. It had been one bizarre trip. Now with the end in sight, there was no turning back and no one to stop them.

Unless, of course, they decided to stop each other.

THIRTY TWO

"Ready, Jason, in five, four, three . . ."

"This is a special NCN News Report. I'm Jason Morris. In a stunning development in the death of millionaire Robert Barker ten days ago, his wife and prime suspect in the killing, Lynn Barker, has been found wandering the streets near her New Liston home. For more on this breaking story, we go to Tanya Greene on location."

"Thanks, Jason. I'm standing in the very spot where Lynn Barker was first seen by several neighbours on this quiet street. I spoke with numerous people who saw Mrs. Barker and each reported she appeared to be disoriented and in a state of shock."

The camera zoomed out to show a man in his forties standing beside Tanya. "Identified murder suspect" was written on the bottom of the screen, along with the word EXCLUSIVE.

"With me is area resident Martin McNall, who spoke with Mrs. Barker a short time ago. Mr. McNall, what was Mrs. Barker's appearance when you first saw her?"

"She was a total wreck," the man said nervously, glancing back at the police cruisers which surrounded the area. "At first, you know, I was kinda frightened to go up to her. She kept mumbling, 'Where do I go? What do I do?' and didn't seem to have a clue what was going on—so I figured I was safe."

"Did she know her own name?"

"That's the funny thing—scary, I guess is a better word. Anyhow, I went right up to her and said, 'Mrs. Barker, are you okay?' and she just turned around and stared at me. It was like she was shell-shocked. I saw that kind of thing in Vietnam, you know."

"Was she carrying any weapons?"

"Not that I saw. Even if she was, I doubt she'd know how to use one. She was that far out of it."

The camera zoomed back into a medium shot of Tanya.

"Tanya, where is Mrs. Barker now?" Jason asked from the studio.

"At this time she's in police custody, apparently being taken to an undisclosed hospital for evaluation."

"Have the police charged her with her husband's murder?"

"I spoke with an officer who stated that due to Mrs. Barker's mental state, she hasn't been formally charged yet. However, upon the advice of the doctors treating her, she will be charged as soon as possible."

"What is the current status of the investigation, Tanya?"

"The police are combing the area of this quiet suburb, hoping to discover clues to Mrs. Barker's whereabouts since the slaying of her husband. Although a massive search has continued since the shooting, no sign of Mrs. Barker or her male accomplice had been found."

"Until today, of course," Jason added.

"Yes, Jason. The police are rather surprised Mrs. Barker has surfaced in such a public manner. Along with the domestic search, police were also pursuing the idea Mrs. Barker had left the country. Today's re-appearance would seem to indicate that was never the case."

"One final question, Tanya. How are the police treating Mrs. Barker's apparent lack of memory and her overall physical appearance today?"

"They are being what I'd call very cautious. Until they speak to Mrs. Barker they're not ruling out the possibility this is a staged performance, laying the groundwork for her legal team, if it comes to that. However, they're also not ruling out some kind of accident which may have impaired Mrs. Barker's memory."

"Thank you for this report, Tanya. We'll continue following these new developments in the Robert Barker murder investigation with updates on the half hour. As well, we'll have a special hour-long edition of *The Newsmakers* tonight at seven. The entire program will be devoted to Lynn Barker's reappearance and its implications on the prosecution's case.

"I'm Jason Morris and this has been a special NCN News Report."

THIRTY THREE

Mitch Carson stepped out of his office and looked frantically across the newsroom.

"Malone!"

"She's not in yet," Arnold Girard responded.

"What do you mean, not in yet?"

"She called to say she'd be down at the Buttons Bar for a couple hours to see if anything transpired."

Carson glared at Girard. Was he telling the truth or angling to get the new Barker assignment? He quickly decided it was big enough for both of them.

"Girard, get down to the Barker reappearance site and keep me posted on anything you find."

Girard grabbed his coat and was out the door in a flash.

Carson watched him leave and remembered Jennifer calling Girard a hack.

"You're probably right, Malone," he said to himself as he entered his office. "But with you AWOL, he's the only hack I've got left."

Stakeouts at any time of Buttons Bar and Thrill were not what

A MEMORABLE MURDER

Jennifer would term fun but seeing a totally different side of the city she called home was, if not entertaining, at least enlightening.

Entering the establishment for the first time, she thought that being a straight woman in a gay and lesbian bar might not be easy. After a drink or two, however, she began to feel quite comfortable. The men left her alone and when a female approached, they'd end up talking to each other as if they were old friends. Generally, when she advised them she was a reporter—a straight reporter—the women opened up more. It was like a bizarre university sorority.

Though the mysterious Raoul was nowhere to be found, any mention of Stanley Unger's name made the women's eyes light up.

Stars in their eyes, Jennifer thought, *and aspirations of hitting it big on television with the help of a major producer.*

It seemed everyone liked Stanley and knew his profession. Jennifer thought he was delusional to believe no one in the straight world would have an inkling of his closeted life.

For her fourth visit, Jennifer decided to go in the morning, as her prey was obviously not a night owl. Once on her usual stool, she sensed a change in the women's attitudes toward her.

Something isn't right, she thought.

Around 10:00 she found out why.

"I hear you've been looking for me."

Jennifer turned and looked into the face of an extremely handsome male in his early 20's who stood six feet tall. She could see why Stanley Unger would be attracted to such a male. She was.

"Only if your name is Raoul."

"Maybe it is and maybe it isn't."

Jennifer wasn't in the mood to play verbal footsie with anyone today.

"And maybe I have the pictures you used to blackmail Stanley Unger," she said bluntly.

Immediately, the bravado drained from Raoul's face. He was clearly terrified.

"I'll give you two options, Raoul. We can stay here and talk and risk having your buddies overhear our conversation. Or we can leave and talk somewhere else—the other side of the state, perhaps. It's your call. Please make it snappy."

"I know a place," Raoul replied nervously.

I bet you do.

Jennifer jumped off her stool and left a ten on the bar.

"Let's go."

A half-hour later, they were sitting in the living room of a house several blocks from the bar.

"It's my brother's place. He's gone for a few days," Raoul stated.

As he had the key to the front door, Jennifer figured he was telling the truth.

"I swear I don't know who they are," Raoul began. "I've never seen either of them at the bar before or since."

"There were two people who set Unger up?"

"A man and a woman. It was strange."

"Did they give you their names?"

"No, we talked for a while and then they handed me an envelope with $1000 in it."

"Not a bad payday for a hustler like you, huh?"

"Hey lady, I'm no hustler," Raoul stated, "but money is money."

"What about the pictures?"

"I didn't know they were going to take pictures. They said they only wanted to watch."

"For $1000 you can arrange to watch two men go at each other?" Jennifer asked in amazement.

"I know guys who will do it for fifty."

"So this deal really is big-time, isn't it?"

"The biggest."

Jennifer felt nauseous.

"Okay, anyway—where did this take place?"

"I can't tell you where exactly. It has two-way mirrors and adjacent rooms. So people can watch in comfort, you know?"

"I certainly don't but that's another topic altogether. So after your little tryst with Unger, what happened?"

"Nothing. I'd already got my money. As for Stanley and the couple, I never saw them again."

"Then how did you know about the blackmail photos?" Jennifer asked, catching Raoul in a lie.

His face tensed.

"I'm telling you I had nothing to do with blackmail."

"Then how—"

"He called the bar."

"Who did?"

"Unger—a day or two later. He called looking for me but I was out of town. When I got back, the bartender said Unger used the word *blackmail* when he was babbling on the phone. I played dumb."

"And you stayed away from the bar."

"Until this morning, yeah."

Jennifer's head was beginning to hurt. First the poolside roller coaster ride with Unger, now this hair-raising tale.

"What about Robert Barker?" she asked, trying to steer the conversation in a new direction.

"He's the dead guy on TV."

"That's it?"

"If you've heard I went to bed with him before he died, you better check your information."

The throbbing intensified.

"Okay, fine. What, if anything, can you tell me about this couple?"

"Not much. Both were white, late 30's maybe, handsome couple. He had a thin moustache and she had . . . Well, to tell the truth, I didn't pay much attention to her."

"Have a thing for moustaches, do you?"

Raoul didn't reply.

"There was one thing I remember about her—something she said a couple of times." He looked off into space trying to remember what exactly it was. After a few agonizing moments, he slapped his hands together. "I got it. Every once in a while she would say something and then add, 'if you know what I mean.'"

Jennifer stared at him dumbfounded.

Seriously? This is what I've been waiting for?

"She would close a sentence with 'if you know what I mean'? Sort of like saying, 'if you catch my drift.'"

"Exactly," Raoul said triumphantly. "It was the way she said it though, like she was being cocky—not intimidating or anything."

"Anything else catch your fancy, aside from the big bucks and the stubble on the guy's upper lip?"

"No, that's about it."

"Then call me a cab."

It was noon when Jennifer finally entered *The Telegraph's* newsroom. As she fell into her desk chair she saw Carson walking her way.

"Mitch, buddy! Did you hear Mrs. Barker was arrested for loitering? I picked that little tidbit off the news station on the cab ride over here."

"Where have you been? I had to send Girard to cover Barker's reappearance," Mitch said testily.

"You sent that pretender to cover my story? How dare you!" Jennifer said in mock protest.

"Let's cut to the chase, shall we? Spill the beans already."

"Okay, here goes. Barker was set up."

"Set up? Which one?"

"Excellent question. I guess that's why you're not only the editor-in-chief, but also the newest member of the Hollingsworth family."

Mitch took a deep breath and exhaled.

"I'm going to silently count to 10 and when I'm finished I will ask you again who set up the Barkers. Do I make myself clear?"

The reporters and copywriters in the room stopped and watched as their boss closed his eyes and presumably started to count.

"Ten," Jennifer said a few seconds later. "Hello, Earth to Mitch." Jennifer looked around at the amused expressions of her colleagues. "Someone call maintenance. Mitch's brain is stuck at the single digits. This is too much of a challenge. Help! Can someone please help us over here?"

Carson slowly opened his eyes and glanced around the room.

"Ten," he said as wild applause erupted. "Now get back to work, all of you!" he ordered. "As for you, Malone, in my office."

Jennifer, trying to conceal a grin, sheepishly stood and with her head bowed in shame, walked three paces behind Carson to his office.

"Are you in one of your moods again, Mitch? 'Cause I currently sense a bit of anger on your part."

"I'm trying to run a paper and I can't do that as well as I'd like if I don't know where my staff is. It's kind of hard putting out a daily when you don't have any reporters."

"*The Star* doesn't seem to have a problem," Jennifer deadpanned.

Up until the very second she saw the corners of his mouth turning upward into a smile, Jennifer wasn't sure if Mitch was going to hit her or fire her.

"A smile! Now that wasn't so hard was it?"

"What did you find out, Ms. Malone?" Mitch asked, leaning back into his chair.

"Ms. Malone? I guess this meeting is officially in session. Okay, I can handle that." Jennifer straightened up in her seat and pulled out her notepad. "I have uncovered how Robert Barker came to be at *The Nation Today* microphone on that fateful morning."

"Which is?"

"It was a blackmail scheme."

"There's been no indication he was being blackmailed."

"He wasn't—the show's producer was." Jennifer flipped ahead in her notebook. "It's a long story. The gist is someone was blackmailing the producer. In order to get some damaging photos back, he arranged for Barker to ask Adams the first question at the outside microphone."

"At which time Barker's head is blown apart," Mitch said finishing Jennifer's thought. "And you can prove this?" Jennifer nodded affirmatively. "But we still don't know who wanted Barker set up, is that right?"

"Or what Barker wanted to say to Adams. I do have some info on the blackmailers, though it's pretty lame. The guy is supposedly in his late thirties with a fashionably hip moustache. The woman is around the same age and has the habit of ending sentences with the phrase, 'if you know what I mean.'"

Mitch mulled over this new information.

"Where does Barker's wife fit into this? Do you think she's hooked up with the blackmailers?"

"The more info that comes to light, the more I'm thinking Lynn Barker may have also been set up."

"To what end? No one seems to have benefitted by this shooting except Adams' presidential campaign, and I seriously doubt he had anything to do with Barker's killing."

"Never underestimate the lure of the Oval Office, Mitch."

"I don't buy it."

"Neither do I. However, until Barker's wife starts talking, Adams is my man."

"Fine. Now what else are you working on—or can you tell me?" he asked sarcastically.

Jennifer leafed back through her notebook and noticed something she'd forgotten all about.

"Whatever happened with the lead on the rental car? I don't remember hearing anything about it."

"As far as I know nothing happened with it. Once the Barker's Volvo was picked up, I think everyone assumed it was the getaway car."

"Well then, to answer your question," Jennifer said as she headed to the door, "I'm off to track down a rented grey Volvo."

"Good luck," Mitch told her. "And call in from time to time!"

After checking the Yellow Pages, Jennifer jotted down the three Queen City Car Rental locations listed. She soon discovered they were all still in business and all had grey Volvos in stock. When asked if they had any 2- to 3-year-old models, she learned that only the airport location stocked those.

Which is the perfect location if you're going to hop a plane after killing your husband during breakfast television.

Parking in the short-term airport garage, Jennifer made her way to the level where all the rental companies stored their vehicles. Checking the overhead signs, Jennifer quickly located the Queen City area and began to walk up and down the lanes. Not finding any Volvos, she stepped into the office and was greeted by an attractive male in his late 20's.

Not as handsome as Michael the security guard or the suit guy at Kingdom Entertainment . . . still, beggars can't be choosers, she thought.

"Can I help you?" Bruce the attendant asked pleasantly.

"I hope so," she said with her thousand-watt smile blazing brightly. "Actually, it's kind of personal."

Bruce's smile wavered.

"Tell me your problem and I'll see if I can help out or not."

"This is really embarrassing. You see I think my husband is having an affair and . . . this isn't easy," she said, trying to act flustered. "Well here's the thing. He said he was going away on business a week and a half ago, but then my brother said he saw him in a grey Volvo driving out of the city. We don't own a Volvo and my brother—he's a police officer and *very* protective of me—he remembered the licence plate and ran it through their computers at work. And wouldn't you know it—it was a rental." She looked at Bruce who appeared lost in thought. "From your company," she added quickly.

"Oh, I see where you're going now," Bruce said with a nervous laugh. "The thing is—"

"I know what you're going to say," Jennifer interrupted him. "Client confidentiality, right?"

"Exactly."

"I'm all for confidentiality, I really am. My problem is my brother."

"The police officer."

"That's the one. You see he doesn't know Darryl and I are kind of on the outs yet. He thinks we're still living happily ever after. So when he saw Darryl driving a rental car when he was supposed to be on business out of state, well, you can imagine how suspicious that looked to him, being—"

"An officer and all," Bruce said, finishing her sentence. "I can sympathize with your situation, ma'am—"

"Lana. You can call me Lana, all my male friends do."

"Lana, right." Was Bruce trying to stop himself from blushing? "As I was saying, I understand your problem. I just don't know how I can help you."

"All I'm asking for is a little favour. If possible, would you be able to check if my husband might have rented a Volvo from here? You see, because if he didn't, I could tell my brother some story so he doesn't pulverize Darryl for something he didn't even do."

241

From the look on Bruce's face, Jennifer knew his company principles were hanging by a thread.

She stepped up to the counter and in barely a whisper said, "I would be more than willing to pay you back for your kindness."

The implication hung in the air for only a moment.

"Maybe this once," Bruce said, his voice faltering slightly.

He checked a cabinet drawer for rental contracts dated the day before and day of the killing.

"We only have one newer Volvo and it's been out twice this month. On the first date you gave me and then yesterday." He scanned one of the agreements in his hand. "Do you know an Alison Strauss?"

"No, why?"

Bruce brought the document to the counter for Jennifer to look at.

"As you can see, on the first date you gave me an Alison Strauss rented the car."

Jennifer's heart began to beat faster.

"How long did she have the vehicle?"

"Let's see here. It looks like only the one day—brought it back the following morning at 8:15."

Remain calm.

"And how many miles did this Miss Strauss drive—does it say?"

"It looks like a pretty short trip."

Jennifer noted the miles driven.

Just enough for a round trip to downtown and back.

"I see her name listed but no address or phone number."

"This is the bottom copy of the agreement. The customer's address is on the top copy that's sent to head office in Michigan."

Jennifer let out a sigh.

"Well, I guess I'll have to make a story up for my brother, won't I?"

"I guess so," Bruce replied, not knowing what to expect next.

"What days do you usually work?" Jennifer asked, her sullen mood changing back to a more cheery one.

"Tuesday through Friday," Bruce said, regaining his optimism.

"I'll give you a call next Tuesday—here if you'd like—and maybe we could get together for a drink or something."

Jennifer doubted that constant scrubbing with a pad of steel wool could wipe off the smile Bruce was now sporting.

"Sure. Here—have one of my cards," he said excitedly. "It's a direct line."

"Will do, Bruce," Jennifer said as she walked out into the garage. "Of course," she said in Bruce's direction, "I'll have to see what my brother thinks of us going out."

Without waiting for a response or having the heart to watch the blood drain from Bruce's pretty face, Jennifer turned and headed to her car.

After finding no listing for Alison Strauss in any of *The Telegraph's* computer databanks, Jennifer decided it was time to cash in a favour from an old friend she'd recently helped out.

"Jeffrey Hamill Investigations."

"Jeffrey, Jennifer Malone here. How did your client like the stuff I sent you?"

"Never used it, sorry to say. Something else dropped into my lap at the last minute."

"You don't say."

"So how can I repay my debt to you today, Malone?"

"I've got a missing person case for you that might break a big story wide open. Interested?"

"Do I like doughnuts? Give me what you've got."

THIRTY FOUR

Senator Adams' day had been the most nerve-racking of his entire life. Immediately following a now standard stump speech, Harold Green had rushed to announce Lynn had been found.

"Where?"

"Near her home in New Liston."

"Is she all right?"

"I think we have a problem," Green replied gravely.

"What kind of problem?"

Had their affair become public somehow?

"She's at a hospital in police custody."

"And?"

"Well, it's like this, Douglas. Presently she has no memory whatsoever and doctors haven't figured out what's caused it."

"Was she in an accident or something?"

"The police are checking that out now."

Frustrated by Green's relatively calm commentary on the situation, Douglas pushed him hard up against a wall, out of view of the clamouring press.

"Look, Harold, although I'm sickened by Lynn's predicament, how does her having no memory present a problem? If she can't remember our affair, I'm certainly not going to remind her at this late stage in the campaign. So what's the issue here?"

Harold gently shrugged Douglas' hands off his shoulders and nervously looked around the hallway. He grabbed Douglas by the arm and escorted him into an empty room.

"First, let's get one thing straight," Green hissed angrily. "I am not your problem, got that? If you'd listened to me, this woman would be no more of a threat to you than a classroom of grade schoolers. But no—I was the idiot who didn't know what true romance was. Do you remember that?"

"Bitch and complain later, Harold. Tell me what the problem with Lynn is."

"I've been on the phone with several doctors — generous supporters mind you—and asked them pointed questions about what to expect in regard to Lynn's amnesia. Every one of them said that, depending on the severity of the blockage in the brain, it could last weeks or even months. That's the good news."

"And the bad news?"

"It could come back immediately, completely intact. Or it might return in dribs and drabs—her brain randomly throwing out a memory here and a recollection there. They may be related to each other or entirely disconnected."

Douglas thought he knew where Green's concern lay.

"So one minute she might recall playing with her childhood dolls and the next—"

"She could blurt out she was making sweet love to Senator Douglas Adams a few days before she blew her husband's head off."

Douglas felt faint. He stumbled to a chair and collapsed into it. There'd be no hush money handed out to any paramedic's kids today.

"This can't be happening," he gasped.

"So far nothing has happened, Douglas, and I intend to keep it that way."

Shocked by this statement, Douglas glared up at Green.

"You're not thinking of—"

"What—killing her? Do you think I'm stupid?" Getting no response, Green continued. "What I'm going to do is send in a specialist we can trust who deals with this type of memory thing. It will make you look sympathetic in the public eye—trying to help Barker's widow. Also, with a mole now planted on the inside, we'll be the first to know when she remembers something."

Douglas mulled over the idea. As usual, he had to hand it to Green. He was the best in the business at fixing these things before they became *real* problems.

"About the image thing. Most people have already condemned Lynn to death row for Robert's murder. Wouldn't we look like we're pandering to the criminal vote or whatever?"

"We take the high road, Douglas. Innocent until proven guilty and all that crap. This will make you look like the greatest humanitarian since Mother Teresa. You're helping someone in need. Who is going to fault you for that—Travers' camp? I don't think so. Anyway, they are going to be too busy kicking themselves for not thinking this up first. Hell, they're still bent out of shape because your statement was read by Morris before they'd even put pen to paper. I'm telling you, Douglas, you can't lose."

"Then call your specialist and fly him to wherever they've got Lynn. Don't issue a press release until he is physically walking through the front doors of that hospital. Because once he's inside, I don't want him to leave."

"My thoughts exactly," Green replied triumphantly, grabbing his cell phone. "I swear, Douglas, nothing can stop us now."

As he went to dial the specialist's number, the phone rang.

"Maybe he's calling us," Green chuckled, pushing the SEND button.

"Put the Senator on."

Green's face went blank. He'd know that voice anywhere. Douglas saw the change in expression and knew something was amiss.

"Who is it?" he demanded.

Green's vacant look remained fixed as he handed the phone over.

"Hello, Mr. President," the throaty female voice said.

Adams body involuntarily shook.

"Look, I don't know who you are," he started in an angry tone, "and frankly I don't want to know—"

"Whoa! Slow down, big boy! We'd better get one thing straight from the very start," the woman's voice interrupted. "It doesn't matter who I am. What matters is that I know what Barker wanted the world to learn about their next President. Now if I somehow let that information slip out to the media . . ."

"I'm sorry. I didn't mean anything by what I said."

"A politician who's sorry. Now that's a switch."

"What is it you want from me?"

"This isn't a secure line, Dougie. In fact, I'm surprised our last conversation hasn't become public yet, if you know what I mean."

"Then what do you want to do?"

"A bit testy this morning, aren't you? I'd thought you'd be doing cartwheels now that your special friend is back in town. I guess I was wrong." The line went silent for several seconds. "There's a phone booth near a refinery outside that hick town you're campaigning in later. Be there by the time Mickey's hands both reach straight up and we can talk more privately."

"Are you insane? I can't cut my appearances short at the drop of a hat."

"Oh, it's my turn to say sorry—I didn't realize you were such a busy man. Forget what I said and go back to campaigning. Only remember this: when you step up on your soapbox proclaiming yourself a family values candidate, you better enjoy it while you can."

The line went dead.

"What?" Green asked, as the cell phone slipped from Douglas' hand.

"She didn't kill Lynn but she's still threatening to kill my campaign."

"Unless what?"

"Unless we cancel our next stop and speak to her on a safe phone outside of town."

"Is she nuts? Our next stop is the Police Association luncheon where they're going to state their full support for you. We can't blow the police off with no notice." Green ran his fingers through his hair. "She's got to be insane."

"Either she is or I am," Douglas said slowly as he rose unsteadily to his feet. "Because we are going to blow off the police and we are going to talk to her."

"Douglas—"

"Just do it!" Adams snapped back. "Before that, call your specialist and get him on a plane now. I don't plan to let this morning turn into a total write-off."

* * *

The following morning, Senator Douglas Adams' face was on the front page of every newspaper and still the lead story on every newscast. His press conference the previous evening, during which he'd delivered his promised bombshell, was attended by every major news organization in the country. There was something big in the air and they didn't dare miss it. That it was also going to take place in a large studio at WCNY only heightened the speculation.

"Ready, in five, four, three . . ."

"This is a special NCN News Report. I'm Jason Morris."

"And I'm Susan Donallee. We are waiting for Senator Douglas Adams, Chairman of the powerful Health and Welfare Committee, and Presidential candidate, to make a statement regarding new developments in the Robert Barker gangland-style slaying investigation. Jason."

"It was 11 days ago that Mr. Barker, majority owner and CEO of Mantis Pharmaceuticals, was shot to death as he was about to speak with Senator Adams during a live broadcast of *The Nation Today*. There is speculation that Senator Adams may have uncovered why the pharmaceutical millionaire was at the outside microphone and what he was about to say."

"Of course, yesterday," Susan broke in, "Lynn Barker, the wife of Robert Barker and the prime suspect in his murder, was found wandering the streets near the couple's home in New Liston. She is currently in police custody at Western General Hospital undergoing extensive neurological testing to determine why she's experiencing complete amnesia. Yesterday, Senator Adams was in—"

"I'm sorry to interrupt, Susan, but Senator Adams has entered the WCNY studio where the press conference is being held, which incidentally is located down the hall from us."

Thanks for that geography lesson, Susan thought.

Determined to have the final word before they cut away, Susan quickly added, "There is no word whether Senator Adams will be answering any questions after making his statement."

The screen cut to the other studio a split-second before Jason gave Susan a stare venomous enough to kill an entire Boy Scout troop during a desert campout.

Their microphones, however, weren't cut as quickly as the images on the screen, allowing the eagerly waiting nation to hear Jason scream,

"You little bitch!" at the top of his lungs, while they watched Senator Adams step up to the podium.

"Good evening," Adams began solemnly, reading his script. "I've called this news conference to disclose disturbing allegations that recently came into my possession. I'd first like to say that the proper authorities in this matter were notified at once by myself and they currently have all the information I'm about to reveal to you.

"As we all know, 11 days ago, Robert Barker was shot and killed during the broadcast of *The Nation Today* program. I was a guest of the show at the time. During the ongoing investigation, no reason was found for Mr. Barker wanting to speak with me via the public airwaves." Adams took a deep breath and added, "Until now."

A low audible shockwave could be heard from the reporters. Having let them wait for several suspenseful seconds, Adams continued reading his prepared statement.

"Documents, copies of which will be distributed to everyone at the conclusion of this press conference, were sent to me anonymously yesterday morning." Adams opened a large envelope and withdrew several sheets of paper. "These documents are copies of original research reports being conducted by Mantis Pharmaceuticals, the company owned by Robert Barker. In these documents are detailed descriptions of research which Mantis was conducting as recently as four weeks ago. As I do not want to glorify this situation in any way, I will only say that some of the drug experiments are unethical in every way, shape and form. Due to the bizarre, and, in some cases, cruel treatment of animals and humans alike—all in the name of science—I strongly urge the media to use extreme discretion when deciding what areas of this research to report."

Another shocked murmur passed through the press corps.

"I have commissioned a panel of inquiry to convene without delay a full investigation of Mantis Pharmaceuticals and its entire research and development program. Until such time as their investigation is completed, citing Section 45.2 of the Federal Health and Welfare Act and as Chairman of the Health and Welfare Committee, effective immediately I have suspended the operating licence of Mantis Pharmaceuticals and all of its subsidiaries."

Sensing his statement was over, the press jumped to their feet and began to simultaneously pepper Adams with questions.

"Who sent you the documents?"

"How did you authenticate the documents?"

"What specific types of research were being conducted?"

"What about Robert Barker's role in this?"

Adams made a gesture with his hands for calm. As the assembled crowd began to quiet down, one reporter spoke up.

"Why was Robert Barker killed?"

Adams' face took on a more disturbed look. He'd expected the question only not so bluntly. He looked out and located the attractive reporter at the rear of the studio.

"What was that question again?"

"Jennifer Malone with *The Telegraph*, sir. I asked why was Robert Barker killed? And do you know what specifically he was planning to say at the microphone?"

"I believe Mr. Barker may have only recently found out about these experiments himself. As an honourable man, he may have decided to fall on his sword, so to speak, bringing up the matter in person with myself. He may also have wanted to apologize for the abuse his company had inflicted while conducting experiments outside its authority."

A brief hush came over the crowd again until Jennifer, clearly mystified by Adams' answer, asked a follow-up question.

"Are you saying that Robert Barker, having only learned that morning—or perhaps the day before—that his company was conducting bizarre clandestine experiments, was so distraught he decided to speak directly to you from a sidewalk microphone during a morning talk show?" Jennifer paused and took a deep breath. "Is that what you're saying?"

Adams stood silent, clearly flustered by Malone's retelling of the incredible tale he'd spun. Without a second thought, he decided to do the only thing a smart politician could when confronted with a similar situation.

Backtrack.

"Ms. Malone, I began my answer with the words, *I believe*. I merely stated one possible reason Mr. Barker would be at that microphone. I have no concrete proof what Mr. Barker was going to say that day. However, having seen the same evidence, I believe that as an upstanding businessman, he was planning on telling the nation how dreadfully sorry he was." Adams paused for effect. "However, it is only one possibility."

And I believe Oswald acted alone, Jennifer thought.

Taking no further questions, a rattled Adams cut the press conference short and quickly departed the studio, followed by the media. Heading out of the building, Jennifer absentmindedly passed the security station and saw a familiar face.

"Michael, how's it going?" she asked, deciding a woman her age who plays hard to get usually doesn't get to play at all.

"Ms. Malone—or is it Miss Mathews tonight?" Michael said with a wide smile.

"Jennifer, Candice, what's the difference? A rose by any other name, right?" She noticed on the station feed monitor that Susan was manning the anchor desk alone. "Where's Jason?"

"You didn't hear?" Michael laughed. "He called Susan a bitch to her face when his microphone was still on. It was the funniest thing I've ever heard."

"First, Unger, now Morris. Who'll be next?" Unable to hear Susan's commentary, Jennifer asked, "Can you turn the sound up on that thing?"

Susan continued to recap Adams' news conference, all the while sporting a mischievous smirk.

"What's your take on all of this?" Jennifer asked Michael.

"Barker had so much money that if he really wanted to confess to the nation, he wouldn't do it during *The Nation Today*. A smart guy like that would have called his own press conference—or better still, would have set up an emergency one-on-one meeting with Adams. Maybe even the President."

"I'm with you."

"Regardless of why he was outside the studio," Michael continued, "Adams still didn't answer your question. We still don't know why Barker was killed. A guilty conscience may have brought him to the microphone but a woman carrying a .22 left him there."

Jennifer smiled at Michael, who returned the gesture in kind.

"What?"

"Nothing," Jennifer said. "Do you still have my number?" Michael pulled out his wallet and handed her the business card. She scratched out her cell number and wrote a second number down. Returning it, she said, "That's my home number. Cell phones are so impersonal."

Without another word, she slung her coat over her arm and walked into the crisp night air.

"You're right, Mikey," she said to herself while heading back to *The Telegraph* building. "A woman with a .22 just left him there. Now if only I can stay focused on that, I think I'll be able to keep my sanity intact."

THIRTY FIVE

The fierce moral dilemma raging within Jeffrey Hamill's head was giving him a migraine. He'd watched Adams' news conference and felt ill as he'd implied Robert Barker wanted to talk shop or apologize for misdeeds.

What nonsense, he'd thought, switching his set off in disgust.

Then came the real kicker: a second press conference was scheduled for today. Another four-alarm barn burner relating to Barker's company—or so it was being billed by the networks.

His phone rang.

"Jeffrey Hamill Investigations."

"You sound tired, Jeffrey. Up late working a marital case?"

"Malone, you're closer to the truth than you know. I presume you're calling about the mysterious Alison Strauss?"

"Am I that transparent?" Jennifer replied flirtatiously.

"Do I like whipped cream on my pumpkin pie?" Both laughed as Hamill shuffled folders on top of his desk. "I've got good news and bad news for you. The good news is I got the driver info from Queen City's head office in Seattle."

"And how did you manage that?"

"Trade secret. Let's say rental places get very nervous when insurance adjusters come a-callin'. Anyway, the licence was a fake from what I can tell. That's the bad news. However, the possible good news is the given address actually exists."

"Here in the city?"

"Nope, a little town called East Haven."

"Never heard of it," Jennifer said, jotting the information in her notebook. "Is it close to anything?"

"The closest place you might call a city is Glenridge."

"What's the address?"

"617 Sheridan Road. That's S-h-e-r-i-d-a-n, not Sheraton like the hotel chain."

"Anything else?"

"Yeah—what big story is this going to break wide open?"

"The biggest," Jennifer replied.

"Then I've got to figure it has to do with the Barker case."

"Did anybody ever suggest you should go into the P.I. business, Jeffrey?"

"Only disgruntled clients. The reason I bring it up is I worked for Barker before he died."

The line went silent, as Hamill figured it would. He'd concluded what he had to do as soon as he heard Jennifer's voice.

It was an omen, he'd thought and in an instant his migraine vanished.

"I know that nugget of information didn't accidentally slip out, Jeffrey," Jennifer said. "Now I admit I skipped a few ethics classes when I took journalism but isn't there some kind of PI-client privilege thingy that has to be kept?"

"You know, I really couldn't say for sure, Malone. I never attended an ethics class in my life. I figured out long ago that if it feels right, do it.

If it doesn't, don't."

"Pretty simple code to live by."

"It's served me well thus far. Anyhow, my client is dead. My obligation of confidentiality was to him, not his estate."

"Have you ever done this before?" Jennifer asked in a near whisper.

"Never, not once. Hey, even private dicks have a set of morals."

"I'm glad to hear that, Jeffrey. So why are we still talking on the phone and not meeting up with each other?"

"Because you've got a big mouth. So shut up and meet me at Bernie's in a half hour."

"I'm covering the press conference right now."

"Cover it from Bernie's—you won't be disappointed."

Bernie's was a greasy spoon that made you feel like you'd travelled back to the 1950's when you stepped in the front door. You expected Richie, Potsie and Ralph Malph from the *Happy Days* television show to drop in for burgers and fries after school.

Jennifer found Hamill wedged into a booth at the back of the restaurant. He'd set up a laptop to watch the streaming video of the press conference.

"I convinced my boss to send Arnold Girard in my place."

"That hack?" Hamill said surprised.

"His reputation is obviously growing," Jennifer replied with a laugh as she sat down.

NCN's coverage began and Hamill turned up the volume.

"Let's see if their big news can top mine but I seriously doubt it will even come close," he said with a sly smile which both confused and intrigued Jennifer.

"We don't know what to expect from this news conference," Susan Donallee began, sitting alone at the anchor desk for a second straight day. "We have been told by Jacob Greenberg, the prominent lawyer who set this conference up, that new information would be divulged regarding Mantis Pharmaceuticals which was closed down yesterday by federal order. Mr. Greenberg also stated in a brief communiqué that details regarding Lynn Barker would also be revealed." Susan looked to her left toward a large-screen monitor, where a man was seen walking to the podium. "We'll now go live to the news conference. Mr. Greenberg is about to address the press."

The screen cut to a close-up of a sharply-dressed man in his early 40's, standing over six feet tall, with a closely-shaved beard and moustache. He smiled at the assembled crowd and withdrew a piece of paper from his jacket.

"My name is Jacob Greenberg, senior partner of the law firm Greenberg and Associates. I will be reading from a prepared statement and will not be taking questions at the conclusion of the statement. Thank you."

He paused to unfold then smooth out his script, which he began to read.

"As of 7:00 last evening, all operations of Mantis Pharmaceuticals were suspended by the federal government, pending an investigation of the company's research and development program. Since the shooting death of Robert Barker, all company operations were overseen by the board of directors until such time as Robert Barker's wife, Lynn Barker, was located. Upon his death, all of Mr. Barker's shares were automatically transferred to his wife, who then became majority owner of Mantis Pharmaceuticals. As has been widely reported, two days ago, Lynn Barker was found wandering the streets near her home with no memory whatsoever. She is currently undergoing extensive testing to determine why she continues to suffer amnesia.

"Yesterday afternoon, my firm was retained by Mr. Jerry Steele, Robert Barker's trusted long time assistant, upon discovering a document in Mr. Barker's personal files. This turned out to be a Power of Attorney contract

made by Lynn Barker unbeknownst to Mr. Steele. In this document, Mr. Steele is named as executor, granting him full discretionary powers if Mrs. Barker became unable, physically or mentally, to handle her affairs."

A murmur of excitement coursed through the press room.

"After speaking with Mrs. Barker's doctors, it was agreed Mrs. Barker is mentally incapable of handling her own affairs at this time. Therefore, until such time as Mrs. Barker regains her memory and is determined to be mentally fit by her physicians, all of Mrs. Barker's personal and business affairs—which now include the operation and ownership of Mantis Pharmaceuticals—will be handled by Jerry Steele." Greenberg paused and added, "This concludes my statement. Copies of the Power of Attorney contract will be distributed at the back of the room. Thank you."

The press were on their feet and hollering questions at Greenberg, who smiled one last time for the cameras and exited the studio.

"What do you think about that, Jeffrey?" Jennifer asked as Hamill closed the laptop.

"I think Douglas Adams is going to be our next President. If that happens this country is going to Hell in a handbasket quicker than you can say 'impeachment.'"

"Adams? What does he have to do with this?"

Hamill pushed a manila envelope across the table to her.

"See for yourself." As Jennifer went to take it, Hamill put his hand on hers. "Along with a surveillance report, I've also made some notes about a strange campaign donation that Jerry Steele informed Barker about three days *before* he was killed. Adams is dirty in more ways than one, Jennifer," Hamill said seriously. "And I've got to think so is Steele. Once you've read this, you'll see why."

"Dirty how?" Jennifer asked, sensing another emotional thrill ride coming on.

Hamill hauled his bulky body out of the booth. Leaning forward, he whispered, "Woodward and Bernstein were right. Follow the money," and walked out of the restaurant.

Jennifer slowly picked up the envelope and noticed her hand shaking. As she stepped out onto the sidewalk, she had the strange sensation she was being watched.

Woodward and Bernstein, she thought. *Could Barker's murder really be as big as Watergate? And if so, did that make Jeffrey her Deep Throat?*

She laughed at the notion. Deep Throat didn't quite fit Jeffrey's personality. Then the memory of Hamill getting out of the booth re-entered her head.

Big Gut on the other hand did have a certain ring to it.

Twenty minutes later she found herself in Mitch Carson's office reviewing Hamill's notes, as well as Lynn Barker's Power of Attorney document.

"It all fits. First, during a night of surveillance with your P.I. buddy, Barker finds out Adams is doing his wife. Then he uncovers Adams is also taking kickbacks from his competitor, Litchfield Industries. No wonder he wanted to speak to Adams. What better way than to confront him on live TV? It was brilliant," Carson gushed jubilantly. "We've got to run this now."

"No way, Mitch," Jennifer replied adamantly. "Not until I check this stuff out further."

"This is gold, pure gold. You want us to sit on this? For how long—a day, a week, until after the election? When? Until those dolts at *The Star* stumble onto it? They'd run a special edition to hit the street at high noon if they had to. And you still want to sit on it?" He shot his arms into the air, infuriated by Jennifer's stance.

"Look, Mitch, Watergate wasn't broken open in one day."

"Watergate? Who cares about Watergate? For one thing, you're not Woodward or Bernstein and we both know I'm not even close to being

Bradlee. Furthermore, if you haven't noticed, *The Telegraph* is not the *Washington Post*."

"If we hold off on this while I check our facts, *it could be, though.*" Jennifer saw Mitch's face brighten, his eyes glossing over at the very thought. "Anyway, there's still no connection between Barker's assistant and the killing. Nothing."

"That one's easy," Mitch said, slowly coming back to reality. "He double-crossed Barker."

"Do you want to elaborate on that for us junior cub reporters present?"

"Steele decides to tell the missus what her husband is going to do. Remember, Barker sat on the bribe from Litchfield for three days. That gave Steele 72 hours to warn and then plot with the missus."

"Plot what—Barker's murder? What would Steele have to gain?"

"Half of Mantis. He strikes a deal with the missus that he will be the getaway driver, in exchange for a percentage of the stock she was bound to inherit." A look of unadulterated excitement came over Mitch's face. "And for insurance, Steele has her sign over her Power of Attorney to him—which of course she does, never figuring on getting bonked in the head after the killing and losing everything." Mitch looked at Jennifer, who appeared extremely bored. "What's wrong?"

"Reality check time. First, the Power of Attorney was signed two weeks before the killing—not three days. Well before Barker knew his wife was bedding down with Senator Adams."

Carson thought that one over.

"Oh sure, it's easy to judge when you have no ideas of your own, Malone."

"And what about the grey Volvo rented to Alison Strauss? And that Stanley Unger was blackmailed four weeks *before* Barker's shooting?"

"Man, do I hate it when you start spewing facts like that!" Mitch howled. "As for Ms. Strauss and her Volvo, I think she's a dead end."

"I don't," Jennifer said stubbornly. "Then there's the bribe from Litchfield Industries to Adams? Maybe they killed Barker for business reasons. Did you see that their stock almost tripled at the opening bell after Adams shut Mantis down? We're talking millions upon millions of dollars here. Overnight."

"What about the affair?" Mitch asked, trying to control his growing anxiety. "It's dynamite, but all we have is Hamill's report."

"I'll find out where Adams was supposed to be at the time he was showing Lynn Barker his commander-in-chief. I'll catch him in a lie. Politicians are dumb that way."

"Also track down anyone who might have seen him before or after his dalliance with the missus."

"I still think we're missing a major piece of this puzzle," Jennifer said.

Mitch continued to pace the room for several moments before slumping into his ratty desk chair.

"I can't believe I'm about to say this, Malone. I'll give you two days for you—and you alone—to confirm these allegations. No one needs to know what you're working on, got that? No one. Then, Thursday evening at 8:00, we'll meet to decide how to proceed."

"Sounds like a plan."

"You'd better hope your private eye isn't running to the tabloids for a quick payday, peddling the same stuff he palmed off on you."

Jennifer rose from the couch and walked to the door.

"Mitch, the only people who are going to make a quick million or two, are you and me."

THIRTY SIX

At the sight of the deserted nurse's station, relief swept over her.

A good sign, she thought as she stepped off the elevator.

After checking the corridors she began down the hall toward Lynn Barker's room. At a small desk outside the room, there was a police officer reading a newspaper. The officer looked up hearing the soft sound of rubber-soled shoes echoing off the bland green walls.

Well, well, who do we have here? he thought.

The woman obviously worked in the hospital but the thing that caught his eye was the woven French braid which hung over her left shoulder. What truly grabbed his attention though was how with each stride the braid bounced lightly against her left breast.

For 3:00 in the morning, it was quite the pleasurable image.

"Evening, officer," she said with a breezy smile.

"Hi," he responded as he stood from behind the desk. "Working pretty late tonight, aren't you . . ." He looked at her hospital nametag, "Miss Gibbons?"

"I got stuck cleaning a man who decided he wanted to check out early. Unfortunately, in all his excitement and the ensuing struggle, he had a bowel movement in his hospital gown." She watched the officer's face scrunch up in disgust. "Let me tell you, it was not a pretty sight."

"I guess not," the officer managed to say.

"That's why I'm a little late. I usually come by when Joe's on duty."

"You know Joe? He's a decent guy. I relieved him at midnight," the officer said casually. "My name is Christopher. Christopher Waterson."

He extended his hand, which she took immediately.

"Angela Gibbons."

They reluctantly let go of each other's hands.

"Well, I really should see if Mrs. Barker's doing okay."

"Can I help at all?" Officer Waterson asked eagerly.

"Not unless you want to clean her bedpan." Waterson's face grimaced again, as she knew it would. "I didn't think so. I'll only be a minute."

"Okay. I'll be right outside the door if you need anything."

She entered the room and made sure the door closed without making a sound. She watched for any change on Lynn Barker's sleeping face. Taking the syringe out of the pocket of her nurse's uniform, she quietly walked to the side of the bed.

Although she'd never done this before, she had seen it in enough movies to have a basic idea of what was required. She took the plastic cap of the syringe off and squeezed the plunger. A shot of liquid jumped out of the needle. She stopped and listened for any movement by Officer Waterson. Hearing nothing, she jammed the needle into the I.V. tube that ran into Lynn Barker's right hand. Once the liquid was completely injected she put the needle's protective cap back on and carefully placed it into her pocket.

The room remained eerily still.

Watching Lynn Barker's chest rise and fall and hearing her calm breathing, she had the strange sensation of losing her own breath. What have I just done? she thought, terrified. Panic began to grip her as she moved toward the door.

"I'm doing this for you, Mrs. Barker," she whispered, "and for Robert. He didn't deserve to die like that."

Suppressing the urge to cry, she stepped into the hall.

The desk was empty.

Where is Waterson? Is he calling for hospital security or police backup? Get out of here now!

The combination of terror and the instinct to run gripped her so tightly she was unable to move.

As she was about to bolt for the nearby stairwell, Officer Waterson turned the corner at the end of the hall.

"Everything all right in there?" he asked.

"Yeah—everything's fine," she replied with an uneasy smile that Waterson didn't appear to notice. "I really have to get to the tenth floor. Another fire to put out before the day shift comes on."

"Are you working again tomorrow?" Waterson asked, getting up the courage to talk to this exceptionally beautiful nurse.

"Are you?"

"I'm here for the next six days. Midnight to eight," he replied hopefully.

"Pretty much the same shift as me," came her reply.

"I was wondering, is it possible to check on Mrs. Barker at the same time tomorrow? You know—so we could talk more. It gets pretty lonely and hospitals have always given me the creeps."

"Sure, why not." She watched as Waterson's face lit up. "But on one condition."

"Name it."

"I usually keep a pretty rigid schedule and if I'm going to drop by, I might get into trouble. So could you keep our little visits confidential? At least until Mrs. Barker is discharged."

How could I refuse a request like that?

"Not a problem," he responded excitedly. "It'll be our little secret."

"Great," she said in a low, almost sultry voice. "Then I guess I'll see you tomorrow night, if that's okay?"

"I can't wait."

Walking away, he was amazed that she was as appealing to look at from the back as from the front. Before disappearing around the corner, she turned and gave him a wave and a smile that sent his heart into near cardiac arrest.

He waved back and strutted like a peacock to his tiny desk, where he picked up the paper. The words, however, had lost their meaning and he began to fantasize about his next meeting with the lovely Nurse Gibbons. By the end of this set of shifts, he was certain they'd be more than just talking during their nightly rendezvous.

In fact, he'd do everything in his power to make sure of it.

"A cop and a nurse," he said aloud. "Man—what a combination."

THIRTY SEVEN

Melanie hadn't talked to him for almost three weeks, not wanting to be connected or seen together in the days leading up to the shooting. Yet as she entered his penthouse apartment, the electricity that had first fuelled their desires months earlier permeated the air.

She walked to the large bay windows and observed the breathtaking view of the city which only the very wealthy could attain.

She thought, *This view, this place, this man, will all be mine shortly.*

"And what are you thinking of now?" the man asked, having entered the room with two wine glasses. "In the window's reflection I see a wide smile on your lips."

Melanie made eye contact with him in their joint reflection.

"I was thinking how lucky we are," she said seductively. "To be at a stage in our lives when our opportunities are limitless. I'm not only talking about the money. I'm talking about the power that'll come with the closest thing to the fountain of youth this world has ever seen—and it's ours for the taking."

"Aren't you going to add, 'if you know what I mean?'" he remarked, handing her a glass, then wrapping his arms around her waist.

Melanie turned and faced the man of her dreams. He was in his late 40's, tall, fit and with the looks of a middle-aged matinee idol. A man whose intricate plot to kill Robert Barker and frame his wife had brought them to this juncture. A man willing to risk everything to make his wildest dreams a reality. A man who would soon rid both of them of Jerry Steele.

"When I'm with you I never have to," Melanie replied, "because you already know what I'm going to say before I say it."

Their eyes locked and they began to kiss like long-lost lovers back from war.

Howard Manard, CEO of Litchfield Industries and soon to be owner of Mantis Pharmaceuticals, set his glass down and swept Melanie off her feet, walking to the master bedroom.

"I have missed you so, Melanie. You can't believe how difficult it's been. I've spent every waking hour following the news and reading the papers, hoping you wouldn't be found out. Praying that idiot Steele wouldn't ruin our well-laid plans."

"With me whispering new ideas into his ear every night after he fell asleep? Nothing was ever in jeopardy, Howard."

"The idea of you two sleeping in the same bed as I languished alone still makes my skin crawl."

"So you missed me that much, huh?"

"More than words, my love," Manard whispered, gently kissing Melanie's neck. Laying her on his bed, he began to unbutton her blouse and inhale her lightly perfumed skin. "What I've planned for our reunion requires more actions than words anyway—if you know what I mean," he added quickly.

Not in the mood to talk in the first place, Melanie gave him an enticing smile and worked on his belt buckle.

By tonight, she thought, *I think we'll both know exactly what you mean, Howard, or we'll have a helluva time trying to figure it out.*

A Memorable Murder

They both awoke drained. Being physically exhausted after making love wasn't new, having experienced it innumerable times since they'd first passed each other in the Litchfield hallways. At the time, Melanie was still looking for work and even with Jerry's help nothing was panning out. Professionally she was feeling like a failure and emotionally she was as frail as a baby bird caught up in a twister. Only days earlier, Robert had informed her he was going back to Lynn and her world seemed ready to blow apart.

Never clear if by chance or divine intervention, a man exited the elevator as she was walked to the Litchfield personnel office. As they neared one another, she felt a wave of electricity pass through her. She wasn't sure if this was caused by being mildly star-stuck with Howard Manard, or if something deeper—something sensual and sexual—was taking place. When their eyes met, she instinctively knew it was the latter.

The following day, she was summoned to Manard's office for a private interview. By that evening, she was at his penthouse showing him what special talents she possessed. As she was leaving to return to Jerry's condo, Manard proposed an offer which she simply could not refuse.

Soon it was announced she'd been hired as a special marketing consultant for Litchfield Industries, working on sensitive projects for the CEO. Instead of going to work each day as Jerry thought, she would drive to Manard's apartment complex and wait for him. When he arrived, they would usually have an hour or so to themselves, during which they'd eat, talk, relax and almost religiously make passionate love. This activity only served to re-energize Manard, who would reluctantly return to the office.

Me, a kept woman? Manard, my sugar daddy? Yeah, whatever, she'd thought when he'd proposed the idea. *It sure beats working.*

The only drawback was Manard's insistence she continue her

relationship with Jerry, for reasons he never fully explained. Although she was mildly interested in Jerry, he was still devoted to her in every way. Figuring the odds of finding two other men as devoted as Jerry and Howard were slim to none, she decided to accept Manard's terms. The fact she was getting paid only made her decision that much easier.

One day, Manard came home looking like death warmed over. When she asked what had happened, Melanie was given an earful about a secret project he'd uncovered at Mantis Pharmaceuticals. He was not only livid at this news but also terrified about the implications for Litchfield.

"Something has to be done," he'd said.

As data from his corporate spies piled up, Manard panicked and terminated 10 product projects, diverting their funds to a new high-security project named Memory One. Using documents purchased from low-level Mantis technicians, the Memory One team duplicated results that had taken Mantis' researchers years to achieve. However, at a critical point, these techs could no longer gain access to the crucial information needed to close the gap between the two companies.

It was then Manard heard that Robert Barker was planning a hearing before the Health and Welfare Committee. It could mean only one thing: Mantis' memory drug was ready for human testing.

In the midst of more ranting and raving, Manard uttered, "I wish Barker were dead!" and by day's end, he and Melanie had figured out how to commit the perfect crime. The only problem: Jerry. When all was said and done though, their plans had drastically changed when old Jerry pulled off *The Nation Today* scheme involving Stanley Unger.

For a fleeting moment as he watched Melanie blow his rival's brains out across the majority of Nielsen families' TV sets, Manard wanted to shake Jerry's hand.

"When are you going to bring this charade with Jerry to an end?" he asked, sweeping the hair away from Melanie's eyes. "I have his money ready to go. All I need is for you to inform him his work was

extraordinary and he should leave the country as soon as possible. Do you think he'll have an issue with that?"

Melanie had anticipated this for quite some time. She was amazed it wasn't brought up the second she'd stepped into the apartment.

"I don't know, Howard," she said sleepily. "Jerry's changed since we started this thing. One day he's as tame as a pussy cat and the next he's a guy cracking a whip over my head. I don't know if giving up control of Mantis is a sure thing for him anymore."

"What?" Manard asked incredulously. "Are you saying he's going to hold the place hostage? He doesn't know the first thing about the pharmaceutical industry and besides, he's an accessory to murder and kidnapping."

"And which of us do you propose call the police with this information—you or me?"

"This is ridiculous," Manard said, sitting upright.

"Slow down, Howard. I said it was a possibility we have to consider. In fact, the whole burning down of the motor lodge made him a bit jumpy. He might want to take the million and run."

"What if I upped the ante to 1.5 million? Do you think he'd have a problem with that?"

"One and a half mil? Hell, I'd drop you for that kind of coin."

THIRTY EIGHT

"How hard could it be to find a person out here?" Jennifer asked herself as she drove past the *Welcome to East Haven - We Love Our Children* sign. It also stated the population as 266, although the numbers were faded and peeled.

On the main street she noted one variety store, one gas station and one combination grocery/pizza/video rental business, which together made up the business district.

Town may have been too grandiose of a word to describe the surroundings, she thought. *Village, however, has a nice authentic ring.*

With one eye on the road, Jennifer pulled out her notebook to where she'd written Alison Strauss' alleged address: 617 Sheridan Road. By the time she looked up from the page, Jennifer was passing the *See You Soon* sign and began to laugh. She made a quick u-turn and drove back into the village.

Before speaking to any of the locals, she figured she'd cruise the few side streets in hopes of finding Sheridan Road on her own. Within two minutes she'd seen everything there was to see in East Haven—except the street she was looking for.

"Hey, how are you today?"

He was barely out of his teens, yet something in the way he'd greeted her at the gas station made her heart flutter. He was a young Brad Pitt. The hair, the smile—those dimples!—were to die for.

So young and innocent, Jennifer thought. *Just what I've been looking for all these years.*

"I'm okay, I guess," she said with a smile. "I'm a bit lost, though."

Brad's twin brother began to laugh.

"I didn't think that was possible here in East Haven. I guess you city folks have a hard time adjusting to peace and quiet, don't you?"

Jennifer returned his smile sheepishly.

"You can't imagine how right you are . . ."

"Nathaniel," he said finishing her sentence.

"Nathaniel, huh? Sounds like a big-city name if you ask me."

It was Nathaniel's turn to blush.

"My dad used to work at a brokerage house."

"Don't worry, I won't hold that against you. By the way, my name is Jennifer."

"Huh, that's funny. So is my girlfriend's."

Lucky girl, Jennifer thought as Nathaniel continued to wipe grease off his hands.

"If your dad was a broker, I take it you haven't lived here too long?"

"About three years."

"I ask because I'm looking for a street that doesn't appear to exist."

"What's the name?"

"Sheridan Road."

"I guess the GPS map people haven't been down lately to update the street names," Nathaniel laughed.

"So there is such a road, only under another name? Do you know what it was changed to?"

"Barclay Street." Jennifer watched as Nathaniel outstretched his muscular arm and followed his gaze to the next street over.

"That's Sheridan Road?"

"Up until two years ago."

"What happened then?"

"It's a long story. The short version is Sheridan was the name of a family that had lived here for generations. They practically owned the whole place. As you can imagine, in a small town like this that never went over too well with the other families."

"Sort of like Mr. Potter and Bedford Falls," Jennifer said, referring to the Christmas classic *It's a Wonderful Life.*

"Who?" Nathaniel asked.

"Never mind, you're too young to remember. Go on, I'm sorry."

"When the last of them died off a couple of years ago, the town council voted to change the name."

"Pretty vindictive, don't you think? Sounds like something that would happen in a big city."

"Yeah, I guess it does, doesn't it?" Nathaniel mused.

"Who is this big shot Barclay? Must be pretty powerful, not to mention vain, to get his name on that sign."

Nathaniel laughed louder than before.

"You're right about that," he said. After inspecting his hands for missed grease, he looked up and said, "I kind of doubt you came all the way out here to discuss country bumpkin politics. What's the number you're looking for on Sheridan?"

"617."

"That's the Mason house."

Again Jennifer followed Nathaniel's gaze and outstretched hand.

"Mason? Are you sure?" Jennifer asked as she looked at the small two-storey bungalow with its tiny front yard. "Because I was looking for someone named Strauss."

"Strauss, huh? Well if they lived there, it hasn't been for at least three years, because the Masons are the only people I know."

Strike one, Jennifer thought.

"Is there anyone who would know who lived in that house before the Masons?"

"Charlie's your best bet," Nathaniel replied without hesitation. "He owns the grocery store."

Jennifer looked toward the store up the street and back at Nathaniel.

"I guess I'll go and talk to him then," she said not really wanting to leave this city-born, country-bred hunk behind. *What I could teach those arms and hands to do,* she thought wistfully. "Next time you see Jennifer—your Jennifer—say '*Hey*' for me, all right?"

"Sure thing."

As she put her car in gear, she looked up at Nathaniel's angelic face.

"And while you're at it, say '*Hey*' to Mr. Barclay when you see him at dinner tonight. Okay?"

The astonished look on Nathaniel's face was quickly replaced by a grin the size of the Grand Canyon.

"I'll do that. I promise."

"Good man," Jennifer said heading off the lot. "I'll be seeing you around."

The short drive didn't erase the image of Nathaniel's shocked expression.

To be young again, she thought, as she entered the East Haven Grocery Store.

It was, of course, what a grocery store should be: small, with three aisles of name-brand products with a meat counter at the back. It was there Jennifer first noticed a man in his late 60's who she guessed was likely Charlie.

"I'll be out in a sec," he offered as he carried a large slab of beef into the back freezer. A short time later he emerged. "Sorry to make you wait, miss. My meat shipment came in a little while ago."

"No problem," Jennifer said in her friendliest tone.

"Is there something in particular you are looking for?" Charlie asked, surveying the shelves on either side of them. "We've got a special on canned vegetables this week. Three for a dollar."

"Actually, Nathaniel at the gas station said you might be able to help me."

"If I can, I will," Charlie declared with an eager smile.

"It's about a house on Sheridan Road—which I've been told is now called Barclay Street."

"Damn shame about that business," Charlie stated, shaking his head. "Did you know that was one of the first roadways ever built here in town? That was back in the 1890's, still, it is part of our history, you know."

"Nathaniel gave me a brief rundown of what happened," Jennifer said, attempting to avoid a rehash of the same story. "The house I was asking about is 617. The Mason place."

"Nice couple the Masons—Mary and Donald. Come in here almost every day."

"But they haven't always lived there, right?"

"They're relatively new to the community, yes. Three years maybe. I say new because hardly anyone ever leaves. We've got families here who go back three, four generations."

"The Strausses left though, didn't they?" Jennifer asked bluntly.

The colour in Charlie's weather-beaten face now appeared bland and pasty.

"Is that who you're looking for?"

"So at one time there was a Strauss family at 617?"

"For quite a while, actually."

"And did they have a daughter?" Jennifer asked hopefully.

The colour abruptly came back into Charlie's cheeks.

"If you can call her that," he said bitterly.

"Was there a problem at home?"

"How can you have a problem at home when you're never at home?"

"She ran away?"

"And broke her mother's heart."

Jennifer glanced at her watch and then at Charlie's distraught face. She knew he had a story that would take much longer to tell than she had time to listen.

"Charlie—do you mind if I call you Charlie?"

"That's my name."

"I don't have a great deal of time right now. You see, I'm looking for an Alison Strauss for an article I'm writing and East Haven is the closest I've come to finding her."

"Did you say *Alison* Strauss?" Charlie said, interrupting Jennifer's sentence.

"Is there a problem?" Jennifer was worried she'd stumbled into another deep dark town secret. "She isn't dead or anything, is she?"

"No, that's not it. It's just I'd forgotten Melanie's middle name."

Jennifer was sure her jaw must be down around her ankles, as a flash of heat burst through her brain.

"Who is Melanie?"

It was Charlie who now looked surprised.

"It's who you're looking for. Alison was her middle name, as in Melanie Alison Strauss."

Jennifer was thunderstruck as another factoid from the Robert Barker shooting popped into her head. Everything in her reporter's mind told her she knew the answer to her next question, and if she was right Robert Barker's killing would be one step closer to being solved.

"Then who is Melanie Fields?" she asked anxiously.

"Fields?" Charlie asked with a quizzical look. "How did you know about Luke Fields?" He took a step forward, cutting the distance between them to less than two feet. "What type of article are you writing anyhow?" he asked coldly.

"I work for *The Telegraph* newspaper," Jennifer said in a rush of words. "Tell me how Alison Strauss and Melanie Fields are related and I'll send you an autographed copy of my article. This is very important."

Charlie took a step back as if he wasn't used to handling the sudden intensity this woman was giving off.

"It's pretty simple, really," he finally said. "Luke Fields was married to Alison's mother, Norma Strauss."

"And he adopted her, right?" Jennifer didn't wait for a response. "And from then on, she was known as Melanie Fields instead of Melanie Strauss. Is that right?"

Charlie looked at her with a puzzled expression, not having the foggiest idea what relevance any of this had.

"What difference does it make now? That was 20 years ago."

Jennifer was dumbfounded.

"Didn't you say this happened three years ago?" she asked, barely keeping the scorn out of her voice.

"No," Charlie replied firmly, "I said the Masons have lived in that house for three years. Prior to that, Luke and Norma Strauss lived there."

"But Alison or Melanie—whoever she was—left a long time ago and never came back, right?"

"Basically."

"And at some point in time, she changed her name from Strauss to Fields. Is that what you're telling me?"

"To the best of my knowledge she changed it when she went to college."

Charlie stared at Jennifer, who didn't seem to notice. She was in a state of shock aboard the Robert Barker Express — an apparently endless ride with no functioning brakes.

"One question, miss," Charlie asked hesitantly, his voice breaking Jennifer's trance-like state.

"Sure, fire away."

"How did you connect Alison Strauss with Melanie Fields without me joining the dots for you?"

Jennifer thought about the witness signature on Lynn Barker's Power of Attorney contract, plus her talk with Raoul.

"It's a very long story and I honestly don't have time to relay it right now. Suffice to say, you've been a great help and I promise I will personally bring my article back down here after it's published."

"I guess I'll have to wait until then, huh?" Charlie said with a shrug of his shoulders. "You know where to find me."

"If you don't hear from me in a few weeks, give me a call. Use the 1-800 number." Jennifer handed him her card. "I really do have to get going. It's been very nice visiting with you, Charlie. You have a wonderful little town here."

Jennifer headed toward the door as Charlie looked at her card.

"*The Telegraph*, huh?" he said. "I guess you've read all about that shooting then. It's hard to believe Lynn Fletcher would grow up to be a cold-hearted killer like that. Pretty sad state of affairs, if you ask me."

Jennifer stopped in her tracks and turned toward Charlie, who now looked like a concerned grandfather.

"Don't you mean Lynn Barker?" she asked.

"Lynn Fletcher, Lynn Barker — what's the difference really? Why — do you know her?"

"Why would you think that?" Jennifer asked, clearly shaken by

Charlie's question.

"I assumed you were trying to find Melanie to ask her about Lynn."

Would this ever end?

"They knew each other?" Jennifer asked, stumbling over her words.

"Heck, they were in the same grade at Glenridge High."

Jennifer's knees almost buckled after that one registered.

"They went to the same school?"

"Yep."

"How can you be so sure?"

"Because I remember Norma telling me how upset Melanie got when Lynn was crowned Prom Queen."

"When was this?"

"In their senior year. Hold on a sec."

Before Jennifer could stop him, Charlie was running down the aisle and disappearing through a back door at the rear of the store. She heard him climb a set of stairs and begin to open and close several doors.

"I really have to get going, Charlie," she said as she began to furiously jot information into her notebook.

"Hold on," Charlie said breathlessly as he emerged through the door. "Before you go take a look at this. It'll prove to you that I'm telling you the truth."

"I believe you, Charlie, I really do. However, I am in a bit of a rush."

Charlie thrust a yearbook into her hand.

"Class of 1986-87."

After her hands stopped shaking, Jennifer laid the book on the checkout counter and began to flip through the pages. In a middle section she found what she was looking for: Lynn in a yellow full-length dress accepting flowers from her King. A plastic tiara sat on her head.

PROM QUEEN Lynn Fletcher and PROM KING Peter Elliot, the caption read.

"You said this was their senior year, right?" Jennifer asked absently as she continued to flip through the pages to find the grad section.

"Senior year, right."

Jennifer took note of all the pubescent faces.

So young and eager, she thought.

She flipped a few pages to one headlined *Legacies*. Listed below were the names of the graduating class and their thoughts about life at Glenridge.

LYNN FLETCHER: I'll always cherish band classes, cheerleading, Mr. Cassidy's English classes, hanging out with Debbie, and winning the regional field hockey championships.

Jennifer turned the page and located Melanie Strauss' parting shot at her small-town existence. Staring up at her in vivid black and white were the words she was certain would single-handedly win her the Pulitzer Prize for investigative reporting.

After Charlie loaned her the yearbook, Jennifer hightailed it to *The Telegraph*, the front-page exclusive already written in her head. The whole trip back, she mentally prepared herself for the battle to be played out with Mitch and a battery of lawyers.

It wasn't every day a presidential frontrunner was accused of being an accessory to murder.

Then again, Jennifer thought as she pulled into the paper's parking lot, *today isn't like every other day.*

She turned the car's engine off and sat in silence to collect her thoughts. She glanced at the yearbook on the passenger seat and picked it up. Turning to the grad section again, she scanned the smiling students in their graduation gowns—boys wearing ties and girls holding bouquets of flowers. Lynn Fletcher looked every bit the part of Miss Popularity. Her smile leapt off the page, her skin was vibrant and there was an aura of invincibility around her.

A few pages over was Melanie Strauss' grad photo. She, too, wore a gown and held loosely-tied flowers but there was no flashy smile and no youthful glow. Although attractive in her own right, the soft focus of the camera lens had been unable to subdue the rage that lay behind her stony eyes. They conveyed one thing: cold, calculating contempt for everyone and everything.

Jennifer returned to the *Legacies* section and still couldn't quite believe her eyes.

MELANIE STRAUSS: Someday, I too will be Prom Queen, if you know what I mean.

Recalling Raoul clearly saying Stanley Unger's female blackmailer used that very phrase, Jennifer knew Senator Adams was not the only one going to be running for cover with the delivery of tomorrow's paper.

If you know what I mean, indeed.

THIRTY NINE

The morning edition of *The Telegraph* contained nothing about Senator Adams. After having been so gung-ho to run Adams' alleged kickbacks from Litchfield Industries and his affair with Lynn Barker two days earlier, Mitch Carson had met a wall of resistance from the legal department. They explained that without corroborating evidence, the paper would be open to a serious slander suit. They also reminded Mitch that a newly-elected President was not a person you wanted to piss off.

However, Jennifer's East Haven information was fit for publication under the headline:

High School Connection Between Suspect and Witness

"Look at this picture!" Melanie yelled, as she threw the paper onto the kitchen table. "I look like a dork!" She picked it up once more and read the byline. "Jennifer Malone—I told you she was trouble!"

Jerry sat calmly on the couch in a rented condo on the outskirts of the city, as their homes had become magnets for journalists covering the Barker saga. He watched as Melanie stared at the graduation picture that graced the top fold and then tore the page to shreds. He was enjoying Melanie's temper tantrum immensely. Although he knew the hole they found themselves in would be difficult to climb out of, seeing Melanie in this state was worth the trouble.

"So they found out you went to school together? Is that a crime?"

"They know my real name, Jerry. Do I have to remind you I used Alison Strauss on the car rental contract?" Melanie walked into the living room and poured herself a double shot of whiskey. After emptying the glass in one gulp, tears welled up in her eyes. "And what if they find that slip, huh? Don't you think the police will put two and two together?"

Jerry let her stew, knowing full well she wanted his input.

"You've already talked to the police and they already know you and Lynn were friends," he finally said. "That's why Lynn had you witness the Power of Attorney. She could trust you. The article means nothing. As for the rental agreement, I'm sure it's locked away in some huge warehouse, never to be found again."

"I wish I could believe you," Melanie said sourly.

"Anyway, with Lynn still not remembering anything, there's no proof she didn't sign the Power of Attorney of her own free will. Without her memory, we're safe."

Melanie continued to brood. Her time with Jerry had become excruciating even before this new development. All she could think about was getting him out of the country where he could control Mantis via that slimy mouthpiece, Jacob Greenberg. Since the shooting, she'd been dreaming of the day she and Howard could live together. No more sneaking around. No more hiding their true feelings.

And best of all, no more Jerry.

Now that all seemed to be in jeopardy.

"I was talking to Manard while you were out getting the papers. His sources on the Hill say there's been no glitches in the Mantis shutdown plan. Everyone of importance is taking a wait-and-see attitude until after the election. No one wants to challenge Adams' wisdom if he's going to

be elected the next President."

"What about the money?" Jerry asked.

"I was getting to that," Melanie replied quickly. "He said and I quote, 'You and Jerry have done an extraordinary job and as a bonus I'm going to give each of you two million dollars,' unquote."

Melanie watched Jerry's eyes closely for his reaction.

"He's not going to kill us and he's now going to pay us double?"

Jerry's expression had revealed nothing.

"There is one catch," Melanie added, thinking feverishly to make one up. "You have to leave the country by the end of the week. Then once things settle down a bit, I'll join you."

Jerry's features changed this time.

"We aren't supposed to leave at all! What would the police think?"

"They would think after all the stress you've been through you needed a vacation—that's what they'd think," Melanie said. "It's not like you're a suspect and with Mantis shut down there's nothing to do anyway."

"What about Lynn? If you haven't forgotten, the only reason I control Mantis is because I'm in charge of her finances while she recovers."

"She's never going to recover, Jerry. Let's face the facts. Her brain is going to be as useful as eyeglasses to a blind person. Set up a care fund and let someone else worry about her. Your responsibility is to her money, not to her personally," Melanie insisted.

Jerry pondered that maybe Manard and Melanie were right. There was no reason to stick around. The longer they stayed in the country, the better the odds they might be accused of some involvement. Leaving Melanie behind wasn't to his liking, although he'd soon have two million reasons to leave her forever.

As she'd said, without Lynn's memory the police could never arrest them for Robert's murder or the kidnapping. They had disassembled and buried the gun, used a false name for the rental car and burned the motor lodge to the ground. In fact, Melanie was in more danger than he was. She was the one Lynn left with for their high school reunion tour. She was the one Lynn had seen at the lodge. She was the one who had supposedly witnessed Lynn's signature.

She's the one going down if Lynn ever wakes up with her memory intact.

Jerry knew these ideas, although highly entertaining, were fanciful musings at best. He was well aware given the opportunity, Melanie would sing like a robin on the first day of spring.

Of course, he'd do the same.

"I'll leave on the first flight after the money is confirmed in my Swiss account," Jerry said with a smile. "Let's get this thing over with."

"I'll call Manard with the news," Melanie said, walking into the kitchen, trying to conceal the grin forming across her lips.

"I think I'll pick up some Chinese take-out to celebrate," Jerry said.

Even better, Melanie thought. *Then I can speak to Howard alone.*

"Sounds great. I'll give you the lowdown when you get back."

Melanie was on the phone the moment Jerry closed the front door.

"Howard, the deal is done," she said eagerly. "Two million in his Swiss account and he'll be out of our lives forever."

"Two million? Are you nuts?" Manard asked. "I said I might—the operative word there being *might*—offer him a million-five. Where did you get two million from that statement?"

Melanie hadn't expected him to be this angry.

"Look," she started abrasively, "it doesn't matter if the payoff is five grand or five million. It's time to pay the piper and get on with the business at hand, which is to perfect Memory One and get it to market. When that happens, an extra few dollars to Jerry Steele will look like chump change. What is your problem, anyway?"

Silence was Manard's initial response.

"I don't have an extra million to throw around, Melanie," he said in a shaky voice.

"You've got to be kidding. Litchfield stock has tripled in the past few days. The company is worth millions more than before the shooting."

"The problem," Manard interrupted, clearly irritated, "is the initial million I was going to pay Jerry has been taken care of—just as Adams' bribe was dealt with. The books have already been cooked. I can't account for another million dollars disappearing so quickly. I'd need a month to do it properly."

"What am I going to tell Jerry?" Melanie asked. "Manard is being a prick and can only pay half now—you'll have to trust him for the rest! Do you know how that sounds, Howard? Huh, do you?"

"You started this!" Manard barked back. "This isn't my problem, it's yours! You should have kept your big mouth shut!"

Melanie could barely hold back her anger, while Manard sat petrified in his office, wondering why he couldn't keep his big mouth shut.

"When Jerry gets back, I'll talk this over with him," Melanie said calmly, although with the tone of an ice princess. "I'll tell him how you're trying to screw us over and maybe we shouldn't trust you anymore. With Jerry in a full-blown rage, I'll tell him to slow down and that everything will work out. Then I'll do what I do best, Howard." Her voice changed from icy cold to seductively hot. "I'll make him feel like the luckiest man on earth."

Silence.

"I'll get the money," Manard said dryly. "Two million by Friday."

* * *

"Who is this Jennifer Malone person again?" Douglas Adams demanded while pacing the hotel room.

"She's a reporter for *The Telegraph*," Harold Green replied, trying to remain composed in light of the information he'd received.

"From the Mantis press conference, right?" Adams asked angrily. "The one who kept asking over and over why Robert Barker was killed." Adams wiped away a drop of sweat from the side of his face. "I don't need this right now, Harold. The election is Tuesday. I see no political advantages in every weekend paper speculating about my love life and what role I played in Barker's death. It's bad enough I shut his company down under false pretences."

"If you had listened to me—" Green began.

"Don't you dare get sanctimonious on me at this late stage!" Adams shot back, pointing a shaky finger in Green's direction. "As I've told you in the past, I hired you for your skills as a campaign manager—not as my priest! Are we clear in that regard?"

Green said nothing, knowing Adams would end up blaming him for answering Lynn's call the night of her knockdown fight with Robert. Due to the police's incompetent handling of Lynn's telephone records, it was only now they'd learned that the last call she'd made before vanishing was to Harold Green's cell phone. He denied any knowledge of such a call and had told Detective Speers he had no idea why she'd have done such a thing. With no further questions, Speers left unsatisfied with Green's answer.

Green immediately went to see Adams to tell him the news. The only problem was that Jennifer Malone—posing as a hotel security officer—had got to him first. In as few words as possible, she'd managed to mention the phone call, the Omni Spirit hotel and a black Lincoln still registered in his dearly departed wife's name.

In a state of unparalleled shock, Adams could barely stand upright by the time Jennifer had asked, "Would you like to comment on this, Senator Adams?" Fortunately, the real hotel security staff arrived and whisked Jennifer out of the building. When Green appeared on the scene, Adams had already consumed several shots of bourbon and was working on a bottle of scotch.

"The police have nothing to connect us to Lynn's disappearance or Robert's killing," Green stated as he poured himself a vodka on the rocks. "Nothing has changed in that area—nothing. If I'd given her your personal line as you flew over the Rockies, then we would have been in big trouble. As we both know, that didn't happen."

"What about this reporter? She knows about the Omni. You should have seen her, Harold. She wasn't fishing for information. It wasn't merely conjecture on her part—she knew. Everything from the hotel to the Lincoln to the time we met. She even revealed the room number." Adams stopped and fell onto a chaise lounge by a window. He looked horrible—tired, unkempt—and felt even worse. "How are we going to combat these allegations once they're printed in tomorrow's paper? I'll be finished."

Green had seen it all before, the desperate candidate whose past had resurfaced to bite him in the ass mere days before an election. It was this aspect of running campaigns that appealed most to Green, whether it was his candidate's derrière swinging in the wind or his opponent's. Although part of the challenge was finding dirt on the other guy, the real test was how you handled the dirt flung in your direction.

In this arena, Harold Green was the one true master.

"She obviously knows about the affair, which itself is unlit dynamite. Without hard evidence though she can't run it," Green explained to his attentive boss. "Now if she were a reporter for a tabloid, you're right, tomorrow's headline would read ADAMS AND LYNN BARKER LOVERS! Fortunately, she works for *The Telegraph*. Their lawyers would tell her such an allegation would be enough for a slander suit—which we'd file the moment the paper hit the ground. It would be her word against yours. Who is the public going to believe: a crime reporter who can't back up her story or the denial of their next President?"

"What if—" Adams began before reconsidering.

Green had made sense, like he always did, Adams thought, albeit grudgingly. Without pictures or sworn affidavits from his bodyguards that evening, Malone had zilch. Even if there were pictures of him entering the Omni, he and Lynn had not been seen together. The only person who could put him with Lynn was Lynn herself and he knew she'd never do that willingly.

A frightening thought came to mind: *What if she remembered their affair and told someone unwillingly?*

"That doctor we sent to treat Lynn, what did he tell you about her condition this morning?"

The abruptness of the question made Green jump in his chair, making him spill some of his drink on his trousers.

"What?"

"Tell me what he said," Adams ordered. "I don't have time to fool around, Harold. What did he say about Lynn's memory?"

Green stared at Adams, whose face was a mixture of conflicting emotions.

"He said her memory had not returned."

"And will it? Will she remember anything by Tuesday?"

Adams' face started to lose colour and he became unsteady on his feet. Green rushed over and helped him into an armchair.

"Do you need a doctor, Douglas?"

"No more doctors," Adams replied through laboured breathing. "All I need to survive is assurance Lynn isn't going to recall our affair."

"She won't, Douglas. The specialist is almost certain of it," Green said in a soothing voice. "It'll take a miracle to unlock her past memories. We're safe. I swear, we're safe."

"Well, if you swear, then I guess everything will be okay," Adams replied sarcastically. "I hope you're right because my heart can't take many more surprises."

FORTY

Jennifer's day had been a frustrating one with her stories on Adams' kickback and affair sitting idle inside her computer. She was also having no luck finding corroborating witnesses or digging up new leads to help her cause.

Lost in thought, she barely registered her phone ringing.

"Turn to page six of *The Post* and you'll find a blackmailer," the heavily accented voice instructed.

"Raoul, is that you?" Jennifer asked.

"Get your hands on today's *Post* and all your questions about Unger will be answered."

"What do you mean?"

The line went dead.

"I don't believe this," she said taking the stairs to the first floor where she exited onto the street. "Lefty, give me a *Post*," she said to the crusty newsstand operator who'd worked the same corner for decades.

"Checking out the competition today?" Lefty asked.

"Yeah, something like that," Jennifer said as she handed over a dollar and walked away. "Page six . . . page six," she muttered as she tried to open the paper without it flying into pieces. Entering the lobby she managed to fold the page over and stared at the smartly-dressed man featured. Upon reading the picture's caption, she began taking the stairs to the newsroom two at a time.

At her desk she frantically dialed the number for Buttons.

"I need to speak to Raoul," she told the bartender. "It's Jennifer Malone at *The Telegraph*."

"I recognized your voice. This is Willy. You know, the girls have been asking about you."

"Tell them I've gone to correct a problem I've had since birth. They'll know what I mean." She waited for Willy to stop laughing before asking about Raoul again.

"I haven't seen him for a couple days."

"Do you know where I can find him?"

"I haven't a clue, sorry."

"If you see or hear from him, could you call me?"

"Sure thing," Willy said as he took down the number.

"Thanks, I really appreciate this."

"It's no problem."

Hanging up Jennifer looked at the picture of Jerry Steele walking down a city sidewalk. Since the Mantis shutdown, he'd pulled a Howard Hughes and was never photographed or seen in public. Somehow *The Post* photographer had been tipped and snapped the picture, probably from a van with tinted windows.

Jennifer tried to recall Raoul's words. He'd said the blackmailer was on page six and all her questions about Stanley Unger would be answered.

This is too crazy, right?

Making her way across the newsroom, she already felt her mental roller coaster gearing up, beginning its ascent into the clouds.

"We've got a new problem."

Mitch looked up from his computer sporting a distressed look.

"Why is it every time you walk in here *we* have a new problem? Can you answer me that?"

"Because I continue to earn my keep, unlike some other reporters around here."

"About that assignment I gave to Girard—" Carson started.

"I think I know who the other blackmailer is," Jennifer said abruptly, interrupting Mitch's feeble attempt to apologize.

"And where did you get this information?" he asked giving his full attention to Jennifer, who threw *The Post* on his desk. "*The Post*? You're taking your cues from these idiots now?"

"On page six you'll find the guy who was with Miss Melanie 'if-you-know-what-I-mean' Fields, a.k.a. Alison Strauss, when they formalized their peep show involving Stanley Unger."

Mitch looked at her skeptically as he continued to turn pages. After examining the picture, he let out a low whistle.

"Jerry Steele and Melanie Fields? Let me get this straight. You're telling me these two—both directly connected to Lynn and Robert Barker—blackmailed Unger to insure Robert appeared on *The Nation Today*?"

"You really should be a police detective with that quick mind of yours, Mitch. Its abilities continue to dazzle me on a daily basis."

"Okay, smartass, here's another thought that popped into my superhuman head: where did you get this information?"

"Well, the fact that there were only four people who knew about the blackmail scheme and you named three of them . . ."

"Raoul, the big button boy, told you this?"

"I know, I know—he's not exactly citizen of the year but he did lead us to Unger and everything he said checked out. So why call me now with this? He's got nothing to gain."

"Unfortunately, neither do we. We still have no real proof, except

Raoul's word."

"I was thinking of seeing Unger again," Jennifer said flatly. "Maybe take the police with me this time."

Mitch didn't reply immediately. Instead, he creased the paper neatly on his desk and tossed it into his garbage can. He then leaned back in his chair and folded his arms behind his head.

"Go ahead, I'm listening."

"I know you're not going to like this idea," Jennifer began slowly, "but I think it's time to bring Speers into this."

"So he can what—interview Raoul between photo sessions?" Mitch inquired cynically.

"Maybe," Jennifer replied. "I was thinking more along the lines of dusting the blackmail photos for prints."

"Then do what with them, Jennifer—ask Steele to come down to the station to get his fingers all inky? It'll never fly."

"What do you propose we do with this information, smart guy?" Jennifer grumbled.

It was one of the few times Mitch had ever seen Jennifer ready to throw in the towel.

"We'll have to sit on it until this whole thing breaks," he said trying to sound optimistic. "First, it's not our responsibility to help the police do their jobs. If they wanted to talk to Unger, they'd have done so. I'm not going to tell Mike Speers how to run his investigation, are you? Besides, even with what you have, it's all hearsay. Great hearsay, but hearsay nevertheless."

Jennifer stood and let out a deep sigh.

"I'm not going to give up on this, if that's what you're thinking."

Mitch laughed.

"If you were to do that, it would make you appear to be human. And where would we be then, huh?"

Jennifer smiled.

"We'd really be lost."

While shuffling the notes that cluttered the top of her desk, the phone rang again.

"Raoul, I'm glad you called back. Where are you? We need to talk."

"Ah . . . my name is not Raoul."

Jennifer didn't recognize the woman's timid voice.

"I'm sorry. I thought you were someone else."

"Maybe this wasn't such a good idea," the woman said nervously.

"No, wait," Jennifer said quickly. "There was a reason you called me. Please don't hang up because I have poor telephone etiquette." There was an uneasy silence on the line until Jennifer asked, "Did you specifically call me or did the switchboard put you through to the newsroom?"

"I . . . ah . . . asked for you," the woman stated apprehensively.

"At least I know this isn't a crank call," Jennifer said, trying to coax the caller out of her shell with some lame humour. "Or this is a crank call and I don't know it yet."

"I called because you're the only female reporter working the Barker killing."

Hello!

Jennifer's grabbed for her notebook.

"I'm sorry about that crank call crack," Jennifer said jotting down the date and time. "It's been one of those days." Silence. "Okay, you obviously know my name, can I get yours?"

"I want to just talk to you first—somewhere private and out of the way."

"Are you in some kind of trouble?" Jennifer asked, sensing the caller feared for her life.

"I will be if anything goes wrong with the experiment—I mean testing," the caller corrected herself.

"Experiment? Testing? I don't like the sounds of that," Jennifer said apprehensively. "Are you sure this isn't a crank call because even if it's kind of slow around here today, I could be—"

"If you meet me in one hour, I'll give you the biggest story of your career."

"When you put it that way, how could I decline?" Jennifer responded. "Only before I leave, I need to know your name." Silence. "I'm not going to tell anyone about you, if that's what you're worried about. As a rule, I never meet up with anybody who doesn't at the very least tell me their name." Silence. "I promise it will remain a secret."

"I'm only going to tell you because I trust you as a woman. I didn't think I could do that with any of the male reporters working at the other dailies."

"I appreciate that, I do," Jennifer said gently. "And I vow I won't betray your trust, I don't work like that. So please, what's your name?"

The caller inhaled deeply before finally answering.

"My name is Alysha Foster and I was Robert Barker's lover at the time he was killed."

FORTY ONE

Jennifer couldn't get the sound of Alysha Foster's sobs out of her head as she drove like a maniac out of the city. Turning into the Missionary Cemetery parking lot, Jennifer could have sworn that only two of the car's wheels were touching the ground.

She glanced across the well-maintained fields and spotted her on a bench near a gigantic tombstone statue.

Who says you can't take it with you? Jennifer thought.

The woman turned and for the first time Jennifer saw she was in her late 20's / early 30's, with hair that hung to the middle of her back, and a slim figure which nicely filled out her dress.

"Alysha?"

"Jennifer?"

"The one and only," Jennifer smiled. She could tell by Alysha's body language she was still nervous about being there. "Why don't we go for a walk? I've got plenty of time to talk if you do."

"Right now I've got all the time in the world," Alysha said, a smile finally escaping from her lips.

They walked and talked informally, getting a feel for one another.

Within minutes, Alysha was certain she'd done the right thing. Starting hesitantly, she described in detail her affair with Robert until his death. She told how devastated she was after his shooting, not being able to tell anyone why she was so distressed. Then, when she had lost her job at Mantis, she'd come unglued.

Although Alysha spoke relatively calmly about how her life had spiraled out of control—*That roller coaster must pick up riders after all*—Jennifer knew this woman was an emotional wreck and could snap at any time.

Better to keep things simple and slow, she decided.

Coming to the end of the long roadway, Jennifer pointed out a bench and suggested they continue to talk there.

"Alysha, although this story has done a number on me as well, I don't think you called me for a counselling session. There's something you think will be helpful to Robert's case, isn't there?"

Alysha looked away and without emotion said, "I've been conducting an experiment on my own that is not only illegal, it's highly unethical." Jennifer remained silent. "As the Senator said at his press conference, that's what we at Mantis do best, right?"

"Then the allegations of questionable experiments are true?"

"No. What I'm saying is that the : a testing I'm doing on Lynn Barker at Western General is highly unethical."

"You're doing experiments on Lynn Barker—right now, as we speak? Is that what I heard?" Jennifer was contemplating the idea that Alysha's phone call was, in fact, a prank. Somehow though, as she'd intuitively known neither Lynn Barker or Stanley Unger were killers, she felt the woman beside her was telling the truth.

"I have a friend who works on Mrs. Barker's floor at the hospital. At night, security is pretty lax and recent cutbacks mean there are very few staff on the floor at any given time. My friend gave me a schedule—a routine—the nurses follow each night. She also made notes about the security guards, including their likes or dislikes."

"I think I know where this is heading," Jennifer interjected. "You somehow gain access into Mrs. Barker's room, right?" Alysha nodded. "What about the police? I thought they had her under virtual house arrest, never letting her out of their sight."

"They do," Alysha answered with a sly smile. "The trick is to be very friendly with them and act like you belong."

"And they'll let you walk in with no questions asked?"

"I'm only in the room for a minute. I say I'm cleaning her bed pan, or some other task involving bodily fluids, which they have no interest in watching."

"So they remain outside," Jennifer added, appreciating the beauty of the scheme, "and once you're in, you inject what—Memoradium?"

Panic swept over Alysha's features as she jumped to her feet.

"Who are you?" she asked as she looked around hysterically, twisting and turning left and right. "I knew I shouldn't have done this! I knew it," she berated herself. "I was only trying to help her, I swear. I wasn't going to hurt her!"

Alysha began to bang her fists against her face.

"Stop that!" Jennifer instructed, trying to catch up with her fleeing source. "I don't know what you're talking about, Alysha. I'm a reporter, not a cop. Trust me!"

Alysha slowed and steadied herself against the nearest tree.

"Don't come any closer," she warned. "How did you know about Memoradium? It was top secret. Only a select few know it exists."

Jennifer could tell the terror on Alysha's face was genuine.

"I only know the name," Jennifer implored, refilling her lungs with much-needed air. "I interviewed the company's PR man, a Kenneth McIntyre, and saw it written on his desk planner. When I asked about it he jumped out of his chair—much like you just did." Both women continued to evaluate the other. "So are you telling me Memoradium actually exists?"

"It does and it's being tested on Lynn Barker."

The words came out of Alysha's mouth defiantly.

Jennifer chastised herself for being so dimwitted.

"You've been sneaking into her room to give her a dose of this stuff? What if it kills her?"

A steely gaze came over Alysha's eyes.

"The experiment will be deemed a failure," she said coolly.

"I don't believe you're doing this for science," Jennifer stated, the gears in her head working furiously. "I think you're doing this to get to the truth about your lover's murder. I can't see you as a cold-hearted scientist, Alysha. It's not your style."

For a moment the rigid expression remained in place but soon the façade faded and Alysha began to cry.

"I loved him more than he loved me, I know that," she sobbed. "It's that . . . he didn't deserve to die that way. All I'm trying to do is set the record straight. If his wife didn't kill him, we'll know to start looking somewhere else for answers."

Jennifer's head began to pound from information overload. If anyone needed to get to the truth, she did.

She walked slowly toward Alysha, who was now slumped against the base of the tree.

"I don't know anything about this wonder drug, except it's supposed to bring back a person's memory. You can tell me all the intricate details later. Just answer this one for me now: Has Mrs. Barker shown any signs of recovering her memory?"

"I don't know," Alysha said, trying to retain her poise. "She's never awake when I'm giving her the drug and I don't dare wake her."

"How many doses do you think she'll need? Two more, five, twenty-five—what?"

"I don't know," Alysha answered. "In the lab, the animals would respond after five or six treatments. My problem is I'm only guessing at the dosage needed for humans. If I had daily access to her I could determine if I should raise or lower the level of the drug."

Jennifer considered this.

"Which is impossible without telling the doctors what you're doing and what they should be looking for, right?"

"If I'm caught they can charge me with attempted murder for giving unapproved drugs to a human being."

"Okay, let's put aside thoughts of criminal charges and think about Lynn for a moment," Jennifer said as she tried to organize her thoughts. "Obviously she's still alive and having no noticeable side effects from the drug, correct?"

"None that I can see."

"And I haven't heard of any either. How many doses have you already shot her up with?"

"Four."

"And you say that lab rats usually start to remember where they left their car keys after five or six shots?"

"Right," Alysha replied with a small smile.

"Then theoretically, keeping all of this extremely simple, one or two more shots might kick-start Lynn's cranium."

"And if it doesn't?"

"I'm going to have to start working on a new story and let all the weasels in this one go about their business."

"Are you calling me a weasel?" Alysha asked, confused by Jennifer's statement.

"No, you are apparently one of the good guys. In fact, you're the only one so far. Senator Adams is covering his butt like it had a bulls-eye tattooed on it. Jerry Steele is only making public appearances as he runs to and from the bank—probably investing in Litchfield Industries. And then there's Jerry's partner, Melanie Fields, who can't decide what to call herself after all these years."

Jennifer discontinued her soliloquy to look at Alysha, who had a puzzled expression on her face. She'd seen the same one a few days earlier inside the East Haven Grocery Store.

"Who is Melanie Fields?" Alysha asked hesitantly.

Jennifer could feel the hair on her neck begin to stand on end.

"Who do you think she is?" she asked, ready to burst from anticipation.

"Once when we were in bed, Robert called me Melanie," Alysha said slowly. "It was the second time we'd slept together. When he should have said, 'Oh, Alysha,' he'd said, 'Oh, Melanie.' He apologized profusely and claimed she was a college girl he'd dated."

"And after all these years her name happened to pop into his mind?" Jennifer asked. "I don't think so."

"Neither did I. It never happened again and I haven't thought about it until now."

"Well I won't forget about it," Jennifer stated. "Ever."

They walked back to the parking lot in silence.

"What are you going to do now?" Alysha asked.

"Hope. Pray. You know, the usual," Jennifer quipped. "What about you? Are you going to play Florence Nightingale again tonight?"

"I only have enough Memoradium for six more doses. When it's gone, that's it. I grabbed it when the feds ordered us out of the lab."

"That was something I was meaning to ask you about," Jennifer said. "Where did all those reports claiming unethical testing come from if no such testing existed?"

"I really don't know, Jennifer. I saw the documents on the news and they were the ones we use but the experiments didn't exist."

"Meaning someone within the company made up the forgeries."

"I guess so, although for what reason I don't know. Memoradium was going to revolutionize the medical world. Why anyone within the

company would want to sabotage that is beyond me."

The names Litchfield Industries and Douglas Adams immediately spring to mind, Jennifer thought.

Alysha stood beside her car looking fragile and lost. Jennifer felt sorry for her. She'd unburdened herself to another woman, only to discover nothing in her life had changed. Jennifer stepped forward and gave her a needed hug.

"I can't tell you what to do, Alysha," Jennifer said, breaking their embrace. "I want an end to this story as much as you do. We're a lot alike in that regard. We both have information that could break this case open, yet are unable to tell anyone. It really is no way to live."

"You can say that again," Alysha said, tilting her head back in an effort to keep tears from cascading down her face.

"Give me a call when there's any news, okay? Here's my card. With any luck, this nightmare will be over in a few days—or even better a few hours, when your wonder drug finally kicks in."

They said their goodbyes and drove off in different directions.

Entering the newsroom, Jennifer saw Mitch walking in her direction.

"What happened? Was she a crackpot or what?" he asked eagerly.

"No more than you and me."

"So there are no new developments in the Barker case then."

"Only that if nothing breaks before the election, I'm off this story."

"You're serious, aren't you?"

"As serious as a bullet to the head, Mitch," Jennifer replied, grabbing some notes off her desk and walking out of the newsroom.

FORTY TWO

ELECTION EVE

"Ready, Susan, in five, four, three . . ."

"Good evening and welcome to *The Newsmakers*. I'm Susan Donallee. Jason Morris is still on assignment."

No matter how many times she'd spoken those words since the infamous *You little bitch* incident, Susan could never quite stop herself from smiling an extra 10 per cent.

"Tonight, on election eve, we examine this year's Presidential campaign. Joining me in the studio are political writer Lisa Whittaker and NCN's Washington correspondent Justin Fitzgerald. Let me start with you, Lisa. Polls indicate that Senator Douglas Adams will defeat President Travers tomorrow. Is there any way President Travers can turn the vote around in less than 24 hours?"

"I don't believe President Travers could turn this election around in 24 days, let alone 24 hours," Lisa said with a small laugh. "Right now, Douglas Adams has the momentum of a runaway locomotive. He's done everything right over the last month and the public has embraced him as an agent for change."

"What are your thoughts, Justin?" Susan asked, turning her attention to one of the media's most eligible bachelors.

"To answer your question, Susan, let me pose another one: What if it had been President Travers guesting on *The Nation Today* instead of Senator Adams?" Justin asked. "Don't you think we'd be talking about all the right moves he's made during the past month, on his way to another landslide victory?"

"That was the turning point of this otherwise dry campaign, no question," Susan interjected. "Do you really think though, that if the tables were turned the President's campaign would have caught fire as Adams' did?"

"I think so," Justin replied without hesitation. "What's being lost on the electorate is that nothing really distinguishes these two men from one another."

"Except a well-executed murder," Lisa agreed. "I think Justin is right."

"The other lost component is the controversy of shutting Mantis Pharmaceuticals down and Senator Adams' role in it," Justin continued. "To me it looked like political opportunism."

"Even with the documents he produced?" Lisa said, a look of disbelief on her face. "If the research records are confirmed, who knows how many lives were saved by Adams' quick action."

"The problem is his investigation panel can't reveal their findings until after tomorrow's election. Unfortunately, what I'm hearing is that no substantial evidence has been found, yet Mantis remains closed."

"If these documents were doctored, what credence do you give to the Senator's claim that Robert Barker wanted to speak to him about the unethical research at a street microphone?"

"He'd have zero credibility, Susan. I have always found that line of reasoning pretty farfetched. The sad reality is we won't learn the truth until Adams is sworn into office."

"I have to agree again with Justin," Lisa said. "Unless someone comes forward with information about Robert Barker's true intentions that morning, we'll have to trust Senator Adams claims. Regrettably, along with his 15 percent tax cut, I have a feeling this charge against Mantis Pharmaceuticals will mysteriously disappear after his inauguration."

"Are you implying Senator Adams may have had more to do with the shutdown of Mantis than acting as a concerned regulator?" Susan asked Lisa.

"All I'm saying is that something about the Barker shooting and the closing of his company remains a real concern to us in the media, and should continue to be to the voters."

"On that point," Susan said, "we'll take a quick break. When we return we will . . ."

Jennifer switched off her set and felt like she might vomit. She had the proof, only no way of getting it out to the public. Looking around her sparsely furnished apartment she knew exactly how Alysha Foster must feel alone with her thoughts.

There is a bright side to this, Jennifer reminded herself. *By tomorrow morning I'll finally be off this stupid ride.*

After consuming a frothy cup of hot chocolate goodness, Jennifer climbed into her bed and quickly fell into a deep calm sleep. Her dreams were a montage of Michael the security guard, Nathaniel the gas jockey and that guy from the Kingdom Entertainment building. She made an unconscious mental note to drop by his third-floor office on her way to work in the morning.

As these pleasant thoughts consumed her sleeping mind, they were unceremoniously dashed away with the persistent ringing of her telephone.

"This had better be Brad Pitt," she said into the phone. "Do you know what time it is?"

"Jennifer, it's me, Alysha. I'm in police custody at the hospital and I didn't have anyone else I could call."

A slap to the face from a complete stranger couldn't have jarred Jennifer awake faster.

"I'll be right there. Don't let them take you out of the hospital until I arrive. Stall them the best you can."

Jennifer jumped into her late model Cavalier and sped through the mildly busy city streets, her heart pounding wildly.

I'm never going to get on another roller coaster in my life, she vowed as she ran a red light. *They could never compare to the Robert Barker Express.*

"My name is Jennifer Malone," she advised the old security guard at the lobby desk. "I'm looking for a woman who is in police custody."

"Do you have her name?" the war veteran asked, looking at his log book.

"Her name is Alysha Foster. How many women do the police currently have detained?"

"I couldn't say. They don't communicate that information to us."

"As far as I know," a deep male voice said behind her, "the police only have one woman in custody."

Jennifer turned to see the troubled face of Detective Michael Speers.

"Detective Speers, what a surprise," she said with a cautious smile. "I'm not on the wrong side of the police tape again, am I?"

"I haven't decided yet," he replied as he studied her stressed features. "How did you get here so fast? For obvious reasons this call didn't go over the air."

"Yeah, we wouldn't want to bump the election off of the front page, would we?" Jennifer asked with mild sarcasm. Speers offered no response. "Actually. . . I'm here at the request of your suspect."

"Why would she call you?"

"Because I could arrange for a *Telegraph* lawyer to be here on short notice."

"And why would you do that?"

306

"Civic duty?"

They studied one another for a moment.

"Off the record, Jennifer," Speers finally said. "How is Alysha Foster mixed up in this? I know you know more than what's written in the paper."

"Completely off the record?" Jennifer asked. Speers nodded his head. "I'm pretty certain I know why Robert Barker was killed."

"You're bluffing," Speers scoffed.

"Let me put it this way, Mike—if nothing is done before the polls close tomorrow night, we're going to elect a President I can prove is not only corrupt but possibly an accomplice in murder as well. Your girl upstairs has some things to say that, if published tonight, may very well bring Adams to his knees."

"I've only got a very sketchy description of what took place in Mrs. Barker's room. This friend of yours was caught red-handed shoving a syringe full of some liquid into the I.V. tube. She's looking at attempted murder from where I stand."

"You're wrong, Mike," Jennifer replied seriously. "She's looking for the truth."

Several minutes later, Speers and Jennifer entered a room on Lynn Barker's floor. Although she knew what to expect, Jennifer was still taken aback at the sight of Alysha dressed in a nurse's uniform. Her face was oatmeal white and tear stains marked her cheeks. When she saw Jennifer she jumped to her feet, scaring the officer in the room, who immediately had his hand on his revolver.

"It's okay, Hackett," Speers said. "Keep it holstered."

"You can't believe how happy I am to see you," Alysha cried.

"Everything's going to be okay," Jennifer said soothingly as she and Alysha embraced. "The lawyer is on his way, however, I've already told Detective Speers what is going on."

Alysha looked even more frightened.

"You told him? How could you do that?"

"It was off the record and you can trust him. Believe me, I know." Alysha's face relaxed slightly. "Let's sit down, okay?"

Lawyer Al Sherratt soon arrived and stated he'd been retained by *The Telegraph* to represent Alysha Foster. With the formalities out of the way, Speers began his questioning.

Against the wishes of her new lawyer, leaving out no details, Alysha recited the same story she'd told Jennifer.

"This Memoradium drug has never been tested on humans, right?" Speers asked.

"Not until now, no," Alysha replied gravely.

"What is Mrs. Barker's condition, Hackett?"

"She's still awake, sir. As far as the doctor on duty is concerned, physically her condition hasn't changed in the past few days."

"No one outside this room knows what you were putting in her I.V., correct?" Speers asked, turning his attention back to Alysha, who acknowledged his question with a slight nod of her head. "So for all we know, this miracle drug could actually be frying the remainder of Mrs. Barker's brain cells as we speak, right?"

"No—I know that wouldn't happen!" Alysha exclaimed. "I've worked with this drug for years and it either helps to unblock restricted cell pathways or it doesn't. There has never been any evidence that it destroys existing cells."

"Hackett, go and tell the doctor on duty we better get a cat scan or whatever they call it, done immediately to determine what effect this drug has had on Mrs. Barker's brain." Hackett left the room and Speers stood, taking his handcuffs out as he did so. "As for you, Miss Foster, I'm placing you under arrest for illegally administering a prohibited drug without a medical licence."

As he walked toward her chair, Alysha began to sob uncontrollably.

"I was only trying to find out who killed Robert. I wouldn't harm anyone."

Speers, with the help of Jennifer, who was equally shaken by the turn of events, brought Alysha to her feet.

"Are the handcuffs necessary, Mike?" Jennifer said angrily as she watched him slap one onto Alysha's wrist.

Before Speers could reply, the door to the room flew open.

"Sir, come quick!" Officer Hackett said. "It's Mrs. Barker!"

Without hesitation, Speers slapped the other handcuff onto the railing of the nearby hospital bed and ran out of the room.

"Oh my God, I've killed her!" Alysha shrieked, collapsing awkwardly onto the bed. "She's dead and I killed her!"

A minute later Speers returned.

"Jennifer!" he bellowed. "You're going to want to see this."

Jennifer was startled by the authority in his voice, which cut through Alysha's continued cries for forgiveness like a switchblade cutting Jello. She told Alysha not to worry and exited the room, following Speers' lead.

Entering Lynn Barker's room, Jennifer hadn't the foggiest idea what she might find. The image of Lynn swinging from a light fixture with a bedsheet wrapped around her neck briefly flickered through her mind. With no memory, no family, your husband's mistress pumping chemicals into your body and a murder rap over your head, who'd blame her for ending it all?

Not me, Jennifer thought.

What she wasn't expecting was to see Lynn Barker sitting on the side of her bed answering her doctor's questions.

"And where do you live?"

"378 Whitecastle Boulevard in New Liston," Lynn said in a voice that cracked with emotion. She looked at the two people who'd entered her room. "I didn't kill my husband, Detective, but I did get my friend Melanie killed. I'll live with that for the rest of my life."

Speers and Jennifer exchanged glances.

It was going to be a very long night.

* * *

"It's Bradshaw from the hospital. You've got a big problem. Lynn Barker woke up and is talking to the police."

"Talking? About what?" Harold Green questioned, although he knew the answer the second he'd heard the specialist's voice.

"About everything—and I mean *everything*."

"Can't you stop her?" Green beseeched, his voice hoarse.

"I can't get near the room now. Even if I could, I'm not risking my life with these trigger-happy cops so I can save your candidate's campaign."

"Then what use are you?" Green threw the cell phone onto the floor, shattering it and made his way to Adams' hotel.

Upon entering his suite, he found the Senator going over the acceptance speech he'd dreamed of reciting his entire life.

"I don't think you'll need that," Green said cheerlessly. "It's over, Douglas. Lynn woke up with her memory intact."

The blood drained away from Adams' face. His reaction was one of resignation though, as if he'd prepared for this moment and was ready to accept his fate.

"You place your bet and you take your chances, Harold," he said cynically. "I bet the wrong way this time, that's all."

"I'm also resigning as your campaign manager," Green said uneasily. "I can't be associated with the charges the police will surely bring in the near future."

Adams bland expression didn't change.

"You always were good at acceptable deniability—or whatever they call it these days. I don't blame you. I'm envious I can't do the same.

Therefore, I accept your resignation. You are free to go."

Green hesitated only a moment before turning and walking from the room. As he entered the elevator, he waited for the sound of a gunshot to ring out.

As the doors closed, however, no such noise invaded his ears. In fact, the only thing he was conscious of was the deafening silence which engulfed the entire floor. It was an uncomfortable sound which he wasn't accustomed to.

Days later, he realized it was the sound of defeat.

FORTY THREE

ELECTION DAY

It had been the most hectic night of Jennifer's life. Keeping up with Speers while frantically writing notes, she soon discovered was as grueling as running a marathon with a leg in a cast. At one point, believing she was hampering their investigation, Officer Hackett asked Speers why he was allowing a reporter to accompany them. Without hesitation, Speers shot back, "This is a matter of national security, Hackett. She's not *accompanying* us anywhere—she's my personal prisoner. Any other questions?"

Once the shock of learning Melanie was not dead had subsided, Lynn Barker revealed everything she could recall of her kidnapping ordeal. Having his suspicions now confirmed, Speers and his best officers then descended on Jerry's rented abode, where Jerry and Melanie were arrested and taken in to be questioned separately.

The morning edition of *The Telegraph* hit the streets two hours later than usual. The first three pages had to be completely reworked for Jennifer's world exclusive. After every new development, no matter where she was Jennifer called the paper, where Mitch Carson personally shaped her observations into a cohesive storyline.

The late-breaking news not only had an immediate effect on the editorial offices at the other papers, it also wrought havoc with the morning television programs. Literally minutes before air time, they had to set aside their entire election day coverage to become bit players in their respective network's coverage regarding Jennifer's story and its widespread implications.

By mid-morning, a special edition of *The Telegraph* was being prepared that would include further developments in the case that only the police and one reporter were privy to.

As if by design, both Jerry and Melanie requested a representative from the District Attorney's office sit in on their interrogation sessions.

"I haven't seen two people who hated each other this much since my Mom left Dad for the town butcher," one of the lawyers told Speers. "They don't want to simply roll on each other, they want to use a steam roller to do it."

The problem was which story to believe. Speers, thankfully, didn't have to make that decision. He charged them with murder, kidnapping, fraud, blackmail and bribing a public official. When Lynn recalled one of the boys who'd helped her escape was named John Hawksworth, he and his friends were quickly tracked down. After learning of the Chandler Motor Lodge fire from the still frightened boys, Speers slapped an additional charge of arson on the pair.

"If nothing else sticks, I'm going to get them for that," Speers told Jennifer, who asked if she could quote him. "Sure, why not? From now on, everything is on the record!"

When *The Telegraph's* second edition hit the streets, a new phenomenon was being reported by the news programs. In almost every district on the east coast, voter turnout was described as practically nonexistent. One political commentator quipped that President Travers might very well be re-elected on the strength of the few million people in the land who didn't own TV sets, radios or buy newspapers.

One thing was certain: the rest of the informed public wasn't giving Adams the benefit of the doubt. In the same manner that Lynn Barker had been tried and convicted in the court of public opinion, so too was Adams. This time, however, no one was predicting a miracle drug might suddenly alter Adams' faltering memory about their affair.

Alysha Foster was released from police custody after promising to appear in court the following Monday.

"By the time the clerk calls your name, Alysha, you'll be regarded as a hero," Jennifer told her later that afternoon. "No judge is ever going to risk his position on the bench by making an example of you. He has to get re-elected like the President."

* * *

With the release of the suspects' conflicting statements to the rest of the media—a full hour after Jennifer had filed her final story containing the same information—Jennifer found herself with Speers in his smallish office, both exhausted by the night's events.

"In the book you'll inevitably write, are you going to portray me as an intelligent investigator who took the necessary risks to apprehend the bad guys? Or . . ." he paused for effect, "as a country hick with the brains of a tree stump?"

Jennifer took a sip of her coffee and let Speers wait a few agonizing seconds before confirming his worst fear.

"Tree stump. Definitely," she said with a laugh.

"There's going to be hell to pay for allowing you to tag along with us last night—guaranteeing you an exclusive. The other papers are going to have a field day grilling me over that."

"Moi—tag along?" Jennifer replied, feigning shock. "If memory serves, Mike, I recall you saying I was your personal prisoner."

"Is that what I said?" Speers said after some thought. "I guess I'm a tree stump after all!"

Jennifer returned to *The Telegraph* building, where she made her way up the back stairs to the newsroom. As she exited into the hallway, as if on cue, she heard it. At first it was a mere rumble of garbled high-pitched voices. As she walked into the room she was confronted by all the reporters and support staff standing on their feet and singing.

"For she's the jolly reporter, for she's the jolly reporter, for she's the jolly reporrrrrrrrter . . . which nobody can deny!"

Whoops and cheers escalated to a fever pitch as everyone began to crowd her, shaking her hand and patting her on the back. For the first time in her career, Jennifer was humbled by this genuine outpouring of support from her peers. She noted that even Arnold Girard seemed happy for her. Then she saw a large cake with a picture of *The Telegraph's* front page on it being wheeled into the room.

She looked around and saw Mitch step out of his office. A huge grin lit up his tired face and he held up his hand for silence.

Once the room's festivities died down to a mild roar, he lifted a glass of champagne off Amy's desk.

"A toast," he proclaimed. "To the best reporter this city has ever— and will ever see. I give you our resident Queen—Jennifer Malone!"

Clapping and cheering broke out anew as all eyes turned back to Jennifer, who stood in stunned awe.

"Speech, speech, speech!" they began to chant.

Jennifer tried to calm the crowd as Mitch had, but no one responded to her gesture.

I guess I'll have to take matters into my own hands, Jennifer thought.

She worked her way through her colleagues to her desk, which she jumped up on, towering over everyone in the room.

"My loyal servants," she hollered above the boisterous noise. "I am deeply touched, although I suspect you already knew that." She waited

for the expected laughter to subside. "As your grateful Queen, I have to tell you that everything that transpired today was a team effort. I couldn't have done any of this without you." She scanned the smiling crowd and added, "Actually, Girard—I did do this without your help but thanks for showing up on time for the party. I'm sure Mitch is going to need someone to *hack* the cake apart. But seriously, folks," she quickly continued, "today is a great day for *The Telegraph* and I thank you for all of this."

Jennifer bowed to the crowd assembled around her desk.

"Just one other thing," she said as she stood upright. "I hope each and every one of you takes a little of this celebration home with you tonight. Because when I win that Pulitzer I'm going to deny ever working in this dump!" she laughed uproariously. "Now by order of the Queen—let them eat cake!"

Jennifer bowed again as everyone cheered her on.

"That was some speech," Mitch said as he helped Jennifer off the desk. "Were you serious about denying ever working at this dump when you become rich and famous?"

Jennifer looked into Carson's eyes which, like hers, appeared to be ready to shed tears of joy.

"Of course not, Mitch," she managed to say. "I love this place. Now as for working for you . . . that's a totally different issue."

Mitch laughed.

"For a moment—a fleeting second, mind you—I thought you were human, Malone."

Jennifer began to laugh along with him.

"Boy, were you wrong."

FORTY FOUR

"Ready, Susan, in five, four, three . . ."

"Good evening, I'm Susan Donallee. Our top story is the reopening of Mantis Pharmaceuticals. The federal investigation of the pharmaceutical giant was halted earlier this morning by President Travers, who began a short vacation after his stunning landslide victory Tuesday. Indicating that no evidence of inhumane research was found, and in light of police statements that the original documents were fraudulent, the President said he had no choice but to rescind the Health and Welfare Committee's order for indefinite closure. That news immediately sent Mantis stocks skyrocketing. The stock continued to climb when new CEO and President Lynn Barker confirmed testing of the new memory wonder drug Memoradium would continue as her husband, the late Robert Barker, had planned.

"In another twist, Lynn Barker's guardian angel and rebel researcher Alysha Foster had the most serious charges against her dropped. She is expected to make a plea deal for one remaining lesser charge, which carries a $500 maximum fine.

"In other related developments, the Health and Welfare Committee

317

held an emergency session last evening and unanimously voted to bar their Chairman, Senator Douglas Adams, from all further meetings. A special panel of inquiry was also commissioned to look into the allegations that Senator Adams received an illegal campaign donation from Nagitoki Pharma, an Asian-based subsidary of Litchfield Industries, this country's second-largest pharmaceutical manufacturer. Howard Manard, the CEO of Litchfield, denies any knowledge of the contribution. He also stated today he does not know murder suspects Jerry Steele or Melanie Fields and calls their conspiracy theory absurd.

"In a written statement to the media, Senator Adams also denied the illegal donation charge. He further stated that the handling of all his election funds was the sole responsibility of his former campaign manager, Harold Green, who could not be reached for comment this afternoon.

"Another casualty of this on-going story is that Stanley Unger, the producer of *The Nation Today*, resigned his post this afternoon. In a news release, he stated he wanted to spend more time with his young family away from the media limelight.

"We have to take a short break, but straight ahead we'll have an exclusive in-depth interview with Jennifer Malone, the newspaper reporter who almost single-handedly solved the Robert Barker murder case. She'll discuss her involvement in the investigation as well as her new book deal, reportedly worth two million dollars.

"And then later, I'll be speaking with three very brave bicycle riding boys about being honoured as heroes this weekend in their hometown.

"So be sure to stay tuned. There's plenty more ahead when *NCN Live* returns."

EPILOGUE

Of all the places Melanie had resided, from the ramshackle house she grew up in to the luxury penthouses to which she had lately grown accustomed, a prison cell ranked the lowest on a list of desired hotspots to spend one's time. The fact she might very well call it HOME the rest of her life was something even her calculating mind could not comprehend.

After years of sacrificing her body (willingly, mind you) to countless men in an attempt to sleep her way to the top, here she was sharing a very tiny space with a 40-something heavily tattooed arsonist named Tori.

This was not how things were supposed to turn out.

"I feel like a celebrity myself just being here with you, Mel—you don't mind me calling you that, right?" Tori asked as she slid comfortably beside her new roommate on the lower bunk. "I had my 15 minutes of fame—or should I say *flame*?— but it's fleeting, you know? One day

you're the crazy bitch who burned down the town's only bookstore on a dare and the next you're locked away in this hole forever, never to be heard from again."

"You got life without parole for setting fire to a bookstore?" Melanie asked slowly. "That town must have been really big readers," she added with a smirk, not yet knowing exactly how to act in this situation.

"Ha! Half the town couldn't read and the other half didn't know the store was there!" Tori laughed, putting her hand on Melanie's right knee. "I got life because the owner—some wannabe writer—had moved above the store. How the hell was I to know that? The newspaper's headline read: **Author In Residence Dead. The End**. I thought that was kinda funny." Tori turned to face Melanie, who was looking at the hand on her knee. "Did you see what the writer did there—the play on words?"

Seriously, this is what my life has come down to? Melanie thought.

This multi-coloured freak of nature did not intimidate her in the least. She'd dealt with various versions of this kind of bully before. The difference this time was not knowing the repercussions of, say, punching the woman in the face to show her exactly who'd be wearing the pants in the relationship. Melanie knew the opportunity would show itself soon enough and she'd be ready. No matter what punishment or humiliation she might have to endure in order to fit in with her fellow sisters, a new Queen Bee had arrived — they just didn't know it yet.

Speaking of relationships and wanting to punch someone in the face, where is that rat bastard Jerry when I need him?

Separated from the moment of their arrest, he had somehow managed to get a plea bargain deal before she could. The real shocker was having Manard and Adams dissing her in the media, claiming never to have made her acquaintance. Suddenly, no one wanted to be associated with the best thing that ever happened to them. Like Tori, they, too, would get their just rewards.

"Do you swear to tell the truth and nothing but the truth?"

"You betcha."

The high-pitched dinner bell vibrated through Cell Block D, a sound Melanie knew she would never get used to.

"Time to get you some grub, superstar," Tori said with a smile as she ran her hand across Melanie's shoulder. "I'll even introduce you to my friends. They're going to like you a lot."

"Whatever," Melanie said with a dismissive hand gesture as she stood, briefly looking away from Tori as their cell door slid open.

She never saw the violent left hook that split her lip and caused her to disintegrate unceremoniously to the hard concrete floor.

"Let's get one thing straight, Kitten," Tori growled, standing over her wounded prey. "In here, you are my bitch and mine alone. Unlike all those phonies you conned outside, I do not forget, forgive or share. And the sooner you realize that, the happier both of us will be. Cross me once and you'll be sorrier than you look right now." With great pleasure, she paused and then added with a smile, "If you know what I mean."

Melanie got awkwardly to her knees, wiped blood from her lip onto the back of her hand and glanced up into Tori's dark, crazed eyes.

Oh yes, she knew exactly what she meant.

THE END

Praise for the
STEVE CASSIDY MYSTERY Series

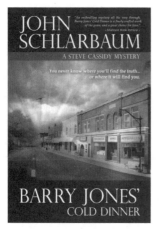

"An enthralling mystery all the way through. *Barry Jones' Cold Dinner* is a finely crafted work of the genre and a great choice for fans."
– THE MIDWEST BOOK REVIEW –

"*Barry Jones' Cold Dinner* has sturdy traditional crime bones. Schlarbaum isn't lacking in wit or an attractive protagonist."
– SUN MEDIA –

After kissing his wife and boys goodbye, Barry Jones departed his small town home and headed to work in the city. He never arrived. Now seven years later, his wife wants the courts to declare her absentee husband dead once and for all. Enter P.I. Steve Cassidy.

"Schlarbaum masterfully creates a mystery where the only thing more intriguing than the plot is the development of Steve Cassidy's character."
- ALAN COOMBS, ASTRAL MEDIA RADIO –

"An entertaining mystery which draws on the elements of humour, romance, and hard-boiled investigation, *When Angels Fail to Fly* is a mystery that'll keep readers reading."
– THE MIDWEST BOOK REVIEW –

When mysterious events happen to Steve Cassidy's loved ones, the police, the press and his friends begin to question his every move. To complicate his life further, a cryptic telephone call begins a new investigation into the bizarre death of a woman keeping a secret.

For more info, videos and to order: www.scannerpublishing.com

Praise for
JOHN SCHLARBAUM'S
Inspirational Books

The Doctor's Bag: A Sentimental Journey is the heartwarming tale of the life of Thomas Sterling and his son Robert. Readers will become enthralled with *The Doctor's Bag* as the intimate story between father and son unfolds, giving new meaning to the actual doctor's bag itself. As the doctor's bag acts as the metaphor between healing and pain from year to year, *The Doctor's Bag* leaves the reader with an enlightening message of life, love and hope. *The Doctor's Bag* is strongly recommended to the general reader and those searching for a gentle, touching, and life changing read.

Aging Gracefully Together: A Story of Love and Marriage is an intimate autobiographical account of one couple's undying love from the time of their engagement through their fifty years of domestic partnership. Captivating readers from first page to last, the story of Henry and Tina Cole's hopes, dreams, joys, heartaches, struggles and triumphs is an inspiring story of love and marriage. *Aging Gracefully Together* showcases a thoughtful and caring relationship and is very highly recommended reading - especially for those who are themselves about to embark upon a lifetime matrimonial journey together.

– THE MIDWEST BOOK REVIEW –-

For more info, videos and to order: www.scannerpublishing.com

About The Author

John Schlarbaum was raised in the town of West Lorne, Ontario. He began his professional writing career while working as a Writer and Field Director for several nationally syndicated television programs. After a fifteen-year career as a Private Investigator, he is now owner and operator of Page 233 Bookstore in Amherstburg, Ontario. He is also working on his next mystery novel.

The first Steve Cassidy Mystery - *Barry Jones' Cold Dinner* - was released in 2008.

The second Steve Cassidy Mystery – *When Angels Fail To Fly* - was released in 2009.